4/22

ATOMIC ANNA

ALSO BY RACHEL BARENBAUM

A Bend in the Stars

ATOMIC ANNA

RACHEL BARENBAUM

GRAND CENTRAL
PUBLISHING

NEW YORK   BOSTON

Copyright © 2022 by Rachel Barenbaum

Jacket design by Jaya Miceli. Jacket photos by Getty Images.
Jacket copyright © 2022 by Hachette Book Group, Inc.

Grand Central Publishing
Hachette Book Group
1290 Avenue of the Americas, New York, NY 10104
grandcentralpublishing.com
twitter.com/grandcentralpub

First Edition: April 2022

Grand Central Publishing is a division of Hachette Book Group, Inc. The Grand Central Publishing name and logo is a trademark of Hachette Book Group, Inc.

The publisher is not responsible for websites (or their content) that are not owned by the publisher.

The Hachette Speakers Bureau provides a wide range of authors for speaking events. To find out more, go to www.hachettespeakersbureau.com or call (866) 376-6591.

Family tree design by Jeff Stiefel

Print book interior design by Jeff Stiefel

Library of Congress Cataloging-in-Publication Data

Names: Barenbaum, Rachel, author.
Title: Atomic Anna / Rachel Barenbaum.
Description: First edition. | New York : Grand Central Publishing, 2022.
Identifiers: LCCN 2021034625 | ISBN 9781538734865 (hardcover) | ISBN
   9781538734889 (ebook)
Subjects: LCGFT: Novels.
Classification: LCC PS3602.A775343 A94 2022 | DDC 813/.6–dc23
LC record available at https://lccn.loc.gov/2021034625

ISBNs: 9781538734865 (hardcover), 9781538734889 (ebook)

Printed in the United States of America

LSC-C

Printing 1, 2022

For Adam,
and for Ezra, Lily, and Jonah

ATOMIC ANNA

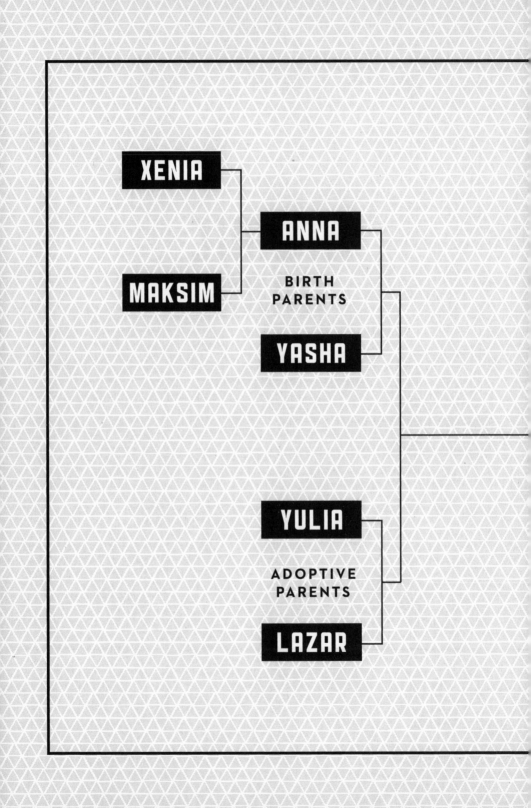

FAMILY TREE

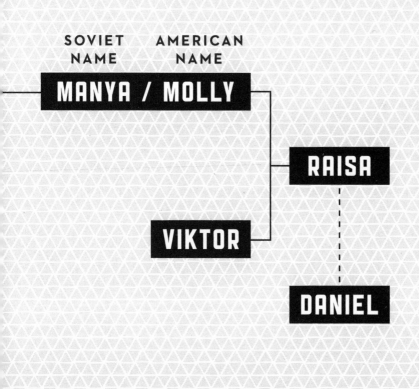

SOVIET NAME   AMERICAN NAME

MANYA / MOLLY

RAISA

VIKTOR

DANIEL

irkei Avot, meaning "Chapters of the Fathers," is a collection of Jewish ethical teachings and stories passed down from generation to generation. It begins with a warning: Be patient in judgment.

PROLOGUE

April 1986

Soviet Union

The scientist Anna Berkova was asleep in her narrow bed in Pripyat, the closed city that housed workers from Chernobyl. She was cold, but then again, she was always cold. The walls in her building were thin. Damp and wind clawed through cracks and she huddled under blankets to escape them. She had fallen asleep working on the amplifier she hoped would increase efficiency at the nuclear power plant, the prototype lying on her chest. It was small and crude, a circuit board covered with diodes and capacitors. She didn't hear the explosion or feel the catastrophic shudder as Reactor No. 4 ripped apart, its insides flayed, releasing the most dangerous substances known to man. Nor did she witness the shock of light that stabbed the dark, because at that exact moment Anna tore through time. It was her first jump—and it was an accident.

When she opened her eyes, she was on her back in the snow, alone, on a mountain, clutching the smoking amplifier. Her head felt like it was being split in two; her hands throbbed. They were burned and raw; she didn't know why. She assumed she was dreaming, but she never felt pain in dreams, only fear when nightmares had her seeing soldiers at her door. It was why she still wore boots to bed, even now as an old woman, so she could run from them like her mother should have run all those years ago. But on that mountain there were no soldiers. She put the amplifier in her pocket and her scorched hands in the snow. That hurt even more. Wind slid through her nightgown and scraped at her skin and with every sensation, she was more convinced this wasn't a dream. This was real. She quickly understood that she needed to find shelter or she would freeze.

She spotted a building in the distance. Smoke stained the sky above, leaking from the chimney. If she could get to that building, inside, she'd be safer. She slipped and clawed her way to her feet and forced herself forward. The building was narrow and long, built with stone. As she stumbled toward it, she passed a spot in the snow that bloomed red with fresh blood trailing in a long line. Her panic grew.

Perhaps the KGB had left her here? It was no secret Gorbachev detested her. Her safety protocols were expensive and slowed production, but without Anna and those protocols there would be no RBMK reactors—and those reactors were Gorbachev's pride. He wouldn't kill her, she assured herself. Besides, if he did, it wouldn't be like this. It would be with a bullet. This was too elaborate.

The front door wasn't locked. Just before she opened it there was a flash. After that, the pain in her head was gone. Relief. She barreled through the entrance, aware of heat as it rolled over her like a wave. She spilled onto a bench. A black parka hung next to her. She put it on and slowly her body warmed. As her temperature rose, so did her terror. The smoke from the chimney meant someone was there, but it was too quiet. She peered down the hall and had the feeling that this complex was familiar, but she couldn't place it. "Hello?" she called. Her voice shook from fear and cold, and only silence hit her back.

She pulled the parka tighter and that was when she realized it was wet. She looked at her charred hands. They were covered in blood. The parka she was wearing was soaked with it. So was a black uniform on the floor. She let out a scream. But again she was met only with silence. "Anyone?" she called.

She crept deeper into the building, down the hallway. The walls were covered in bright murals. Adrenaline had her mind working faster than her body, and as she stumbled through, she caught glimpses of the art, of what seemed to be three superwomen with capes and high boots.

In the kitchen, the table was toppled. Chairs were overturned. Anna grabbed a knife, held it up as best she could. That was when she recognized the lead-lined box from her laboratory flung into the corner, covered with warning stickers she had created. The box was made to hold pellets of enriched uranium oxide, the fuel used in the RBMK reactors.

She heard a moan. "Anna?"

Anna jumped back, stabbed the knife into the air in a wild gesture. She scanned the room, searched for a threat, for someone, tried to think who could do this. "Anna," a woman's voice said again, and Anna saw her, a stranger lying in a puddle of blood next to a picture window that looked out over the ice-covered mountains. She appeared to have been shot in the chest, to be bleeding out. Anna dropped to her knees at the woman's side and tried to apply pressure with blood-soaked towels already next to her. It was all she knew to do.

"What happened? Is anyone else here?" Anna asked, frantic. She looked at the woman's face, tried to place it, but she didn't recognize her. "How did you know my name?" Blood gushed from the woman's chest, spilled over Anna's hands as she pressed harder to try to stop it. Her panic rose. Surely whoever did this would hunt Anna next.

"Why are we here?" Anna asked, and then saw two pendants around the stranger's neck, golden bears. One bear was on its haunches, ready to fight. The other was on all fours, resting, at peace. She looked down at her own matching necklace dangling between them. Anna's mother had given Anna the bears just before she was taken. They were unique, a wedding present to her own mother, and Anna had never seen those pendants anywhere else. "Where did you get that necklace?" Anna asked. "Who are you?"

"You gave it to me. Or you will." The woman's voice was a rasp. "Anna, we failed."

"What are you talking about? What's happening?"

"I'm Manya. Your daughter."

Anna's elbows buckled, her hands slipped, and she had to remind herself to keep pressure on the wound. Anna hadn't seen her daughter since she was a baby. This had to be a cruel trick. Anna had spent years staring at any girl or woman who was the right age, sure that if they happened across each other, she would recognize her daughter. But this woman didn't resemble who she imagined her Manya to be. Anna forced herself to look closer. She tried to find a trace of Yasha or of her own self in her features, her voice, but fear and panic made it impossible to see. "Manya?" A surge of sadness paralyzed Anna as she realized the irony of what might be unfolding, the idea that she might only see her daughter on the two ends of her life, as a baby and a corpse. Tears drenched her cheeks, fell on the woman and mixed with all that blood. "Are you really Manya?"

"You gave me the bears, said you would trust me if you saw them." The woman's voice was softer now. She didn't have much time. "You said if I told you about the cake, your tenth birthday, you would know me." A queasy sensation hit Anna when she heard the word *cake*. The woman was fading, paler even than she had been a minute earlier. "We're running out of time. This is your first jump. Your amplifier, it pulled you through a ripple in space-time. It's December 8, 1992." The woman's eyes fluttered. Anna shook her to keep her awake.

"Time travel? I actually did it?" Anna whispered. "This is 1992?"

"Yes, but we failed." The woman gasped for air. "This is your station. The one you designed. Yasha built it. For you."

It was beginning to make sense now, why it felt familiar.

"We failed. Again," the woman whispered. "You have to try again. For Raisa. You promised to save Raisa."

"Who is Raisa?"

"Your granddaughter."

Anna shook her head. It was too much to take in and she was trying to parse facts from the emotions roiling through her, the fear and regret, sadness and confusion, making it hard to think clearly. The woman— her daughter, Manya, maybe—grabbed Anna's hand. It was warm and slick, covered in blood.

"Chernobyl melted down. Reactor Number Four." The woman's voice was even weaker.

"It couldn't melt down. I designed it. Oversaw the safety protocols myself," Anna said.

"The impossible is always possible." A ghost of a smile crossed the woman's face. "You told me that." And then, "The reaction caused the jump. We're out of time." She gasped. "Save Raisa. Remember you promised." The woman struggled to hand Anna a worn photograph just as everything around Anna turned into static, as if she were watching television and the antenna needed to be adjusted. She was sucked into a place with no light at all. Her legs and arms lengthened and stretched. She was sure she was dying and she screamed because she couldn't leave, not yet, only the sound was lost in the dark.

"Anna," a voice said. Anna opened her eyes. Vera, her nurse, was standing over her, back in her cold, damp bedroom in Pripyat. Vera had been assigned to Anna seven years ago even though she didn't need her. Young, dark-haired and all heart, Vera was more spy than attendant. The Soviets watched all their best scientists with *nurses* like Vera. "You screamed," Vera said. "What are you wearing? What happened to your hands?"

Anna looked down to see that she was still wearing the parka from the mountain. She'd been too cold to take it off even if it was soaked in blood. She was holding the photograph in her burned, tortured hands, now blistered and bleeding.

"Can I help you take off your boots at least?"

"Leave me alone," Anna said. "I tell you all the time, leave me be. I don't need your help." She turned away, reeling from the shock of what she'd just seen, to look at the old photograph. There in the picture was the family she hadn't contacted in decades. Yulia and Lazar. They were older, but there was no question it was them. They stood in front of a store's plate glass window. The woman from the mountain—Manya, yes, it had to be Manya, Anna decided—was next to them. She was smiling, holding a baby. Baby Raisa, Anna's granddaughter. A date was scribbled in the bottom corner: 1971. Anna started rocking back and forth, tried to make sense of everything that was happening. Manya. The memory of the birthday cake and the bears, they were all real, proof—of what?

"The explosion, it was violent. It shook the building. Did you hit your head?" Vera asked, bringing Anna back. "At least let me bandage your hands."

"What explosion?"

"Something happened at Chernobyl. There's a terrible fire."

"It melted down," Anna said, remembering what Manya had predicted. Anna hadn't believed her then. But now she looked toward the window and saw an eerie blue light streaming through the glass. She stumbled out of bed to take a closer look, and her foot crunched on something. It was the amplifier. It must have fallen from her pocket. The circuit board was charred. Anna ran her fingers over the melted diodes and capacitors. Her mind raced. Berlin. That was where she first thought about the theory of ripples in space-time—of time travel. Anna blinked and realized she believed that whatever had happened on the mountain was in the future. But Chernobyl was now. Anna was the chief engineer and those reactors were her responsibility. Instead of seeing the silhouette of illuminated towers, she saw a column of fire topped by a blue beam of light like a spike splitting the sky, and Anna knew this wasn't just a fire. The reactor really was melting down just as Manya had told her it would. Tens of thousands, maybe hundreds of thousands of people would die, and it was Anna's fault.

"No, no!" Anna cried, feeling overwhelmed and terrified by the mountain and Manya, and now this. She leaned against the wall to steady herself. Crowds had formed in the courtyard below. All of Pripyat had come out. It looked like they were in the rain, but it wasn't rain. It was radioactive ash coating the lawn, the streets and cars, and worst of all, the people. Children were laughing and dancing. They were playing in poison and no one was stopping them. Anna wanted to run outside and warn them, but it was too late. It had already been on their skin, sucked into their lungs. She knew these children, the crowds, they would all be dead within a week.

"What did I do?" Guilt and shame took hold, and then the phone rang and she knew exactly why, and what would happen next. All the blame and punishment would fall on her. Arrest, torture, death.

"No, she wasn't at the lab. She didn't do anything wrong," Vera said into the receiver. Anna shoved clothing into a bag along with the singed amplifier. She was still holding that photograph of Manya, Raisa, Yulia, and Lazar.

Anna had only one option. It was a risk, but everything was a risk now. She had to go to that mountain, to the cosmic ray station she'd designed all those years ago, so she could go back in time and stop all of this, put the world back the way it should be.

PART I

If not now, when?

—Pirkei Avot

MOLLY

Philadelphia

t cost two hundred," Papa said in his thick accent, waving his arm at the exhaust belching from the truck that had just pulled away. He pointed to the pile it had left behind: concrete blocks, mortar, wooden beams, and nails. Everything lay in a disjointed heap next to the back door of their butcher shop. Manya, though no one called her Manya anymore, stood next to him and her mother, staring at the delivery. She was ten years old and constantly frustrated by her parents' choices, like this one, always trying to help them make better ones. It was why she had renamed herself Molly when she started kindergarten. Her parents, Yulia and Lazar, embraced this decision, praised her for it because *Manya* was Soviet, *Molly* was American, and while they didn't agree on much, all three of them were eager to leave the USSR behind. Now her parents were convinced this pile of construction materials would help them live like real Americans, and Molly needed them to understand that was ridiculous.

She held up the issue of *Life* magazine that had inspired the purchase. The man on the cover wore something called a civilian fallout suit. She imagined him laughing at their family for buying all of this, the supplies *Life* said every household needed to build their personal shelter. Her parents read *Life* as a set of instructions on what Americans were supposed to think and do. Since Hires advertised on its pages, they bought the root beer. Same with Kellogg's Corn Flakes, Johnson & Johnson bandages, and General Electric's television. And because the magazine said they were supposed to be scared of nuclear bombs, they were scared and preparing to survive—with the schematics from the latest issue.

"No one else in the United States is really doing this," Molly said.

Mama stood with her arm around Molly's shoulders. Molly wiggled for space, tired of Mama always being too close, but her mother only held her tighter. "Every American *is* doing this, or it wouldn't be in the magazine," Mama said.

"They're not. It's stupid." Just saying the word *stupid* made Molly feel better, loosened the knot tied in her gut from the frustration with her parents, with this project. The shelter wouldn't magically make them like everyone else. Anyway, *she* felt American. It was her parents and their bad ideas, like this one, that held them back.

"Two hundred, for this? For nothing." Papa spat on the ground.

"It cost two hundred *dollars*," Mama said in her perfect American accent, correcting his English. Mama was a linguist, and night after night, for years, she had tried to teach Papa so he could blend in like she did. Molly was embarrassed that he couldn't do it, that kids at school laughed at him. "Lazar, add 'dollars' or 'bucks.' And don't roll the *r*."

"The door," he said to Molly. She opened it and the hinge creaked. The rusted bell overhead rang. "It cost two hundred dollars," he said, still with a thick accent. He picked up a concrete block from the pile and went inside. Mama followed, carrying a sack of mortar. A white cloud puffed around her from a hole in the bag.

"Can I go play now?" Molly asked. It was Saturday. The store was closed, and all the other kids would be in the park. It wasn't fair that she couldn't be outside with them, having fun. "Please?"

"No. Start carrying supplies down to the basement," Papa called.

"Check the list," Mama said at the same time, wanting Molly to compare the list of what they'd ordered to the actual materials dumped behind their store.

"American kids play at the park on Saturday," Molly said. She let go of the handle, the door slammed, and that knot in her gut tightened again.

When Mama came back up from the basement, the fringes of her hair were dusted white with mortar. "It's the sabbath and Yom Kippur. You're not going anywhere," she said to Molly.

"We don't even go to synagogue. What does it matter?"

"We're Jewish. It matters." Mama kissed the top of Molly's head.

"Stop touching me."

"I can't stop. I'm your mother. Now check the list. Make sure we weren't cheated."

"No one's cheating us." Molly groaned and looked back at the magazine. Across from the list was a drawing, a cutout of the finished shelter. It depicted two parents and two children inside. The little girl was brushing her straight hair. The father was lighting a cigarette and the mother was tucking the little boy into one of the bunk beds. The shelves were filled with canned goods and first-aid supplies. They were all smiling. *It's fake*, Molly thought. No one stuck in that shelter would be happy while the world outside was melting. She knew it because she had seen pictures of what those bombs did.

Mama looked over Molly's shoulder at the family in the drawing and her voice changed, fell. "The four of them look perfect. But they're not real. Don't believe in the glitz and polish."

"I know, I know," Molly said. She rolled her eyes, anticipating what was coming next.

"The veneer wears away, just—"

"Like it did in Berlin," Molly said, finishing the sentence. Mama always talked about Berlin that way, told Molly that when she got there in 1937 it was a city filled with life and dreams, but when she left in 1941 it was a terrifying shell. And she warned it could happen to the United States, too. "If you don't believe in this stupid picture, why are we building the shelter?"

"Because your father believes, and we do things for people we love." She took a deep breath, started walking back inside with another sack. "Keep working."

Work. It was the one thing her parents agreed on: Above all else, working hard was the way forward, no matter where you lived or what you wanted. It was why if Molly wasn't at school, Mama watched her do homework or stationed her at the cash register, unless they needed her help with slaughtering and slicing. But kids in America played in the park on the weekend. They didn't work. Building wasn't what Molly was supposed to be doing, and now her stomach was so tight she needed water. A drink always helped.

She went inside to what Mama called their home but was really just a room in the back of their butcher shop, separated by a curtain and crammed with rosebushes Mama adored and Molly hated. Molly's bed was stuffed in one corner and Mama and Papa's bed was in the other. They had a small stove and a counter with a tiny half sink. Their sheets came from Sears because they advertised in *Life*. The walls were covered in posters from national parks like Yellowstone. She filled a glass, drank, and felt a little better. But she still thought she should not have to spend her weekends working, listening to her parents tugging one way and another. She took a deep breath and yelled down the basement stairs, "I'm going to the park." Then she ran as fast as she could, shaking and thrilled that she was breaking their rules, crashing through the door so hard the bell clanged and shook. She heard Mama call after her, but by then Molly was too far away and she didn't look back. They wouldn't chase her or make a scene. They couldn't risk it because they weren't in America legally. They needed to hide in plain sight, her parents said, and in that moment, Molly loved taking advantage of it. She ran as fast as her saddle shoes would carry her, skirt flying and braids coming loose. It was a release to put space between her and that butcher shop. Every step loosened the pain.

They lived in a part of Northeast Philadelphia some called Little Russia, where all their neighbors were refuseniks like them, Soviet Jews forbidden to emigrate but who found a way to escape. No one knew who had legal papers and who didn't, and no one asked. But instead of living like they were now free, Molly thought, they all lived like caged animals in a neighborhood that must be just like the one they left. Everyone spoke Russian and ate borscht and herring, slurped soup bones and marrow. The store signs were in Cyrillic. The bread at the bakery was dark and coarse and the dresses at Svetlana's shop were thick and out of style. The baker called to Molly as she ran. So did the man who owned the shoe shop. They all knew her. Five blocks away, Little Russia collided with an Irish community, and the children all crashed into one another at school and at the park. Bigger kids had tight-knit groups defined by their roots. Smaller kids, like Molly, didn't care. Her best friend, Catherine, was as Irish as could be, and they laughed at the fact that they both had blond hair and blue eyes.

The park had a chain-link fence around one side. Molly ran her hands along the steel, still shaking from the thrill of disobeying her parents. She hurried past older boys playing basketball and the girls standing in circles. She went straight for the swings.

"Hey," she said to Catherine, who was already there. Molly started pumping her legs.

"Freak," Catherine replied. Her pigtails bobbed.

"I know you are but what am I?" Molly stuck her tongue out and they both giggled.

"Did you tell your mom your birthday cupcakes you brought to school yesterday were weird?" Mama used Soviet flour, which felt like grit. She bought it from the baker across the street because it was cheaper. She said no one would taste the difference, but the cupcakes tasted like they had been rolled in sand and everyone spat them out.

"I liked them," Molly lied.

They played tag and climbed on the jungle gym, skipped through hopscotch and double Dutch with other girls. By the time Molly left it was starting to get dark, and she walked home slowly, thinking about how angry her parents were going to be. They had no right to be mad, she told herself. She was sure that the kids in *Life*, the ones pictured in the shelter, if they had been real, wouldn't have helped their parents build it. They probably would have gone out and played baseball or biked around while their father hammered it together and their mother baked cookies. Why did Mama even mention Yom Kippur? Americans celebrated Christmas. If Molly's parents wanted a *real* American family, they should have let her play like a normal kid, forget about being Jewish.

Across the street from their store, she saw the baker lugging a box out to the corner. It looked heavy and he called her over, asked for help. "Thank you," he said when Molly grabbed one end. He grunted and they eased the damp, warped box to the ground.

"What is it?" Molly asked.

"Comic books. Got soaked when a pipe broke." He lifted the lid and handed her one. It was wrinkled and moist, like the box. She had always thought comic books were for boys, never looked at any closely, but this one was different. There was a girl on the cover. She was about Molly's age and she looked strong, standing with her hands on her hips like she was in charge.

"This is beautiful," Molly said. She flipped through, couldn't take her eyes off the pages, the main character. The colors were bright and the girl appeared to be smart. Her eyes were wide, and she seemed to know what was coming and was ready for it, had already planned her next move, and even the next one after that. "I've never seen a comic book with a girl."

"That's Mary Marvel. I was gonna leave this here for whoever picked it up. You wanna take some home with you?" Yes, of course she did. He handed her a stack. "I have others in the basement, boxes that stayed dry. Let me know if you want more." She thanked him and crossed the street. Mama spotted her, ran outside, and flung her arms around Molly.

"We were so scared," she said, kissing Molly's head and hands, arms and shoulders, anything she could reach, while Molly tried to pull away. Mama's long blond hair fell on Molly and mixed with hers, indistinguishable. There was no blood shared between them, but their coloring was the same. People told Molly how much she looked like her mother all the time. It took all Molly had not to tell them their connection was a lie, because she wasn't supposed to tell anyone she was adopted. Her real mother was named Anna and Anna still lived in the Soviet Union. She had given Molly away, and Molly wasn't allowed to talk about her because she was dangerous. Mama and Papa refused to tell her what that meant, but she understood she couldn't cross that line. Besides, Mama loved it when people talked about how much she and Molly looked alike, and Molly loved seeing Mama's expression when the subject came up, the only time her lips broke into a full smile.

"Yulia, you should be yelling at her, not kissing her," Papa said.

"I thought she was gone." Mama held Molly even tighter.

"We're in America," Molly said. "Of course I was fine."

"People disappear here, too," Papa said.

"I was only at the park. I told you where I was going."

Mama pulled back enough for Molly to see that her face was blotchy and red, covered in tears. "You can't run away. Do you understand?" Her voice turned hard, and Molly knew a punishment was coming.

"You're cleaning the display cases for a week. Go to bed." Then, "Wait. What's in your hand?"

"Comics."

Mama shrugged like it didn't matter, then kissed Molly again. "I was so scared."

"You're scared all the time," Molly said. "Catherine's parents aren't ever scared."

"I'm sure Catherine's parents never had to live through what we did. We never want you to know why we're scared," Papa said. Molly kicked at a chunk of sawdust on the floor. Papa continued, "Mollushka, we can be anything in America. We have opportunities here that Jews, Soviets, don't have. But it's fragile and we must be careful. That's why we worry."

"What do you mean it's fragile?"

"We'll explain when you're older," Mama said.

But Molly was tired of her parents putting off explanations. "What happened in the Soviet Union? What is so fragile?" Her voice got louder.

"Go to bed."

"Why should I listen?" She clenched her fists to the sides of her head, squeezed her eyes shut because this was frustrating, infuriating. "Talk to me about what happened. Why should I do anything you say when you don't tell me? Your shelter is stupid. You're stupid. You're not even my real parents." She said it because she knew it would hurt.

"Watch that tongue," Papa said in an even tone, not rising to her anger. "Bed."

"I hate you. I hate this store." She kept going, harder because she couldn't stop herself by then. "My real parents would never do this to me."

"You don't know that," Mama said, unfazed. "Double math assignments tomorrow."

Molly wanted to yell and scream more, but by then her stomach hurt so much she couldn't breathe. She bent over to ease the pain, to suck in air, and when she looked up, Mama and Papa were already carrying a candle and their small table through the curtain, out to the front of the store. The steel roll-downs were closed to protect the glass front and they made the space entirely dark. When Mama and Papa wanted privacy, they sat together out there, drinking vodka by candlelight next to the cooler that held slaughtered chickens, herring, chunks of beef. The hum of the refrigerator drowned their voices so Molly could never hear what they said. She pictured them huddling, whispering about her punishment. "I hate you," she yelled one more time. They didn't respond, and she flung herself onto her mattress and cried. She tried to be loud, hoped her parents would come to comfort her, to apologize, but they didn't.

When her tears were gone, she looked up at the webbed cracks in the ceiling, a hundred lines crooked across the old plaster, and she remembered the comic books from the baker. Molly pulled her flashlight out from under the corner of her mattress and began reading. Mary and her twin brother, Captain Marvel, were separated at birth. At the age of twelve they were reunited, and Mary realized her superpowers. While both used the same word, *Shazam*, to invoke those powers, her brother's powers came from Solomon, Hercules, Atlas, Zeus, Achilles, and Mercury, while Mary's came from Selena, Hippolyta, Ariadne, Zephyrus, Aurora, and Minerva. A comic book with a powerful girl at the center and all kinds of superhero adventures took her mind off the anger. Molly read page after page.

At one point she heard Mama speaking in a loud voice and Molly stopped cold. "Anna cares about science. Yes, she built the atomic bomb for the Soviets, but for her it was a lab experiment. I know her. She wouldn't build a weapon to kill people. Not our Anna, not Molly's mother. She just wouldn't do it. She built it, they stole it and now they're using it to threaten America. That's what's happening. She lost control of her own science." Molly's heart sped up, her body tensed, and she tried to make sense of what she'd just heard. Her birth mother, Anna, built the atomic bomb? Maybe Molly had heard wrong. Surely her parents couldn't have kept a secret like that. Molly strained to hear more, almost fell off her bed by leaning so far over the side. Mama continued, "It's always been about those ripples she saw. Space-time, then gamma rays. She never imagined people would be building shelters, terrified like this. She wanted to make the world better."

"Don't be naive," Papa said, his voice also louder than usual, as if he was finally mad. "She had to know. There's only one reason you build a weapon. To kill. Period. And if you design it, build it, you're guilty. She's guilty. Anna is guilty."

"Shh," Mama said, and their voices dropped. Molly leaned back and felt the weight of what she had just heard like an anvil on her chest. She didn't understand everything. *Space-time*, *gamma rays*, and *ripples* were all new words, but her instinct was to defend her birth mother. Surely Molly didn't come from a woman who could build a bomb to kill millions of people. But her parents didn't lie to each other—which meant Molly's birth mother built the Soviet atomic bomb, the reason behind that stupid shelter in their basement.

"No, no, no," Molly said. Her brain was spinning with too many ideas, all underlined with a new kind of panic that if her birth mother built a nuclear bomb, then she was a murderer, or she would be because when countries have bombs they use them. That's what Molly had seen in all those books at school. Weapons were always used. Surely Mama was right, Molly tried to tell herself. Anna wasn't a villain. If she built the bomb, she couldn't have ever wanted to use it. If her mother were a murderer, Molly would know. Wouldn't she? Molly went around and around in circles before she convinced herself that Anna was like the superheroes Molly had been reading about. Her power was her brain. She used her brain for good, and evil characters, the Soviets, took what she did and used it for bad. "That's it," she said out loud, convincing herself. "Anna needs to fight them so her work is only used for good.

For good guys." The notion helped settle her a bit. She turned off her flashlight, stuffed it back under the mattress, and rolled herself into a tight ball. She tried to imagine Anna in a cape and boots flying over Billy Penn on top of city hall, racing to catch the bomb before it fell on their city. She listed all the ways Anna could save the world with nuclear powers, imagined what it would look like for her to fight and regain control of her work. Molly must have fallen asleep, somehow, because the next thing she knew, Mama was kissing her, telling her it was time to wake up and get ready to open the shop.

"You scared us yesterday," Mama said at breakfast. She and Molly were at the table. Papa stood nearby at their tiny stove. "We can't lose you." Molly rubbed her eyes, was waking up slowly. "We can't always do what we want—"

Molly interrupted, "I heard you talking about Anna. Is it true she built the bomb?" Mama's face went white. "You don't think she's a bad guy. Right?" Molly pushed.

"It's complicated."

"Then it's true. She did it?" Molly kept going. "Papa said she's guilty."

"Your papa sees in black and white. I envy him for that. I love him for that." Mama's voice was quiet, shaken. She kissed the top of Molly's head. "We'll talk about it later."

Molly knew that when Mama said that they were done, she wouldn't talk about it again, only Molly wanted more. She pushed. "Anna built the atomic bomb for the Soviets. Is that why we ran?" Mama was on her feet before Molly even finished the question. She walked to Papa and he handed her a steaming glass mug. Papa's Soviet mugs, coffee, and blackened cezve pot that brewed on the stove were the only un-American things they refused to give up. "Papa, I heard you talking about Anna. She built the bomb. You never told me."

His face had turned the color of ash and his fingers shook. "You weren't supposed to know."

"But I know. You have to tell me more."

"We…we can't." He turned and walked through the curtain to the front of the shop. Mama followed and the conversation was over.

When the store opened, her parents put Molly at the cash register, a job she hated because she had to talk to customers. Her only relief came during lulls when she could read her new comic books. The baker had given her all twelve issues in the *Mary Marvel* series. Molly read every crinkled copy that day. Mary Marvel could fly. Bullets bounced off her. She could conjure lightning. Molly couldn't get enough because she'd never seen such a powerful, smart girl, and Mary had Molly dreaming she could be just as strong and confident.

"I've never seen you read for so long," Papa said after the late day rush. His voice was bright and lively, as if their morning conversation hadn't happened.

Molly couldn't let it go. "My birth mother is a superhero," she said, defiant. Her papa's earlier disgust, the word *guilty* were both still running through her head, keeping her angry. "Her power is building bombs—for good. I know it has to be for good. I heard you last night. Why do you hate her?"

"I don't hate her." His voice softened, was tender even, and it surprised her. "I love Anna, actually. She's my family—not by blood, but the bond is just as strong. Family is complicated. You know that." He picked up a broom, began sweeping sawdust. "We have better things ahead of us here in America. No need to stew in the past."

But Molly wasn't done. "What about my birth father? Who is he? Did he help?" Mama came through the curtain. Her heels stabbed the linoleum as she walked.

"Your papa's right. Better to look forward," Mama said.

"Please," Molly begged. "Just tell me something about them."

"Never mention them again." Mama's voice went terrifyingly still. "Do your math work."

"I hate math. Americans hate math. Only Soviets think numbers are worth anything."

"That's what foolish Americans say. Yuri Gagarin. How do you think he traveled to space? Math and science. And hard work. It's rewarded in this country. It's how we're going to build our stores. A whole chain," Papa said. He held out his hands, made a sweeping motion as if showcasing the future. "By the time I retire, you'll have a dozen shops to manage."

"I don't want to be a butcher."

"Of course you do," Papa said. "And you'll need math to run the books and check statements, so do your math work."

Molly shivered and picked up her workbook. She always tried to do the problems, but she never excelled the way her parents expected. When she looked at a triangle, she didn't see a hypotenuse or the area that fell inside those three lines. She saw the silhouette, the jagged cut in white space on the page. She saw the way light illuminated and hid, magnified and laid the truth bare. Molly tried to explain that geometry's rules used the wrong perspective to explain the world. Numbers weren't a skeleton that described the universe. Light was the source that allowed them to put all the pieces together, only Papa didn't understand, could never comprehend the way Molly's mind worked. "Come on, Molly, we went through this, what theorem, what's the formula? You're brilliant. You can do this," he'd said to her over and over. His frustration made her feel like she wasn't good enough. Papa would tell her if she couldn't figure out how to calculate the angles of a triangle, she wouldn't get good grades and all those dreams he had for her would die. She wanted to cry and yell, but if she did, he would give her more work. The only defense she could think of came from Mary Marvel.

"Shazam!"

Papa leaned back and told her to stop the nonsense, but she said it again. "Shazam."

"I have no patience for this," Papa said. He went through the curtain to the back.

Mama kissed her. "It will be okay. Just keep trying." That only made Molly angrier. She couldn't change the way she saw that triangle.

"Shazam," Molly said the next time her parents wanted her to change her clothes to blend in at school, yelled at her to tighten the bow in her ponytail. "Shazam," she said at the playground when kids teased her because she never had peanut butter and jelly for lunch, only salami. "Shazam," she said when a customer argued that she hadn't given the right change even though she had. Each time she said it, she stood a little taller. She asked the baker for more comic books and fell in love with Merry, the Girl of a Thousand Gimmicks, and Wonder Woman, featuring the Amazon origin story. The world of comics was dominated by characters, shapes, and feelings. And unlike math, they made sense.

At eleven years old, Molly read and reread every issue she could get her hands on, and then started tracing the ones she loved best. Following their lines even inspired her to make her own, and unlike schoolwork, drawing came easily. When she drew, the pain she felt dulled with every line she added to the page. When classmates saw her art, they stopped and stared. "*You* made that?" a boy on the bus asked. "Tell me who helped you," her math teacher said.

Molly made women her central characters because she couldn't find enough women superheroes, and the ones she drew were the companions she wanted. She could imagine herself among them, being clever like them, and it made her feel less alone. She named the main character Atomic Anna after her birth mother, gave her a red outfit with the flaming cape she'd imagined the very first night she understood Anna was a superhero. Atomic Anna wore a mask because Molly couldn't draw her face. She had no idea what her mother looked like. She gave Anna powers she imagined an atomic character could have: X-ray vision, fire bolts like bombs that could both explode buildings and create power for people who needed it. Anna could create orbs that hung like lights over cities so bad guys couldn't hide. Her radiation was only deadly when she chose for it to be, and she slept inside a nuclear reactor.

Atomic Anna was never beaten or thrown into refrigerators like female characters in other comic books. She was the hero and her team was all women, a group Molly called the Radioactives. Mighty Minerva was the superhero who wore all white. She was an artist who designed the cases and devices that held Anna's science. She had the power to make her drawings come to life. If she needed a laser gun, she could draw one and pick it up off the page. Rocket Raisa was the third woman on the team. She was named after Mama's sister, Ruth, and her superpower was speed. She could fly and run faster than anyone or anything on earth.

The more Molly drew, the more she could escape into the *Atomic Anna* universe. Her comic books helped her ignore her parents, who were watching over her more closely than ever. By 1963, the second anniversary of the Bay of Pigs was coming and her mother started guessing at dates when the riots and backlash against Soviet Americans would begin. "We used to predict pogroms; this is no different," Mama said.

"This is America. There are no pogroms," Molly argued.

"Just because it hasn't happened doesn't mean it won't. Why are you bent over again?"

"It hurts."

"What hurts?" Mama asked. Molly couldn't explain the pain. It was easier to say it was in her gut or stomach, but it was more general than that. It was a queasiness that came and went with a dozen emotions that swirled around inside her so quickly she couldn't pin them down to name them for her parents or the doctor.

"I told you I can't describe it," Molly said.

"Fine." Mama was exasperated, but Molly didn't know what else to say. "It's Shabbat. Help me get ready." That meant help making the chicken soup and challah they had every week. Papa had grown up eating a special, secret meal on Friday nights, so Mama insisted on their observing the tradition now that in America they could do so openly.

* * *

By 1964, as Molly was growing into her teenage years, Mama started spending more time making sure Molly's sweaters were plain and her skirts were long. She wanted Molly to look like a typical American teen, not a beauty. One night, Mama and Papa were huddled by the thrumming display case, next to the chicken, with a candle, and when Molly went to them to say good night, Mama looked her up and down and said, "Boys are trouble. Being attractive is not what you want. Stay away from them for a few more years." It was snowing. The streets were quiet save for plows that ground past, scraping the road. There was a bottle of champagne on the rickety table. Molly had never seen her parents drink any alcohol but vodka.

"Yuck. Boys are yuck," Molly said, even though she wasn't sure she still felt that way. She used to think that, but things were changing inside her in a way that felt overwhelming. She pointed to the bottle. "What's the occasion?"

"Anna's birthday. We always celebrate."

"I didn't know that."

Mama stood up and turned on the radio. They were playing some kind of piano music that sounded old to Molly, but Mama's face lit up. "We used to dance to this," Mama said. "Anna and I. In Berlin."

"Is that where she met my father?" Molly asked. She had to try.

Mama ignored her question but refilled her own glass and Papa's, then pulled out a third from behind the register, added a splash of champagne, and handed it to Molly. "A celebration of Anna." The three of them held their glasses up and Molly drank, thrilled they were finally pulling her into their circle. The champagne bubbles danced over her tongue, tickled her mouth. She had tasted vodka before, when her parents weren't looking, and it burned her throat. This champagne was nothing like that. It was beautiful and sweet. She loved it as much as she loved the way her parents were acting. Mama took Papa's hand and pulled him to her so they were dancing. They looked carefree, like she had never witnessed before, as if they could finally enjoy themselves, and for a moment Molly could imagine them younger, lighter. "Mollushka, join us," Mama said. She held out her hand.

"I didn't know you dance," Molly said.

Mama winked as they twirled and turned. "Parents can't tell their children everything."

"Happy birthday, Annushka," Papa said. He poured more champagne for him and Mama.

"Was my father tall?" Molly asked.

"Don't ask about Yasha," Mama said.

"Yasha? That's his name." Mama had slipped. Molly pounced. "Is he still alive?"

"He's probably still chasing Anna," Papa said.

"Enough," Mama said. She turned the music up and they danced long past Molly's bedtime. Molly had never been happier with her parents. She finally felt like they could throw off the weight of the past and instead experience its joy, the hope of a real future.

*　*　*

By the spring of 1965, business was good. Molly's parents had long since finished the shelter and instead of leaving it open and empty, ready to use at a moment's notice, they filled it with supplies for the butcher shop because they needed to keep more stock on hand. They could also finally afford a down payment on a real home. Mama wanted to be closer to downtown Philadelphia, and so she and Papa wore their best clothes and polished their shoes to attend open houses. They were always greeted with smiles and ushered inside, but as soon as Papa opened his mouth and the real estate agents heard his accent, they hurried her parents out and never returned their calls. Even with Joseph McCarthy in the rearview mirror, no one wanted a possible Communist for a neighbor. Only Little Russia would have them, but even that wasn't simple. When they applied for a mortgage, the banks refused. Papa's cousin Andrey was the only one who would help, the one who had always helped. Yulia, Lazar, and Molly had snuck into the United States through Canada. Without proper papers, they didn't have a way to get a driver's license, a bank account, or a passport, had no hope of opening their own shop except through Andrey. He was the one who, for a fee, secured everything they needed to become perfect fake Americans: birth certificates, social security numbers, and the store itself. They hated him for charging them—his own family—so much, and loved him for what he gave them: hope. Papa dreaded accepting his help with a mortgage, but there was no other way and so they borrowed from him again, agreeing to pay exorbitant interest plus a larger piece of their shop's profits.

Being rejected by American banks and relying on Andrey's shady money crushed Papa, but Mama smiled as everything came together. They landed in one of the row houses blocks from the butcher shop. It was narrow and red brick with a cement path rolling from the door to the sidewalk. The wall-to-wall carpet looked like mustard to Molly, but Mama called it gold. "We would never have had so much space in the USSR," she said. Then she added quietly, "Not in Berlin, either." But the happier she was, the more unhappy Papa seemed.

"Maybe America is a delusion like *Pravda* warned," he said, scowling.

* * *

At fourteen, Molly found it easier to be alone than to be with other kids. By then, the girls were changing; at least other girls were. Molly's chest was flat and that pain in her gut hadn't let up. Still, she and

Catherine were at least friendly until a new swimming pool opened in the neighborhood. The rules there were different from at the playground because mothers sat on the side and didn't let their children mix, making sure the Irish and Soviets kept their distance. Molly tried stuffing her bathing suit so it looked like she had bigger breasts while she was sunbathing, but one of the boys saw the tissues sticking out and he made fun of her for it. Everyone laughed. Catherine was worst of all, bringing Molly a box of Kleenex the next day in school. That was the end of their friendship, and Molly tried to tell herself it would be all right, that trying to fit in was exhausting anyway. It was easier to live in her artwork, to imagine the life of a superhero, and so Molly spent more time drawing, getting better and better.

*　*　*

"You look like a perfect American," Papa told Molly one night when she was fifteen. She couldn't tell if he was proud or angry, still holding on to the American dream or giving it up. They were in the living room. Papa was watching television and Mama was straightening Molly's hair on the ironing board. She moved in long strokes, starting as close to the roots as she could. Molly hated the sound of the singe when the iron came down, all the times her scalp had been seared.

"I'm not really American, not like the kids in school."

"Of course you are."

"No one else eats salami that looks like ours," she said.

"That's because they don't know from real salami," Papa said.

Molly dragged her hair out from under the iron. It fell hot on her back and she leaned to the side to keep it away from her skin while it cooled. "I wasn't done," Mama said.

"I'm done," Molly said. "You keep wanting to blend in but I'm sick and tired of it. Why can't I go to the soph hop next week? Pasha invited me."

"You need to study," Mama said. "Enough with the art. Put your time where it matters."

"Art matters."

"It will never put food on the table," Papa said.

Mama tried to kiss her, but Molly stepped away, fought back the only way she knew how. "Why didn't Anna and Yasha come with you?" And, "You dance and get drunk on her birthday. You're so much fun then. Why aren't you like that more?"

"Celebrating isn't living. It's hiding for a night. That's all," Mama said.

"Maybe we should hide more. There's nothing else for us in America," Papa said.

"What?" Mama went pale. He reached for the vodka bottle on the side table next to him and took a swig. He fell into a silence as a jingle for toothpaste crept into the room. A perfect freckled boy smiled at them. Mama looked shattered. Molly was afraid to move. Light from the television reflected on Papa's face, making him look yellow and then red. Molly knew he had never doubted the country that way before.

"We can't be anything we want here. It's all a lie. A sham," he said.

"What's happened?" Mama unplugged the iron and sat next to him.

"The bank said no to another store. That's the fifth one to refuse me."

"Why didn't you say something earlier?"

"I'm saying it now. We can't open a second store, let alone a chain. Ever."

"Andrey can help," Mama said.

"I won't accept another penny from that crook." Papa took another long drink. Molly thought she might throw up. "Maybe you're right, have always been right. All this country is good for is hiding."

"You don't mean that," Mama said. But Molly saw he did. She stared at her father with this new perspective. His black hair was pushed back, his eyes bloodshot. For the first time she saw the wrinkles in his forehead, around his mouth, and it made her uncomfortable that she hadn't seen them before. His love for America, his faith in the dream had always been a constant, something she could depend on. Without it, she wasn't sure she recognized him, understood him.

"You're just giving up?" Molly asked. "You always told me to push. To find the answer."

"They won," Papa said.

"Who won?" Molly asked.

"The Americans. I can't be one of them. Not ever. I'm an almost." He twirled the bottle, ran his finger over the peeling label. "I'm smart enough to try for what I want, to plan and go for it, but I missed it. See, I *almost* had it. Most of the world is filled with *almosts*. I will die an almost." Molly knew then that he was drunk, told herself he could change his mind in the morning.

"Papa, this isn't you," Molly said, wanting him to fight her.

"Your mama knew." He let out a sound between a laugh and a sigh. "All these years, she's known. America is like Berlin. The luster is wearing off," he continued. "If anyone asks for your papers at school, tell them they are at home. Then run. When they ask for papers, that's the end." His bottom lip was trembling. "I've wasted years on a stupid dream."

"We're in America, Papa. They don't ask for papers. And the war, it's over."

"What about Vietnam?"

"It's not the same."

"Are you sure? One day they will start asking for papers."

Molly's stomach clenched down and she ran for the bathroom, made it just in time. Her dinner and lunch came out in a giant burst that left her stomach hurting so badly she curled on the floor next to the toilet. The next morning, she started drawing invisible jets for Atomic Anna, dreaming they would carry both her and Anna away.

* * *

"Nuclear weapons should be destroyed. All of them," Molly said to her parents when she was sixteen. They were in the store waiting for a delivery truck. Molly was learning about World War II in history class and it forced her to think about her mother, what her mother had done. When Molly was younger, she had been more forgiving. She'd believed Anna worked on the bomb because of her love of science, wanting to understand laws governing the physical universe, but now she sided with Papa because she understood what had happened, found it harder to believe Anna could research and build something so destructive in a vacuum. Anyone brilliant enough to build a weapon like that had to know it would be used. That made Anna a murderer.

"They're a deterrent. No one will use them again," Papa said.

"That's not what you used to think. If we have them, it's just a matter of time before we use them. You don't believe that anymore?"

"People change," Papa said. He sounded tired.

"Then tell me about Anna and Yasha. Why did they send me away?" The truck they were waiting for pulled up and her parents went out to meet it, in effect ignoring her question. They still kept a wall up between the present in America and the past in Germany and the USSR, and the fact that Molly could never break through made her as angry and lonely as ever. She slammed through the curtain to the back of the butcher shop, grabbed her cigarettes from behind the stack of waxed paper where she hid them, and walked out to the alley. She had already set up an array of paints, planned to create a mural after the delivery, and decided to skip helping. She'd smoke instead, then paint. Her parents detested her cigarettes as much as they detested talking about Anna, and Molly wasn't embarrassed to admit that was why she lit up as often as she could.

When she had been younger it was easier to paint her birth mother as a superhero, to make Atomic Anna all good, but now Molly gave Anna flaws. In one issue she was out for revenge, wanted to kill the general who ordered his country to use an atomic bomb. In another she couldn't control her anger, which led to a nuclear power station melting down, killing thousands. Molly's drawings were more detailed now and she knew they were impressive, but she didn't show them to anyone anymore. At school kids teased her for still reading and drawing comics. They told her they were childish. At home her parents told Molly her art was a waste. Instead of drawing, she needed to spend time getting healthy. She wasn't eating enough, they said.

* * *

By the time junior year was approaching, Molly's parents were talking to her about college constantly, but Molly had bigger, better dreams. She was going to leave Philadelphia the day she got her high school diploma and go to New York City to work for the *East Village Other*. *EVO* was part of the underground comix movement, a newspaper filled with pages of psychedelic swirls, bawdy language, and doctored photographs. Best of all, it was bursting with outrageous comics that included *Captain High* and *Gentle's Tripout*, along with a feature called Slum Goddess. It was an underground publication and she got her hands on her first copy by accident. The overweight guy with the greasy hair who ran a comic shop near Little Russia handed it to her because he knew she was always looking for comics with women. "You don't get more *womanly* than this," he said as he handed it to her, laughing. After that, she called the *EVO* offices and begged the assistant who answered the phone to send issues. Trina Robbins was her favorite artist. She wrote about partying with Jim Morrison and the Byrds, and drew gorgeous comics that challenged tradition. Robbins rallied against expectations that women were meant just to marry and have children, that only men read and drew comics, and Molly wanted to work with her, to learn from her. All she needed to do was get herself to New York and she knew she could make it happen.

* * *

Viktor arrived at their butcher shop on July 1, 1969, thick with self-confidence and a swagger exaggerated by his leather jacket, which made him look like someone who never backed down from a fight. And when Molly saw him, she was sure she had found her ticket out of Little Russia. He came the day a hurricane was bearing down on the city. Molly was hunkering with her parents in the store because they couldn't afford to lose it and they were there to do whatever it took to save it. They'd even just renamed the butcher shop, called it the Russian Market, and expanded their shelves, started offering foods like tinned fish and sauces that tasted like they could have come straight from the USSR. Wind rattled the windows and the roll-down security gates. Papa tried to cover the sound with the radio, but the Gershwin tunes were interrupted by so many storm warnings it didn't help. Molly sat in the corner where they had stored canned goods before they all sold out in the rush leading up to the storm. She was wearing bell-bottom jeans and had her knees pulled up in front of her, a pad of paper resting on her thighs. She'd gotten halfway through a sketch. The Radioactives were battling the evil TNTs on a cold mountainside. Molly was lost in constructing the landscape until someone banged the steel gate.

"Coming," Papa called. His voice was higher than usual and by the way he hurried she could tell he thought it was bad news. He had warned Molly they were likely to be evacuated, but she didn't think he was right. He was always jumping to conclusions now, thinking the worst. Papa turned the first dead bolt, then the second, and unfurled the gate. A gust of wind blew Molly's page and the smell of sewage seeped inside. She caught a glimpse of the street. Water was already spilling from the gutters.

"Andrey wants his money." Molly heard a man with a Russian accent she didn't recognize. Papa stepped aside and let him in, then closed the door quickly. The music blared a flurry of piano notes clashing like the storm. Molly leaned to the side to get a look. Her first impression was that he was big. Most men wore their hair long, but his was shaved to the scalp. He had dark eyes and a white button-down shirt with a black leather jacket. She guessed he was around twenty-five years old.

"Who the hell are you?" Lazar asked.

"Viktor. Andrey's new *assistant*." Papa's face changed, went dark. Some days Papa yelled at his cousin, said he was stealing from his own family. Other days he thanked him for everything he did. "The money?" Viktor said.

"Wait here." Papa threaded past the display cases and a rosebush and slipped behind the counter. Molly couldn't take her eyes off of Viktor. Men like him, men without wedding rings, who were well-dressed, never came into the store. Nor were there men like him at school, only boys. When he noticed her staring, he smiled. Her face flushed, and he nodded as if to return the compliment and that made her skin feel even hotter. She put a hand on her hair, tried to smooth it back. She hadn't ironed it and her untamed curls were loose and wild, and suddenly she regretted that she was wearing sloppy clothing. In contrast, the pleats in his pants were sharp and his shave so close his face looked raw.

"It was a good month," Papa said, coming back with a thick envelope. A gust of wind hit the building and blew the door open. Molly hurried to grab it before it banged too hard and broke the glass. "Tell Andrey next time it can wait a day," Papa said. The overhead lights flickered.

"What were you doing?" Viktor asked. He pointed to the notebook in Molly's hand.

"Wasting talent," Papa said.

"Drawing," Molly said at the same time.

"Drawing what?"

"A comic book." Molly covered her sketch with her hand and cleared her throat. Next to him she felt like a child, and she realized that she cared what he thought; she wanted him to see her as a woman. She smoothed her hair again.

"Superman?" He smiled. "I love Superman."

"Not Superman. Atomic Anna. She's...she's my creation."

She held out her sketch and he stood close enough that his arm pressed against hers. He used a finger to trace the line of the mountains, his nail hovering over the page, careful not to touch or smudge it. "It's beautiful. You are very good. It's your mountains that give away your talent. They are cold and harsh. Too many artists try to be romantic instead of real."

"Lazar," Yulia called from the basement where she was looking for extra mops and rags. Something fell downstairs and she called again, more urgently, "Can you help?"

"You'd better be gone when I get back," Papa said. After he disappeared through the curtain, Viktor took a step toward the door but Molly was faster. She slid in front of him. She hadn't planned it, and her confidence surprised her. Her tongue felt heavy. Her skin tingled and he didn't ask her to move. He was interested, she figured, and she kept going, felt like they had a connection, spoke quickly before she changed her mind. "I, uh...I need a ride on July fourth. What do you think, would you drive me?" She looked at the curtain. Her parents were still downstairs. "New York City. I need to be there by nine a.m. I...I know it sounds crazy. You don't even know me. But you work for Andrey. He's my family. And you drive. That's how you got here. And I need a ride. I can pay you. If you don't charge much." She was embarrassed that she was babbling but couldn't stop. "You're probably busy but I thought just in case. Maybe."

"Okay," he said, and his grin grew even wider. "I'll meet you here at seven a.m." He didn't even ask her why. He touched her hip with one finger to gently push her to the side. The move was so quiet and fast, and Molly felt it the way she imagined one of Atomic Anna's electric shocks would hit her, as something that prickled and left her reeling and wanting more at the same time. Then he was gone.

Since Molly had lost Catherine, she hadn't made other friends. She was lonely and once her breasts had finally grown, the only people who looked at her were boys. To everyone else, she was invisible. She wondered what it would be like to date, to have someone to laugh with or even to sit with in the lunchroom. She saw the way Mama and Papa touched, the way couples giggled in the hallway, and Molly wanted that, but she wanted something more, too. She wanted someone who appreciated her as an artist, who saw the bigger world beyond them, and she had tried to find it. She snuck out a few times to go on dates and told the boys about her dreams of drawing professionally. Michael with the too-big lips and too-small jeans told her, "Be happy with what you have. You don't need New York." Evgeny, whose dad ran a travel agency, said, "Be a secretary, that's good work." She refused every second date, never experienced any of the feelings she wanted to feel with those boys, never felt her skin tingle the way it just had with Viktor.

"What did he say?" Papa asked as he stepped back through the curtain. He was out of breath from the stairs, holding two mops and a bucket. "Your cheeks are red."

"Nothing." She looked at her sketch, traced her finger over the mountains the way Viktor had and tried to hide her smile. It had all happened so quickly and it had her on fire. This must be the way the Radioactives felt after a mission.

Mama came through the curtain. A smear of dirt was on her forehead. Papa used a tissue to clean it off for her. Mama would have been gorgeous if she wanted to, but just as she'd taught Molly, she made herself inconspicuous. She kept her lean figure covered with loose dresses and all her blond hair was tied into a scarf. Lipstick was her only nod toward vanity. Mama looked from Papa to Molly. "What happened?"

"Andrey's new *assistant* came. He looked at her sketch." Papa rolled his eyes. "He's bad news like all of Andrey's boys."

"How can you say that?" Molly said. "You barely said anything to him and—"

"Don't," Mama said, cutting her off.

"Don't what?" Molly's voice was loud. Her anger always came so quickly with her parents now.

"You know exactly *what*. I can see it. You think he's exciting and handsome."

Because he was. Still, Molly couldn't stand the way Mama always seemed to know what she was thinking. Mama continued, "When I was your age, I thought a man would help me escape, too. He sent me to Germany."

"What man?"

"The point is, I was wrong."

"Germany worked for you. You met Anna. Wouldn't have me without it."

Mama pressed her lips into that straight line Molly hated because it meant Mama was done. The pain in Molly's side cut deep. She pressed hard to tamp it down, to be able to push further. "Tell me something about Germany, about Anna. Was she brilliant or was she a fool? She built a bomb to murder millions and I don't know where that leaves her. And, and you talk about what you did at my age in these bursts. It makes me feel like you're comparing us, me and Anna, me and you, and I hate it." She could never tell if the comparisons were a way to hold Molly up or drag her down.

"Anna, she got us out. She saved us. That's all you need to understand."

"How? From what I know, I think she's a coward. A heartless coward who left us, and you're afraid to admit it." Mama still didn't look angry and that infuriated Molly. "I'll be like my real father, Yasha, not like Anna," she said in a strong, loud voice.

At that, Mama finally answered. "Never, ever say that."

Three days later, Molly snuck out of the house at six a.m. and waited for Viktor in front of the store. She was so nervous and excited she had barely slept, had to redo her mascara twice because her hands were shaking. She wore her favorite polka dot dress with the short sleeves and even shorter hemline. She had her portfolio in a bag slung over her shoulder and her hair was big and wavy with a headband holding it off her face, the way Trina Robbins wore hers. Viktor's Cadillac purred to a stop right in front of her one hour later. She took a deep breath and anticipated the conversation they were about to have. She had imagined it a million times, had even rehearsed in front of her mirror. *You came back,* was going to be her opening line, but she wanted it to sound off-the-cuff, bored even. To achieve that effect, she shouldn't have stared at him, but she couldn't help it. She watched him cut the engine and look at his reflection in the rearview mirror. Then he pulled something from his glove box—cologne? He shook it on his hands and ran it over his smooth, shaved head. When he climbed out of the car, he was wearing the same black leather jacket and creased pants, only this time he had a black eye. His aviator sunglasses didn't cover it well.

"I hope you haven't been waiting for long," he called out in Russian. His smirk looked both devilish and sexy and already he had her off balance because she had been planning to speak first. She crossed the street. When he didn't come around to open the door for her, she realized she wanted him to, but it was no big deal. She got in by herself.

"You're hurt," she said in Russian.

"Andrey. I run errands. They don't always go as planned."

Molly nodded like she understood because she wanted to seem older and more sophisticated than she was, but she had no idea what the errands could be. The car smelled like his cologne. It was too much, but at the same time she liked it. She pointed to his eye. "Did you see a doctor?"

"Not for this." He lit a cigarette and took a long, slow pull. "New York City?"

She nodded. "Statler Hilton hotel. It's…it's near Madison Square Garden." That's what the advertisement said. She hoped it sounded like she knew more than she did, willed herself to speak slower, only she was nervous and sweating. It wasn't even hot yet.

"What's there?"

"Comics."

"You need a ride to buy more comics?"

"No, there's a convention. I mean, I'm hoping I can find a job." She held up her bag. "I'm bringing my portfolio."

"You're running away? I can't take you if that's what you're doing. Andrey'll kill me."

She smiled, but in a way she *was* running. She planned on coming back today, but if it all worked out, she'd be gone soon. Again, he had gotten her right away, like her art, and it had her spinning. "No, that's not exactly it."

"Okay. If that's your line, I'll take it. I can play dumb later." He slid the key into the car, turned the ignition on. "You want to get paid for your art. I understand that. Your parents don't respect it, that's why you're doing this. Right?" She nodded and looked out the window. She wanted to ask how he saw her so clearly when most people acted like she didn't exist, or just ignored her. But she hesitated because she wasn't used to being understood. He continued, "You're nervous about today? I understand that, too. It means you know this is a big deal." He waited for her to respond, but all she could think to do was look away and pretend she wasn't reeling. "You're close with your parents? Andrey talks about them, says they're good people."

"Does Andrey know you're here, driving me?"

"No one knows unless you told them." She shifted in the seat to face him. He flashed that wicked smile and Molly felt something give inside her. She had been right from the beginning; they had a connection, a real connection. "Andrey told me once you're the smartest girl he's ever met. When I came the other day, I wanted to see you for myself." He offered her a cigarette and she took it. "When I saw your art, I knew he was right."

"How can he say that? How can anyone judge brains?" It was something Molly had started to wonder about a lot, like whether Anna was smart or a fool. And it wasn't clear why her parents insisted Molly was brilliant when they hated her art and she couldn't get a decent grade at school. Now Andrey, a cousin she barely knew, was saying the same. They were all throwing the word around—*brilliant*. But none of them could really judge. "Let me ask you something. If you build a powerful, genius machine but use it for something stupid, are you smart or an idiot?"

She braced herself for him to laugh the way kids did when she said things like that, but he didn't. He took it in and seemed like he was thinking about it, considering an answer. "I don't know," he said. "Like you said, how can anyone judge brains?"

"Exactly," she said. The word came out as a whisper because he really was taking her seriously. "No one else gets that. I mean, when I asked before. At school. No one got it."

"Then they're the idiots." He pressed the accelerator. The wheels spun out, caught, and the car jerked into the center of the street. The rubber squealed. He looked at her as he headed toward the stop sign on the corner and drove straight through without slowing down. "You're American or Soviet? Andrey wasn't sure what you'd say."

"Both," she said. She couldn't remember the USSR but didn't feel at home in the US, either. Her documents were fake. If she was caught, she could be sent back. She couldn't remember a day in her life when her parents weren't looking over their shoulders, teaching her to do the same, or when her gut wasn't turned into knots from all that fear, from not knowing. "I keep a suitcase packed under my bed."

"What?" he asked.

"I mean, it's no big deal," she tried to walk it back.

"No, that's not what I mean. I do the same."

And Molly sucked air between her teeth from the shock that she had found someone so similar to her. "In case we have to run," she said. He nodded and she kept talking, said things she had never dared to say before. "It's confusing to be neither. American or Soviet. My parents speak English when they're out of the house and try to pass as American-born, at least my mom does, but in our store all our customers speak Russian, and my parents play the part of refusenik."

"But what are *you?*"

She paused. "No one's ever asked. But I'm American. I'm sure of that."

"What does that mean?"

"I guess…I'm not suspicious of everyone. What about you? Are you more American or Soviet?"

"You think I'll say Soviet, don't you? Everyone does because I don't speak English well. But maybe you understand, maybe you're the first to understand that doesn't make me one or the other. It's how I think that matters, and that makes me all American. Like you." He looked at her and swerved. Another car honked and he gave them the finger. "I will be a big man here in the United States. The American dream will make me rich."

"My dad used to say that," she said, her voice flat. She always deflated inside when she thought about what had happened to Papa.

"Your papa is an honest man. That's what Andrey says. I respect that a lot, but I won't be a big man with an honest business. I can hustle, as they say." He took a hard turn. She pressed into the car door. "That's my dream and I never told anyone that before. You're easy to talk to."

"You are, too." She smiled. "What hustle?"

"Don't know yet," he said with a laugh. At the next red light, he stopped the car and turned to take a good, long look at her. "You don't sound like a high school student. Don't look like one, either."

"I certainly don't feel like one." She held his gaze, thought about the fact that she had always felt different from her peers, like she had never quite fit, and so it made sense that she didn't resemble a high school student.

He reached for her hand and the air around them felt like it buzzed. "I get it." The light turned green. Viktor moved them forward.

"It's beautiful here," he said. "Even with all the graffiti and drugs, it's beautiful. The USSR is gray. Here, it's green."

"Where is your family?"

"The Soviet Union," he said.

"You miss them?"

"Yes, but Andrey saved them. The money I make, most of it goes to them. Now at least they're eating. Every day. You know, you speak like a real Soviet. Your accent, I mean."

"I'm a Jew. So I could never be a *real* Soviet."

"Me too," he said, and she leaned back in surprise. The car climbed onto the expressway, and two exits farther north, he pulled into a gas station. Instead of filling the tank, he went to a pay phone on the side of the building and turned his back to Molly. She watched him from the car, excited for the morning she was having, eager for the day still to come. The call seemed to start off normal enough, but then it became clear Viktor was arguing. He ran his hands over his scalp angrily, and Molly began to feel uncomfortable, nervous, because she thought about the fact that she didn't know who he was calling, why he was upset, or really anything about him. She had assumed he'd put the entire day aside for her, for their trip, but now she realized that was a mistake. Childish, even. Viktor had responsibilities. And today wasn't important to him the way it was to Molly. Of course he hadn't put everything on hold for her, for a stranger. She put her hand on the door to leave, reasoned she'd hitchhike or find a bus, but then Viktor turned to face her. He smiled, mouthed the words *I'm sorry*, and she stayed. Brilliant or idiot, she couldn't find the answer.

When he was done, he got into the car and looked at her. "I'm so sorry," he said. "Something happened. Andrey needs me to take care of it."

"So, you can't take me to New York?" The disappointment was in her voice and she didn't care that he heard it. She realized that she wanted him to hear it, to make it up to her.

"Not today. But I can another time. I can already see you're sad about it. You'd be a terrible poker player."

"I get it," she said, looking out the window. She told herself she could still climb out of the car, find her own way there.

He must have seen her hesitating. "Do you want me to ask a friend to drive you?"

"No." She wasn't going to New York with a total stranger.

"I can make it up to you. I just can't say no to Andrey. It's complicated." He put the car in reverse but didn't move. "Do you want to get out?" She did, but she had an even stronger urge to stay. No one had ever looked at her as closely as Viktor did, made her feel like they understood her, let alone admired her art. And while logic told her not to stay just because of a man, somewhere deeper she felt logic didn't apply.

"There's a connection between us, isn't there? I mean, that sounds ridiculous. But I think I feel it." He wasn't disagreeing or laughing. He was listening, really listening. "I saw you were angry out there. Now you're not. Whatever happened is bad, but you're still trying to help me get to New York instead of running off to do whatever you need to do." She reached for his cigarettes on the seat between them and lit one, inhaled so the paper and tobacco burned. Next to him, she wasn't bent over in pain. Her gut wasn't throbbing.

"I feel it. That connection," he said.

"I'll give you a chance to take me another time," she said.

"Good. Then I promise to help you become the artist you're destined to be." She believed him and smiled because what it came down to was that he made her feel lighter, better.

The next morning Molly told herself it was better she didn't go to New York. She'd snuck back inside without her parents noticing she'd been gone, so she didn't get into trouble. Plus, no one just showed up and got a job. Best to send samples, let them get to know her work, and so she went through her portfolio to decide what to send. Her early sketches of Anna weren't as good as the work she did now, so she decided to redraft them, the story of how Anna became *Atomic Anna*. It happened during an experiment gone wrong. The first frame showed an old Anna in her laboratory, her skin wrinkled, holding a cane. The text explained that she was born with a rare blood disorder. In the next frame, Anna began an experiment with a machine meant to stop nuclear blasts. She had a wall of high-tech NASA-style computer screens near her. They were all red, revealing that the test was failing. Her machine wasn't stopping an atomic explosion. The fourth frame showed the machine and her lab in flames, with Anna as the only survivor. Her blood disorder had saved her. In the fifth and final frame, Anna stood triumphant. Her cane was gone, along with her wrinkles. She had become Atomic Anna, saved and fueled by atomic energy. As she redrew the comic, Molly decided she loved thinking of her birth mother this way, as a survivor and a hero. It was easier than facing what she had actually done, having to grapple with whether she was the good guy or bad guy. That uncertainty about her mother weighed on her every single day.

ANNA

July 1986

Six Years Before Molly Dies on Mount Aragats

Mount Aragats

After the meltdown at Chernobyl, it took Anna three months to make it to Mount Aragats, the site of the cosmic ray station she and Yasha had conceived. As she traveled, there were stretches when she thought the KGB was closing in on her and she hid, others when she felt safe enough to move, and all along the way she watched the country change. At first citizens were oblivious to what had happened, going about their lives as usual, but as the news leached across the USSR, children stopped playing in the parks; people started closing their shutters and drawing their curtains as if that would protect them from the radiation.

Anna had designed the station in 1949, and even though she hadn't seen the plans in decades, she remembered it like she'd worked on it yesterday, knew exactly where to go. She headed south to Kiev, then southeast, skirting the Black Sea and into the Armenian Soviet Socialist Republic, where Mount Aragats lay near the Turkish border. She had to be careful, use forms of transportation that didn't require identification that would alert Gorbachev's men and make it easy for them to arrest her and blame her for the meltdown.

Moving through the country, she had long stretches alone when she could think about Yasha and the station. Their dreams had been ambitious, but that was decades ago, back when they were still together. She didn't think he'd ever build it without her. The idea had come to Anna while she and Yasha were on vacation at Lake Baikal. They were staying in a rustic dacha on the edge of the water where they were surrounded by trees and doused by sun. Work, their lab, and all the pressures they had felt during the war slipped away, replaced by days spent making love and lounging in the sheets. For the first time in years, she had found herself dreaming again, going back to a theory that came to her in Berlin: ripples in space-time. She explained it to Yasha while they lay wrapped in a blanket, naked, in a hammock on the front porch. The hammock creaked and swung.

"Einstein thinks a lot about time," she said. Yasha held a pear, sliced off a wedge and offered it to her. It was late in the day, on the edge of night, and he felt warm and solid, stronger than she had anticipated when they first met. "I had an idea about a decade ago about time and Einstein's theories. I've been too busy to go back to it." She took the slice and licked a drop of juice dripping on the side. "Time is relative, Einstein says, because gravity changes time. Take a black hole. It's all gravity. If you could stand on the edge for ten minutes and then instantly go back to Earth, you would only be ten minutes older but on Earth, without that same amount of gravity, twenty or fifty years might have passed. Everyone on Earth would be twenty or fifty years older. You see, at the black hole, time is different. Take that a step further: If time is relative, then there's no difference between the past, the present, and the future because they are all happening at the same time."

"That's too much for me," Yasha said, and he trailed a finger along her collarbone. "But it is incredibly sexy that you think that way."

"Just listen," Anna said, laughing. She grabbed his hand to make him stop. "I had this idea in Berlin. If time is different in one place from another, then we can travel through it. Not in a straight line. Through ripples in time, the waves that are already all around us." He told her he didn't understand, and she kept going. "Think of time like a piece of spaghetti. If we run our fingers across a straight, raw noodle, we have to touch the entire thing, go over the entire noodle to get from one end to the other. But if we cook it, we can bend the noodle and jump from one end to the other without going over the whole thing." She took a deep breath. "There are already ripples in space-time; some could even be produced with large explosions—in theory. I think we can travel through time on waves, maybe even on gamma rays—think of them as the cooked noodle. In effect, we can use them to time travel."

"You're linking gravity and electromagnetism?" he asked, sitting up. He looked like he was considering it, but then he shook his head. "It can't be done."

"I'm saying *maybe* it can. *Maybe* we can cut through gravitational waves using electromagnetism. *Maybe* there is a full unified field theory waiting to be uncovered. And if I can't detect the waves on my own, maybe I can make them. I think a nuclear explosion would do it, give me the gamma rays I need to travel through the ripples in space-time. I'd just need to contain them so they don't fry me first." She sat up. "I could build an amplifier to increase the size and intensity of the gamma waves while controlling them, then jump forward or backward."

"But how would you do it, control the explosion so it doesn't kill? And stop confusing the theories."

"I don't know. I'd need a lab, a wide-open space where I could study cosmic rays, electromagnetism. Nuclear might be too dangerous. I just don't know yet." She smiled. "And confusing the theories is the whole point."

He told her to design it, to put her ideas on paper, that they could work on it together.

"I'll build it for you one day, for us, the Anna Maksimovna Berkova and Yasha Ivanovich Berlitsky Cosmic Ray Station," he said, and he kissed her, slid his hand under the blanket along her stomach, down to her thighs.

The Soviets always needed more weapons and no one else believed her theories. The whole project was put on hold. But if she'd jumped through time, then the ripples in space-time were real, and her theory was plausible—there was a way to unite gravity and electromagnetism. The *if* was the variable, *if* she had traveled through time. In the days and weeks that had passed since the meltdown, doubt had taken hold. Perhaps she'd been too quick to draw conclusions. She wouldn't let herself believe, really believe, until she saw the station. Or didn't. And as she crossed the country, she went around and around, arguing with herself over what she would find.

When she finally arrived at the base of the mountain, the town there was quiet. No one seemed to take notice that an old woman had arrived and started asking about what loomed above. A local showed her the way to the path leading up Aragats, and as she hiked, her nerves heightened with every step. She tried to stay calm, tried to loosen her chest. It was impossible. She was petrified of finding the station and just as petrified of finding nothing at all. It took a few hours to make it up to the top, and when she finally walked through heavy larches and a carpet of leaves mixed with ice, the station appeared through a clearing and it took her breath away. She dropped to her knees and burst into tears. It was real. All real. All her worrying, her arguments with herself were pointless because there it was. And it was exactly what she had seen the night she'd jumped from Pripyat, only now without the snow. She took in the main compound in its full glory along with the six towers, the observatories she had designed, dotting the area in a semicircle. Yasha had done it, he'd really done it, she realized, and awe and terror swept over her. This meant time travel was something she could actually achieve. After all the years of theorizing, this was proof. Even more, it implied she could stop Chernobyl from melting down. But then her stomach dropped. It also meant Manya, her Manya, had been there dying. And Raisa. Manya had said they'd failed to save her. It meant Anna had to save Raisa even though she didn't understand why or how. The weight of it all kept her on her knees for a long time before she even thought to search for signs of Yasha, the KGB, or soldiers, but when she did look around, she saw nothing and no one. The complex appeared deserted.

She pulled herself together, made her way toward the main compound, slowly, and looked down at her hands. They weren't burned this time. Her head wasn't throbbing. A single caretaker met Anna at the entrance. He said his name was Artush, that he was a local who had been there since construction started in 1963. "1963," Anna said. That meant Yasha had worked on it for years without telling her. She stepped back, trying to process it all.

Artush had a thick mustache and a nervous smile. He bent to the side to look behind her. "Is anyone with you?"

"No," she said. "Who are you looking for?"

"Dr. Yasha Berlitsky. This is his facility, his top-secret laboratory, but he hasn't been here in years." Artush looked over to the other side. "You walked? I don't see any vehicles. You really came alone? How did you find it?"

She sensed Artush was scared of Yasha and she understood why. Yasha had a soft side he showed to Anna, but even that hadn't lasted for long. "He doesn't know I'm here."

Artush hesitated, but then he sighed and opened the door. "Well, I have orders to let you in, Dr. Berkova. He told me that if you came, I should give you anything you need."

That was when she started to feel the first pangs of real fear. "How did you know my name, what I looked like?" All she could see was the small entryway and she recognized it, flashed back to the bloodstained parka and uniform, the toppled table and chairs, to Manya bleeding in the kitchen.

"Do you need to sit?" Artush asked. "You are pale. You're shaking."

"Is this a trap?" She was asking herself as much as Artush.

"I was wondering the same. But I'm all alone," he said. He held her elbow to steady her as she took a slow, careful step over the threshold. "I'll show you how I knew you."

There were no coats hanging this time. No blood. "It's real," she whispered, still in shock, roiled by dozens of emotions. She was angry at Yasha for keeping this from her, disappointed in herself that she hadn't found it earlier, and excited that she would have the chance to stop Chernobyl. Underlying it all was a profound sadness that this was where her daughter was going to die if she didn't change the future, and that this was a place that could have held another future, another kind of life, for her and Yasha.

"I really think you should sit," Artush said. "You don't seem well."

"I'm fine. Just show me how you knew me," she said.

They continued down the hall. "Yasha has a desk. He arranged it so he can come anytime, whenever he needs, but he hasn't been since construction stopped. No one has." They were halfway down the hall and she stopped, stared at the walls. When she had been there before, they were covered with murals of superwomen. These walls were bare and gray. Wires hung down from an unfinished ceiling. Spots of plaster were unpainted. "What happened?" She pointed to the walls. Artush explained that work had stopped as quickly as it started. One day the crew just up and left. After that, Yasha disappeared, but Artush stayed because it was his job and also because he was scared. "If he came back and I wasn't here..." He shook his head. "All the workers were threatened with death if they ever spoke about this place." He looked around nervously. "He really doesn't know you're here?"

"No," and then, "These walls. They had murals, didn't they?"

"Murals?" Artush asked. "No. They've always been like this. Come,

Yasha has a photograph of you and him on his desk. You're in front of a lake. You're younger, but I know it's you. And he told me your name. I looked you up, read about your work." He offered Anna a tissue from his pocket and she took it, wiped her eyes, hadn't even realized she was crying. She knew the photograph from his description, knew it was from that vacation they'd taken, the one where he said he'd build this station for her—for them. She remembered the photographer, the moment the shutter clicked. In the kitchen, the table had a single plate set, a loaf of bread half-gone. A samovar steamed in the corner. Nothing was broken or toppled and the view from the picture window was glorious, with mountains rising up into an endless blue sky. And yet Anna shivered, stared at the floor in front of that window. She kneeled down and touched the wood, ran her fingers over the coarse grain, and felt like splinters were pushing under her skin, deep inside.

"I won't let it happen," she whispered. "None of it can happen."

She spotted Yasha's desk in the corner and made her way to it. The photograph sat in the middle. The frame was silver, polished and gleaming. Yasha had his arms around her, smiling as they stood in front of the dacha. The hammock was behind them. The logs that made the cabin looked rougher than she remembered, and she and Yasha looked so young. For a moment she could feel the sun blazing off the lake, warming her while they stood there, posing, squinting. Yasha had held her so tight she felt every bit of him against her back. *I love you*, he'd whispered after the photo was taken, before he let her go.

The last time she saw Yasha was in Moscow in 1971. She was dining at a restaurant with her colleague Valery Legasov, one of the few men who ever requested to work with her, who wasn't intimidated by a woman knowing more than he did. She and Valery were eating, and the room was full and loud. Yasha had stormed in, chest pushing forward, filled with fury and jealousy. He didn't have to accuse her of having an affair because she knew that's what he thought. She told him to go home. Anna and Valery were friends, nothing else. She had pushed Yasha out of the restaurant, mortified.

Anna faced Artush. "Did you know we're still married?" She laughed. It was a bitter sound because thinking about him now, she remembered Yasha's position and realized he was likely leading the charge to find her. Luckily he was too conceited, too self-assured to believe Anna would discover this station on her own. "We're safe. He'd never look for me here," she told Artush. Anna blew her nose and put the tissue in her pocket. That was when she felt another photograph, the one she'd brought back from the jump. The corner was worn from Anna holding it so often. Standing there, looking at it, she let memories of Yulia and Lazar come pouring back. All these years she had been fighting to keep them away, Yasha, Yulia, Lazar, and Manya, and now they were all there, forcing their way to the front of her mind, and it scared her more than she would have anticipated. But oh, how Anna missed Yulia. She would have known what to do next. "Outthink them," Yulia liked to say. "You'll never be stronger, but you will always be smarter."

Anna put the photograph of her and Yasha in a drawer and turned to Artush. "Can you show me the equipment Yasha stored here?" December 8, 1992, was her deadline. She had six and a half years to change the future and she had to get started.

✳ ✳ ✳

Anna turned one of the six cosmic watchtowers into her laboratory. It was a single room identical to the others, with a wooden floor and walls that rose to waist height, windows that soared from there to the ceiling so there was a clear 360-degree view of the sloped forest and the mountains. Snow made them look soft, but their cliffs and ice meant the reality was they were deadly. There was also a chimney and stove, a pile of wood Artush kept replenished. She tacked the photograph her daughter had given her to the wall, the one with Yulia, Lazar, Molly, and

Raisa standing in front of a butcher shop, and threw herself into work with a ferocity she hadn't had in years, starting with the amplifier. It was the key to time travel and she needed to adapt the design she had been holding when Chernobyl melted down, build something that could work with less power. She wanted to save all those people, but also, she needed to stop the memories that were coming for her and taking hold, memories she could lock away in her mind when she worked.

She left the mountain only once, in 1987, to meet Valery Legasov. They had worked together on atomic weapons and she trusted him more than anyone else in the Soviet Union. Plus, he had access to the fuel she needed for her time machine, uranium pellets. They met in a café at the base of the mountain. When she saw him, she gasped. He had lost so much weight his cheekbones jutted out like rods coated in skin that was too thin and too pale. His hair had fallen out in clumps, and patches sprung from the sides. "I'm running the cleanup at Chernobyl," he said as explanation, and she hugged him, not wanting to let go. Eventually he pushed away to cough into a handkerchief, a fit that left the cloth soaked in blood.

"I'm sorry," she said.

"I don't regret anything. I'm the best man for the job. You know that." He leaned down and pulled a heavy box off the floor along with a rosebush that he put on the table between them. "I thought you might need a pick-me-up. And I remembered you loved your rosebushes."

"Thank you," she said, leaning forward to smell one of the three blooms on the plant. It was a pale pink, near its end, but the smell still took her back to memories of living in the small flat with Yulia, Lazar, and Malka. But nothing lasted forever and there was no question Valery was near death. "Are you scared?" she asked. She was. Seeing him like that made the accident real in a way it hadn't been for her before. All her work on worst-case scenarios and disaster mitigation had always been theoretical. With Valery in front of her, dying, a tangle of guilt and regret took hold, left her fingertips tingling. If only she'd spent more time on the enclosure for the reactor, building a stronger concrete barrier, constructing more failsafes...

"I know you're thinking about what you could have done differently, but the answer is nothing. There was no way to anticipate what happened, the way it happened. And as for being scared, am I scared that they'll catch me for stealing this? No." He smiled and held up the heavy box he'd brought for her. Her lips tugged toward a smile; it was like him to joke even when facing death. "A bullet would be a relief from the pain I'm in now." He coughed again, more blood. "I *am* terrified that the other reactors will melt down, but I'm not afraid of dying. That's what you really meant, wasn't it?"

She nodded.

"You read it was AZ-5?"

She had. AZ-5 was the final measure to shut down the reactor, to insert all control rods, but Anna had miscalculated. She hadn't anticipated what would happen during the first split second after the rods descended. It was what had destroyed the reactor.

"It's my fault," she whispered.

"You led dozens of engineers who checked and rechecked every detail. Everyone missed it."

"But I was in charge."

"We all make mistakes." A waiter brought them tea. "You're alone again, aren't you?" he asked. "You always look like this, sad, when you're by yourself."

"I've always been alone."

"You had Vera for a few years."

Anna blew air out from her lips as if to dismiss him, but even as she did, she realized there was something to what he said. "You see everything, don't you?"

He grinned again, his skin stretching so thin. "You're brilliant, Anna. And you're blind. Vera was by your side at every meal. You walked together every afternoon."

"It was her job."

"A job she chose. Like me. I chose to work with you."

"Is she dead? She went to help, didn't she?"

Valery nodded, and when Anna's tears started, he said, "I took care of her family. Sent them to America, to your family. I knew Yulia and Lazar would help her mother and brother." He dug into his pocket. "Here. This is the address, where I sent them."

"What about her father?" Anna was thinking about the photo Vera had kept on her nightstand, a photo of her family, holding tight to one another, standing at the end of their long haphazard driveway.

"He died looking for her." He shook his head. "I'm sorry. I thought you knew."

They sat in silence while Anna cried, began to mourn. She thought about their walks together, their conversations, the way Vera smiled. She knew how close Vera's family was, that two deaths would hit her mother and brother hard, and she felt for them. After a while, Anna went back to what Valery had done, to Yulia and Lazar. Even in her grief, those names had power over her, made her nervous and excited. "How did you find them?"

"You told me once you thought Lazar and Yulia took Manya to Philadelphia. It wasn't hard to locate them after that." He paused to cough, sending more blood into a handkerchief. "Don't worry. I didn't tell Yasha."

She picked up the carafe on the table and poured more water for him. Of course he would never tell Yasha anything. There was a long pause. Other people in the café joked and lounged, smoked cigarettes. They all had time. They would all live while Valery wouldn't, while Vera and her father didn't, she thought. Dwelling on all the death made a sadness open in Anna that she had closed long ago. Now, re-exposed, it flooded back. Quietly Anna said, "Yasha found blaming me easier than blaming himself for Manya, for losing her."

"Leave it behind you. Look forward. You know they think you're dead? You've been officially classified as deceased, killed in the accident?"

"I had no idea." She leaned back, thinking about all the precautions she'd taken, all the time she'd spent hiding while traveling. "So no one's looking for me?"

"Not a soul," he said, and smiled. "Before she died, Vera said you'd run to the lab to help save people, and since no one found your body, it was easy to make assumptions." His voice dropped lower, racked with sadness. "It was chaos, Anna. Dozens of people just disappeared like that, lost in the rubble and destruction. Now tell me, why am I here?"

She moved to the edge of her seat, tried to push away the grief and guilt weighing on her. "The night the reactor melted down, something happened." She took a deep breath and began, told him about her theory from Berlin, the cosmic ray station, and then about her amplifier. "When Reactor Number Four melted down, I traveled through those ripples in space-time," she said. "That night I jumped to Aragats, to the station, and found my daughter dying. I was watching Manya bleed to death in 1992."

"Anna," he said, shaking his head. "1992. Time travel? You know, I thought through a dozen reasons why you'd ask me to come here, and time travel wasn't one of them. I mean, it never occurred to me that what you're describing would be anything but science fiction."

"But you believe me?" She leaned so far forward she was half on the table by then. "I know it sounds..." She stopped, couldn't think of the right word. Then, "Impossible."

"If it were any other person in the world, I would dismiss it, but not you." He lit a cigarette and went quiet for a long time. "I understand now why you wanted the fuel," he finally said. "You want to save your daughter."

She shook her head. He misunderstood. "This isn't about Manya. This is about Chernobyl. I want to save all those people. And you."

"But Manya?"

"Don't you see, she was there. On Aragats with me. If I stop Chernobyl, then we never go to that mountain, she's never shot, killed. By stopping the accident, I save her, too. And you."

"Come on," Valery said. "You're not thinking clearly. If you stop the meltdown, you save all those people, and me. But you can't be sure you're saving Manya."

"What are you saying? Of course I'd be saving Manya."

"List out the facts. You don't know what she was doing there. You haven't seen her in decades. What would bring her back here? Surely she didn't come just to help you. Manya knows if she's caught in the USSR she would be arrested for leaving illegally. Her life would be ruined. No, if she risked coming here then something made her leave America. Something terrible."

Anna leaned back and crossed her arms over her chest. Valery often did that, saw things more clearly than she did. "You're right," she said quietly. "Manya told me to save Raisa. My granddaughter. She said we failed, that I promised to save her. Maybe she comes for Raisa."

"There you go." He nodded and reached for another cigarette. A woman at the front of the café began playing an accordion. Valery continued, "I don't have much time, so I can only point out what's obvious. Assume Raisa will come here. Why? If she and Manya come to the USSR, then they are both desperate. If you choose to save everyone at Chernobyl, then you are choosing your work, that power plant over Manya and Raisa. That's how I see it."

"You're simplifying a situation that isn't simple."

"I'm not. If you can even build this, go back and fix AZ-5, or do whatever needs to be done, what happens to Raisa? Whatever reason Manya had for coming here probably won't disappear. AZ-5 and Chernobyl have nothing to do with Raisa or Manya. They're in America. Chernobyl is in the USSR. If you fix the reactors, you won't be helping your family. Even worse, if you fix the reactors and Manya and Raisa still come to the USSR, if Manya still comes looking for you, she won't come to a deserted mountain. She will go to Pripyat, and surely there she'd be caught." Valery sipped his tea. "I know you. You want to think you can fix everything, and it's easier that way, to look at it as a situation where you can do both. Only you can't. You're going to have to choose."

"I'll make time for both."

"December 8, 1992, is the date Manya gave you? It's not much time. Building something like a time machine would take decades, if it can even be done. You're going to spend every minute on it and I'm warning you, be ready to decide. You're going to have to choose."

"There has to be another way."

"What if there isn't? Not making a choice is a choice itself."

*　*　*

Back on Aragats, Anna put the rosebush next to her desk and plunged into the task of designing and building the time machine. She told herself not to worry about Manya or Raisa. If and when her daughter came to Aragats, Anna would help her, but that might be years away. Anna reasoned it was possible the problem Manya needed help solving hadn't even happened yet—wouldn't happen until 1992. Besides, without a time machine there was nothing she could do to change anything or save anyone, and so she pushed on, calibrating the amplifier to work with less power than the one that had pulled her through to 1992. Each step was smaller than she wanted. Errors and mistakes cost her months, and while she knew that was all a part of the process, she didn't have time to spare. Months melted into years and every day she was weighed down by Valery's words, waiting for Manya. She watched the trailhead for her daughter endlessly, jumped when the trees rustled, thinking she was coming, but she never did. Anna told herself again and again that choosing to stop the meltdown first was the right decision. Manya and Raisa would come later.

By October 10, 1991, Anna was ready for her first full-scale experiment. She was going to step through a ripple and travel back in time to her laboratory in Chernobyl. So far, through experiments she had learned that the law of twos applied to her machine. First, she could jump for only two hours. After that, the amplifier pulled her back to her starting point. Second, she could jump to a particular year only two times before the ripple became too flat to enter or leave again. Now she stepped up to her time machine and entered the coordinates for her lab at Chernobyl, for January 5, 1985. If it worked as planned, she would find herself and explain that AZ-5 would fail in April 1986.

In Anna's dreams her time machine was sleek and modern, but in reality it was a hodge-podge of pieces. The power source, the center of the contained explosion that generated the gamma wave, was held in a metal shoebox-style container. The control board was built into a regular-looking computer that was connected by a slew of wires to a small, generic keyboard and monitor. The amplifier was the size and shape of a large jewelry box. Anna put it in a satchel, slung it over her shoulder for her jump, and activated the machine by pulling a trigger attached to the side of the power source. The reaction was immediate. There was a flash of light. Then came a thud; the boards under her shook. Anna saw the gamma waves expanding as if the space around her were a pond and she had dropped a pebble so everything around her shivered in gentle waves. The waves were contained so they weren't irradiating her, just giving her access to ripples in space-time. She felt herself stretching, gravity pulling. For a moment she thought her legs would be dragged through the floorboards. Her vision turned static so she saw only black and white lines and then she was aware that she was lying on cold, damp cement. Her satchel and amplifier were still slung over her shoulder, at her side. She couldn't open her eyes because her skull felt like it was being crushed and she was sure she was dying.

Eventually she managed to look around, to figure out she was in the cement stairwell near her lab. She was lucky it was nighttime, deserted, as she lay there writhing on the ground while snow blew in through the ventilation slits above. She tried to open her mouth, but she couldn't say a word because of the searing pain in her head.

Two hours passed, feeling like two decades, and then she was pulled back to 1991 and instantly the pain in her skull disappeared, replaced by the duller throbbing from burns on her hands. She thought the way her head had hurt was similar to what she'd felt when she'd jumped from Pripyat to Aragats that first time, only much more intense, and that didn't make sense. She dismissed the idea, tried again. After another jump to 1985 and two more excruciating hours of pain in that cold stairwell, she concluded something she had suspected, another rule of time travel: Two versions of the same person from different time periods couldn't be in close proximity to one another. The pain came because she was too close to the Anna living in 1985.

Anna tried to think through alternative ways to contact herself in the past, considered writing herself a letter, making a tape recording, but none of those ideas would work because she knew her 1985 self wouldn't trust them. She needed a person to help, the only person she could ever truly trust. Yulia.

PART II

Which is the straight path a person should choose for themselves?

—Pirkei Avot

ANNA

October 1991

One Year Before Molly Dies on Mount Aragats

Mount Aragats

Yulia, it turned out, was easy enough for Anna to find. She used the address Valery had given her in Philadelphia, and once she decided to go, she spent more time than she had in years choosing her clothing, doing her hair. She plugged the coordinates into her machine and then she hesitated. Thinking about Yulia made Anna's hands shake, her skin tingle. She felt younger again, and older at the same time, contrasting how she used to feel in Berlin and Moscow with her wrinkled complexion in the mirror on Aragats. She was both the same and different, and she wasn't sure how Yulia would have changed. If only she could skip over the terrifying, emotional parts of whatever reunion was about to come and go straight back to the way they used to be.

Anna looked at the sad rosebush in the corner. It had died months earlier, but she couldn't bring herself to get rid of it because it reminded her of Valery, of Berlin, of times in life she'd loved. "Here we go," she said to the roses, and then she pulled the trigger. There was the flash, the thud, the static, and then she stepped into Philadelphia in 1975, into the middle of a street. A wide black car was headed straight for her. She jumped. The car swerved and missed her. She made her way to the sidewalk and hunched over, put her hands on her knees so she could catch her breath. The satchel with her amplifier hung at her side. *Safe*, she thought. *I'm safe*. The sidewalk and street around her were cleaner than Moscow, and louder. People jostled past in clothing that was brighter and softer than she was used to seeing. She felt lucky that no one seemed to notice her, which meant she blended in well enough and could make her way forward. She looked for a street sign, a marker to tell her which way to go, and then she heard Lazar's voice. It had been decades, but she knew it as well as anything and the effect was immediate. She stumbled toward it. Her blood raced and for a split second she was back in Moscow, in their flat. He was on the floor next to his sister, Malka, learning English with Yulia.

"Have fun," he called now in English. His thick accent sounded exactly the same as it had back then. And when she saw him, he didn't look that different: a little older, a little more hunched perhaps, but still Lazar. She watched him wave to two women holding a little girl's hand and she knew by the look on his face, by the way he stared at them as if nothing else mattered, that he was staring at his family. Anna hurried closer and caught a glimpse of Yulia just before she stepped onto a bus. She looked young, *was* young, almost twenty years younger than Anna was at that moment. Seeing the youthful Yulia had Anna imagining the two of them dancing, flirting, drinking. The other woman had to be Manya, the child Raisa. Anna hurried to follow them, snuck onto the bus through the back door. The stopwatch around her neck said one hour and fifty-five minutes was all she had left. A young man offered her his seat. She took it, her eyes glued to Yulia in the front. When Anna first met her, Yulia was the woman everyone watched in a room. She would throw her head back and laugh, cross her legs and pull her skirt just a little too high. But there on the bus Anna didn't see any remnants of that Yulia. Instead, she saw a woman in a dark coat with hair tucked under a hat, like half a dozen other women around her. She blended in so well that if Anna hadn't heard Lazar or seen Yulia's face, she never would have known it was her.

Anna moved closer as people got off the bus, but she didn't want to confront Yulia there in front of a crowd. She would wait until they got off. The bus bumped over potholes and slinked between tall buildings. More than anything, Anna wanted to touch Yulia, put her hand on her shoulder or arm, her waist, only she knew it was better to be patient, to wait.

Yulia, Manya, and Raisa got off in the center of the city. Anna tried to follow but four people were in front of her and by the time she stepped off, Anna caught only a glimpse of the three of them going inside a department store called Wanamaker's. Anna spent an hour searching for them there, a daze of marble, Christmas music, and too much perfume. By the time she found them in the children's department, she was frantic and disheveled. She scolded herself for not thinking to start there. Manya and Raisa were in line to ride a small train suspended from the ceiling. Yulia stood alone. Anna had only ten minutes left until the amplifier would pull her back to Aragats. She didn't have time to waste. "Yulia," Anna said, elbowing past the women between them. Yulia looked right at her and gasped. When Anna had imagined this moment, she'd thought of Yulia running to her, of them hugging, kissing, and crying, but Yulia didn't move. She looked scared, unsure of herself, of Anna.

"I'm real," Anna said. Perhaps Yulia believed she was seeing things. Anna had certainly imagined seeing Yulia before, in the supermarket, at a lake. Places she could never be. "I'm real," she said again. This time she took a closer look at her old friend. Yulia was all sharp angles where previously she had been soft. Her clothing covered her instead of clinging to her curves to put her on display. And where the Yulia Anna had met in Berlin wouldn't have hesitated to reach for Anna, now she was still. But then Yulia blinked and grabbed Anna and they both held on as tight as they could. Anna felt safe again, the way she had all those years ago, like she could finally give herself over to someone else again, to talk and to share, and there was so much she wanted to say.

"You're safe? You're free?" Yulia said. Anna felt tears pouring down her cheeks. She hadn't cried in years before Aragats and now she seemed to fall into a blubbering mess far too often. Yulia used her thumbs to wipe Anna's wet cheeks, then braided their fingers together.

Anna's words came in an anxious staccato. Her heart beat so fast she couldn't fill her lungs or manage a strong voice. On top of it all she felt the pressure of time, that she needed to fit more than she could into the minutes they had together. "I . . . I saw you get on the bus, saw Lazar. I don't have long. I came because I need your help."

"With them? That's your daughter and your granddaughter," Yulia said, looking over her shoulder at Manya and Raisa.

"I know that's them, but no. I don't need them, I need you. I built it. My time machine," Anna said. It was hard for her to untangle the words. The proximity to Yulia had her spinning. "I missed you."

"Are you dying? You look like something's not right. You're too old."

"No. That's not it. I built the time machine and I used it. I came because—"

"You wanted to see Manya? She's Molly now and—" Yulia stopped. "What do you mean you built your time machine?" Her face went pale. She pointed to the stopwatch around Anna's neck. "Why do you have that?"

"For my machine, to track how long I have." As Anna said it, the enormity of what she had done overtook her. She hadn't paused to celebrate, didn't have anyone to share it with. "I really did it," she said, louder this time, letting a little excitement through while still trying to stay focused and clear, to commit every second to memory so she could hold on to this moment and revisit it later, on Aragats, again and again.

"Shh," Yulia said. She held a finger to her lips. "Take a moment."

"That's the thing. I don't have a moment. I came for Manya, but it's not what you think."

"Yasha?" Yulia said the name as a hiss. "Does he know you're here? Where she is?"

"No. He has no idea. You're safe. There's been an accident…" She tried to tell Yulia about the meltdown at the power plant, that she needed Yulia's help to stop it because she couldn't go back herself—and now was the time because they were just building the facility, they could still change the design of AZ-5.

"Wait. Wait," Yulia said, her smile melting away. "This is a lot to take in."

"I know. I'm sorry. There's no other way. I came because I need your help. Manya—"

"Molly," Yulia said. "Call her Molly." Anna didn't have time to ask about the new name. Yulia dropped Anna's hands and looked at Molly. "She's been through a lot. She's still so fragile. Surely you want to see her more than you want to fix something at work, don't you?"

"It's not just *fixing* my work. This is about saving tens of thousands, hundreds of thousands of lives." Anna took a deep breath. "If we help all of these people, we help Molly and Raisa, too. There just isn't time to focus on only Molly and Raisa. Not yet."

"There's always time for your own flesh and blood. Molly needs you. Now. She needs all of us. She's barely hanging on. I don't know if I can hold her together, if I can take it again if she runs or goes back to Viktor. And Raisa—"

"Runs? Where?" *Is this the year Molly comes to Aragats?* Anna asked herself. No, it was too early. Anna desperately needed Yulia to understand. "Yulia, listen to me. Manya, no, Molly, and Raisa will need me in 1992. But first, Reactor Number Four is going to melt down on April 26, 1986, and I need you to come back to the Soviet Union so you can help stop it. Find me now, the Anna living in 1975, and tell her what to do to keep it from happening. Tell her AZ-5 won't work.

We will help Molly and Raisa later." Anna gestured to her body. "This is an older me, you can see that. You know what I'm telling you now is real, right?" She waited for Yulia to respond. And waited. But she only saw anger cross Yulia's face, the way her lips pressed into a straight, hard line. Anna tried again. "We can—"

"Didn't you hear me? Your family needs you now." Yulia sounded disgusted. "Not in 1992. Today. I can't go anywhere. Nor should you."

"Please."

Yulia took a step away. "You came all this way, built this incredible machine, did this miraculous thing. You found me, your daughter, and your granddaughter and all you can say is you want me to help you with work? Can you hear yourself? Are you out of your mind?"

"Did you hear how many people are going to die?"

"I am telling you your daughter is barely hanging on. Did you even look at them, really look at them?" She pointed to Molly, to the train Raisa was riding, passing by. "Don't you want to talk to them? All you can think about is you, even after all this time. What about us? Do you know what we've been through? You haven't even asked. And did you think about what would happen to me if I went back? You know they'd catch me, torture me. Kill me. I'd never make it to any closed city." Anna opened her mouth to explain the scale of the disaster, to describe the horror so Yulia would understand that it was worth the risk, that she could find a way, but Yulia held up a hand to keep Anna from speaking. Angry red streaks were climbing up Yulia's neck and tight lines formed around her eyes as they narrowed. "I don't care what you think you need because you obviously don't know. It's our family that needs *you*. I need you. Here."

Anna thought about Valery, how he had warned her that she was framing her whole plan the wrong way, that she would have to choose. She couldn't stop Chernobyl and save her family. She had dismissed him because what he said was too hard to face. And maybe, she realized now, the truth was that she couldn't walk away from the chance to stop

Chernobyl. Not even her family could change her mind and she hated that, but she couldn't help it. "I only have until December 8, 1992," she said, still trying to bring Yulia around.

"Who knows what will happen between now and 1992? Molly could be dead long before then." Yulia's voice was now dripping with fury. "Suppose I believe you. That you built it, that it works. You came all this way to ask me to help you put your life back in order, the lives of strangers, without even asking about the lives of the people in your own family. How could you?"

"People are going to die," Anna said, but her voice wasn't strong anymore.

"Have you forgotten what I always told you? Just because you can doesn't mean you should. Annushka, move on. Whatever happened, leave it alone. Come back and help *us*. Have you even thought about Mollushka since you sent us away?"

"I gave her to you. It was best for all of us."

"Now things are different. She's sober today, but I don't know how long it will last, what will happen tomorrow. If you're going to change something, change her life. Molly wants *you*."

Anna didn't know how to respond, what else to say. There were too many places to start, emotions to cover, and she was almost out of time. In her pocket was a piece of paper with the coordinates for the station. She tried to hand them to Yulia. "I'm not taking that," Yulia said. "Whatever that is, I'm not taking that. Not unless you stay."

"I can't."

"Who are you?" Anna startled at the voice coming from behind her. When she turned, she saw it was Molly. Not the broken, dying Molly she'd be in 1992, but a stronger, healthy Molly from 1975. "What's wrong, Mama?" Molly asked, and Anna breathed her in. She smelled like Yulia's perfume and she looked like her, too, fair and blond and beautiful. She had Yasha's eyes, but she had Anna's mother's curls and mien. Anna's mother, Xenia, had been brusque, to the point, and stronger than anyone else Anna had ever met. She'd never wasted time and already Anna could see Molly didn't, either. "Tell me what's happening," Molly said.

"You're perfect," Anna whispered. She took a step back to steady herself. She hadn't expected to have the urge to hold her daughter and kiss her, but she did.

Molly looked from Yulia to Anna. "Have we met?" And then, pointing to Anna's neck, "I've seen that watch. I'm sure I've seen it. And that necklace."

Anna remembered to check the time, started to panic when she saw how little was left. She felt the weight of the amplifier in the satchel digging into her shoulder. "Please, help me," she said desperately. "Find me. Here." She now held out the paper to Molly.

"Who are you?" Molly asked again, refusing the paper, looking even more confused.

Raisa ran toward them then. "Mama! Mama!" she yelled. She had wandered over to a toy firetruck, was coming back. She had the same infectious smile she had in the photograph tucked away in Anna's pocket, the same perfect cheeks.

In another heartbeat, Anna felt the tug of gravity, saw the static. She dropped the paper at Yulia's feet and said, "I'm out of time." She was sucked into the dark and when she opened her eyes again, Artush stood over her. Her hands were scorched raw. The room, her machine, all of it was a blur in the middle of the excruciating pain.

"She's not here," Artush said. He shook Anna. "Stop screaming. She's not here."

"What?" Her hands ached. Her arms, too. "Who?"

"You were yelling for Yulia, the one who sends the letters and pictures. She's not here."

"You know about Yulia?"

He looked at her strangely. "Of course. Her letters are all over the walls." He pointed to one side of the watchtower. When Anna had left, it had been wallpapered with her sketches and calculations for the time machine. Now it was covered in letters and there was no mistaking the curled, beautiful handwriting. Dotting spaces between letters were photographs of Manya and of Raisa as a baby, growing into a little girl and then a big girl. In the middle of it all still hung the original photo from Molly, the one taken in front of the butcher shop. "She writes every month. I pick up the letters at the café. There's a new one on your desk."

"But I've only been here since 1986. These are older."

"After you showed up, a pile came in a huge box. Don't you remember? You said something about them being written for years, saved up. I think they start in 1975." Artush took the satchel holding her amplifier, placed it in the corner, and Anna stumbled to her feet, to the newest envelope. She couldn't slide her fingers under the flap. They were too injured. Artush helped. He had never come so close.

"What are you doing?" she asked.

"You always ask me to help when your hands are burned. They're getting worse, you know. And healing slowly now."

"My hands?" She looked at them, shook her head. "Why is your hair different?"

"It's not." She was sure it was shorter and maybe darker. She closed her eyes, thought through what had happened. The letters, his haircut, the difference in his behavior—these differences had to be the result of her time travel. She had altered the past and therefore the future, her present. It scared her because she hadn't anticipated it, didn't know how much she had changed.

Artush handed her the newest photographs from the envelope. Yulia and Lazar looked older than they had been when Anna was in Philadelphia. They stood next to a young woman who was an older version of the child Anna had just seen at the department store: Raisa. Her face was the same, but the sweet dress was gone. So, too, was the smile Anna had seen just before she was pulled back to Aragats. Raisa had a scar on her forehead. She looked angry. She was thin and pale. She wore a black leather jacket and thick black makeup. The bottom half of her head was shaved. Anna turned the photograph over. *Raisa, twenty years old* was scrawled on the back. The photograph had been taken on the day she earned her high school degree. *She finally did it,* Yulia had written, as if to suggest relief or surprise.

"I need some time," Anna said to Artush. She turned and saw he was already halfway through the hatch, on his way down the ladder. Anna had jumped to 1975. It was now 1991 and she understood Yulia would never come back to the Soviet Union. Instead, she'd used the address to send letters trying to lure Anna to America. It seemed she'd started writing the day Anna found her in the department store and now Anna had years' worth of correspondence to read, photos to review.

As Anna began to parse through the decades of communication, she saw right away that just as Yulia had told her, her family was drowning. *Help us,* Yulia wrote again and again. She needed Anna—Molly and Raisa needed Anna. *Together we can save Mollushka and Raisa,* Yulia wrote. *Together.* And Anna felt the full weight of guilt crash on her back, guilt for abandoning them, for choosing to stop the meltdown over them. She could still help, maybe, and get back to them. Close the distance between them. Since the day they'd met, all Anna had ever wanted was to be closer to Yulia.

△ △ △

When Anna and Yulia met in Berlin in 1938, each was at the top of her field but completely alone in the world. General Goncharov had sent Anna, the Soviet Union's premier expert on radioactivity, to Germany as part of a Soviet program to bring scientific glory to their country. He didn't label her a spy, but in effect, that was what she was. He gave her the name and address of her assigned roommate, a woman Anna assumed was on a similar mission, and sent her on her way. Her new flat was on a loud street dotted with cafés and bars. Her building was five stories of carved stone and heavy wood. When she arrived, she heard water running, and so she rapped her knuckles on the door, hard. "Hello?" a woman called from inside. The water stopped. A lightbulb, hung on a string over the landing, swayed. Shadows shifted at strange angles.

"Hello," Anna called back. She cleared her throat, thought about what she wanted to say in German. She had only been studying the language for a year in preparation and it was still hard for her to speak. "I am your new roommate."

"Fucking Russian accent. Don't say another word," the woman inside yelled back in perfect German. There was the sound of sloshing water and Anna realized she was holding her breath. A chain rattled on the other side. "You're Anna Maksimovna Berkova," the woman said as she swept the door open. Anna didn't even have a chance to respond before she was dragged inside. The fog from not sleeping and hours of travel evaporated when Anna got her first good look at her new roommate. She was Anna's height, tall, but where Anna was dark, she was light. She had wide blue eyes with mascara flaked beneath them. Drops of water from her wet golden hair spilled onto the floor. "I'm Yulia Aronovna Kramarova. You probably know that. Goncharov said you were coming. Your German is as terrible as I suspect, isn't it?"

"It will improve."

Yulia laughed. "Only if I help. Which I will." She waved her hand around the room. "Russian in the flat, that's fine. Everywhere else, German. Only German." Yulia walked back toward what had to be the bathroom. She was wearing a threadbare silk robe and left a wake of perfume behind her. She continued in Russian. "The neighbors know we're Soviets, that's bad enough. I like to think we can make them forget so long as we don't speak Russian or act Russian." She turned the sink on. There were other noises and Anna realized she hadn't been in a room with a woman getting dressed for years, since Mama was taken.

The sounds came back as memories: a lid being unscrewed from a jar of cream and then being placed on a counter, a brush struggling through tangled hair. There was a slip on the floor, a skirt on one of the two beds. All of it felt unfamiliar yet comforting. *"Parles-tu français?"* Yulia called in perfect French.

"Oui," was all Anna could manage. Yulia kept speaking. Anna had a hard time following, let alone replying. Her French was better than her German, but there was a formula for each language, a structure that Anna needed to think through. She couldn't oscillate between them without preparing.

"Fine, back to Russian," Yulia said. "I've lost you already. You're not answering any of my questions." She emerged from the bathroom in a dark pleated skirt and a flowered top with puffed sleeves, all fitted to her body. "You like it? I made it myself. I can make you something similar if we scrounge up enough fabric. I won't say I enjoy sewing, but it's the only way to make do. We have to dress German. Everything modern and chic." She smoothed the pleats on one side. "Tell me, why did Goncharov send you? What's your special power?"

"I don't have a special power." Anna wasn't used to anyone being so forthcoming and she was trying to find her bearings.

"My special power is languages. Obvious, *non?*" Yulia said something in another tongue, then another. Then she laughed. "Don't be shy, what is your power?"

"Chemistry, I guess. And physics," Anna said.

"Are you going to take off your coat and hat?" Yulia grinned and Anna realized she was still standing at the entrance. She stepped forward and took it all in. The flat was one cramped room. Anna could walk from one end to the other in eight steps. It was furnished with two beds covered with moth-eaten blankets, a rickety table, and a beaten brown rug. There was a hutch on one side that looked like it served as their kitchen. It had two glasses and two plates on a shelf and a small sink to the side. "It's beautiful, isn't it?" Yulia asked. She pointed to the window. "Our view, I mean. We can look out over the city. At night it's teeming with handsome soldiers."

Anna put her coat on one of the chairs, rested her hat on top. "Not soldiers. Nazis."

Yulia was holding a tube of lipstick and a knife, using the blade as a mirror. "Yes, of course, Nazis. They are horrid. You're a Jew, aren't you? Only a Jew would say it like that." She didn't even pause, kept speaking quickly. "I'm a Jew. Not according to my papers, but Goncharov knows the truth. He made all of this possible."

"How can you speak freely? What if someone hears?" Anna asked nervously.

"Ah, so you *are* a Jew. I knew it. Look, our papers say we're Soviets, not Jews, right? I assume yours have been altered, that Goncharov made you promises, too. The Nazis will never know. And we can admire a handsome man even if we know he's vile." She searched in a bag and pulled out blush. "Most times I see an attractive Nazi, I take in his looks and then I imagine how I'd torture him before I'd kill him. It's what they would do to us. Why can't I wish them the same?" She clicked the lid open and picked up a powder puff. Anna wanted to tell Yulia she could never look at a Nazi as handsome even if she could stomach the idea of killing him or anyone, which she couldn't. "Don't look so surprised. I'm only being honest. My mother disappeared from our village. Goncharov told me Papa didn't make it out of Lubyanka. Both my parents were called enemies of the people. Political dissidents. That's why they killed them. What about your parents?"

"My father escaped with me. They only took my mother."

"What year?"

"1917. She is a hero." Why had she said so much? It was because Yulia had her off balance, losing control. Anna tried to think of a way to slow down the conversation, but Yulia was too fast, kept pushing.

"You've heard from her, then? Where do they have her?"

"I don't need to hear from her to know she's alive."

Yulia gave a knowing look. "Whatever we need to tell ourselves."

"I shouldn't have said anything," Anna said anxiously.

"Don't worry about it. This is Berlin. What happens here, we'll forget later."

Anna tried to press her lips into a smile, but she was trembling. She hadn't talked about her mother in over a decade and now, just like that, she told a stranger about her and practically admitted she was a Jew. She had paid such a high price to erase the label. Papa had made her swear she would never even say the word again, and one day outside of the country and she had already failed. Not that she even really felt Jewish—it was only a word to her, a word that pushed her down. She knew nothing about the religion or traditions or even the languages. That identity had been erased from her papers along with her mother and now she only felt Soviet. It didn't make sense that she'd trusted Yulia so easily. There was no evidence showing she was trustworthy; it was something Anna felt, and she wasn't used to emotions being her guide. She looked down, realized she had balled her skirt up into her fists.

"It's okay," Yulia said. "You're safe. I won't repeat it. Ever. I can't or I'd die, too, be accused of being an accomplice or some other bullshit. We have to hide each other's secrets. We're the same that way, aren't we? It makes us friends and allies even though we're strangers. Let's just forget about it and have fun." Anna didn't even know what Yulia meant, have fun. "Come on. Let me add a little lipstick to your lips, some perfume, and I'll show you a real city. The world beyond the USSR. You won't believe how much we miss up there."

"I can't," Anna said.

"Of course you can." Yulia kneeled in front of Anna and put a hand on her knee. She untangled her skirt from her fist and smoothed it back down. "I come on strong. I know. I can't help it." Anna focused on Yulia's hand touching her leg. Mama was the last person who'd touched her that way, who had come that close, and thinking about that made some of the pain Anna had hidden deep inside come back. She felt her face flush. But she was too tired to do this now.

"Stop touching me," Anna said. Her voice sounded cold and she saw Yulia flinch.

"I'm sorry," Yulia said. She withdrew quickly. "Did someone hurt you?"

"No. It's not that."

"But you don't want to be touched."

"It's not that, either." She did want to be touched, to be close to someone again. She just didn't want to think about her mother, not then. "I had to fight to get here," Anna said. It was the simplest explanation she could offer. And it was true. She had fought her classmates on the playground and at the park; the professor who tried to ridicule her in front of all her peers; all the men who had told her she didn't belong. "I can't lose it."

"We both had to fight. Not only with our fists, right?" Yulia nodded and Anna knew she understood. Yulia held up the lipstick. "I'll go slow." She brushed it along the full length of Anna's lips without touching any other part of her body. It felt tacky, but Anna realized she loved the sensation. "You're gorgeous." Yulia beamed. "Let's go."

Outside they switched to German. Anna could understand most but was having as much trouble with the language as she did with the fact that Yulia kept talking and wouldn't stop. "There's so much to teach you about life here. You won't believe how different it is. I know, I know. You're going to tell me you were happy there. I thought the same. What else did I know?" No, Anna thought, that's where they were different. Anna had never thought she was happy. Nor did she think she was sad. She was surviving, not thinking about anything other than staying alive. Walking with Yulia now, she realized she had been numb. Yulia continued, "Americans are evil. Capitalism is death, blah, blah. They say all that garbage but I'm telling you, you won't regret your time in Berlin. We have to live in the moment." They were on the street by then. A tram clacked past. Couples strolled by. Nazis stumbled, drunk and cackling. All of it was excess: laughter and adornment in multitudes, all under the shadows of the Third Reich flags.

"Remember, nobody knows who we are. We can be anyone at all here. Follow my lead." And Anna did. They went into a café. It was crowded, teeming with smoke and music. It felt foreign to Anna, and that made her hesitate because foreign could be dangerous, could lead her to do the wrong thing. "Should I slap you to get the blood flowing?" Yulia asked. "Come on. Wake up. Live a little." She dragged Anna deeper inside.

"They're…they're all—"

"Happy?" Yulia lowered her voice so Anna had to strain to hear against the noise of the bar. "Hitler's only struck fear into the hearts of Jews, and no Jew would come near this café." Then Yulia whispered, "Never order vodka. In Berlin we drink beer." She waved at a waiter, who cleared a table for them and brought two steins filled to the brim. "Tell me about your work," Yulia said.

"I can't."

Yulia held up her stein to toast. "Fair enough, for now. You're good at whatever you do. I'm sure of it. You're probably Goncharov's best hope. Something he can showcase to Stalin, a way for him to gain power and prestige. We're his props, you see. He will stand on our backs to reach greatness."

"Aren't you terrified to speak that way?"

"No one can hear. Plus, they're all too busy looking at my legs." Yulia threw her head back and laughed, a full-throated roar that made Anna smile. "If Goncharov wants me, he can take me. I have nothing left anyway. I told you, my parents are dead. My sister, too. I have no other family."

"How do you do it?" Anna asked. "Sit here without a care in the world. Looking like the Germans, acting like the Germans."

"I just hide my fear better than you. And I told you, sounding like them is my special power. Looking like them, or anyone, comes easily. I have no idea how, I just do it, mimic the accents, the facial expressions and hand motions. Can you explain how you solve an equation or whatever?" She took another sip of her beer. "Give me any language and one month and I can fool anyone, make them think I'm a local."

"That's impossible."

"No it's not. I bet you're not so different. People think when you calculate answers quickly, or find an answer they can't, that you're cheating—don't they?" A man across the room called out to her and she threw her head back and laughed. "Rolfe! Come and meet my new roommate." He pulled up a chair, and then two more men also joined. All of them were competing for Yulia's attention. It reminded Anna of the way she used to see Mama's followers gather around her, only these men were wearing Nazi uniforms. When Yulia stood up to dance, Anna went home.

The next morning, Anna woke up early, as always, and got to work on a problem she had been puzzling through, one she wanted to present to Otto Hahn, her new collaborator in Berlin. It was Sunday and she planned to spend the entire day working. At noon a set of bells rang from a nearby church, and Yulia rolled over. "Is it that late already?" she groaned. "I want to show you the city." She got up and stretched. Whereas Anna dressed entirely behind the closed door, Yulia stripped down next to her bed and walked to the bathroom in nothing at all. Anna couldn't help but stare. She hadn't seen a naked woman since Mama. Yulia's hips were rounder than Anna expected, her curves softer, and Anna found herself touching her own hips, running a hand over her own backside. She looked away because her heart was racing. But maybe like Yulia said, this was finally living.

"I didn't realize that I missed speaking Russian until last night," Yulia called from the bathroom. "We need to get to work on a new dress for you. You look like a babushka."

"I don't have breasts like you."

"I told you, you're gorgeous."

Once Yulia was dressed, she showed Anna how to apply lipstick, even gave her a tube. For the first time in years, Anna wasn't thinking about her work.

"You'll be my project," Yulia said. "I've been lonely."

"With all those men swarming, I find that hard to believe."

"Come on. They're Nazis." She sighed. "Maybe we both need each other."

* * *

On Monday morning, Anna made her way to her new lab. In his letters, Otto Hahn had directed her to look for him in his office. It was nestled in a gray four-story building where every angle and corner was sharp. Anna found him hunched on a stool. In profile, Hahn was smaller and thinner than she'd imagined. He was focused on a square of wax, cutting through the layers. "Professor? I'm Dr. Anna Berkova."

He looked up with the knife in his hand. "Yes, the Soviet. Please." Anna's first impression was that this brilliant scientist looked dull. His eyes didn't glow with intelligence. His shoulders weren't broad with the weight of ideas. But then when he smiled there was warmth in it that Anna hadn't seen in any of her colleagues. "I've been waiting for you."

"I'm not late."

"Not at all. We're thrilled to have you, me and my colleague Dr. Lise Meitner. She'll be here soon. You know her?"

"Of course." Meitner was the real reason Anna had wanted to come. She was the scientist who secured the greatest advances attributed to Hahn's lab.

"Lise is a Jew. That's bad right now. You're a Soviet. It may not be better. I don't know. Perhaps you'll both have to leave."

Anna tried to look undisturbed, but there was the word again, *Jew*.

For Anna it went together with *Soviet*. She was a Soviet Jew even if he didn't know it, and all she could think was *Born a Jew, die a Jew*. "It shouldn't be a problem. I have papers."

"Papers mean nothing. But I've forgotten my manners. Dr. Anna Berkova, it is an honor to meet you. You're a genius. You know more about radioactivity than I do and we need your help, desperately. Please." He pulled out another stool for her. "We can't ignore the fact that these are dangerous times. War is coming. Tell me, why did you apply to work with me now?"

"I want answers," Anna said. It was the truth. "I came because our understanding of radioactivity isn't complete. We're missing something, something important, and together we can find it. Why did you invite me?"

"Because I think the same. Even more, if scientists can't rise above hateful politics, who will?" He looked behind her at the door, spoke in almost a whisper. "There are Germans in this building who are not open-minded like I am. If you are in danger, I have ways of helping." He cleared his throat and spoke in a louder voice then, pointed to the square of wax. "I have uranium in here. I want to understand its nucleus. Together, we must understand an atom from its essence, not its historical path."

"Precisely," Anna agreed. "Past explanations, the belief that an atom is immutable, are wrong. Uranium shows that, but how? And why? That's what I want to find."

"Yes," Otto said. "Lise and I, we found that in radioactive elements particles break away from the nucleus. They shoot out at high speeds. You know that, of course. We were trying to prove the hypothesis that atoms decay in a process similar to erosion. Like a pebble caught in a river, they shed one layer at a time. I'm certain of it, but I need proof. That's where you and I will begin. Tell me, what fascinates you about radioactivity?"

No one had ever asked her that before. She sat back and thought for a moment. It wasn't that she didn't have an answer. It was that for years no one had cared what she thought. Her male colleagues disregarded her opinion even when they benefited from her work. And now, finally, she had an audience and she wanted to be clear. "The notion that so many things exist in a perpetual state of decay, that they are always changing and metamorphizing, is incredible." She thought about how she'd watched decay her entire life. Her family deteriorated. Russia crumbled in civil war. Now the Soviet Union was in disrepair, departments, policies, and punishments falling to pieces. It was all for the greater good, there was a goal—but the path wasn't enviable. "Radioactive elements want to be stable. It's why they shed their outer layers. Don't we all want that, stability?"

Otto, Lise, and Anna fell into a routine, working twelve and fourteen hours a day. They didn't speak much because they didn't need to. Science was a means of communication. Experiments were a language Anna understood better than anyone. She drew into her shell and the only person who could pull her out at the end of the day was Yulia. Yulia jabbered at her the minute she stepped into their flat, asking about everything. She wanted to know how Anna survived the revolution, how she enjoyed having papers without her Jewish stamp, and that was only the beginning.

"You keep calling yourself a Jew," Anna said one night over dinner, boiled potatoes. "You do nothing Jewish."

"Do you have to be observant to be a Jew? Can't we embrace certain sides of ourselves in private, and other sides in public?" Anna had never conceived of herself as being composed of distinct parts. She tried to make sense of that idea while Yulia continued, "Being Jewish is in our blood. We can't escape it, so we might as well embrace it together." She took out a silver cigarette case. "Tell me about all those notes and equations you're always scribbling."

"What language are you working on now?" Anna countered, thinking it was better not to answer. Unlike Anna, Yulia didn't dodge questions. She opened herself to all of Anna's inquiries and even started introducing Anna as her sister when they were out. Anna was surprised by how much she loved that. She had never had a friend, barely had a family. Being called Yulia's sister meant this bond Anna felt was real and stable, and she held on tight.

One night in late 1938, Anna and Yulia sat on the edge of their window, smoking, drinking, and looking out on the people dancing in the café below. It was near dawn and Yulia sat so close their pinkie fingers touched. "My family was from a village near Kiev," Yulia said into the silence. "My parents were sure we would die from a pogrom or starve. They sent us, my sister and I, to Petrograd to find work. I've never told anyone about what happened." She spread her fingers over Anna's and locked them together. "I've never even wanted to tell anyone before, but now I have you. I need you to know." A tear spilled off her chin, her smile fell away, and for the first time Anna thought she might be looking at the real Yulia, the one behind all those questions and glamour. Yulia continued, "I was so hungry. Hungry enough that my stomach was distended. My hair was falling out. Have you been that hungry?"

No, Anna hadn't.

"That kind of hunger haunts you," Yulia said, holding out her hands. They were shaking. "See, the memory brings back the fear, the way I felt when I was so hungry I had to leave my parents. I know over a dozen languages and not one can help me describe the feeling. Nor how I felt when my sister died."

"What was her name?" Anna asked.

"Ruth. She was smarter than me. She was fourteen. I was twelve. Papa came for us a few months after he sent us away, said he made a mistake." She stopped and took a long pull on the vodka bottle between them. "That factory owner had connections. We were good workers and he wanted to keep us under his thumb. When he saw Papa, he accused him of hideous things. Of being an enemy of the people." She dropped her head. "Arrested, sentenced, and murdered in a day. For what? Trying to bring his daughters home. I never told anyone."

"You said your parents were political prisoners."

"It's easier that way, isn't it? They came for Mama not long after. In our village. She disappeared. I have no idea how they killed her, or how the factory owner had that kind of power. Mama couldn't even read a newspaper, let alone plan a rebellion against Stalin. All she wanted was food, a better life for her daughters."

"I'm so sorry," Anna said. She pulled Yulia into her arms and held her tight. It was the first time they'd ever been that close for so long, and there was a security in it, in feeling Yulia's skin and body pressed against hers. Yulia must have felt it, too, because she held on. "And Ruth?" Anna asked.

"We couldn't go back to that factory, so we found another. There was a famine. Peasants flooded in looking for work, like us, and there were so many languages. Without trying, I learned one, then another. I helped workers understand, translated directions, learned to read their papers. The foreman saw what I did and took me off the looms, made me an interpreter. Goncharov was the foreman's uncle. He heard about me." Yulia squeezed Anna's hand. "And now here we are."

"You didn't tell me what happened to Ruth."

"No. It's hard." She sucked in a tangled sob. "She was seventeen by then. I was fifteen. The looms. She was caught. She...she tried to fix one. It crushed her in a single revolution." Yulia's tears had been a slow trickle, but now they came in hard waves and she crumpled, all her weight falling into Anna. "Ruthele used to hold me like this."

"Do you think it's your fault?" Anna asked.

"I know it is. I could have taught her languages so she could work like me."

"You couldn't."

Yulia sobbed. "It should...have been...me...Ruth...She was good."

"You had no power."

"How do you know?"

"Because I've felt the same for my mother for years. I should have stood up to the men who took her. I should have made her run. There are millions of things I've thought I should have done, but like you, I had no power." She stopped. "Maybe I have no power now, either. But I won't make her mistakes."

"Power." Yulia's shoulders still shook. "Why does it always come down to power?"

* * *

After that night, Yulia and Anna stopped staying out as late. Instead, they came home and talked, and Anna found herself telling Yulia about her family, her life back in the Soviet Union. Once she started, Anna couldn't hold back. For the first time she talked about her last night with her mother before everything fell apart. It had been Anna's birthday and her parents threw a party for her, just the three of them. It was the best and worst night of Anna's life. The next morning, Xenia, her mama, was gone, marching with the revolution. By nightfall the day after that, the Czar's men had her, and Anna and her father ran to the train station, to a new life. Letting the secret out felt like a weight had lifted, but it was also terrifying because it reminded her what it felt like to be that little girl. All the emotions and fear she had bottled up for so long came out and left her feeling like an empty, shaking shell, more vulnerable than she had ever been, because now she saw she could still come undone. "My mother, I love her and I hate her for what she did, for leaving us," Anna said after she'd taken time to recover. They were sitting on their windowsill smoking. Yulia kissed the top of her head.

"She didn't leave. She was taken," Yulia said. "You really believe your mother's alive?"

She hesitated. "I need to believe it. Do you understand?"

"I do." Yulia squeezed her hand. "I do."

"That night in our flat, celebrating my tenth birthday, Mama was focused on me. She laughed all night, and she rarely laughed. Papa, too. He spent so much time saving rations for that cake. And it was awful, made with potatoes mixed with a bit of flour. But it was the best food I've ever eaten. That night—when I need it, I go back to it again and again. It makes me feel better." She took a deep breath. "After Mama disappeared, Papa turned into a drunk."

"You were lucky to have that birthday party. Some people don't even get that much."

"It's why I love science," Anna said. "There's an answer. An absolute. When Mama is finally free, will she try to find me? Or is Mama gone? I can make a case for either. There's no way to know. But when it comes to math and science there's an answer."

* * *

One day in early 1939, Anna woke up with a start. Her hands were sweaty even before she could focus, caught up in excitement and exhaustion. The night before, she'd thought she had made a breakthrough in her work on radioactivity, in understanding its decay. She grabbed her notes, splayed over her moth-eaten blanket, and went through them again. Yes, she was sure she was right. She had to get to her lab, to tell Otto. He was the only one left who would understand. Lise Meitner had fled Germany, fearing for her life because she was a Jew. Anna's realization was that they had been framing radioactivity the wrong way. The nucleus didn't erode—it split. *Split*. The word was small, but the ramifications were tremendous.

The process was called fission and it was extraordinary because not only did the nucleus cleave in two, but the by-product was energy. Enormous energy. One atom splitting was enough to make a single grain of sand jump. An atom is minuscule compared to a grain of sand.

Imagine what a cluster of splitting nuclei could do. If she could harness the energy, she could create power plants, batteries, and that was only the beginning. As the atom split, it caused a wave, like a sound wave, only it was an energy wave that warped space. She called it a nuclear ripple and hypothesized that just as sound could be turned up or down, a nuclear ripple could also be magnified or shrunk. That meant a small reaction could be used to generate enormous power.

"You make so much noise, Annechka," Yulia moaned from the other side of the room. "At least hand me a cigarette. My head hurts."

"You're hungover. Drink water," Anna replied. She shoved her notes into her bag.

"You're being short with me."

"I'm not."

"You are. You don't even realize it. It means you're preoccupied, that you're not sleeping." And then, "It's my job to watch over you."

Yulia was propped up on her elbows with the eye mask she wore to bed pushed up on her forehead. Her eyes were smeared with eyeliner. Even disheveled and hungover, she was beautiful. "Drink," Anna said, softer now, handing her a full glass.

Yulia took the water. Wind batted snowflakes against the window. A tram clattered at the other end of the street and Anna hurried downstairs to catch it, running past lampposts emblazoned with swastikas. While she was used to the cold seeping under her coat, that morning it ripped through the wool with a sharper edge than usual. The smell of rust or something rotten was thicker than it had been the day before. The only people on the street were men in uniform. All of them carried guns. They made Anna curl forward and wish she were invisible. She had heard rumors about what was happening. The ghettos were real. The trains were, too, and they terrified her most of all. People were disappearing in Germany the way they disappeared in Russia and the Soviet Union, the way Mama had disappeared. No Jews were coming back.

The tram door opened, and Anna climbed the steps. It was crowded and she was forced to take a seat across from a soldier. She couldn't see his face, but she noticed that the shoulder pads on his coat slid down his thin frame, making it look too big, like it was his father's. The tram clacked. The car jerked forward and Anna faced the window. How high were the peaks and troughs in the nuclear ripple?

The horrifying noise came before the impact. The sound of screeching metal was so high-pitched she felt it rumble in her gut. Instinct made her crouch into a ball and cover her head. There was no way to avoid the crash she could feel coming, and with that realization, even as she knew time was racing, it simultaneously slowed. She hovered, experienced every second as if it were an hour, floating out of her seat with her hands still on her head. She made out the stitches in the leather on the bench, the rivets welded in the floor and along the sides of the car, the specks of dust floating with her around the lights. She even took note of the seams on that too-big coat that enveloped the soldier. Every detail, every speck was clearer than it had ever been. Then as quickly as time had slowed, it slammed forward. Anna's head banged the seat in front of her. The pain was immediate, radiating from her skull down through her neck all the way to her toes, making her go numb. Then she was on her side, lying on the window. That had her confused. Shouldn't gravity have her the other way up?

Someone screamed. Smoke made it hard to breathe. Her head. It throbbed. She reached a hand up to touch the edge of her scalp. Even through her gloves she felt it was slick. Blood. She smelled the iron in it, the same scent she'd picked up running to the stop. Now it mixed with smoke.

The soldier. He was still across from her. His eyes were wide, only he didn't blink. Or breathe. It took her another moment to realize his too-big coat had caught on the pole between them and hanged him, maybe even as he tried to escape. It had snapped his neck so his head sat at a crooked angle. Even worse, he wasn't across from her. He was dangling above her. The tram car had flipped. She wanted to scream but the smoke was too thick.

Blood trickled over her forehead, down the side of her nose and into a puddle. She watched the drops melt into a pool. Like water, they rippled. The waves were clear, peaks and troughs. The image reminded her of Hahn's diagrams of an atom, of his depictions of the layers surrounding the nucleus. A drop. To a ripple. And back to still. An action and a reaction.

"Ma'am," a man said. She couldn't see his face. His hands pulled her arm. They were gruff. Quick. "We must get out of here. Now. It's burning."

He walked her across the windows. The sound of glass grinding on stone mixed with crying, Anna's crying. The man heaved her through the side door and another man pulled her up and lowered her to the street. Other people were as bloody and bruised as Anna. Bystanders, shopkeepers, and Nazis were kneeling and climbing on the toppled car, pulling more people through the windows. Sirens blared.

Anna stumbled across the cobblestones and found herself under an arch, in an arcade where a café had chairs and tables set for customers. She took a seat facing the tram, the crowd. From her new perspective it was clear the car had skipped the track. Perhaps it was ice, or speed. Or both. Either way, the accident had caused the electric lines above to spark. One of the swastika flags above caught fire. It waved so close to another that a line of flags was high with flames. It would have been safest for her to run, but she was still too stunned to move. She dropped her head in her hands and stared down at the cobbled walk. The leap from the tracks wasn't isolated. Its effect was running down the street, one flag burning after another, one action leading to another. It was like a drop of liquid falling into a puddle, like her own blood—ripples. After the sand jumped, there was also a ripple. It was a tiny ripple. Why did it distort space? Was it a wrinkle in the fabric of space? Maybe. Einstein had written about the theory of space-time, had suggested there might be a way to rip or distort the fabric of the universe—and that was similar to what she witnessed. Her brain was working in overdrive, filling with ideas, one spilling to another, all going back to her realization that one atom splitting was enough to make a single grain of sand jump. The power in that was awe-inspiring. And a cluster of splitting nuclei, she realized, could come from a nuclear explosion—a bomb. Would that explosion give her access to ripples in space-time, a way to see time as bent, not linear.

"Ma'am? Can you hear me? We need to take you to the hospital," a man said. He wore an apron, must have worked at a café. He reached toward her with a towel to help with the blood coming down the side of her face. She flinched and he pulled back. "I understand your fear. We'll get them. Don't worry."

She was confused. "Who?"

"The Jewish scum who did this. We will make them pay," the man said. Anna had to force herself not to recoil from his touch, his words.

"Did you see someone sabotage the tracks? How do you know it was a Jew?"

"How else could such a tragedy occur?"

"It was an accident. The tram took the curve too fast given the ice."

"Stop making excuses for them." He dropped the towel in her lap. Anna held her breath. The familiar fear of being discovered came roaring back. Even as she sat there with her German hairdo and German clothing, was there something Jewish about her that he might recognize? Would she be blamed? She closed her eyes and cradled her forehead in her hands. Her head had never hurt so much. Around her people ran and yelled. A fire brigade worked to stanch the flames, to pull all the burning flags to the ground. Anna went back to the screech. To the jolt. That was where she stopped. Where time slowed. In the moment after she hit her head, she hovered. Why? And what did that have to do with her blood dropping in a puddle, rippling? She thought back to the notion of a nucleus surrounded by layers of electrons. She knew she was confusing disparate events, but there was a reason for it. She could feel she was on the edge of a big idea. To find it, she went back to the beginning, to what she knew.

Fission. Atoms split. When that happens they release enormous amounts of energy that can be channeled toward ripples in space-time, ripples like the drop of blood that fell into the puddle. Space and time were connected. Einstein said they were part of the same fabric, only he couldn't find a way to incorporate gravity and electromagnetism. But maybe Anna could, could find a way to use electromagnetic waves to access ripples in space-time—to bend time. Most people laughed at Einstein, but Anna didn't, never Anna.

△ △ △

Anna, her dark hair now gray and her straight back now stooped, leaned back in her chair in the watchtower on Mount Aragats and looked over at her time machine, the photo she'd tacked to the wall of her family standing in front of their store, and her pathetic, dead rosebush. Her work in Berlin was over fifty years ago, but it felt closer now that she had so many letters and pictures from Yulia plastered on the walls. They told the story of Molly's life falling apart, then Raisa's, and Anna understood she would use her work from the past to save their future. Yulia, Anna's Yulia, hadn't doubted Anna for a second, and after all the times and countless ways she'd saved Anna, it was time for Anna to save Yulia. Valery was right, Anna needed to choose. She would change her course. She would choose her family.

MOLLY

Philadelphia

I still need to go to New York," Molly said to Viktor two weeks after she started riding home with him from school. Her parents didn't like her taking rides from Viktor and that made it more of a thrill. It helped that kids at school looked impressed when she got into his car, that even Catherine looked jealous.

"I'll take you. Soon," Viktor said. "I promise."

"You said that before," she said in a voice that made it clear she was losing patience.

"Because I mean it. I will take you." He pointed to the new Russian Market sign in front of them. "Why don't your parents like me?"

"Who cares?"

"Seriously, Andrey says your parents are good people. You know, an all-American family. I have no one here. My family is all in the USSR. I want yours to like me."

She didn't have the heart to tell him they would never like him or accept him. They only wanted her to be with a rocket scientist or a doctor. Just a few days ago, after Shabbat dinner, while Molly was helping with the dishes, Mama had said, "I see that boy driving past our store all the time. Stop wasting time with him."

"Maybe I like him." Molly had picked up a plate to dry as Mama washed.

"You don't know what you like. You're too young." Mama turned off the water and faced Molly. The long green rubber gloves she wore dripped. "At your age, I had already lost my sister and my parents. I was alone. I want better for you."

"I didn't know," Molly said, her voice quiet with surprise as she leaned on the counter. She'd had no idea Mama had been so young. "Will you tell me about your sister?"

"Ruth died in Petrograd. That was the name of the city then." She dropped her chin to her chest. "Crushed in a loom. She left me all alone."

Molly went still, didn't dare move, afraid she'd break the moment, hoping Mama would say more while also struggling to hold the weight of what she had just shared. But Mama turned back to the sink, pushed the soup pot on its side. Dirty water splashed over the edge.

"Why didn't you ever tell me?"

"There never seems to be a good time to talk about any of it. I saw things no one ever should. So did your father, and Anna."

"Can you tell me more?"

"Not now." Molly felt the familiar tug of anger as her mother shut down again and went back to scrubbing. "Holding on to the past, the bad parts of the past, isn't worth it. Get your diploma, go to university, and you will have a whole world open to you here."

"But I don't want that life. I want to draw, publish my comics."

"That's a hobby. Not a career. And that boy," Mama said, her voice dangerously quiet now. "That boy. He will distract you. Tell you lies. Make you promises. I've seen enough to know. You will never be an artist with him. I promise you that."

But Molly knew her mother was wrong. Being around Viktor was exciting like nothing else Molly had ever experienced. He made her feel like she could do anything and become anyone. When she was in his car, or in a room with him, the air was different; she was finally rising out of her teenage self. He saw her for who she was, and every time she was with him, she thought about his long fingers and the way their heat made her loosen when he touched her, the way her skin sang.

One day after school, instead of driving Molly home, Viktor took her to a diner. It was polished stainless steel on the outside and speckled linoleum and Formica on the inside. Speakers blared something old, a guitar with a woman crooning. They looked out on a bus depot where a network of trolley lines hung like a spiderweb overhead. Viktor sat across from Molly and, as always, wore his leather coat and sunglasses. Today his knuckles were swollen. His shoulders, his presence took up the entire booth.

"How is your art?" he asked. "Did the magazine write back?"

"Not yet."

"They will."

She shrugged and felt a pang, a pinch of pain, realized she was admitting what had been eating at her, that EVO hadn't jumped when they saw her work, hadn't called and asked her to come to the office right away as she'd hoped they would. Now she knew getting published by EVO, or even working for them, wasn't going to be fast or easy. "They might not even like my work," she admitted without looking him in the eye.

"Of course they will. You're a brilliant American. Americans like Americans." There was that word again. *Brilliant.* The chain that was always being wrapped around her, that she couldn't stand.

The waitress came and Molly ordered a large orange juice. It was expensive and her parents never let her order it. She wanted to see what Viktor would do, if he'd pay for it. He didn't blink.

"Coffee. Black. Very hot," Viktor said. "You have salmon?"

The waitress smiled. "We got fish sticks and tuna."

"Your lettuce is fresh?" Viktor asked. The waitress nodded and laughed. "Then I'll have lettuce. Just lettuce and carrots. No dressing unless you have olive oil."

"Canola not good enough for you?" She laughed even louder.

"Lettuce at a diner?" Molly asked.

"It's healthy. Health is important." He put a fist on his chest. "It is the secret to a long life, but really it is not so secret. Mollushka, what else do you want?" She shook her head to say nothing because usually her stomach couldn't take much, but with Viktor she felt better, stronger, and she changed her mind, ordered a hamburger and french fries.

After the waitress left, Molly pointed to the bus depot. "How do you stay healthy with all the pollution in this city? And your smoking?"

"I go to the ocean as much as possible. Swimming in salt water cleanses the body." She wanted to tell him she didn't believe the Atlantic had that kind of power, but he never said anything like that to her. He believed in her and so she decided to believe in him, too. "I'll teach you to be healthier," Viktor said. "You, you can teach me to be a better American." She liked thinking they could help each other, and when the food came she ate every last bite.

Soon Molly started counting the hours and minutes until she saw Viktor. He began coming to the butcher shop every Saturday night when they closed, taking her out. They went to more diners and restaurants, ones that served salmon and lettuce. He always asked to see her sketchbook and if she had heard back from *EVO*. He took her to a Sixers game and she explained the rules. As they walked together, he put his hand on her lower back, just at the top of her skirt or pants. His touch made her jolt to life. He kissed her neck first, before her lips. He kissed her arms, her wrists, her knees. She loved the thrill of his lips on her skin, that he didn't kiss her the way she saw high school boys kissing girls, rushed and hungry. Instead, his kisses around her body were controlled and slow, meant to make her want more. Every time he touched her, she thought about them having sex and knew he did, too. Still, he didn't push. Molly enjoyed herself even more when he started taking her to clubs where he knew the bouncers. Classes and homework fell away.

"You'll regret him," Mama said as she and Molly fought about Viktor again and again.

The more Molly fought with her parents, the more her stomach hurt and the less she ate, unless she was with Viktor. She started losing weight, hemmed her skirts shorter, and began unbuttoning an extra button on her blouses. She stopped ironing her hair. Instead, she kept it loose, her curls wild. Best of all, she was drawing more than ever. Molly erased Rocket Raisa's lab coat and gave her a white leotard top with a short gold skirt to match. The character donned knee-high gold boots and her hair became a thick white mane worn in a ponytail high on the crown of her head. She slimmed Mighty Minerva's waist, made her bust bigger and started using brighter colors and bolder lines. And she let Anna go for blood when she wanted revenge instead of pulling back. Molly wanted Anna to be as free as Viktor made her feel.

The only thing restraining Molly, keeping her from feeling like she was flying, was the fact that she hadn't heard back from *EVO*. She sent more samples, and more, but still nothing. When Viktor asked her what was happening she said she wanted to dance instead of talking about it. It was easier to push the rejection away because that was what it was— rejection. Silence meant they didn't want her, and if *EVO* wouldn't take her art, well, she didn't have a backup plan. The weight of that pulled her down hard and so she avoided it. The only thing she knew for certain was that she wasn't going to college. She didn't need to deal with another place where her parents expected her to be brilliant, where she was surrounded by people who mistook her disinterest for lack of smarts and gave her bad grades. She threw out every application her parents put on her desk, her bed, the table.

One Saturday night, Viktor picked her up early. He took her to a club that had a stage and a live band. Viktor asked her for the first time if she wanted a drink. "Champagne," she said with a shy smile, because she'd loved it from that first taste on Anna's birthday.

He handed her one glass, then another. After three glasses she was gloriously numb, all of her pain gone, and she tried her first shot of vodka. Later, he took her out to his car, parked under a dark overpass, a spot she would never go on her own. When they got to the car, she followed him into the back seat. *This is it*, she thought. *Finally*. She was going to lose her virginity. She slipped her panties off, was so nervous she banged her knee against the door. "Don't worry, I'll take care of you," he said as he kissed her neck, her stomach.

Molly straddled him. He had already unbuckled his pants and pulled them down. She didn't see him do it. It was possible she was drunker than she thought, and for a split second she thought about stopping, but she decided she wanted this. He trailed kisses down the side of her neck, slid the strap of her tank top off her shoulder and cupped her breast, slowly licked her nipple. She felt herself opening up into adulthood, like she had all the powers of a real woman, and that gave her as much pleasure as Viktor kissing her, touching her. "When do you get your period?" he asked as he brushed his fingertips across her back, making her shiver.

"Another week." Was that right? She knew she should ask him to wear a condom, only things were happening quickly, and it felt so good.

"Fuck it," he said. "I don't care. We'll take care of it if we need to."

She agreed because she didn't want him to stop. And then he was inside her. She felt herself stretch, felt him moving. The thought that she was losing her virginity, being the wild daughter her parents worked to tame, increased her pleasure even more.

"I'm having sex," she said once, twice. "I love it."

"Yes," Viktor said. "Yes." She tried to hold on to it, feel it so next time she would know what to do to make it better. Afterward he pulled a tissue box out from behind the seat to clean up the blood. "Are you okay?" he asked. He kissed the top of her head.

"Perfect," she said, and closed her eyes. She thought about the locker room, hearing other girls talk about sex and how she could talk about it now, too. She was done being a little girl. "It was time."

Viktor looked confused. "Time for what?"

"Time that happened," she said.

He laughed and pulled her into his lap to hold her. "I love you."

"You don't have to say that."

"No. But I mean it. I've never met anyone like you." She knew he was waiting for her to say it back, but she wasn't able to. She loved being with him and around him, but she didn't love him. She knew because she saw love in her parents, in the quiet between them where they spoke without words, in the way they anticipated each other, did for each other. She and Viktor didn't have that; they had fun—not love—and Molly was happy with that. Besides, all she wanted to think about was the fact that she wasn't a virgin. She could leave high school behind. She could move to New York City and live her own kind of life.

Afterward, as she made her way back inside the house, Papa was waiting for her, and she felt guilty that she had been out so late, hadn't told them where she'd gone, because she knew her parents worried all the time. And she wondered if Papa could see that she was different, that she'd had sex. "You don't need that boy," Papa said as she tried to glide quietly toward the stairs. His voice was soft, not angry the way Molly expected. "You can do anything, like your superheroes. You have so much talent. Don't waste it on him."

"You hate *Atomic Anna*," she said without looking at him.

"Yes, but you don't. Listen, Mollushka." He walked over to her and put an arm around her shoulders. "America is hard. The Soviet Union is harder. Wherever you live, you need to work for what you want. This Viktor wants everything served up on a platter."

"You don't know him."

"You think I was born a parent? That I haven't been in love, seen the world in different ways?" He took a deep breath. "I lived what felt like a thousand years before I came here and had you, enough to understand when things need to end—and this, between you two, it needs to end. What do you have left outside of him?"

"My art."

"You'll need more than that."

* * *

Molly and Viktor started going out on weeknights as well as weekends. Molly was called into the principal's office because she was failing English and French. She convinced herself it didn't matter. She hadn't heard a word from *EVO* yet, but like Viktor kept telling her, she would. She was sure she had a different future where high school didn't matter, where no one cared if she went to college anyway.

It was May when Viktor offered her a bump. They were at a club. He said it casually, as if he were offering her a glass of water instead of cocaine. The music was loud. She was wearing a new short skirt he'd bought for her, one she put on after she was out of the house. He was wearing his leather jacket, holding his arms out to block people from brushing against her. "No pressure," he said. "I just thought it would be a good time."

Molly knew kids in her class were *doing drugs* but didn't know what that meant. Were they smoking pot? Using needles? In health ed, the gym teacher showed films where kids overdosed, but it was his job to scare them. This was Viktor, a man she trusted, saying it was no big deal.

"You've tried it?" she asked. He nodded. "It's not healthy, like your salmon and lettuce."

He laughed. "I do my calisthenics. I eat properly. A little vodka. A little cocaine. It's okay." He took her hand, led her into the men's bathroom, and showed her what to do. The rush was instantaneous and more intense than anything she'd ever felt in her life. Every remnant of pain she had dulled with alcohol lifted out of her body. Every anxious thought that sat in her mind, even those buried deep enough so she didn't have to look at them, disappeared. High, there was nothing she couldn't or wouldn't do. She was convinced she would be the greatest artist ever. It wasn't euphoria, it was better than that. Nothing that had ever made her sad could touch her. Nothing that had ever angered her could come close. Only it didn't last long enough. The comedown started before she was ready, and even as she felt it slipping away, she knew she wanted more and that Viktor would give it to her.

* * *

Viktor came for Molly in the middle of the night three weeks later, just before her high school graduation. She woke up to him stroking her arm. At first she didn't recognize him. Adrenaline made her jump out of bed, grabbing the first thing she could find, a pen, to defend herself. She held it to ward him off, but then her eyes focused and she saw it was Viktor. "What the hell?" she whispered. Her voice was sharp. "How did you get in? What do you want?" She looked at the door. It was closed. No light had turned on; her parents hadn't heard anything. She turned on her reading lamp to get a better look at him. His eyes were red-rimmed and bloodshot.

"I climbed in the dining room window." His arms were up in surrender and he sounded sad, worried in a way he never had before. "I'm sorry."

"You're in trouble?" She couldn't think of any other reason he would be there.

"I—I can only ask you once."

"What?" She reached for her bathrobe and pulled it on. Even though he had seen her naked dozens of times, in that moment, in her pajamas, she needed to cover herself.

He took a deep, long breath and dropped to his knees. "Will you run away with me?"

"What are you talking about? What happened?"

"I have to run. And I can't come back." He took her hand. "Marry me?"

She was still trying to make sense of it all. "I... I—"

"You know I love you. You haven't said it, but you feel it. I know it. And if it were up to me, it would be different, but I don't have a choice. Andrey, if he finds me, he will kill me. I stole from him. I can pay him back, just not now. Run with me. Marry me?"

"I'm eighteen! Last week we were fighting about the prom. You said you wanted the all-American experience." She had refused to take him.

"I know." He bit his bottom lip. "It's almost been a year, and for me it's enough. We are the same. I know we both want the same thing."

"What's that?" They had spent most of their time together partying, not talking, and Molly realized she had no idea what he wanted, only that he liked his car, drugs, and America. She didn't know if he wanted kids or not. She barely even knew what she wanted. Her desires were painted in broad strokes: independence, New York, becoming a comic artist. She loved being with Viktor because he helped her escape all the confusion in her head. But that wasn't being in love, living for one another the way her parents did. "What do you want?"

"You. A simple life. I'll pay Andrey back and we'll put this behind us, figure out the rest together."

"But what is the rest?"

"It's not important because we love each other."

"Do we?" She saw the words hit him like a truck. He flinched, and she felt bad. She hurried to do something. "You make me feel more alive than anyone ever has," she said, because that was true.

He brightened. "I feel the same. And I know you're scared. It's why you're hesitating, but don't let fear make your decisions. I'll give you everything you want."

"Why do we have to get married?"

"I can't ask you to run away with me without asking you to marry me. It's not right."

"You're old-fashioned," she said, and laughed quietly. This man who worked for Andrey, who stole from Andrey, who introduced her to drugs and alcohol and sex, was old-fashioned.

He flashed his wicked grin. "Your parents will respect me if I marry you. And I really do love you. Run with me and you can spend every day on your art. I know this is right."

She didn't, but Viktor was the only one who saw her for who she was, for what she wanted. Graduation was around the corner, and what was she going to do? Work in the butcher shop? She wasn't even sure she had the grades to graduate. If she stayed, she would keep fighting with her parents. She could run to New York, but she didn't have any money. Where would she sleep and how would she eat? Viktor was offering her a way to make the dream happen. She already knew he wouldn't try to stop her or push her to waste time in school. Besides, the idea of running, of picking up and going, was a thrill that already had her whole body tingling. Wasn't that what someone daring and visionary like Trina Robbins would do? "I'll go, but I won't marry you right now."

"You're saying yes?"

"To running away with you. That's all. I'm going to be an artist."

"Of course you are." His lack of hesitation, his firm belief was all she needed to know it was the right decision. Viktor kissed her, pressed his tongue so deep she had to lean away to breathe. She was shaking from excitement. She was finally making a decision about her life on her own. She could hear Mama's voice saying some decisions couldn't be undone, but Molly didn't believe that. She had her whole life in front of her.

Molly threw clothing into her backpack. She took eyeliners and lipsticks and the high heels she squirreled away in her closet. In a separate bag she packed her pens and markers, paints and sketch pads. She took issues of *Atomic Anna*. Her art bag was three times the size of her clothing bag and Viktor asked to carry it for her, but she wouldn't let him touch it. They crept downstairs. The note she left on the dining room table was simple: *I'm leaving with Viktor. I'll call when we're settled.* At least it would keep Mama from panicking.

"Are you ready?" Viktor said.

Molly looked down at the note, picked up the piece of paper, and kissed it. She took a deep breath to make sure she would remember the smell of fried onions that always lingered and mixed with Mama's lavender perfume. She looked at the divots on the couch where her parents sat, the side table crowded with mugs and an ashtray. If only her parents had listened to what she wanted, to who she wanted to be. "It's better this way," she whispered, even though she wasn't sure. "I'm ready."

ANNA

Mount Aragats

nna read every one of Yulia's letters enough times that she memorized them all. The photographs, too. Yulia had sent bundles of them and Anna studied them enough to know Molly stopped having ink-stained fingers in 1969; that Molly lost weight toward the end of high school, was too thin after Viktor appeared. There were no photos of Molly in Atlantic City, only ones when she returned. In those she was pregnant and looked like she was in anguish. Molly smiled again once Raisa was born, and every photograph showed little Raisa holding tight to her mother or grandparents. Then there was a gap and Raisa reappeared after two years in foster care. The change in her appearance broke Anna's heart. It was as if the smile Anna had seen on Raisa in the department store had never existed. By the time she was a teenager she was wearing thick black eyeliner and lipstick. Her nails were black to match, her head shaved and her scowl filled with pain. She stopped caring about school, Yulia wrote, or about anything.

Please. Help us, Yulia pleaded in letter after letter. Anna fell asleep imagining Raisa's face, the too-thick makeup and angry eyes, and woke to nightmares of Molly dying in an alley like the drug addicts Anna had seen in Soviet newspapers showing American depravity. And while visions of Molly and Raisa haunted her, it was Yulia who tortured her most. Anna had sent Yulia to America for a better life, for a future she could never have in the USSR, but the life she'd given Yulia seemed disastrous. Yulia wasn't happy, none of them were, and where Yulia had always found a way to rise in the past, even in the worst of times, in America she was only sinking. Anna knew it was her fault because she was the one who pushed them to go, to take Molly. She tried to make a list of all the things she could have done to help but always came back to the same conclusion: She should have gone with them.

Anna slipped a finger under the flap of the latest letter, one that had just arrived. A photograph fell out along with a single slip of paper. The photo was of a man wearing a leather jacket. His head was shaved, his shoulders broad, and even though he was smiling, there was something in his eyes that made Anna uneasy. He had his arm slung around Molly like he was holding her in place, like a weight. On the back Yulia had written: *This is Viktor and Molly. Annushka, you know what it feels like to have a man change your life in the wrong way. Please. Help us. Use your machine to keep him away.* Yulia scrawled an address on the back, along with a date, and that's when Anna knew where her next jump would take her because, yes, she knew what it was to have a man change your life in the wrong way.

△ △ △

Yasha entered Anna's life in 1943. Anna didn't even see him coming as she stood in an unmarked Soviet building she knew to be the new Laboratory No. 2, the so-called secret heart of atomic research and development. Goncharov was dead. And war had spread so much chaos that Anna was having a hard time finding a way back into the atomic labs. She had spent months pleading her case, begging for permission and support to continue her work. What she had done with Otto Hahn was revolutionary and there was no question she could help her country use it to stop Hitler. Above all, that was what they needed to do—stop Hitler. Before she and Yulia left Berlin, they had seen what the Nazis were doing to Jews, witnessed them brutalizing men and women, stripping them and beating them in the streets. Their hair and beards were shaved. They were raped and violated, sent into ghettos and killed in mass graves. Yulia had reminded Anna constantly that they could be next, if they were discovered to be Jews. By the time Otto and Anna realized their work could be weaponized, Hitler's men had thought the same and started to pressure them to turn their research into a bomb, to work with a man named Werner Heisenberg. Anna had sabotaged her notes, written mistakes into her equations, and then she and Yulia had fled. Now back in the USSR, Anna had to build the bomb before Germany did. It was the only way to stop Hitler, but the Soviets weren't giving her a lab, putting her to work.

At the reception desk, she asked to speak to Comrade Igor Vasilyevich Kurchatov, the man in charge of the Soviet nuclear initiative. This was the fifth time Anna had skipped her work on the street-cleaning crew to come to this office, to beg for an audience with him. Soon she would be fired for missing another shift, accused of social parasitism, but it was worth that risk. She couldn't give up, and waited to be denied again. A thin blond woman sitting at the switchboard held up a finger, asking Anna to wait. Outside, the streets of Moscow were cluttered with rubble. Too many buildings had been decimated by the Luftwaffe; streets were lined with antitank battlements that looked like rusted crosses tipped on their sides. Noticeboards were tacked up listing the dead and announcing Stalin's victories. Inside, it was quiet.

"I only need five minutes with Comrade Kurchatov. He will want to talk to me."

Not long after that, a man appeared from a side door, the same man who spoke to Anna every time she came. He wore a lab coat and had a small gun in a holster. He took her arm, gently, and guided her down the hall. His features were compact, eyebrows, nose, and mouth all too close together while his forehead and chin were high and long. His eyes looked young, but his sideburns were speckled gray. He tilted his head when he spoke to her like he was trying to signal that he trusted her, was on her side. "I've read your papers," he whispered. Their footsteps echoed on the marble floor. "They're impressive."

"You believe me, then? That I worked with Hahn? That I can build a bomb?"

He smiled and dared to lean closer. "It's not up to me." He stopped in front of an office and hesitated. "They're always listening," he murmured, and waved his hand around them. Then he straightened his back and opened the door to a small office. It was tidy and gray with sagging fixtures. In a split second, his soft edges were replaced by hard orders. "Sit," he said after he took his place at a dull, steel desk that took up most of the space.

Anna eased into the chair opposite him and started speaking even before the man took out his notebook and pen. "The Germans are working on an atomic bomb. Hitler will have it soon. I know because I was there. With Otto Hahn. Hitler's man, Werner Heisenberg, threatened to use our science. I tried to sabotage it. Then I ran." Anna leaned over the blotter. Her hands were clenched in fists. She had to make this man see that they were losing valuable time. "Hitler must be stopped and I can do it. Let me speak to Comrade Kurchatov. Please."

"I told you last time you were here. That name, Kurchatov, is not familiar to me," the man replied. He wouldn't look at her and she knew he was lying.

"Comrade Kurchatov," Anna said. "He sent you to question me, didn't he? His laboratory is here in this building. Please, tell him he needs my help to build a bomb. I just need to get to work."

"You were in Germany for a long time. Are you a spy?"

"I told you, Goncharov sent me to spy for him."

He frowned. "Goncharov passed away. No one can verify your story."

"Come on!" She pounded the desk with her fist and then she took a deep breath, tried to bring herself back under control. *Steady*, she told herself. She handed him a piece of paper, the same note she gave him every time she came. "Give this to Comrade Kurchatov." Anna stood to go, and the man walked around the desk to follow. He had never done that before.

Once they were back in the hall, alone, he took her arm again and whispered, "You did well in persisting, showing your dedication." He pressed something into her hand, and she slipped it into her pocket without acknowledgment.

Outside, the cold smacked her. She knew it was coming but it still caught her off guard. She wore boots she had taken from a dead soldier, a skirt hemmed in two times because she had lost so much weight, plus three sweaters under her coat, and it wasn't enough. She shivered, waved to Yulia across the street, leaning against a pile of rubble, smoking.

"They denied he's there again?" Yulia asked. "They'll never believe you. A Soviet woman who escaped Germany and came home?" Yulia handed Anna a cigarette. "Good thing they don't know you're a Jew, too." She laughed.

They started walking and once they turned the corner, Anna reached into her pocket for whatever the man had given her. It was a theater ticket. "That's odd," Anna said. She held it out to Yulia. "He gave me this, slipped it into my hand on my way out."

Yulia took it from Anna. "A play by Bulgakov. *The Days of the Turbins*." She smiled. "A Stalin favorite. Whites become Reds."

"Why only one ticket?" Anna asked.

"He's asking you out on a date." Yulia grinned. "Is he handsome?"

"It isn't like that," Anna said. "I don't want to get him into bed. I want him to let me work. If I were a man, they wouldn't treat me this way."

"So, you want to be a man now?" Yulia teased. Anna smiled. "Didn't the other scientists in Berlin say you were more man and monster than human? You hated it."

"Otto never did. Why can't a woman be powerful? I just want to be a scientist they respect because I'm good. My sex shouldn't have anything to do with it." She grinned then, couldn't help it. "I don't ever want to be a man. Look at all the terrible things they do."

Yulia reached for Anna's hand. "Good. You're far too kind to be a man."

"You're the only person to ever think of me as kind."

"That's because I'm the only one who gets to see your heart." Yulia took a long pull on her cigarette. "If you gave them our address, they'll come for you."

The way she said it made Anna go even colder. "We should have a plan," Anna said. "If you really think they'll come for me. It could be good, but if I'm arrested, you need to run."

"This will be different from your mother."

"What if it's not?"

"If they take you, we'll go. Malka, Lazar, and I will go to America."

"They're family now, too?" Anna asked. The Adelsons, Lazar and Malka, had lived across the hall with their parents until their mother and father were killed waiting in a bread line. Shrapnel from a bomb took them. Lazar was twenty-five, the chief engineer at a tank factory, which was why he wasn't conscripted. His sister was fifteen, still in school. After Yulia heard about their parents, saw Lazar struggle to raise his sister alone, she invited them to live with her and Anna. They had been with Anna and Yulia for half a year, but during war six months felt like six years.

"Yes, they're our family now." And Anna thought that was right.

"America is worse than a gulag," Anna said. "You've seen the articles in the newspapers talking about the greed and excess, the love of money. It's no different from Berlin, and look what happened there."

"Of course it's different. There's no Hitler."

"They're a disaster."

"I'm not saying the glitter won't come off of America. I just mean we could live openly as Jews. Get away from the bombs. They're not hemmed in like Europe." Yulia pulled Anna close, and their hips bumped. Anna wanted Yulia even closer, wanted to revel in the warm tingling she felt when she held Yulia, when she imagined Yulia pressing against her the way she'd pressed against men in the bars in Germany, but she knew Yulia didn't think of her that way. "You're my sister," Yulia said time and again. Anna would force a smile and never say she wanted more, because she knew Yulia didn't. And besides, a relationship between them would be illegal. Even if Yulia had wanted that, they couldn't risk it. Anna had no choice but to accept what they had. Yulia squeezed her hand. "We have each other," she said.

"We do."

They made their way between armaments and rubble. The streets were quiet, everyone terrified to show themselves, terrified they would become a target. They lived across the street from a building that had been split in two the day the Adelson parents were killed. One half had fallen, exposing the other side, which still housed intact bedrooms and kitchens as if they were looking into a life-sized dollhouse. The rubble, Yulia reasoned, kept them safe. When the Germans flew over, they thought they had already destroyed the area and left it alone. So far, she had been correct.

"So…will you go to the theater with him?" Yulia asked. "You should. When was the last time you went out?"

"I'd rather be in our flat with you." She already knew she wouldn't go.

They entered their building quietly. It was an older gray structure that was a square made up of smaller squares: a square lobby, square flats, and even a square stairwell. Up three flights and they were home.

Lazar lay on the floor, reading. Malka was on her feet, running to greet them. The walls were yellow and the carpet a faded red. The couch that doubled as Anna's bed was pushed against the far wall. Yulia's bed was perpendicular to that. They had given the bedroom to Lazar and Malka when they moved in so Anna could stay up late to work. While all the furnishings were worn, it was clean and warm, a home. And Anna loved it. When she'd left the Soviet Union for Berlin she'd had nothing but a bare room. Now she had a family.

"You're home," Malka exclaimed with relief. She ran over, hugging them hard, kissing them, like she always did when they returned. Anna guessed Malka watched from the window, waiting for them to come home the way Anna used to wait for her mother.

"We're fine," Anna said.

"So are we," Lazar said. He frowned at his sister. Anna had heard him more than once whispering to her in the corner, urging her to stop trembling, to be brave like him. And he certainly was putting on a strong front. He had changed, grown up since his parents died and moved from being a son to the man in their apartment, the one who was protective, pushing them to stay inside while he went out for food and coal. His appearance had altered to match his role. He'd grown a beard, worked to strengthen his body through calisthenics, and even developed a deeper voice. Unlike her brother, Malka had stayed small, still childlike.

"Will you go over my English with me?" Malka asked Yulia.

"Of course."

"She needs to be good at it," Lazar said. "One day we'll leave this hellhole and go to America."

"Not without us," Yulia said.

At the same time, Anna said, "That country is a den of corruption and lies. I'd never step foot on their soil."

"Don't you think that some of the lies come from Stalin?" Lazar challenged. Anna turned her back, refused to respond. They'd had this argument dozens of times.

As Anna worked peeling potatoes, her mind went to the place that felt safest, that was a comfort—her work. Otto, Lise, and Anna had been working hard to find a way to control a nuclear explosion. They knew how to split an atom. In theory they could split many atoms, but how could they create a chain reaction they could control? Anna's theory was that a runaway reaction, a meltdown of a core, would create an event she called gravitational collapse. Otto said that was impossible, but she argued he was wrong and it could be catastrophic. Figuring out how to control the explosion was the key to building an atomic bomb. She needed to design some sort of amplifier as a mechanism to contain the size of the blast. Every time she thought about it, she went back to her accident on the tram, to the ripples she saw, to the idea of using them both as a weapon and for time travel. If only she had a lab, a space to experiment, she could make real progress.

Anna added salt to the cabbage and potatoes boiling on the stove. That was when she noticed something new in the apartment, a row of four half-broken vases by the window. Twigs that looked dead poked out of wet soil. "What is that?" she asked.

"Malka's new collection," Lazar said.

"Our mother loved roses," Malka said. "I'm growing them for her. I stole a few from a bombed park. You'll see. They'll be beautiful one day."

* * *

One month after Anna's last visit to Laboratory No. 2, Malka burst through the front door. "Look! Look!" she said, smiling and waving something small around. "Tickets. Four tickets were left on our doorstep! For a performance tonight!"

"Tickets?" Yulia looked at Anna. "To a play. Four this time?"

Anna shivered. Of course he knew she'd need four. "What play?" she asked.

"It's called *Ivan Vasilievich*," Malka read. "A play about a time machine. It says the performance is a secret."

"Secret? Then it's too dangerous to go. Besides, time travel is nonsense," Lazar said. "Even if it wasn't, we're in the middle of a war and they're still putting on plays? What the hell is wrong with people in this country? If you're going to break the law, do it for something worthwhile."

"Literature, the stage, these are a means to addressing problems in a way people can understand and digest," Yulia said. "It's beautiful, something the world needs more of. The fact that it's an illegal performance makes it even more worthwhile."

"It does seem off that the tickets are for an illegal performance," Anna said, agreeing with Lazar. She wanted to think that through, try to understand what it meant, but Yulia went to the radio and turned it on. It was the hour when the state-sponsored orchestra played, and she took Lazar's hand, spun him into the middle of the room, started dancing. "Feel the music."

His cheeks flushed as he twirled with her. Yulia held him tight and Anna was struck by the small gesture—she had never seen her touch him before. And now she took a closer look at Lazar, noticed for the first time that he was a striking young man. "Enjoy it," Yulia said. She spun him between the roses. Malka's collection had grown and its perfume covered the odors from the dying city.

"Dancing and plays are fun, but they don't help when I'm hungry. They don't pay for the food we need," he said.

"You can express that frustration as we dance," Yulia said, and twirled him faster.

Lazar didn't resist but kept talking. "I want debates! *Real* discussion about better ways to get food to the hungry, how we can win this goddamned war." And then, "Maybe I should fight."

Yulia stopped as soon as he said it.

"And die like everyone else?" Anna asked.

"Time travel?" Malka interrupted. She was always the peacemaker. "The play is about time travel. Can you believe it?"

"You said you found the tickets at the door?" Anna asked, and Malka nodded. There was no question the tickets were from the man at Laboratory No. 2 because no one else had ever given her a ticket before. Did the tickets mean she was closer to Comrade Kurchatov? Or was it a test to see if she'd attend, enjoy a performance knowing it was illegal? When the music stopped Yulia came and stood next to her.

"You think they're from him, the man who speaks to you every time you ask for Comrade Kurchatov?" Yulia said, and Anna nodded. "I told you they would come for you."

"He wears a lab coat and carries a gun. It's odd, isn't it? I don't know if he's a soldier or a scientist."

"I can't say anything makes much sense right now." Yulia shrugged. "But I think we should go. It will be fun."

"I've been thinking about time travel again," Anna said. They hadn't discussed it since leaving Berlin.

Lazar called from across the room, "It's impossible."

"If you could go back, what would you change?" Malka asked.

"Nothing," Yulia said. "Because if I did, I wouldn't know any of you."

"What if you could kill Hitler?" Lazar asked. "I'd do it. Not just to end the war but because I'd want to torture him. I'd make his death painful and hideous."

"What if you could save Ruth?" Anna asked Yulia.

"I wouldn't want to do it. It wouldn't be worth the cost." Yulia forced a smile. "If I did, my life would be different. We never would have met. None of us would have met. And who knows what else would be different. All of life is a trade-off. Nothing can stay the same forever."

"If I could go back, I'd save both our parents, too," Lazar said.

"Same," Malka said.

"You've really thought about time travel?" Lazar asked Anna. "As in something you think you might be able to make happen?"

"Maybe. In theory," Anna admitted.

"If a time machine were real, it would be used as a weapon," Yulia said. "The deadliest, worst weapon ever built. Worse than your bomb, even. But here's the thing. You can keep building a bigger and bigger bomb, but someone else will always have an even bigger one. You can never be stronger, but you will always be smarter. Outthink your enemy. That's how you win."

"And yet you support me building the bomb."

"To stop Hitler," Yulia agreed.

"You want to work to build an atomic bomb?" Lazar asked. "You never told us."

"I don't like to talk about it," Anna said. She spoke quietly and quickly. "It's…it's an extension of my research. At least it's possible. I mean, it's something I could do now that I understand fission."

"An atomic bomb and a time machine," Lazar said, seeming to think it over. Eventually, he shook his head. "If you build an atomic bomb, that would make you as bad as Hitler. Wouldn't it? Think of all the people you'd kill."

"Maybe not. It could be a deterrent." She faced him. "It could save millions of people by scaring them out of war."

"That just sounds naive," Malka said. "If you have a gun, you'll use it. That's what our mother said, and she was right about everything. If we have a bomb, we'll use it."

"Same with a time machine," Yulia said. "If you ever build it, once it's in the world, it would be used as a weapon and kill countless people. Think about it; by changing lives in the past, you'd erase people today. In an altered timeline, their parents might never meet. Then they'd never be born." She stopped. "Who judges what to change and what to keep?"

"So you're in favor of Anna building an atomic weapon but not a time machine—another kind of weapon?" Lazar asked and Yulia nodded. There was a pause as he seemed to consider her position. "She's right. A bomb isn't as bad. Going back in time to change anything is playing God."

"But what if you controlled it so only a few people had access?" Anna pushed. "Decisions by committee?"

"Those people would be playing God by committee. You can never control science. Once it's out in the world, it belongs to everyone. That's why you have to build the bomb but you can still avoid building the time machine," Yulia said. "You taught me that. Think about Otto's lab. How quickly Heisenberg swooped in. Even if you could hide it, why should *you* decide how to use it? What gives *you* that power?"

"There are no good answers," Lazar said. "And actually, now that I think about it, I wouldn't use it to kill Hitler or save my parents. Even if it accomplishes one good thing, disaster would be inevitable."

"Just because you can doesn't mean you should," Yulia said.

"Can't we stop fighting and go to the play?" Malka asked. "It starts in a few hours."

Before anyone could answer, there was a knock at the door. Anna opened it, expecting to find a neighbor begging for food, but instead it was the man from Laboratory No 2. The one with the compact features, wide forehead, and gun at his hip.

"Who is it?" Yulia asked.

"My name is Yasha Berlitsky."

△ △ △

On Aragats, Anna looked back down at the photograph and slip of paper that came in the most recent letter from Yulia, at her beautiful, curled handwriting. Viktor was going to ruin Molly and Raisa just as Yasha had ruined her—and Anna could help. She could make her family her priority. She went to her machine and dialed the coordinates and date on the back of the photo. The only problem was that the last numbers were smudged. She wasn't sure if the date was 1970 or 1986. Anna started with the earlier date. She pulled the trigger and found herself standing in front of a prison. A billboard looming in the distance showed an advertisement for an Atlantic City casino.

MOLLY

Atlantic City

Three months into her new life in Atlantic City, Molly was home-sick. The feeling snuck up on her and took her by surprise. When she had first arrived, she wanted to cut herself off from her parents and their influence, to stop thinking about them. She'd lugged an old desk she found on the street up to the apartment above the coin-op she and Viktor managed and set up her workstation. She laid out her sketch pad, arranged her pens, paints, and markers, and started drawing. That first week she drew *Atomic Anna* morning and night, and when Viktor asked her why she worked all the time, she realized she didn't have a good reason. She was out of her parents' house but still laboring with the intensity they expected.

The next morning, instead of waking up early to draw, Molly suggested she and Viktor start a new ritual, swimming before the beaches opened, when it felt like they had the entire Atlantic to themselves. It was glorious. Being in the water naked, with Viktor, far from school and her parents, made her feel stronger than she had ever felt, and she decided even more change would keep this feeling going. Instead of counting the quarters they earned and calculating the full sum in her head, she used a calculator. Instead of eating a healthy dinner, she drank champagne, and they started going to clubs and dancing three, then four nights a week. She added cocaine to the mix more and more often, and soon she and Viktor were sleeping in late and staying out later. The pain in her gut faded to nearly nothing, and after delirious nights she couldn't always remember what had happened the next morning, but she knew her life was coming together, that this was how she was supposed to live—even if she didn't have time for her art. When she was high, she told herself there was no rush, she would get back to *Atomic Anna*. Then, when she let herself come down, when she woke up sober, the pain returned and she reached for bottles of booze, not her pens and pencils. The paper in her sketch pad yellowed from disuse and looking at the bowed pages made the pain worse, which drove her to drink more. Instead of drawing *Atomic Anna*, she mopped the floors in the coin-op while Viktor began dealing. When they started seeing profits, they were able to furnish their place, buying a pair of blue-and-white lamps she put on either side of the brown velour pull-out couch that doubled as their bed.

It was Viktor who helped Molly realize she missed her parents. "If I had a family like yours, I'd miss them, too," he said as he stroked her arm. It was noon and they were tangled in the sheets. The bar in the middle of the bed bit into Molly's spine. She shifted to the edge, took the cigarette from Viktor's hand, inhaled, and thought about what he said.

"Why do you think I miss them?" she asked.

"When we're out, all you do is talk about them. You tell whoever will listen about how they're disappointed in you. Last night you said that before you left, they had started buying you more paint. That it was too little too late." He stared at her. "You didn't tell me that, babe."

She shrugged but only because she didn't want to keep talking about it with Viktor. She was embarrassed that she'd brought her parents up when she was high, even more that she didn't remember. Besides, he wouldn't understand. He couldn't, because she wasn't sure she did, either. She had spent her whole life pushing away from them, and now she wanted them back? That just didn't make sense. She tried telling herself she was glossing over the past because it was easier to live that way, that buying her more paint didn't mean anything. But she knew it did. When she had to change a lightbulb in the coin-op, she thought about the way Mama lugged the ladder from the back closet to change the bulbs over the counter. When a pipe burst in the apartment upstairs and leaked through their ceiling, she thought about the way the three of them sloshed water over the bloodstained floor after they had finished butchering chickens on Friday mornings, and how she missed seeing the regulars hurrying to buy dinner for Friday nights. She hated how often thoughts of her parents came to her, that she couldn't keep them away. She knew she couldn't contact them because it was too dangerous. Viktor kept reminding her that Andrey could track him down through her parents, was probably at their butcher shop once a week asking for her new address.

When Viktor passed out on their bed, drunk one night two weeks later, she took out a jelly jar of quarters collected from the coin-op and tiptoed down the stairs. She was more nervous than she wanted to admit, even though she could do what she wanted. Viktor did, she reasoned. Out the back door she started walking to the closest phone booth, passing the church lady who walked the boardwalk every Sunday to collect addicts, to try to get them into rehab.

"Mama," Molly said when Yulia answered.

"Mollushka! Lazar, it's Mollushka. She's alive. Pick up. Pick up." Instead of rolling her eyes like she would have before she left, Molly felt tears starting.

"I didn't mean to scare you," she said. "I'm sorry."

"Give her the number," Papa yelled. "We're bugged."

"You're not bugged. No one is listening," Molly said. "I just miss you."

"Give me your number. I'll call back in fifteen minutes from a pay phone," Mama said. Molly read her the number off the phone and hung up. Her parents were being their ridiculous selves and this time she loved it. She leaned back against the glass and waited for them to call back. The streetlight blinked. The phone book next to her was torn and damp. A man walked past and eyed her. Another whistled. Seconds ground to minutes. A police car skidded around the corner, lights flashing, siren blaring. Then an old woman appeared, running toward the phone booth. Her hair was a mess. Her clothing was odd and her hands were bright red. It took a moment for Molly to see they were burned. The woman ran straight up to the glass and Molly was sure she would run through it. But she stopped. She had a strange, antique stopwatch around her neck, along with a delicate double bear pendant, and she had a strange, old-fashioned bag over her shoulder.

"Don't go back," the old woman said in Russian. "Take Raisa and leave him."

"Who's Raisa?" Molly asked. She was startled at the Russian, and something told her she knew this woman. She waited for a response, but she realized she was engaging with a lunatic and the fact was there was nothing familiar about her. Plenty of ex-Soviets lived in the neighborhood. Still, the name Raisa made her pause. It was beautiful. Perfect, even. And the name of one of her comic book characters— Rocket Raisa. "Leave me alone," Molly yelled.

"Don't go back. You have to listen to me. I've spent nearly two hours looking for you, started at the prison. I don't know why. But I found you and you must listen." The woman was spewing nonsense, looked like she was going to say more, but then suddenly there was a flash of light. Molly reared back as the woman was surrounded by white and black static, the kind you see on TV when the antenna isn't right. She stretched like a noodle and then she disappeared.

"What the fuck?" Molly wasn't sure if she had imagined the whole thing or if it really happened. She had done so much cocaine the night before, maybe it had messed with her mind. Or maybe she was just tired. She hadn't been sleeping and she saw strange things sometimes when she didn't sleep. That had to be it, she told herself. The phone rang, startling her out of her thoughts about the strange woman, and she picked up on the first ring. "Mama, are you okay?" Molly said.

"That's what we want to know. Are you okay? You can come home," Mama said all in one breath, quickly. It wasn't what Molly was expecting. There was no anger, no accusations. She imagined Papa standing over her mother, sharing the receiver the way they did whenever important calls came, like the last time the bank called after he applied for a loan. How they stood there tense and scared. She could still see the way Papa had crumpled as the denial came and Mama holding him up.

"We love you," Mama said. The words made Molly feel calm in a way only drugs had made her feel before and she realized she loved them, too. She really did.

"I love you. And I'm fine," Molly said. Her voice shook but she was smiling, happiness washing through her at hearing their voices.

"Mollushka, we miss you," Papa said.

"So much," Mama agreed.

"We just want you to be safe. Come home, please," Papa pleaded.

"At least come for dinner. For Shabbat this week," Mama said. Molly wanted to say she couldn't, but the truth was she wouldn't and so she said nothing. And they waited. She thought about all the things she wanted to tell them: how she'd left to make something of herself, to find a place where she felt like she belonged. And she wanted to tell them that even though she hadn't expected it, she missed them, talked about them more than she even knew.

"Are you happy?" Mama finally asked.

No, she almost said, but she stopped herself because the answer surprised her, and she couldn't say it out loud. "I can't give up."

"It's not giving up. Don't think about it like that," Papa said. But she did.

"I hear your voice. You're tired," Mama said. "You're not sleeping."

Molly both loved and hated that her mother knew. "I'm fine," Molly said.

"Where are you? We can't talk for long. You understand? Andrey has been asking for Viktor. Viktor stole a lot of money. Andrey comes here looking for you, for Viktor."

"I can't tell you where we are. But tell him Viktor will pay him back. Soon."

"Tell us what you're doing. How are your comics?"

"Why didn't you ever ask that when I lived at home?"

"We don't want to waste the time fighting," Mama said. "Tell us about your new life." Mama was right, that was easier. So she told them about the coin-op and how Viktor supported her art. "He believes in *Atomic Anna*."

"Did they reject you, that New York publication?" Papa asked.

"No, I just...I mean...They haven't gotten back to me yet. But they will."

"Of course," Mama said. Molly waited for her to ask how much she was drawing, was relieved when she didn't because she didn't want to lie, nor did she want to admit that she was usually too high and too drunk to pick up a pen.

She bent at the waist because the pain that hadn't been bad since she'd left was coming back, hard. She didn't want to say goodbye yet. She still wanted to keep them close, on the phone, for as long as she could, but the truth was she had nothing else to say. "I should go."

"Not yet," Mama said, sounding sad. "Please. Another minute."

Molly couldn't take another minute. It hurt too much. "I'll call every month. I promise." For a split second she thought about telling them she wanted to come home, that she'd changed her mind, but then she imagined Papa being rejected again by another bank and she hung the receiver back in the cradle and crumpled down to her knees. As she leaned on the glass, she told herself it was time to stop making excuses, time to go to New York.

PART III

He who seeks a name loses his name.

—Pirkei Avot

MOLLY

Atlantic City

A fter her phone call with Mama and Papa, Molly tried to draw, tried to force herself to come up with something new to send to *EVO*, but nothing worthwhile came to her. Every plot she hatched ended with Atomic Anna defeating an enemy and wanting revenge—and Atomic Anna and Mighty Minerva arguing over whether revenge was ever worthwhile or justified. Molly didn't have an answer, and that kept her from drawing a single line, let alone adding Rocket Raisa into the mix. She ran her fingers over the edge of the desk and thought about Atomic Anna and the Radioactives. Perhaps the problem was that Molly was still thinking of them like children, where clean lines mattered. Adults didn't have that kind of clarity. She'd begun to see how they lived more in the gray because she was finally living as an adult. She decided it was time to embrace that new and improved Molly and even convinced herself that once she dressed as her new adult self she would relax enough to find her characters, to draw again.

Even more, she would show herself, and her parents, that she had made the right decision.

In one giant sweep she tore everything from her closet, her jeans and T-shirts, tank tops and knee-length skirts, and hauled them to the Salvation Army. Viktor was thriving as a drug dealer by then, and she went to his safe and took out more money than she had ever spent on clothing and went to Philadelphia to raid Wanamaker's, the fanciest department store she knew. She and Mama went there as a special treat for lunch and their Christmas show every December.

Molly picked out platform shoes, tight pants, strapless tops, and big earrings. She tried them all on, twirling in front of the mirror, and didn't bother changing back into her old clothes. "I want lipstick, mascara, blush. Everything," she said to the woman at the cosmetics counter. She spoke with a Russian accent, trying it on like the new clothing to see if she liked it on this new version of herself, and she found that having grown up with everyone around her speaking with that accent, it felt natural.

Molly wobbled outside on the sidewalks in her new heels and went to the best comic shop in Philadelphia, South Street Comix. There she jumped up and down when she saw a copy of Trina Robbins's latest, a one-shot underground comic book put together by a group of women. It was called *It Ain't Me, Babe* and the cover featured traditional female characters like Little Lulu, Wonder Woman, and Sheena all raising their arms, running to fight for women's liberation. On the bus she read and reread the issue. When she walked back into their coin-op, she watched Viktor take her in. He started at her chest, looked down, and came back to her breasts. She wasn't wearing a bra. The woman in the dressing room insisted the strapless shirts were worn without bras and now she understood why. She reveled in Viktor's gaze, letting him stare for as long as he wanted. "Mollushka?" Viktor said. "What happened?"

"I needed a change."

He gestured to her body, from head to toe. "I don't want other men looking at you."

"It's not about men. It's about me," she said, thinking that was exactly what Trina would say. Molly took his hand and twirled him in a circle. "We're going dancing tonight. I'm getting ready for New York." She took him to a disco bar. He wore his usual jeans and leather jacket and held her hand so tight her fingertips went white, but he didn't try to rein this new Molly in. He kept pace, stride for stride. At the bar, Viktor ordered champagne and vodka. He took her to a corner and cut up two lines of cocaine. The high was more electric than it had been before and the familiar pain in her gut fell away to a dull throb.

She sat back to take in the new, light feeling, her head resting on the vinyl-lined booth. "Is revenge pointless?" she asked Viktor. He put a hand to his ear, signaling he couldn't hear. "Can a hero go too far?" she yelled.

"You're too deep for me," he said, and scooted closer to kiss her. Molly was the one who dragged him to the bathroom. Door closed. She straddled him right there while women just beyond the rusted stall primped their hair, touched up their lipstick, and she didn't care. She threw her head back and moaned with pleasure, because this was what she wanted and there was no reason she shouldn't enjoy it. When they came out of the stall, Viktor was still adjusting his belt. Molly tumbled toward the sink and reached into her purse for her lipstick. In the mirror, she watched Viktor wink and then walk away. She raked her fingers through her hair and puffed it higher with a comb, thrilled at the thought that she'd just done something Trina Robbins would do. She didn't notice how quiet it had gotten, how empty, and then she saw a woman standing across from her. She had red hair so flat it looked like Molly's when Mama ironed it. She wore shorts and high silver boots. "Vik's with you now?" the woman asked in Russian. "Did he tell you he wants a simple life? That he'll pay Andrey back and put this all behind you?"

"Who are you?"

"Doesn't matter. Just know you're not the first. Are you running a car shop, a gas station? He's a mechanic, you know. Aside from the drugs, he fixes things." The lipstick slipped from Molly's fingers, clattered on the fake porcelain. The questions crowded the air in the bathroom and made it hard to fill her lungs. "Come on," the woman said. "You're not really surprised, are you?" And that realization was what hurt: She wasn't surprised, not really. And she wished she were sober, that all the doubts and thoughts in her head were more organized so she could piece through them and ask a coherent question.

"You and I, we're not the same kind of person," Molly managed. The woman burst into a deep, loud laugh and made Molly feel defensive, nervous. Molly was struggling to put together a reply, to prove that even if Viktor had been that way in the past, she was special—they were special together. Weren't they? But Molly didn't really know anything about how Viktor used to be. By the time Molly opened her mouth to say more, the woman had turned and made her way to the door, her boots clicking as she walked. Molly hurried after her, but she was gone.

"Viktor?" She used her elbows to push her way through the crowd. "Viktor!" she yelled, louder this time. She didn't know why she'd never asked Viktor about past women, or his past at all. Of course she knew there had been many others, but he loved her. He was the one who used that word, not her. "Viktor?" She pushed toward the bar.

"You okay?" the bartender asked. He handed her a glass of water. "Bad line?"

"Maybe." She blinked and thought she saw Viktor with the redhead in a corner, but it wasn't him. The worry growing inside her hurt as much as any pain she had felt with her parents, maybe even worse because she didn't want this new and improved Molly to be taken in by a man. She was better than that.

"Baby, relax," Viktor said. He caught her elbow and she jumped back, spilled the water. "I was outside smoking."

"Who was she?" Molly asked. She was out of breath, felt betrayed, no, jealous, and she'd never been jealous before, didn't want to be that kind of woman. But the redhead's words were too precise, her message too exact. Maybe it wasn't jealousy. Maybe she felt stupid, swindled, but she didn't want to think about that for long.

"She's no one you should worry about."

"Don't lie to me," Molly said. "She said I wasn't the first."

"She's no one."

"I told you not to lie to me," Molly said. She ripped her arm away.

"She used to be my girlfriend a long time ago. Forget about her." He leaned down and kissed her, a gesture that felt as practiced as flicking a cigarette butt.

* * *

Molly took the memory of the woman in the silver boots and tucked it away, told herself that soon enough she'd be working in New York, away from Viktor. She loved her new self and so she dug in deeper and showed off her Soviet roots by using commentary she had heard from her parents and their customers. "Everyone here is fat. Too much food," she said at their coin-op. And "I never felt the cold until I came here and had heat. Americans are soft." When Viktor heard, he laughed, never contradicted her or teased her for playing a game.

The only thing digging into her roots didn't help her find was answers for *Atomic Anna*. Molly couldn't figure out the ethical code of a superhero, whether Atomic Anna would want revenge, whether it was justified or not. Without that answer, Molly was convinced she couldn't draw and so she went harder into the Atlantic City disco scene with Viktor. They stayed out until sunrise five, then six nights a week, drinking and snorting even more. Molly told herself she was partying because it was what she read about in magazines, what famous people like Liza Minnelli did in New York when they needed inspiration, but the hangovers were getting harder to manage. Viktor made sure there was always orange juice in the refrigerator, told her it was healthy and it would help her recover, but even that became too sweet, too much. She only felt better when she drank more alcohol and she didn't fight that because drinking made her numb and she loved feeling numb most of all.

For Thanksgiving they went to Molly's favorite club, the Mood Room, where Viktor was the exclusive dealer. It had been months since Molly had drawn anything. "I want to show you something," Viktor said, his arms around her waist. He kissed the bottom of her ear and led her down a hallway with carpeted walls. She was already drunk, stumbling. The door at the end was puke brown and had a crooked sign that said MANAGER. Viktor pulled out a key. "Joey said we could use his office for a little while. I thought it would be fun." Molly kissed him before he finished with the lock and knew what was coming. Viktor was always finding new places for them to have sex. It kept things interesting and intense, still an experiment rather than anything permanent, which was perfect because this life, and Viktor, were still parts she was trying on. But after he closed the door behind them, he didn't touch her. He went to the desk and pulled out a syringe.

"Are you serious?" Molly said. She looked over her shoulder, nervous.

"I know, I know." Viktor nodded. He ran his hand over his scalp. "I told you I'd never use the needle, but it's not a big deal. I just, I need to expand my business. We want to pay Andrey back, right?" When she didn't answer, he started speaking faster. "This, this is what people want. Plus, it sucks them in."

She stepped back. Seeing him with the syringe made her think of the users she'd seen shooting up in the alley near the coin-op. They were emaciated, with missing teeth and dirty clothes. Many of them were so out of it they couldn't even focus when she asked if they needed help. "You said it was a hard line."

"Yeah, but times change. Anyway, I'm only sampling the product.

I need to know what I've got, don't I? How about all your lady artists drawing comics? You know they're on this stuff, right?" He pulled out a spoon and a baggie. "Want to try it with me or not? Just once." He filled the spoon, clicked a lighter to life. The outsize glow took over the pathetically small room. The smell made her feel like she was choking. "One time won't kill us."

She didn't want to, but maybe she did. That smell wasn't so bad now. She took it in, let it sit in her lungs and massage her from the inside. He was right. The people she idolized, the ones drawing comics, they did drugs. But they also drew a lot. Still, a needle felt like another level. "Well?" Viktor asked. He drew the liquid from the spoon into the syringe.

"No," she said, but her voice was weak, and she knew he could sense she was close to giving in. He flashed that wolfish grin she loved, could never resist.

"Come on, baby girl," he said. He still held the syringe. His hand was steady and he pulled off his belt, started wrapping it around his arm.

"'Baby girl'?" He had never called her that. It gave her pause.

"Just came to me. You're my baby girl. I birthed you into this new life."

"I don't want to be a baby." He laughed, but she was being serious, felt her skin prickling. "I mean it. I made myself into this new Molly."

"Relax. It's my way of saying I'm here to take care of you."

"Just don't call me that. I don't want you to take care of me."

"Well, you used my money for those new clothes. My drugs. My apartment."

"You want me to pay you back? Is that what this is about?"

"No. I'm happy to give you more, but don't forget that. I'm giving it to you."

The words hurt. She wasn't a child. But then she caught her reflection in the mirror on the back of the door, her smudged makeup. He was right. He had seen right through the new Molly. She had never had a job outside of the butcher shop, never had a boss or a paycheck.

She didn't even have a high school diploma. *EVO* hadn't taken her. No one had. "I'll earn things myself one day." She hated that she sounded so tired.

The next morning, Molly sat at her desk and thought about her promise to herself, that she would face the blank page and draw, only her hands were shaking. Instead of facing Anna, she poured a glass of vodka and mixed it with orange juice. After that, her hands went still, and she tried to draw but erased every line she started. The tip of her pencil snapped because she was pressing too hard and Molly gave up. She told herself she'd come back to it later. She didn't. Weeks blended into a month and Molly snorted all the cocaine Viktor gave her, reveled in a world where nothing could go wrong. Even better, when she was high, she could ease herself into a fantasy where she was the star at a table in a hotel ballroom in the middle of Comic-Con. She imagined the stained carpet and ashtrays, the costumes the women waiting in line would wear to look like her characters, like Atomic Anna, Mighty Minerva, and Rocket Raisa. Molly could dream that she was finally earning her own way.

By January 1971, alcohol and cocaine were her best friends, the loves of her life, and all she thought about and tasted. Only something inside started to change. She felt nauseated all the time, could barely hold down a meal. Even more, she started to limp from a shooting pain running down her leg. She told herself it was nothing, but Viktor was worried, insisted she see a doctor. He drove her to a clinic near the boardwalk where the physicians only took cash. The office had blue walls and scuffed white linoleum. When Molly sat on the cold examination table the room was so small there wasn't space for her to straighten her legs. Viktor wanted to come in with her, but she refused to let him. "Some things are private," she said, and sent him home. Whatever was coming, she wanted to know first because once she walked into that office, she realized how bad she felt, that something really was wrong.

And that had her sweating. She didn't want to die. She hadn't done anything and she would leave nothing behind. Absolutely nothing.

"Can you tell me what's going on?" the doctor said when he came into the room, speaking before he even closed the door. The name tag on his white coat said BERNSTUN. He was young and frail-looking with greasy hair. "Are you pregnant?" *Pregnant.* The word brought with it pain and panic. She shook her head. It hadn't even occurred to her. Pregnant. But the idea was hitting her like the worst comedown she could imagine. "When was your last period?"

"I'm on the pill."

"Do you take it every day?" She missed pills, but not often. Besides, she told him she was there because of the pain. "It could be connected. We'll give you a test. You'll know before you leave. The pain, it could be sciatica. It's early, but maybe." He babbled more and she stopped listening. Pregnant. She knew that was it, didn't need the test results, even though he gave them to her not long after.

"Just stay clean and sober for seven more months," the doctor had said, as if it were nothing, like she could just stop the drinking, the cocaine. She used to tell herself she could, but she knew the truth.

"I want an abortion."

"That's illegal," he said, but he handed her a piece of paper with a phone number scrawled across the top and winked. She closed her eyes, imagined a coat hanger and a dirty table. She didn't know if that was really what it would be like, but she did know too many women died in botched procedures. "If you drink or get high, it could kill the fetus. But that would be lucky, if you want an abortion, right?" He smirked and she wanted to slap him. She could tell he saw her as a junkie or a drunk, a pathetic woman who would never be anything, and she hated him for that, maybe because she was scared he might be right. She started to cry. He handed her a tissue and kept talking. "If the fetus isn't killed it could have brain damage or physical abnormalities. If any of that happens, no one will adopt."

She balled her hands into fists, wanted to claw his face, tear his skin because she was so angry while he seemed to be reciting lines he had memorized, completely devoid of any feeling.

"How can you speak to me this way?" she said, gasping for air. "Like it's nothing?"

"I assure you I know it's not nothing," he said. "I've seen a lot of women in your position. If you want to make this work, it's going to practically kill you. You have to go cold turkey. I'm being honest, trying to help." He stood up and handed her brochures for a rehab clinic, for AA and NA. She'd seen such brochures before. The woman who walked the boardwalk left them in the coin-op. "You'll need all the help you can get. Take this minute by minute." He stood up to leave.

"Wait." She knew that the moment he walked out, she would be alone, and her situation would somehow be real in a different way. Her hands shook so hard she had to sit on them.

"You can still have a future, a whole life in front of you. The man who brought you in, your boyfriend or husband—I could tell he was high. If you really want to help this child, give it a chance at a decent life. Don't go back to him." He left and she was alone in the too-small room, crying and out of control.

When Molly thought about her future, she never imagined herself as a parent. It wasn't that she didn't want to be one, it just wasn't something she dreamed about. She didn't want to be tied to a child, changing diapers, begging for babysitters. Even worse, she had no idea how she would pay for all those diapers or baby food. Viktor was right, he still gave her everything she had. She hadn't earned a single penny on her own. Didn't even know if Viktor wanted a child. The only thing she knew for sure was that she couldn't bring a baby into her current life, but that still didn't tell her what she should do. Seven months sounded like a lifetime and no time at all. A nurse came into the room and asked her to leave, helped her outside. Molly walked in a daze, couldn't even remember getting on the bus. She stared at the brochures but didn't read them, folded them and unfolded them. She watched the boardwalk rise, caught glimpses through the gaps where the streets and buildings split. Seagulls circled overhead. They were free, she thought. Creatures that had the world open to them.

Viktor was waiting for her in front of their coin-op. "I'm pregnant." She blurted it out, worried she might lose her courage if she didn't. He pulled her close, held her tight, and she tumbled back into hysterical tears. "It's okay. We'll make it work. We'll get married. I'll take care of you and the baby." He was saying all the right things, but his voice was weak, and as much as she wanted to believe him, she didn't. She couldn't, wouldn't even if he sounded convincing. Their entire existence together revolved around getting high and getting other people high.

He kept talking, building imaginary plans, describing a crib and a nursery, a new place. She couldn't help but think he was performing the role of the father, going through the motions, and she had to stop him. "I'm leaving," she said, and her voice came out strangled and cold. She knew if she said more, opened up more, she might change her mind. Viktor tried to argue, but she pushed him away and started walking and did the only thing she could think to do. She called her parents.

It was blistering cold when Molly boarded the bus. She was shaking so hard she couldn't walk straight. Minute by minute, the doctor had said, and Molly repeated it to herself as the bus bounded along the expressway. All she could think about and taste was vodka, but she wouldn't let herself touch it. Instead, she rubbed her belly, kept watching through the window. Ice had bleached the trees and snow mounds were black from exhaust. She was scared her parents wouldn't meet her at the bus or let her come home, but even those fears were nothing compared to her need for a drink or a line. Anything to escape the tremors and the feeling that she was dying.

In Philadelphia, Molly recognized her mother's profile from across the parking lot and hurried toward her as fast as she could. It had been only eight months since she'd seen her parents, but Mama looked different, older. Her lipstick was darker, and so were the circles under her eyes. Mama held out her arms and Molly began crying before either of them even had a chance to say a word. Guilt, relief, and sadness came over her; she was seeing what she'd let her life become. "I still have a future, don't I?" Molly was clinging to what the doctor said.

"Yes. You can be anything, just like your superheroes," Mama said.

"Anything," Papa agreed. "We love you."

At home, withdrawal was a haze of pain and vomit and uncontrollable sadness that swept her under for the next week, maybe more. She couldn't keep track of time or even remember if she was eating or showering. When she came up for air, finally, her father was sitting next to her bed, holding her hand. He smiled and ran a cold cloth across her brow. She felt ashamed and relieved. The sheets were damp with sweat, as were her clothes. "We'll take the child, if that's what you want," he said.

She didn't want him to just wash his hands of her, of the mistakes she'd made, but at the same time, why should she force him to deal with her blunders? Being an adult meant facing consequences. "I don't know what I want yet."

Mama walked in, leaned on the door. "We'll raise the baby together."

"You could still be an artist," Papa said.

"You hated me drawing," Molly said.

"I...It scared me." Papa's voice was quiet. She knew he was working to keep it controlled, to keep away from the subject of Viktor. "Numbers, formulas, I understand. If you're an artist, all those critics can tell you you're a genius and list the reasons why, but they can use those same reasons to call you a fool. Idiocy or brilliance determined by a whim. I don't want that for you."

"That's it?" she asked. She closed her eyes, still felt the pull of the drugs and alcohol and used all her strength to push it away, to concentrate on the conversation. "All this time, you didn't want me to be an artist because you were afraid of what people would say? You thought I couldn't take rejection?"

"I grew up in the shadow of chance. Who gets a bullet today, and who gets bread. We never knew what anyone was thinking." Papa's voice was almost a whisper. "I thought it would be different in America, and it is in some ways, but in others it's exactly the same."

Molly felt ashamed that she had never considered that Papa's objections to her choices could stem from anything more than disappointment. She had never realized he was trying to protect her. "Papa, America's not the Soviet Union. And math's no different than art. A proof only holds if people agree on your logic."

Papa kissed the top of her head. "I was wrong. We were wrong. Now that you're home, you can draw. We'll help you, help the baby. We know better than most that you can always restart your life."

* * *

Molly started going to AA and NA meetings the very first day she could get out of bed. She also decided revenge was never worth a superhero's time. It was better to move on, and so she started drawing again and resumed her shifts at the Russian Market, only instead of having her slaughtering in the back, her parents had her sitting at the cash register in front. As her belly grew, it was all the customers and neighbors talked about when they were in the store. "Are you sleeping?" "Can you eat anything?" "Did you try bone broth?" Or worse, they tiptoed around asking where she had been, avoided asking about her art. She nodded and smiled, told them all she was sleeping and eating fine, it was just time to come home. She could never explain to them what she was really feeling. It wasn't nausea, not anymore. The pain had morphed into the ache of loss. She had lost Viktor. She had lost time, having spent it on him. She had lost her childhood, too, she realized, her dreams, the idea of who and what she would become. She sat at the cash register in a kind of mourning. Sometimes she called her sponsor every hour, sometimes every half hour. She went to meetings at least twice a day.

"The past is never worth revisiting. I should know," Mama said to Molly one afternoon when Molly was out back, smoking. She allowed herself one precious cigarette every twenty-four hours. It was raining and dark, but not cold. Her stomach extended so far by then that she was wearing maternity pants.

"It doesn't matter. We can't go back anyway," Molly said.

"No, but we can look at the now, tomorrow. And when I look out, I want you to know I'm proud of you." Hearing that was an unexpected shot of strength for Molly, what she needed to make it through another ten minutes, maybe an hour. She hated thinking about how thin the thread holding her together was. Sometimes she would hear the crinkle of a plastic bag or look at a glass bottle and think about vodka or cocaine, smell it, feel it. She made herself rub her belly when that happened, was never as prepared as she wanted to be to fight the urge, because when it crashed on her, it was like a wave she misjudged. It took her under and she had to fight just to breathe while it dragged her out. She couldn't let herself go anywhere near parts of Philadelphia where she might find it or she would use again. She didn't have the strength to say no and so she rarely left home or the butcher shop except for the meetings. There she told the group about Viktor, and they were the only ones to ask if she missed him.

"No," she said. "I miss the idea of him, that he gave me the feeling of being numb."

Her parents stopped telling her she was making mistakes. They stopped pushing her to be more, to make different choices. It was hard for them to change that way. She saw it in how they still started to say something, "Mollushka, you could—" and then stopped themselves. She loved them more for working so hard, for pushing themselves to nod and listen. Because of it, she had never felt more comfortable in her own skin while sober. A few months after she came back home, Molly was sitting in the living room in the near dark, watching the streetlight shadows through the window, willing herself not to think about vodka. She gripped a half-finished issue of *Atomic Anna* in her fist. Papa came in and turned the television on.

"Mollushka, you have to move your body. To stop is death." He took a deep breath as if to steady himself. "After my parents died, we had to keep moving. The sadness can kill like a bullet, but the pain is worse. I started Soviet calisthenics to make myself stronger."

"How did they die?" she asked tentatively, hopeful that he might tell her something.

"I should have told you a long time ago." He shook his head. "We made so many mistakes. It was in a bread line. A bomb fell while they were waiting for food during the war. Mama and Anna invited Malka and I to live with them. I was a grown man, but what did I know about raising Malka, or cooking? We needed them as much as they needed us. As four we were stronger than two."

"I didn't know," Molly said quietly. She couldn't help but feel grateful and elated that he was sharing. "How did you find out? They just didn't come home?"

"We heard the bombs, the planes. It sounded like a freight train running through my head and when they hit, everything shook. The walls, the ceiling, my heart. I knew I was breathing but it was pitch black and I didn't know if I would make it out of the basement, outside again." He bit his lip and wiped a tear away. "When they gave the all clear, I walked in a line, followed everyone back up the stairs, back to our apartment. Our building was untouched. Meanwhile the one across the street was sheared in two. Malka and I waited, waited, and waited." He reached for Molly's hand and she held on tight. She had never seen this side of him, never heard so much from him.

"What happened to Malka?"

"She used to dream with me about coming to America, but when the time came she refused. She said she would never leave the USSR. I don't know what changed her mind. She's a party member now, running grocery stores, overseeing shipments and rations. I miss her every day."

"I love you," Molly said suddenly.

"I love you, too. Keep moving." She looked down at his hands, realized how calloused they were from work, how tired he was from carrying the weight of all he had endured. She understood now in a way she never had before that his actions came from love. "Keep moving," he said again. "Have you heard of Jack LaLanne?"

"The exercise man?" Molly laughed. "Of course."

"Watch him. He might help."

* * *

Her first contractions started after a phone call with Viktor. They had fought. He wanted her to come back to Atlantic City, promised he'd go stone-cold sober. "Viktor, you don't know what it means to be clean," she said. "You can't promise you'll stop. It's not that easy."

"Of course it is. I'm not an addict." His pleas continued and with every lie, Molly was more certain she'd made the right choice.

"Goodbye," she said, and hung up. What hurt the most was that he believed what he was saying, that he wanted to be clean, only the truth was he wanted the drugs more. Mama came and sat with her on the couch, wrapped an arm around Molly and kissed her, held her tight, and finally Molly leaned on her.

"I made so many mistakes," Molly said.

"You're doing the right thing now," Mama said. "We're proud." Mama and Papa had been saying that since she came home. They also bought her more pens and paper when she ran out, even hung her

144

work around the house, and seeing her comics on the walls filled her with pride, reminded her that she could still become an artist.

"I'm sober, but I'll always be an alcoholic and an addict," she said. It was what she had learned at meetings.

"I know." Mama turned the television on. It was time for Jack LaLanne and Molly had started watching him every night. It was the middle of summer and they were in a heat wave. Molly felt bloated and had sweated through her shirt. Two hours later, on August 12, 1971, her water broke. During the birth, Molly didn't hold back. She screamed with all her might and it had nothing to do with the child tearing her apart. It was her old self pulling her to pieces, and as she pushed it away, she made room for the baby. And when the child finally came, the relief was a euphoria that no drug had ever made her feel. Molly had yelled herself hoarse, slain her body, popped a blood vessel in her eye, and now she and her daughter had a new life. Finally, Molly could sleep. When she woke up, Mama handed her the baby. Molly waited to be struck with love, only she wasn't and that made her panic. "I don't love her," Molly said, her voice a scratch.

"It takes time," Mama said.

"But I should—"

"Shh," Mama interrupted. "It takes time to love. Any mother who can't admit that is lying. You want to protect her?" Molly nodded. "Then love will come. What's her name?"

"Raisa Adelson," Molly said. She stared at her daughter, was sure the name was perfect. "Raisa. After your sister, Ruth." Like Rocket Raisa.

Molly's love for Raisa came on slow and steady. At first, she woke to feed and change her because it was her duty, but once the baby smiled and cooed, reached for her, Molly felt the tug other mothers described. She started taking Raisa with her to the butcher shop, sitting up front at the cash register. When the baby's first word was *Mama*, Molly's heart opened a little further and she devoted her days to her daughter.

Every hour, every minute when Raisa was awake, Molly focused on her, pushed alcohol and cocaine away from her mind. But when she slept, or at night when the house and neighborhood were still, when Molly was alone, her mind wandered. She dreamed about clubs and dancing, partying and drugs. She missed being someone outside of the baby, outside of the house and the butcher shop. She still went to meetings and called her sponsor. Jack LaLanne helped, too. He was on late at night, when everyone else was asleep, and she liked to think he was broadcasting just for her. She never did the exercises. She just watched the hypnotic way he moved his body. He did the same thing over and over. When she wasn't watching Jack LaLanne, she watched Raisa.

Raisa was a mix of Molly and Viktor. Her hair was brown and her eyes were dark. She was stubborn like Molly and quiet, always watching. She cried whenever anyone left her alone and she started doing jigsaw puzzles before she could toddle across the room. When Raisa took her first steps with her perfect, pudgy fingers wrapped so tight around Molly's, it made Molly realize how much her daughter needed her—how much they needed each other.

Molly took Raisa to the park and to the swimming pool. She read to her all the time, classic fairy tales but also her own original *Atomic Annas*, which her parents had stored for her in neat, organized bins in her old room. At night, after she put Raisa to bed, she drew. Whatever had her blocked in Atlantic City was gone, and stepping back into comics felt as natural as breathing. The stories poured out of her. Anna no longer needed revenge. She just moved on and fought the bad guys. Rocket Raisa became Mighty Minerva's daughter and Molly drew her with obsidian eyes and long black hair, the way she imagined a grown Raisa would look. In Molly's mind, Raisa wouldn't make any of the mistakes Molly made. She would grow into a woman who carved her own way into the world, who paid her own bills.

When Raisa was four years old, Molly and her mother took Raisa to Wanamaker's to restart their family winter tradition, the one Molly adored. Viktor hadn't called since their last fight the night Molly went into labor. Not once had he shown up at the store or dared set foot near the house. Still, he was in the background. Just as she could still taste vodka and cocaine, she sometimes thought she saw him ducking around a corner or peeking through the window. It was never him, just the ghost of him. Going to Wanamaker's, having fun the way she used to have fun with her mother, would help, she told herself. The more she dwelled on good, the further away the past fell.

It was December and the store was glorious, shrouded in twinkling lights and gold and silver tinsel. The restaurant buzzed with children. Molly ordered extra ice cream and she and Raisa and Mama shared it all. Raisa squealed with delight when they leaned over the balcony to watch the Nutcracker light show. Afterward, Molly and Mama took Raisa down to the toy department. It was hot and more crowded than the rest of the store with kids laughing, crying, and begging. A mini train ran just below the ceiling, its tracks following the perimeter of the department, and Molly pushed Raisa to try it.

"Don't make me go alone," Raisa said.

"You'll be fine. I'm right here," Molly reassured her. It saddened and frustrated her how often Raisa said that. Maybe her daughter sensed something Molly couldn't.

Once Raisa had taken her seat on the train and the engine started, Molly looked for Mama. She was in a corner talking to an unfamiliar woman, and that worried Molly because Mama never spoke to strangers. The woman wore a long, outdated coat. Her face was shadowed, but her frame showed her old age, with her shoulders bent like hooks, and the hair that jutted out from under her hat was so white it was translucent. Molly walked toward them but didn't go too far because she'd promised Raisa. Closer, she saw the woman wore a stopwatch and two pendants, two golden bears. Molly recognized them from somewhere, but she couldn't place them. Mama was talking, looked upset, and Molly tried to hear but with all the kids around them it was too loud; she caught only fragments. The woman was speaking Russian. She had an old bag slung over her shoulder.

"I...I saw you get on the bus, saw Lazar. I don't have long. I came because I need your help." A child next to Molly started to wail and she missed the next part of the conversation, only heard the stranger saying, "I built it. My time machine—" Then the train passed overhead, drowning another stretch of conversation.

Mama took a step away and said, "You came all this way, built this incredible machine, did this miraculous thing. You found me, your daughter, and your granddaughter and all you can say is you want me to help you with work? Can you hear yourself? Are you out of your mind?" Mama looked furious, the way she looked whenever Molly mentioned Viktor.

"Mama!" Raisa called as the train stopped and Molly hurried to pick her up. She wanted to get back to her mother, to the stranger. It was clearly important, whatever was happening. Molly was sweating and her blouse made her feel hemmed in when she wanted to be free to move quickly. Holding Raisa, she elbowed her way through the crowd.

"If you're going to change something, change her life. Molly wants *you*," Mama said to the stranger.

"What's happening?" Raisa asked, and Molly missed more of her mother's conversation.

"Shh," she said to Raisa, and pulled them both in line with the stranger. "Who are you?" Molly cut in. She put Raisa down. "What's wrong, Mama?" The two women went still and stared. The stranger's skin was pale and her eyes went wide. For a second, Molly thought she might know the woman. "Tell me what's happening."

"You're perfect," the stranger whispered, taking a step back.

Molly looked from Yulia to the stranger. "Have we met?" And then, "I've seen that watch. I'm sure I've seen it. And that necklace."

The stranger looked at the time. "Please, help me. Find me. Here."

She tried to hand Molly a piece of paper. A long line of numbers was scribbled on it in old-fashioned handwriting. Molly didn't take it.

"Who are you?" Molly asked again.

"Mama! Mama!" Raisa called. Her voice was high-pitched with fear. She had wandered off to look at a truck and gone farther than she wanted. Now she was running toward Molly, who leaned down, ready to catch her. Only there was a flash of light and Raisa tripped. She fell into the side of one of the displays and started screaming. "Mama!" Raisa yelled. There was blood running down her forehead, splattering her dress. Molly ran to her, sure the deep-looking cut would scar. When she looked up, Mama was already coming toward them and the other woman was gone. So was the scrap of paper. Mama told Molly to forget about the stranger, she was no one. But there was something about her Molly couldn't shake. When she got home, she sketched the two bears the woman wore as a necklace and Mama framed the drawing, hung it in the dining room.

ANNA

Mount Aragats

amn it. Damn it," Anna cursed. She was back in the watchtower after having found her daughter in the phone booth, in a terrible neighborhood but in good health. It seemed like Molly hadn't recognized the name Raisa, which meant she must not have given birth yet. It was too early. Anna had read the smudged date wrong. She should have gone to 1986. Anna took a deep breath and looked down at her hands. They were burned and ached, but that pain was manageable. She still wasn't sure what the burns were from or how to stop them. She looked around the tower; nothing seemed different. The letters were still there. The photos, too. The building, all of it was the same. She had been lucky; it could have been a huge mistake, but she hadn't changed anything in that jump. "Damn it." She would have to try again. Adrenaline and anger made her eager, unable to summon the patience to wait for her hands to heal. She had to jump to December 1986—after Chernobyl.

She went to her machine, entered the coordinates, slung her bag with the amplifier over her shoulder, and pulled the trigger. There was the familiar thud. The boards under her shook. Then the flash, the ripple. Her vision turned to static and she landed at the prison again, and now she knew it wasn't a mistake. The facility must have expanded since Anna's last jump, as this time the coordinates placed her inside, in a hallway fronting a long row of cells.

Anna stood slowly, dizziness hitting her. That hadn't happened before, but she'd never jumped twice in a day, either. She also wasn't sure if she felt weaker or if she was just tired. She took a few minutes to rest, waited for the dizziness to pass, and then she started searching for Manya. No. She stopped midstep. Manya went by her American name. Anna couldn't remember it, but she told herself she would recognize it when she saw it or heard it. Staring at the bars, the cells, made her think of her own mother. Mama had been taken to a prison. Anna knew that meant she was likely beaten while Anna and Papa ran to the train station. Anna was furious they had run without her, felt like they were leaving her. "What if she comes home, looks for us?" she had asked as Papa dug into his pockets and handed over their last kopecks for tickets. "She'll find us," he'd said with a look that told Anna Mama wasn't coming back.

She blinked, pushed the memory away to focus on finding her daughter. There was a list of prisoners on the wall in front of each cell. She read the one closest to her and saw MOLLY ADELSON. That was her daughter, that was Manya.

The cell was simple, with two bunk beds, four inmates. All of them were asleep. Anna zeroed in on Molly, who was in a bottom bunk with her head near the bars. She looked sick. She lay on her side, shaking and soaked in sweat. Anna's heart broke. She dropped to her knees, and since she couldn't go inside the cell, she reached through the bars and ran a finger over a lock of Molly's hair. Even her curl felt too rough, undone. Anna thought about what Yulia had said in that department store, that Molly needed Anna. Yulia had been trying to tell her she could prevent this, and Anna hadn't listened, she'd been too pigheaded, too focused on Chernobyl. She leaned closer so her face pressed on the bars, and taking Molly in like that, in the cell, something Anna had buried for a long time shifted. It was a longing for what she'd had in Moscow during the war, even for what she'd felt with Yasha during their first few years as a couple—family. But all of that was tied together with an overwhelming wave of guilt for what she'd done with Molly.

Back in Moscow when Anna had sent her away, she knew in theory that she'd never see her daughter again, but she didn't understand the full meaning, not then. She had been trapped in a fog since giving birth. Having the baby affected her mind in a way no one understood. She couldn't think straight, and at the same time her body wouldn't cooperate. She was bleeding on one end and leaking milk on the other, so exhausted she fell asleep at her desk without being close to any solutions. She didn't recognize herself in the mirror or even in her notes. That was the worst part, finding mistakes in her lab reports. She was the one who had always yelled at others for being sloppy, and after the baby, Anna was the one making the errors. Yasha, Lazar, and Yulia all told her to give it time, that she needed to let herself recover, but Anna knew it was more serious and deeper than that. She had a doting husband, a good home, a great position in a lab, and a beautiful new baby. Why couldn't she stop crying? There was no neat, clear answer or solution. When she brought it up to Yasha, he only smiled and kissed her, told her it was natural, and that made her angry. She told him she thought it all meant she shouldn't, *couldn't* be a mother, and instead of listening, he forced her to spend more time with the baby, to take a longer break from the lab. He was her superior by then, another man promoted over her, and she couldn't push back. Stepping away from work only made things worse, made her begin to dread holding and touching her child. She tried to tell Yasha and Yulia she didn't feel normal, that something wasn't right, but neither of them listened. If only they had.

She kissed her fingertips and placed them on Molly's head. "I'm sorry," she said. "I made so many mistakes." Molly didn't move. "You can heal. You can still make something of yourself," Anna whispered. Molly rolled onto her back, her arm falling over the edge of the bed. Anna saw a line of fully exposed bruises and scars in shades of red and yellow, a trail of needle marks. "It's my fault. All my fault," Anna said, finally understanding the consequences of all her bad decisions. But why hadn't anyone tried to help her, recognized she was broken back then?

"Who are you?" Molly moaned. She struggled to sit up on her elbows, to look at Anna, and when she finally faced her, Anna was struck by how much Molly resembled her own mother. Blond and strong, Molly could have been Xenia's twin. "How'd you get in here?" Molly wiped her eyes. Her hands were unsteady. "Holy shit, am I dead? Are you a ghost?"

"Shh."

"It's the drugs," Molly muttered, and turned over. "Hallucinating." She mumbled something about one year of heroin feeling like a life-time, that the drug was too easy to get in prison. "Nothing else to do anyway."

"Molly, I'm real. And I'm here."

Molly startled, let out a small yelp. Another prisoner stirred. She pushed herself up higher and said, "I've seen you. Before. At Wanamaker's, didn't I? The day Raisa split her head?" Molly's eyes weren't focused. She kept blinking. "Wait. The phone booth. Was that you, too? I thought it was. I don't know. Maybe just more dreams." She pointed to Anna's neck, to the bear pendants and the stopwatch. "But I recognize those."

"I am going to erase this so it never happens. You don't have to live this life." Anna reached for Molly's hand, but Molly pulled away. "We can get rid of Viktor."

"What the fuck does that mean? He's dead."

"I can keep him out of your life."

"He's not in my life anymore. I just told you he's dead."

"I mean I can change things so he's never been in your life. So you two never meet."

"What? I'd never want that. I need him."

"You don't." Anna hesitated because she recognized that feeling, that emptiness that made Molly think she couldn't stand on her own feet. She'd felt it after the fog lifted, after she really understood all she'd lost—everyone she loved. "You're stronger than you think. Tell me when you met him. I can go back and change the day completely."

"Sure, okay. Just twirl your fairy godmother wand and make it all go away." She laughed and shook her head. "What the fuck?"

"I'm real," Anna said, pleading. "Please, believe me. Tell me what to change."

"I already told you I'd never want that. If you take Viktor I won't have Raisa." Molly moved over, leaned back against the wall, seeming more awake. "I've messed up most of my life. Everything but her. You can't take Viktor or you take Raisa." She paused. "I can't believe I'm even having this conversation. You can't erase people or change the past. Life doesn't work that way."

"What if it did?"

Molly's laugh was full of bitterness. "Even if you could change something, there's no one moment where everything went wrong. I have a long list of bad decisions. No one can help me, not even with all the magic in the world. Just let me die. Leave me alone."

"I won't do that. I won't leave you again." And then, "I can prove to you that I'm real. Ask me anything."

"Where did you meet my mother?"

"Berlin. We were roommates." Molly's eyes opened wider.

"How about my father?"

"He and his sister lived next door to us in Moscow. Their parents were killed during an air raid while they waited in line for bread. Yulia and I took them in. We were—" Anna felt the tug of a smile. "We were a little family." She didn't know what else to do or say. She waited for Molly to speak, didn't move while Molly reached through the bars and touched Anna's face, rubbed her thumb over her cheek. "You're Anna? You're actually Anna?"

"Yes. Your birth mother." The admission seemed to hit them equally hard as they both froze.

Finally, Molly spoke. "Tell me a story. If you're really Anna, tell me about my mama. How did you meet her?"

"I told you. I met her in Berlin. We were roommates."

"No. Tell me something she can't," Molly said. Anna leaned back to think. She needed distance because somehow their proximity was bringing back that old feeling of chaos, of her brain not working the way she needed it to. "Just start anywhere."

"Anywhere," Anna said, and took a deep breath. "Yulia loved you like her own the moment you were born. She was there. She even held you before I did. And I was so grateful. I think I knew even when the umbilical cord was still attached that she was meant to be your mother." Molly was hanging on every word and so Anna continued, "Before that, in Berlin, when it was just the two of us, Yulia saved me. She pulled me out of a depression I didn't know had taken hold. My mother was captured, my father was a drunk, and when I showed up in Berlin, I was lonely and lost and didn't even know it. Yulia showed me how to go out and be in the world, how to laugh. She showed me how to love. I loved her from the first night I landed in that city, even as she bombarded me with endless chatter and all of her languages. Maybe even because of it. No one had spoken to me like that in years." Anna stopped to take a deep breath. "My German was so bad. Yulia helped me practice. She made me feel...feel special and important, like a beautiful woman." Anna went on and told Molly about the cafés and dancing in Berlin, their escape back to the USSR. She found herself sharing details like the way Yulia applied lipstick using a knife as a mirror, the way the

Nazi flags turned their blood cold, and even the tram crash leading to her amplifier and time travel. She even took the device out of her bag to show her daughter. She wanted to say more, to keep going, but time melted away and then she felt the suck of gravity. Her two hours were gone. "Find me. You must. When you get out, come to me. It's how we save Raisa." Her legs, then her whole body, felt heavy. The ripples appeared and stretched and Anna was pulled back to Aragats.

When she opened her eyes, Anna was lying on the watchtower's cold floor, and she felt someone close by. It always took a while for her to come back together, to stand up, but at that moment she felt worse than usual. Her body was still too heavy and her mind slow. She told herself jumping twice in a day was a bad idea.

"Anna?" a woman said, and Anna's heart sped up. She knew that voice. She tried to sit; her palms slipped just as she saw a flash of blond hair and then pain in her hands had her writhing. When she opened her eyes again, Molly was standing near her. Not the Molly she had just seen, strung out and high in prison, but an older, sober Molly. Her cheeks were pink and round, and her hair was thick and brushed.

"Molly? You're really here?" Anna said. She tried to reach to touch her, but the burns were too severe, the skin hurt too much to move, and she pulled it back. Molly kneeled close and offered Anna a glass of water, helped her drink.

"You went to the prison, didn't you? You warned me this would happen, that we had two separate timelines that still needed to converge."

Anna finished the water, took a deep breath. "What do you mean?"

"In my timeline, the life I know, we've been on this mountain together for four years. Before this jump, you told me you were going to visit Mama, but when you come back from seeing her you're usually relaxed and smiling. Right now, you look terrified. And surprised. I'm guessing this is where we come together, that you were just at the prison." She walked across the room and used a pitcher to refill the water glass. "I remember that night so well. I was sure I was dreaming, hallucinating. It took me a week to realize it was real. Heroin was so easy to come by in prison, I was hooked and high most of the time, even that night. You asked, what would I change? Somehow, I remembered seeing you in Wanamaker's. That day, when you were talking to Mama, I overheard you use the words *time machine*. In prison, all these pieces started to come together. I realized you were real. Time travel was real and I could actually change the future. You weren't lying. I could do something. Not for me, for Raisa. That's what you said. Being here together, this is how we save Raisa."

Anna's head was still heavy, spinning. Had it worked? Had she done what she was supposed to? "So you just got clean?"

"It wasn't that easy," Molly said with a forced laugh. "It's still not easy. Minute by minute I'm sober. I've thought about jumping off the cliff on the far side of the clearing a dozen times. You probably don't remember us talking about it because that was in my timeline, not yours." She stopped. "Actually, if you're just coming back from the prison, you don't know anything about our time together." She helped Anna drink more water. "Do you feel okay?"

"Tired," Anna said. "Please, tell me more."

"You're dying."

"What?" Anna's eyes went wide. "What do you mean?"

"You figured it out a few months ago. Each jump, it decays your cells, breaks them down, the ones in your brain in particular. Your brain is getting weaker. And it's taking longer for your hands to recover. I don't understand the science, only that you've been sampling your blood. You forget things, often. Am I right?" Anna nodded, slowly. She thought back to the prison, how she couldn't remember Molly's American name. Were there other things, too? "You're afraid you don't have many jumps left in you—and you won't let me near the machine to jump for you because you don't want it to kill me, too. You probably

want to know more, but maybe we should talk later. You need to rest."
She pointed to a cot in the corner, one Anna had never seen before.
Molly helped her to her feet and walked her over to the bed.

"Where are my roses?" Anna asked. She stared at the empty space
where the old dead bush used to sit.

"Long gone. It was dead when I got here. Besides, I told you, no
more roses. Mama had too many; now I can't stand the smell." Molly
pulled a cigarette from her pocket, lit it with Anna's lighter from her
desk drawer like she had done it hundreds of times before.

"They were Malka's," Anna said.

"I know. Mama could never move on; everything was about what
happened before, even though they barely talked about it. They barely
even told me about Malka. Is she still alive?"

"I hope," Anna said. "She's in Kiev. Or was, last I heard. Before
my last jump." Anna leaned into the bed, noticed another difference
in the tower. When she'd left, the walls had been covered with Yulia's
letters and photos. Now those were all gone, replaced by murals like
the ones Anna saw during her first jump. They featured superheroes,
three women.

Anna took a deep breath. "How long have you been here?"

"Four years. I already told you that."

Right. She remembered. "You didn't believe me when I said I could
change your life."

"Come on, I was high! But then you told me about my mother, that
she saved you in Berlin, and I knew you weren't lying, that I wasn't
hallucinating. When I got out, I had nothing to go back to. I'd lost
Raisa to foster care. You saw those pictures. My baby was a wreck, and
it was my fault. Foster care plus all the drugs she saw with me and
Viktor, it was enough to fuck anyone up. She deserved better than that.
And you said I could erase the past. That I just needed to tell you what
to change. Mama helped me find you. She saved that piece of paper
you tried to give us at Wanamaker's. I came here because I didn't know

where else to go." Molly finished her cigarette, stubbed it out in an ashtray Anna didn't recognize. "You don't have a single memory of our time together, do you?"

"I can't," Anna said. "I didn't live it. Another me was here, an iteration of myself who no longer exists. It's the time travel paradox inherent in parallel existence." She looked down at her burned hands. They were shaking, and her brain was trying to catch up to all this new information.

"Yeah, yeah. We've been over this a thousand times. Now that you're here, I'm supposed to fill you in. We don't talk much. I think you're scared of me. At least you act like you are. And I'm still angry at you for a long list of reasons, starting with the fact that you pushed me, Mama, and Papa out of your life and never came for us. But I'll help you. That's our deal. I'm here for Raisa, and as long as I help you with Chernobyl, you'll help me save Raisa."

"What happened to Raisa?"

"Foster care. I just told you." She dropped her chin to her chest. "You want the details, I know. I messed up in court when I was sentenced. It all happened so fast, and I was in withdrawal. I didn't say the right thing to the judge. He thought I was telling him not to give Raisa to my dad, so they put her in foster care. Once she was in the system, it took my parents a long time to get her back. One home didn't feed her enough; the other had two drunk parents that beat her. By the time Mama and Papa got hold of her, she was set to follow in my pathetic footsteps. And then you found me. You changed my life. Just not the way you thought you would." She pointed to the murals. "I'm drawing again. When I came you asked me to draw. You said it would help. Like math soothes you, drawing soothes me. You were right."

"You're still angry with me?" Anna asked. Her voice was higher than she wanted.

"Sometimes. It's complicated. Everything in our family is complicated. Maybe it was getting better. I don't know. You were nicer before you jumped. Now you're cold again." Anna didn't know what that meant, and Molly must have seen that somehow. She explained, "I mean, you were different before. Like, right now, you're leaning back, away from me. The old you, you leaned toward me." She forced another chuckle. "You don't remember any of our fights, our reckoning is what I called it, because they never happened for you. But they happened for me. And we worked through some stuff and you leaned forward. It wasn't much, just a little body language, but when you draw you realize those subtle cues tell a story without words."

"What would we fight about?" Anna asked.

"Everything." Molly headed for the hatch, to start down the ladder. "Anyway, you're tired. Get some rest."

"Don't go," Anna said. Her voice sounded panicked and she realized she didn't want space yet. She still had questions. She wanted to know what else had changed. She wanted to know more about what Molly meant when she said Anna was cold again, that she was nicer before. And she wanted to know if Molly knew she was going to die in 1992. "Tell me more about Raisa. Did we talk about 1992?"

"Come and get me when you're ready." Molly heaved the hatch open. "You'll heal and try again. That's one of your superpowers. You never give up."

"How long will I need to recover?"

"I don't know." Molly shrugged. "Your burns are really bad. Maybe a few months this time until you can jump again. For now, get some sleep. When you're ready, find me. The next jump is for Raisa. You promised."

MOLLY

Philadelphia

Viktor walked into the butcher shop on a Friday morning when Molly was alone. Papa was out delivering in their new van. Mama was home with five-year-old Raisa while Raisa took her morning nap. It was a sunny day that looked like it should have been warm, but cold unexpectedly stabbed the late fall and left Molly shivering. Viktor looked her up and down.

"You're even more gorgeous," was the first thing he said. He held flowers and chocolates and she knew he was there to charm her, and her first thought was that she was excited for it. For a flash she was a teenager again, feeling that high she got when he walked into their store for the first time during the hurricane. Just as quickly she flashed to their first date at the diner, the hamburger and fries, then to the thrum of a bass the first time he took her to a club. The memories were a jolt of excitement and her sponsor had warned her about this, that the past could bring it on, that Viktor was a trigger.

"What are you doing here?" she asked, reminding herself to be careful, that she hadn't heard a word from him in five years. He had changed, lost the hollow look in his eyes, had filled out and was back to the way he was when they first met, not emaciated like he was when she left. He stepped closer, a body length away. He wore a dark brown suit and matching vest with a wide, open white collar. His skin gleamed and she had the urge to touch it. She crossed her arms tight around her.

"I'm sober," he said. "I'm back to salmon and lettuce and swimming. And I settled everything with Andrey. I've come for you and our daughter."

"I'm happy here," she said, and she thought it sounded like she was trying to convince herself. But maybe only because he was making her nervous. She really *was* happy, wasn't she? She stopped herself from answering, from going down that hole, and instead thought about the advice her sponsor gave her. *Think about the bad*, she would say. *Think about how much harder it is to climb back up than it is to fall down*. Molly leaned on the counter for balance. Viktor hadn't called or even sent a toy since Raisa was born. "What do you even know about Raisa?"

"Andrey showed me pictures."

"How do I know you're not lying?"

"You can ask him."

"I mean about the drugs. How do I know you're sober?"

He pulled out a bronze-and-green chip, held it out for her to see, flipped it between his knuckles. "I went through the program," he said. "Six months. This is my reward." She looked him over closely. He wasn't trembling or fidgeting. His eyes were clear, not bloodshot.

"Can you walk across the room? Touch your toes?"

He walked to the counter to put the flowers and chocolates down and she caught the smell of his aftershave and cigarettes, felt something she hadn't felt in years. She loved and hated that. "I'll take any test you want." He walked across the linoleum, from one black square to another in a straight line. Then he touched his toes, touched his nose. He knew the drill. "Stone-cold sober," he said.

"What do you want?"

"I want you back. And Raisa. I want you to come with me to Atlantic City, to our apartment. You don't want to do this alone. You need me."

"I'm not alone. I have my parents."

"Come on. I know you. You must be bored out of your mind." He gestured around the store. "You need more than this. Always have. Let me help. I even keep orange juice in the refrigerator, hoping you'll come back." He held up the coin.

"Then why didn't you call even once?"

"I'm an idiot. Please? Give me a chance. I won this for you."

"You don't *win* sobriety."

"Maybe," he said. "Is that yours?" He pointed to a framed comic strip hanging on the wall. It was Molly's first publication. A local newspaper, the *Roxborough Press*, had bought it. They didn't ask for the series, just a one-off, but it made her feel like she was on top of the world. "It's really good. You've gotten better," he said, stepping closer. "Give me one dinner?"

The excitement she used to feel around him came bubbling back even as she tried to tamp it down. The feelings were just too strong. Her whole body was crackling, disobeying her. "Come to my parents' tonight for Shabbat dinner."

"Since when do you do that?"

"Since I'm back. My whole childhood."

"You never told me that."

There were lots of things she'd never told him, and things he'd never told her. She realized then that was likely one of the reasons she loved being with him, that they didn't really talk. None of her past sat between them, weighed down any decisions. "We were living in the moment, weren't we?" she said.

"Yes. And we both loved it. I know that." He winked. "Raisa will be there?"

For a second, Molly had tucked Raisa away, not thought about her because she'd become her old self. "I don't want her meeting you yet," she said quickly.

After Viktor left, she collapsed, leaned her elbows on the counter and dropped her head into her hands. How quickly she fell into her old habits, even stopped thinking about her daughter. She told herself not to be a fool, to think about the comedowns, the sadness, the way she looked in that mirror at the Mood Room.

Later, Molly made dinner with Mama to keep herself busy while Papa gave Raisa her bath. They turned leftover chicken necks and backs into soup, pounded old, stale matzo that hadn't sold at Passover, mixed it with chicken fat to make matzo balls. The main course was more chicken in an olive and prune sauce, seasoned with rosemary. She focused on every step, every ingredient, because it kept her mind away from that feeling she got around Viktor, that tingling she loved but knew she should hate.

Mama must have known Molly was on edge. "This is a bad idea," she warned. "We can send him away, tell him you changed your mind."

"No. I want to see him."

"For the right reasons?"

"What is the right reason?" she asked. She put down the knife she was using to slice carrots. The cutting board hung over the edge of the counter and Mama pushed it back.

"To say goodbye. That's the right reason. If you don't say goodbye, you're saying yes."

Molly told her she was wrong, that there was an in-between. "Raisa deserves to have her father around." Molly of all people knew that. She'd hated growing up without her birth parents in her life. But she didn't dare admit to her mother how she had tucked Raisa away when she saw Viktor, how quickly she'd melted into her old self.

Viktor came while Molly was upstairs putting Raisa to bed. She heard Mama's voice, cold and controlled, thanking him for flowers. Then Papa, yelling.

"Take it outside!" Papa roared. "No alcohol in this house."

"It's for you and Yulia. Not Molly or me."

"Not in the house."

Molly bent and kissed Raisa's head, closed the *Atomic Anna* they were reading. It was an early issue in which Anna builds her new laboratory.

"I said no!" Papa said, louder, angrier.

"Who's here?" Raisa asked. She had her arms around Molly so tight they felt like a rope cutting off her circulation. Molly peeled her away and kissed her tiny hands.

"Just a guest," she said. "I love you more than anything. You know that, right?" Raisa leaned over and kissed Molly. Her lips were so soft, and Molly loved how her daughter trusted her, how she looked to Molly for answers to everything. "Sweet dreams," Molly said, tucking Raisa in.

"The store is looking great, sir," Viktor said to Papa as Molly came down the stairs. Her cheeks were warm and flushed and she tried to calm the feelings producing all that color by thinking about the way Viktor had called her his baby girl. "I really like what you did with it," Viktor bellowed, and Molly stopped midway on the staircase. Viktor had told her he was sober, but his voice was just a little too loud, too jovial, and she knew what it meant. But, no, she convinced herself she was overreacting. He wasn't that stupid. He wasn't drunk, just nervous; clean and sober and nervous. Right?

"Good, you're here," Mama said when she saw Molly. "Let's eat and finish this."

"I don't want to rush," Molly said quietly. Viktor was watching her, and she couldn't help but enjoy him taking her in, look at the patch of skin showing where his shirt was unbuttoned below his neck. She shivered, remembering the way he used to lick her neck.

"Be careful," Mama whispered to her. "You've worked so hard."

Molly shook her head, forced herself back to an image of Viktor holding a syringe. She walked to him to say hello and kissed his cheek because she didn't know what else to do. He took advantage of her being so close. He grabbed her waist and pulled her in, wouldn't let her retreat.

Papa shook his head, looking disgusted. "Enough. Soup is ready."

They sat on four sides of the dining room table, spaced out so wide she couldn't touch anyone else unless she leaned over the table. They slurped soup in silence broken by the clash of spoons against china. "Molly sold her first comic," Papa said. "She never drew a thing when you two were together. Here she has the space. She's sober."

"Papa..." Molly said.

"It's okay," Viktor said. "I'd be that way with my daughter, too. With Raisa." He wiped his mouth with the white linen napkin, one of their Shabbat napkins. "I saw it framed in the butcher shop. It was stunning. Molly, you're so talented." She smiled despite knowing it was an easy compliment that anyone could have lobbed at her. But with Viktor it was different because only he understood how much it meant to her to sell her first panel. He opened his mouth to say more, and Mama cut him off by taking his bowl before he was even done. His eyes met Molly's and his smile grew. It was him saying he was proud, and it felt good.

"Your daughter is brilliant like her mother," Mama said after she had served the chicken. "You wouldn't know because you've never met her."

"I'm not surpr—"

"Pass the potatoes," Papa said.

"Can't you let him finish his sentence?" Molly asked. Mama tutted and Molly became aware of the growing pain in her gut. She turned to Viktor. "How is the coin-op?"

"Fine," he said. He cut a sliver of meat off the bone. "I bought you a drafting table. It's under the skylight in our apartment."

"Your apartment," Mama corrected. "*You* live there, alone."

"Hopefully not for long."

"She knows better than to go with you. You're an addict and a fool," Papa said.

"She's bored here. She has to be." Viktor gestured around the room. "She was born for more than this, for a life as an artist."

"She's a mother now," Mama said.

They were talking about her like she wasn't in the room. "Bored," Molly whispered to herself. The word clicked because he was right. But boring was okay for now because she was sober, she told herself. She could imagine her sponsor telling her the same, that only addicts think boring is a problem. Boring is content and happy, or it can be. "Raisa needs me," she said to Viktor. "She depends on me."

"I see it in you," he said. "You need more."

"Enough." Molly banged her hand on the table. "Stop talking like that."

Viktor leaned back, put his hands up. "Fine. Then I'll just say this: I'm sorry for not being there for you and Raisa. I'm sorry, baby girl."

"I've told you not to call me that."

"It's my way of showing how much I love you."

"I've had it," Mama said. She stood up, started collecting dishes. A fork slid off the edge of a plate, hit the floor.

"I'm good for this family," Viktor said. "Whether you like it or not, I'm Raisa's father."

"Dinner is over," Papa said.

"She's not going with you," Mama said.

"Stop talking for me. All of you," Molly said. She was angry at her parents for trying to control the situation, her decisions; for the way they spoke to Viktor. And she was angry at Viktor for the way he spoke to her. She shook her head, needed to get back to the calm, to the quiet. Yes, her life was boring, but she was in control and she couldn't lose that. "I can make my own decisions," Molly said.

"Mollushka, please. Ask him to leave." Papa's voice was pleading. "For Raisa."

"You don't believe in me," she said, looking from Mama to Papa. "You think just like that I'll go back to using?"

"It's not that."

"Then why are you treating me like a child again?"

"We're not," Mama said.

"You're different around him. Your mother and I, we see it. Like before."

"Can't you see I'm stronger now?"

"With us, yes," he said. "What if we weren't here?" The question cut deep enough that she bent farther forward, pressed her hand into her side to relieve the pain.

"Mollushka, being sober can never be something you do on your own," Mama said.

"Being sober is something only *I* can do," Molly said in a loud voice, because she realized then how little they thought she had done. Her sponsor always told her being sober was on her. It was her decision, her job. She was proud of that, and she couldn't let them take that away. "*I* did it. I quit," she said. "And he's Raisa's father. *I* decide if he has a right to be in her life."

Viktor turned to Molly. "You hate that I call you baby girl, but they're the ones who treat you like a child. Come on, Molly. Come home with me." He reached for her hand, but he missed and knocked a water glass over.

Papa stood up. "Get the hell out of my house," he said. "You are not sober."

Maybe he slipped because he was nervous, Molly reasoned. If so, he'd be sober again tomorrow because it was important, she told herself, knowing her sponsor would say she wasn't fooling anyone with her excuses. Still, she wanted to believe. She'd tasted that feeling again, slid back into memories of what it felt like to be desired, to live a different life, and it was powerful. She wasn't sure she wanted to tuck it back away. The word *bored* rattled in her brain. Raisa was five. She'd be fine, wouldn't she? And if Viktor had slipped, she could understand why; the pressure of coming to dinner was a lot. That's right. He could call his sponsor, get back on the wagon.

"Molly, can't you see what they're doing?" Viktor said. Too many possibilities were swirling. "You don't need this. You have bigger dreams than this house, this life. Come back with me. This time I'll take you to New York."

Even though she didn't believe him, she didn't say no.

The next morning, Viktor walked back into the butcher shop and Molly jumped in surprise. She was sure he would have run back to Atlantic City. "I knew you'd be waiting for me," he said, flashing that wicked grin of his, and for the second time in two days, feelings Molly hadn't experienced in years rose to the surface. She could imagine being seventeen again, when she could still dream about making it in the city. She waited for him to make his case, to push himself on her, but he didn't say anything. He put another box of her favorite chocolates on the counter along with another bunch of flowers, kissed her cheek, and left. It wasn't until he'd been gone a good ten minutes that she realized it had happened again: She'd tucked Raisa away.

He came every morning for an entire month, leaving candy and flowers and kissing her cheek. The card on the chocolate box said the same thing every day: *I'm sorry. Please come home.*

At first, Mama threw the flowers and the boxes out. Papa threatened to stand guard at the door to bar him from coming back, but the more they fought against him, the more Molly wanted to see him, the more she fought for him. She knew it was her old instincts kicking in, and she knew they were dangerous, but they were exciting, too, and she hadn't been excited in years. "Don't you trust me?" she asked her parents.

"It's the drugs we don't trust," Mama said.

"But I like seeing him," she admitted one night as she fished the flowers from the trash. The store was closed. The metal gates were rolled down and it was dark and quiet. "Stop trying to protect me, treating me like a child."

"Don't blame us. Not again," Papa said, but of course it was them making things worse. They didn't realize what they were doing. They even went back to correcting her and criticizing her the way they had before she'd left.

"Not like that," Mama said when Molly washed Raisa's hair. "You're making tangles; rub this way." And "Mollushka, give Raisa an extra jacket. It's cold today." Or "Did she brush her teeth?"

"Stop watching over me, telling me how to do everything," Molly said. They apologized, said they were worried. Around and around they went in circles, correcting her, arguing and second-guessing her. Viktor never did that. He always let her be who she was.

The Roxborough paper bought another one of Molly's comics, and even though her parents congratulated her and framed it, they started reading through the classifieds, suggesting other jobs. "Don't you think I can make it as an artist?" she asked. They nodded and kept circling openings: secretary, office assistant, or babysitter. The more they pushed the jobs, the more she thought about Viktor. She could barely breathe, the pain was getting so bad.

Molly took Raisa to Atlantic City in February of 1977 after a fight with her parents. They had been arguing constantly and she couldn't take it anymore, could barely eat or sleep. She had to get away, and while she knew Viktor wasn't the best answer, at least he was *an* answer. She told herself she could handle it, that she could stay sober. Besides, it was only for a little while, until she sold more comics and could afford a place of her own. She told Raisa they were only trying it out as she packed their suitcases. The little girl stood there crying silent tears. She didn't shake or whimper like other kids, and Molly was torn between feeling proud and upset that her daughter was forced to be that strong. "It's okay to be sad," she said to Raisa when they boarded the bus. She held her daughter on her lap, kissed her hair, her cheeks. She was still amazed at how soft her skin was, that she always smelled like sugar and flour, not chicken fat like Molly. "You can tell me what you're thinking." But Raisa didn't open her mouth and Molly hugged her even tighter. "I'm excited," she whispered, and she realized she wasn't lying for Raisa's sake. She was tingling with hope, the promise of a better chance this time, only when they arrived at the apartment it looked duller and less polished than she remembered. It was strewn with empty vodka bottles. Her clothes were still in the closet and the drafting table Viktor had mentioned was nowhere in sight. Molly slept on the pull-out couch holding Raisa that night. The little girl was so scared she wouldn't go to the bathroom alone or let Molly out of her sight for a second.

"I miss Baba and Pop-Pop," she said when Molly tucked her and her teddy bear in.

"Let's give it one more day," Molly said.

One day led to another and another. Molly didn't want to be there, but she didn't want to go home, either. She needed to move forward, and here, with Viktor, she could at least have more space to figure out what forward meant. Besides, there were AA and NA meetings in Atlantic City that she could join. With Viktor sober, they could talk it all through, she told herself—only he didn't sober up. Molly stayed with Raisa on the couch for months. She should have been angry with him, but the real truth was that she was jealous. He was using, but it was under control. His body was healthy. He was functioning and feeling good while she was barely holding on. *I'll get there,* she told herself. She just needed time, except Viktor was never around to take Raisa for a few hours after school or on weekends, not like Mama and Papa. She wasn't sure she would have trusted him anyway.

"Let's go out, have some fun," he said to Molly after she put Raisa to bed one night.

"We can't leave a five-year-old home alone."

"She won't know the difference and you won't regret it." But she knew Raisa would. Her daughter was smart that way, figured things out long before a kid her age should.

Viktor came home high and happy, again and again, and Molly couldn't stand it. She was on the edge, telling herself she was stronger than him. She tried to draw to make herself feel better, but with Raisa feeling more comfortable and running around, there was no peace. And when there were moments of quiet, Molly's body ached for that high, for that release, and she pushed herself to watch Jack LaLanne again, to even try his exercises herself.

She found her first real distraction by accident when a stray copy of the *Inquirer* blew into her feet at the beach. The lead headline caught her eye, announcing that the Atlantic Nuclear Power Plant was coming to New Jersey. The plant was supposed to be two reactors eleven miles from Atlantic City on a set of man-made islands. Molly had never learned much about nuclear power, only enough to give *Atomic Anna* its story lines, but she knew putting something that powerful near Atlantic City, her home, her daughter, was dangerous. To fight it, she needed information. She started going to the library with Raisa. And Raisa, who refused to stay in the children's room without Molly, sat with her mother in the adult section. Molly read every book and magazine she could addressing nuclear science, the atomic bomb, and the fallout from explosions. There was a lot that went over her head, but what she understood was that many scientists argued a nuclear power plant could be built safely. That in the long term it was cleaner, more efficient, and even cheaper than coal. But even Molly could see that this Atlantic City project was idiotic. There was no way to shore up anything on the coast, let alone on a man-made island, to protect it from the hurricanes and storms that battered New Jersey. Even worse, they wanted to build the thing in Florida and bring it up on a barge. "Fools," she said in the library, and Raisa flinched.

"Baba Yulia wouldn't call someone a fool," Raisa said. "I miss her."

"Me too, but Philadelphia is too far away for us to see them," Molly said. At first, she had called every Sunday with Raisa, but Raisa started crying on the phone, begging her grandparents to come and pick them up, and Molly couldn't let that happen, so she began calling alone. Molly felt guilty keeping Raisa away, but she couldn't stand the pleading, the idea that she might be making a mistake.

To drown out the doubt, Molly began throwing herself into organizing against the power plant. It gave her something to do. She supported nuclear power in theory but didn't trust the government to run the Atlantic facility they proposed. In addition to organizing, Molly drew comics where the Radioactives swooped in to save Atlantic City, to stop a meltdown. She drew other story lines where they destroyed the plant in Florida, the man-made island, and the barge carrying the parts north. At every stage of proposed plant development, her team of superheroes set out to stop it. And like the Radioactives, in real life, Molly did everything she could. She planned town halls and meetings, went to every open public hearing she could to protest and object. All the time at the library paid off as Raisa got to know the librarians and they started offering to watch her. Raisa knew them well enough to be happy to stay with them. She had learned to read quickly, and they helped find her books to devour.

Molly kept a list of people who came to her meetings or helped by writing letters. At first only one or two people showed up or replied to the flyers she posted around the boardwalk, but then the number grew to six, then ten, then twenty. With each new follower she felt a renewed sense of purpose. She didn't need to work as a secretary or babysitter because she was going to change the world.

But the work was exhausting. "I have something that can give you energy, make you feel better," Viktor said one night, ten months after Molly moved back. He held up a bottle of pills and shook them.

"I'm not doing drugs," she said, but her voice wasn't steady, and she knew he heard it.

"I don't want you falling off the wagon, either. These keep you awake. That's all."

It was fall, but it was snowing outside and their apartment was hot because the heater was on overdrive. Steam poured out of the radiators and there was no way to stop it without turning it off and freezing. Molly could barely keep her eyes open or think straight, but she couldn't sleep, either. The itch for a hit was too strong. The urge to dull the pain that was constant again was all-consuming. "I need my head clear," she said, arguing with herself more than Viktor. "And I need to work harder. Put in more hours. If this power plant is built and it melts down, Raisa will die."

"Then take a pill and keep fighting," Viktor said.

"Get away," she said too loudly, and clapped her hand on her mouth. Raisa was asleep on the couch, which she now had to herself. Molly was back in the bedroom with Viktor, orgasms being her only high. Viktor put the pills on the kitchen table.

"Take it or flush it," he said, and left. Then it was just Molly and that bottle of pills, and while the container was small, it took over the entire apartment. At first, she stayed on the other side of the room, but she stared at it. The clock pushed forward one hour. She didn't look away. Instead, she got closer. Two hours and she moved along the edge of the kitchen.

"Just flush it," she said. She took another step closer, inched to the edge of the counter, then to the fridge. "Flush it," she said again, even as the distance between her and that bottle decreased. Even when she sat down at the table, she told herself to walk away, but she couldn't. She thought about Raisa and her parents. She thought about Viktor and her art, all she had done to stop the nuclear power plant. She had shown everyone, even herself, that she could be someone, that she could do something. That paper in Roxborough had even published three more *Atomic Anna* panels. *You deserve a reward*, she told herself. And it was only a pill. *Just one.* She would stay in control this time.

She swallowed it without water, imagined it running down her throat, leaking into her blood. Twenty minutes later she didn't feel numb and the pain in her gut didn't go away, but she did feel new energy surging. She jumped to her feet and ran through some of the old Jack LaLanne exercises. By the time Raisa was up and ready for school, Molly felt like she could jog with her all the way there.

Since she wasn't high in the way she used to be, Molly told herself it was okay to take more pills. Viktor was happy to bring a supply and she started writing dozens of letters every day in protest of the power plant. One year dragged into another and she and her group made such strong arguments, the project was postponed, and Molly's supporters started peeling away. "Postponed doesn't mean canceled," she said to her followers, but they disagreed, told her it was the best outcome they could hope for. "We need to block the entrance to city hall to let them know we're not done until it's *canceled*," she said, and they told her to go ahead without them. She needed the project. Without it she had nothing. The rejection by her supporters made her feel empty again, pushed her back to a minute-by-minute life. She started attending four meetings a day. Her sponsor pleaded with Molly to leave Atlantic City, to leave Viktor. *Do it for Raisa*, she said, but Molly couldn't leave. She had done more in Atlantic City than she ever had in Philly. *Postponed is not canceled*, she wrote over and over as she kept at the letters. And *I'm not addicted*, she told herself when she swallowed pills before breakfast, or was it dinner?

* * *

By fall of 1981 Molly was taking more pills than she wanted, but she was sure she was okay. After all, Raisa was thriving. Every morning, the girl skipped herself to school. She was so grown-up, so self-sufficient. Molly was proud of her, certain it was because she had made the right decision in moving them to Atlantic City, in keeping Raisa from her grandparents. And she wanted to keep her happy, which was why Molly didn't mention her arrests. Twice she had been taken in for protesting without a permit, and both times they found cocaine on her. Not much. Just enough to boost the pills she was taking, too. She was on probation and keeping it together.

"This is going to be it," she told Viktor the night before the big rally she had been planning for a month. It was the biggest event she had worked on in years. She had fifteen people committed to come. He handed her a pill to keep her awake, so she could finish her signs. Raisa was sitting in front of the television with her back to them. Molly made sure she didn't see the vodka, just a sip to down the pill. Not enough to make her drunk. Viktor went out and left more pills in a container by the sink, and Molly went back to making signs, working through the night.

"Mama?" Raisa said. "Mama, are you listening?" It was six in the morning and Molly was still painting signs. There were piles all around the apartment. "Breakfast?" Raisa said.

"Raisele, don't wait for me. Go eat at school. Don't they give you pancakes?"

"It's not for me, Mama. It's for you. You have to eat."

"What?" Molly shook her head. "I did eat."

"You didn't. I'm positive. You didn't have dinner. I don't think you ate anything yesterday. There were no dishes in the sink."

"Do you want me to pack you a lunch? Is that what this is about?"

"They give me lunch at school." That's right. Raisa got a better lunch at school than Molly ever had, a real American lunch.

"I bet it's delicious," Molly said.

"I hate that everyone knows I get free lunch."

"So what?"

"It means we're poor."

"No. That's not why. It's better food and they're jealous." Molly smiled, reached down and smoothed Raisa's dark hair, took her hand

and kissed her fingers. Molly loved those fingers, those hands. They were still thick and round, touched with baby fat. Her palms, too, even though there wasn't a lick of actual fat on her. It was the end of childhood that hadn't yet washed away. "You're getting so big."

"Mama, I asked if you liked that show last night on television? *The Greatest American Hero.* He was funny. Wasn't he?"

"Sure." She couldn't remember what Raisa was talking about.

"I made you a new poster."

"Thank you, sweetheart. What is that?" Raisa was packing her backpack for school; she had a thick math book that looked far too advanced for a child. Molly reached over and took it from her. "I told you not to bother with math. It's a waste. You have other talents."

"Maybe I like math?" Raisa said quietly. Molly sighed. Suddenly she was so tired. She wanted to lie down, but there was no time for that. She had to finish the posters, get to the protest. She needed another pill. "Do you know where I left my medication?"

"Next to the sink," Raisa said. "Can I come with you today?"

The pills. There they were. "Thank you." She was lucky Raisa was so independent and smart. Molly felt the pill sliding down her throat, knew it would only be a few minutes until she started to feel the first wave of energy. She should be good for the entire protest, at least until lunch. "I'm going to get dressed and get going. Don't be late for school," Molly said. Did she already kiss Raisa goodbye? She kissed her one more time just in case.

Molly put on jeans and a blazer she'd found at the Salvation Army. It made her look professional, and that was important because what you were wearing when you were arrested mattered. She brushed her hair, added lipstick, and was on her way to city hall. It was cold but the walk felt short. Even with the stack of signs tucked under her arm, she made good time. "Today's the day." She could feel that she'd make a real difference, was gaining momentum again. Next week, she'd have even more people involved.

As she got closer to city hall, the wind kicked up and sand blew, bit at her face. She thought she might hear people already, chanting and yelling, but as she got closer, she saw the lawn in front of the building was empty; she must have mistaken the seagulls for voices. Molly was the first to arrive. She leaned against the black fence on the perimeter and waited. Fifteen minutes later, Viktor came around the corner with half a dozen men who worked for him. None of them were on Molly's list of people she expected and her heart fell. She knew Viktor was paying them to come. "I don't need your help," she told him.

"Can't I support my woman?"

"Don't call me your woman." She looked down the street, around the corner, for the people who had told her they were coming, but there was no one and it was getting late.

"Do you want us to go?" Viktor asked.

Timing for these things, she had learned, was important. She needed workers to see the protestors when they got to the parking lot. "Fine, you can stay," she said. She handed out the signs to Viktor's crew and stepped up to the front of the group. She raised her hands over her head. It always made her feel powerful when she stood that way, a natural rush, and even though all those men were there because of Viktor, she still felt it. She started chanting. "Hee, hee, ho, ho, all nukes have got to go. Hee, hee, ho, ho, all nukes have got to go." The group joined in and they got louder. It wasn't the roar she had hoped for, but it was something.

The parking lot next to city hall started to fill. When the mayor arrived, two police officers escorted him. His suit looked cheap and gray. His tie was too thin. Molly was sure he would walk around to the back entrance, slip past without facing the protestors, but he walked straight for them. Molly started yelling even louder, pumping the sign in her hands.

"Thank you for coming," the mayor said, facing her with an awful smile. Sun glinted off his bald spot, made his gray hair look thin. "I appreciate your sentiments. Your sincerity."

"Stop the power plant," Molly yelled. "You're killing our children."

"We're not building anything. The whole idea's on hold."

"That's not good enough!" Molly screamed. "Cancel it."

"Lady, it's as good as dead. There's no money in it."

She felt rage because he wasn't listening. Until the plant was officially canceled, the fight wasn't over. Maybe if she could get closer, she could make him understand. Without thinking it through, she used her sign to smack the policeman standing between her and the mayor. In response, another cop shoved her to the ground, hard.

Next thing Molly knew, she heard Viktor yell, "No one touches my girlfriend!"

"Gun!" yelled an officer off to the side. Molly didn't see it, only made out the image of cops tackling Viktor, slamming him down. She heard a crack as his head connected with the ground, and then he went silent—and that was when Molly knew it was bad, because Viktor was never quiet.

"Leave him alone!" she yelled. She couldn't remember ever feeling so scared, so helpless. And dizzy. When she tried to stand up to get to Viktor, a cop grabbed her, dragged her toward a black-and-white. She caught a glimpse of Viktor then, lying on the ground, not moving, blood pouring from his head. "Help him. He needs a doctor."

"Shut up," the cop who had her said. Off to the side of the car, he patted her down and found pills on her. Damn it. She hadn't meant to bring them, couldn't even remember putting them in her pocket. Then he shoved her into the back seat. All the while she twisted and turned, fought to get a look at Viktor, but she couldn't see what was happening.

"Viktor!" she yelled. Her voice sounded desperate and it went nowhere, bounced around the vinyl and plastic and made her ears ring. "Help him," she said again when the cop climbed into the front seat. He smirked, told her to relax.

At central booking, the blazer didn't do a damn thing. They threw her into lockup with prostitutes and drug addicts, the same cell she had seen before. She sank down onto the piss-stained floor.

Since it was her third offense and she was already on probation, Molly was sentenced to seven years, the maximum. It was only after her sentencing hearing that her lawyer told her Viktor was dead. He said it quickly, like he was in a hurry, as if he were telling her the score of the game last night. "What?" she said, stunned.

"Dead. He hit his head. Report said it was an accident." The lawyer was looking at the back of the courtroom, at his next client. "Is there someone you want to call?"

"Dead?" she said.

"Your dad? You want to call your dad?" the lawyer asked. "Your daughter, is that where you want her to go, to your dad?"

"No. No." She was too angry to explain that she was objecting to what had happened to Viktor, furious that this man who was supposed to be her attorney couldn't even stop to listen. If only she had her pills, they'd help her clear her mind. Viktor was dead. "He's dead. They killed him," she said, shaking and out of control. "They killed him."

"Your Honor, Ms. Adelson says her father is dead. Someone killed him." He leaned back down to Molly. "Is there anyone else to take your daughter?"

"He's dead," was all Molly could say. Her head was spinning. Her thoughts were incomplete. She didn't realize that was the moment she needed to correct them, to tell them her father was alive and to declare her parents as Raisa's guardians.

"Raisa Adelson is hereby remanded to foster care," was the last thing she heard the judge say before they hauled Molly away and locked her up.

ANNA

April 1992

Eight Months Before Molly Dies on Mount Aragats

Mount Aragats

nna and Molly were up in Anna's watchtower, getting Anna ready to jump to Raisa. Molly handed Anna her heavy satchel with the amplifier, and Anna thanked her. Then she leaned forward and kissed Molly on the cheek. It was awkward, the first time she dared to get that close to her daughter, and while Molly didn't pull away, she didn't lean in, either. "Thank you, for doing this, for helping Raisa," Molly whispered. She leaned back and Anna was too uncomfortable to say or do anything else. She wasn't used to intimacy or her daughter, and she was embarrassed by what she'd done. Every day she tried to be the kinder, warmer Anna that Molly had known, but felt like she was failing miserably.

"I'm proud of you," Anna said.

"I don't want to do this now," Molly said. She'd learned how to enter coordinates into the time machine, how to activate it, and she turned away to get started. When she gave the signal, Anna pulled the trigger and jumped to 1981. She landed on an empty beach next to the boardwalk in Atlantic City, shivering in wind that ripped over the sand and made October feel like November. Her hands were blistered and burned again. They throbbed, but it didn't matter. All that mattered was Raisa, and she was coming. Molly had been clear, this was their agreement. Anna would save Raisa and then Molly would help Anna stop Chernobyl. But as Anna stood there waiting, she realized there was no formula dictating what she had to do or should do. The outcome was something she couldn't control. There were too many variables, countless things that could go wrong, and she was terrified of the uncertainty.

She was also petrified for Raisa, for what her granddaughter was about to face. Anna had been the same age, ten years old, the day she lost her own mother, the day the soldiers dragged Xenia away. She knew the pain and fear Raisa was about to experience, and thinking about it was making Anna feel nauseated. She forced herself to put those feelings out of her mind, to concentrate on her mission, keeping Raisa out of foster care, and checked the stopwatch around her neck. Anna and Molly had planned meticulously for this meeting, and now that it was so close, Anna had to fight away the memories and emotions threatening to paralyze her.

She took a deep breath and surveyed the beach. A splintered ramp rolled over the dunes. The boardwalk beyond sat in the shadow of clapboard houses that looked like they were sinking. *Focus*, Yulia would say, but Anna couldn't. Her mind raced. Minutes ground past, an hour. Molly wasn't sure exactly when Raisa would come but knew this was the right window. Any minute, Raisa could make her way across the ramp and look down on the ocean, on Anna. When she did, Anna was supposed to set their plan in motion.

A seagull circled overhead. Anna reached into her bag and pulled out the comic book for Raisa. She tried to picture her granddaughter in the yellow raincoat and green sneakers Molly had described. Anna knew she would want to hold open her arms for Raisa and tell her she was going to be okay, that if Anna could survive, Raisa could, too, but Anna couldn't do any of that. She was a stranger to this little girl. She had to keep her distance.

The wind hissed. She tasted salt. She looked up and there was Raisa standing on the boardwalk. She was pitched forward, using all her weight to drag a wagon. Molly had told Anna Raisa's wagon would be filled with protest signs, and she saw the childish, misshapen curves spelling out NUCLEAR POWER, NO THANKS.

"Raisa," Anna yelled, then cringed. She shouldn't have said her name. Not yet. Luckily, Raisa didn't hear but held a hand up to her ear. Anna stared at Raisa's full cheeks, relieved they hadn't faded to the sharp angles Anna saw in the photos Yulia had sent.

"Do you need help?" Raisa yelled. "Your hands are bleeding." Anna cursed silently for having forgotten to keep them behind her back. The girl was staring at her and she hurried closer so they could stop yelling. "Your clothes are weird. You look like you came from an old TV show. And what's in that weird bag on your shoulder?"

Their interaction was supposed to be brief, but standing there in front of her granddaughter, Anna didn't want it to end yet. She barely even knew Molly. She needed another few minutes with Raisa. She stepped closer. "Can I tell you something interesting about waves?"

"I know a lot about the ocean."

"I'm sure you do." Anna smiled, proud of Raisa's confidence. "Waves in the ocean are like light. The way they travel is peculiar. If you try to catch one, what happens?"

"It's hard," Raisa said. She paused. "You think about this, too?"

"What do you mean?"

"I mean, I think about it a lot. If you run after a wave, it's going fast. It's hard to catch, but if you catch it, it appears to slow down." Her smile grew. "No one ever listens to me when I talk about this. You want to keep hearing about it?" Anna nodded. She couldn't believe Raisa had already gotten this far. "This is where it's really weird." Raisa's sweet, thin voice was rising with excitement. "If I travel next to the wave, if I block everything else out, it would look like the wave is frozen in time, like it's not moving at all. Can you even imagine? If we could catch up to a wave, it would look like it wasn't moving. It's crazy!" Raisa stopped and seemed to think for a few minutes. "Those waves, it's like they're sharp. Like they're glass and if you break through, you'd shatter the glass and they'd hurt you. Maybe cut your skin and make you bleed. I tried to talk about it with the librarian, but she didn't understand. Do you?"

"I do." Anna barely got the words out. She was speechless. Those ideas, what her granddaughter was talking about, were the beginning of Einstein's work. "Who taught you that?"

"No one. I read a lot of books, but I haven't found it anywhere yet."

A smile tugged at Anna's lips and grew. "Keep working on it," she said. "I have something for you." She held out the comic book, a new issue of *Atomic Anna*. Inside was a note from Molly with Yulia and Lazar's phone number and address.

"I can't take anything from strangers. Not even my mom's comic book." Raisa put her hands behind her. "How did you get that?"

"I know your mom. She gave it to me. And this is important. When the police arrest your mother, call your grandparents."

"What are you talking about, arrest my mom?" She narrowed her eyes. "My mom doesn't give her comic books to anyone. And how do you know about my grandparents? We haven't spoken to them in years." She looked like she might cry. "I shouldn't even talk to you. My mom says only perverts are on the beach when it's cold like this." All of Raisa's confidence had melted away and suddenly she looked like the scared ten-year-old she was. Anna had crossed a line and she felt Raisa turn away before she did it. Anna had to be fast. She hurried up the ramp. She was lucky Raisa's wagon was heavy. It gave her time to catch her granddaughter. She grabbed the back of the wagon and slid the comic book in between two signs while Raisa strained to tear it away.

"I'm sorry I scared you. I don't—want you—to be scared." Anna panted. Her hands left blood on the rusted metal. Her mind was working too slowly, couldn't piece together what she needed to say next. It was the deterioration from too many jumps.

"I have to help my mom. Go away. She's protesting."

"Right." Anna's words came back to her. "I know you're going to the protest. Your mother was awake all night again. You're frightened. I understand. Believe me, I understand. But you need to listen." Anna took a deep breath. "When your mother is arrested, promise me you will call your grandparents. Their phone number is in here." She pointed to the comic book. As she did, Raisa jerked the wagon backward. "If you don't call, they'll put you in a foster home."

"Get away. Pervert!" A wheel caught and it gave Anna an extra few seconds.

"Call them," Anna said. There was so much more she wanted to tell Raisa, things she had never dared to say out loud before. Things that her granddaughter wouldn't understand, at least not yet. She wanted to tell her the Soviet Union was lonely and miserable and as much as Anna had wanted to leave, she couldn't. She wanted to say she regretted never meeting Raisa before, that she was sorry she had pushed Molly away. Most of all, she wanted to tell Raisa she was proud of her—that she believed in her. And she wanted to say all these things because it was what she knew to be true and because it was what she had always longed to hear when they took Xenia, her own mother. "Promise me you will call your grandparents."

That was when Anna's time ran out. The wind picked up and her feet felt heavy, as if being pressed into the boards. She opened her mouth to say one more thing as Raisa reached for a handful of sand on the side of the boardwalk and flung it into Anna's eyes. Anna crumpled and dropped to her knees, and she couldn't even feel any pain, only pride. Raisa was already the fighter she needed to be. "Now on to Chernobyl," she said, already planning her next jump with Molly. The static came and Anna's body was pulled. It lengthened and when she opened her eyes again, she was back in the tower and she knew she had done enough because there was a new photograph on her desk, Yulia in front of a van with her arm around a young Raisa. In the photo, Raisa was the same age she'd been on the beach. She wore the same green sneakers and a frown. Yulia's smile told her Raisa never went to foster care.

"We did it," Anna said. Molly was at the desk. She came down to the floor, next to Anna.

"Did what? You were supposed to visit Valery. We're almost out of fuel."

"I wasn't with Valery," Anna said, and smiled. They had been in different timelines again, and now Anna was converging into Molly's— a world that was better for her granddaughter. "We saved Raisa." Molly looked confused and Anna understood. In Molly's timeline, Raisa had never veered down a wrong path, and Anna felt better than she had in a long time. "I promised you I would save her. I did."

Molly sighed. "You're confused again. We're working to stop Chernobyl, not save Raisa." She handed Anna an envelope. "It's another letter from Mama. And a photo. An old one. It's me, Mama, Papa, and Raisa standing in front of the old butcher shop back from when Raisa was a baby."

"I know the photo," she gasped, and pointed to the identical photo that still hung in the middle of all the other photos Yulia had sent over the years. Only now she noticed all those photos were different from the ones that had been there before she'd jumped to Raisa. They didn't tell the story of Raisa falling. They told the story of her growing stronger and being happier than she'd ever looked in the other photos. Still sitting in the center was the photo from Anna's first jump.

"That's weird. It's like time turning back on itself." Molly paused and seemed to think about something. "It's like the ouroboros, the snake eating its own tail. You have the picture from your first jump, now it's here, the original and—"

"I won't let it repeat," Anna said. "If that's what you're thinking." Silence stretched between them as Anna examined her hands, thought about her granddaughter and what she'd said about the waves. "Raisa's incredible, isn't she?"

"She is," Molly agreed.

"I think she's going to help us, help me fix my machine. She's already thinking about waves, the way they interact with the universe, our world."

Molly glared at Anna and stepped back, stood taller as if preparing to fight. "I told you before, I won't let you bring her into this."

"But she said the waves were like glass, implied they're dangerous. She knows something."

"Leave her alone."

PART IV

By virtue of three things does the world endure: truth, justice, and peace.

—Pirkei Avot

ANNA

Mount Aragats

After saving Raisa, Anna watched as her burned hands healed and thought about what Raisa had said, that the waves looked like glass. She'd said if you break through, you'd shatter the glass and they'd hurt you, maybe cut your skin and make you bleed. And it occurred to Anna that her granddaughter understood exactly what was happening to Anna as she traveled through time. Her hands were burned from brushing the ripples as she jumped. She must have been breaking through and the radiation was too much. It was killing her. She needed to find a way to angle inside of them, not brush them as she jumped. She tried to reason her way through the idea only as she recovered from the superficial injuries, her mind continued its decline. She could remember the deeper past easily, and that she was working to stop the meltdown at Chernobyl, but sometimes she couldn't recall the day-to-day, and it was frustrating her, making it harder to concentrate. Often she had to read her notes just to piece things together.

December 8, 1992, was coming, quickly. She needed to finish before then, make sure she and Molly were far away from that mountain and whatever disaster Anna had glimpsed on her first jump.

Aside from her mental deterioration, she was also facing the fact that she didn't have enough uranium to support more than a few more jumps. To stop Chernobyl, she was going to need help—she was going to need Raisa. There was no question her granddaughter was the one to do it, who could help her fix her machine and make it work with the small bit of fuel they had left. Standing on the beach as Raisa described catching waves the way Einstein described catching light, Anna knew that she was brilliant, that she was interested, and that she would understand ripples in space-time in a way no one else could. Most important of all, Anna could trust her. She was family. She wanted Molly to agree.

Anna found Molly in the kitchen, standing at the sink in a bathrobe, stirring a mug of tea. Anna held the envelope with the photo from Yulia, the one taken in front of the butcher shop, and watched Molly for a moment. She looked different from the way Anna remembered her before the jump to the beach. Her hair was shorter, cropped, the way it was when Anna found her dying on the floor. The murals Molly had painted in the main compound were different, too, and the walls and ceilings were finished, all the wires tucked away so now it looked the way it did the first time she jumped to Aragats. Anna realized that likely meant this was it. They were in the timeline in which Molly would die unless Anna stopped it. "You left the stove on," Molly said. Her spoon clinked against the mug. "You could have burned the whole place down."

"I'm sorry," Anna said. She held up the envelope. "I'm going to hang this here in the kitchen."

"You really love that photo," Molly said.

"I do. I…I have stared at it for a long time."

"I know. You told me you found it during your first jump." Anna wondered how much she'd told Molly about that jump. In previous timelines she'd never dared tell Molly she was going to die in 1992, but had this been different? She would have to find out somehow. Molly didn't seem to notice Anna hesitating. She was busy making herself tea. There was food on the table. "Will you eat with me?" Anna asked.

"We don't eat together." Molly's words were harsh, her tone cold. Molly had been much more distant to Anna in this timeline. They hadn't had their reckoning, as former Molly would have said.

"We could try," Anna said. She pulled out a chair for Molly, sat in the one next to it. A blizzard was battering the station. The wind howled.

"When the storm stops, I'll take the snowmobile down and get us more food. Artush is off for a few weeks."

"We have a snowmobile?" Anna said.

"Yes. In the back shed." And then, "You forgot, didn't you?" Anna nodded and tacked the photograph to the wall. Then she pressed her fingertips into her forehead, tried to remember seeing it before, to decide if it had been there in her previous timeline, too. All her life she had been the one with answers and explanations, but now she had none and she felt lost, unmoored, was continually trying to make sense of things. Molly continued, "Before you jumped, you asked me to work on designs for the amplifier. You said the one you built is too big and heavy. You were having a hard time lugging it around in that satchel. I've been sketching other ways to disguise it."

"That sounds like exactly what I need," Anna said. Molly was waiting, looking at her, and she knew she was supposed to say something but she wasn't sure where to start. The silence was stretching on too long. "I'm sorry," she said. "I don't remember asking. Maybe because I was living in a different timeline."

"You want to stop Chernobyl, you remember that much?" Anna nodded, told her of course that hadn't changed. "You came to me in prison and said you needed my help. You assured me you could help me sober up, stay sober once I got out of prison. You said you would do anything for me, for Mama. And that I could have a purpose again, that I could help you stop the Chernobyl disaster, that the impossible is always possible." Anna kept nodding. It all sounded logical for a universe in which she didn't need to help Raisa. Molly needed a reason to come, something to bring her to Aragats so she could heal. "I'm here to help with design. Hold on, I'll show you what I have." She handed Anna a comic book and pointed to the cover. Atomic Anna was standing with her hands on her hips. Her cape blew behind her and there was a small black box strapped to her belt, the size and shape of a pack of cigarettes. Molly pointed to it. "It's going to look like this." Anna ran a finger over the drawing and thought it looked perfect. Molly shifted closer. "It's hard for you, isn't it? Not remembering, or not knowing what happened before."

"You have no idea," Anna said. "The problem is I don't know if I'm forgetting or just never lived it in the first place. Not being able to depend on my own mind, I'm scared it could make me go mad." She dropped her hands from her forehead and looked at Molly. "Tell me about Raisa."

"She's at the top of her class, looking into graduate schools. She's gotten together with Vera's brother, Daniel. She wants to study astrophysics. Of course, that's no surprise. She's been reading *Atomic Anna* her whole life." She smiled. "I hated math. She loves it and I couldn't be more proud."

"Maybe she can help with the time machine and Chern—"

"No." Molly's voice had an edge to it Anna hadn't heard before. She narrowed her eyes. "We've been through this. I told you, no." Molly grabbed *Atomic Anna*. "Don't you dare go near her."

"I'm sorry," Anna said. But there was no way she could leave Raisa out of it. Raisa was the only person in the world who could help, and Molly had just given Anna an idea. Raisa had been reading the comics her whole life. That was how Anna could reach her, get her assistance.

She just had to be careful. "Mollushka," she called as Molly started walking away, "I need a favor."

"What now?"

"Will you draw the changes I'm making to my machine, put them into your comics, along with my new math? I think it will help me remember." Molly hesitated. "Please?"

"I can try," Molly said. "If it will help."

More than you know, Anna thought.

RAISA

Philadelphia

When Raisa was sixteen years old, she had been living with her grandparents for six years, in a slice of Northeast Philly they called Little Russia. The streets were lined with row homes separated by walls so thin there was no privacy and invisible borders so thick she didn't need to use a word of English until she stepped into a classroom at school. She never saw her mother because she'd been told she was still in prison and Raisa refused to visit. Papa was long dead, and now Raisa passed every waking hour either at school or with her grandparents working at their store, the Russian Market. She oscillated between the two worlds on a schedule set by the school bell and a pair of church bells recorded in Moscow that blared on the Russian radio station her grandmother played at all hours.

"Please, no more meat or broth. I need to leave," Raisa said to her babushka. She pushed the bowl away. She was due at a math competition in two hours and if she didn't leave soon, she'd be late. They were seated in the kitchen at their Formica table, so close together their knees knocked. The whole space was cramped like that. The refrigerator was flush with the stove, which nestled against a counter that in turn spilled into a sink only one plate wide. Babushka often complained she didn't have room to breathe while she cooked, but Raisa liked the lack of space, knowing her grandmother was close. It was the only thing that helped her calm down, and she needed that. She had always been nervous. Her whole life she was sure something bad would happen. Call it a premonition or just an anxious disposition, but it had also proven to be true. She had already lost both her parents and didn't have any other family in America. The fact was, if Raisa lost her grandparents, she would have no one and so she needed to be as close to them as she could.

"You're not late. You could leave in another hour and still be on time," Baba said.

"I like to be early." Sixty minutes early for every event, so she could get her bearings.

"Fix my machine, then," Baba said, pointing to the radio.

"It's broken again?"

"Can't you hear?" Baba said. Her words were sharp, but Raisa was used to that. Baba had never lost the edge she'd developed in the war she and Pop-Pop survived. It protected her soft underbelly, and a heart as big as Raisa could imagine. Baba wore bright lipstick and painted her nails to match. She was seventy-seven years old, but she moved fast and talked even faster, and her skin was still tight. She walked for an hour every day and stood so straight most of their customers at the butcher shop thought Pop-Pop had robbed the cradle, even though Baba was eight years older. All of this made them different. Raisa was different, too, because unlike other kids, she had to work, and she didn't live with her parents. She hid the fact that her mother was in prison from kids at school, made up a lie around Mama being a world-renowned artist. For a while they'd believed her. When their questions grew more intense, she stopped answering and eventually they stopped asking. No one cared anyway because no one took much notice of Raisa. She was quiet, and as long as she faded into the background, everyone was happy to leave her there. She was fine with that.

Raisa heard the static on the radio and went to the counter to examine it. It was a cheap model. She had built an antenna and a booster for it so her grandparents could listen to the Russian station they loved, the one broadcast from New Jersey, but Raisa didn't have a soldering iron. She'd used clamps to hold the wires together and they often came loose. She bent over the transistors. "It could be the fluorescents. I told you they interfere," she said. She pointed to the ceiling, to the brown fixture. "Wait." Raisa exhaled. "Here it is. You took the clamp off."

"I did not," Baba said, but she was smiling.

Raisa groaned. "You did it on purpose!" Her grandmother was particularly skilled at knowing how to distract her when she needed it. She called it "redirecting Raisa's energy." Raisa rethreaded the wire and clamped it back in place. The announcer's voice came in clear. He was talking about Boris Yeltsin.

"I'm so proud of you for this math competition," Baba said.

Raisa nodded. Both of her grandparents had told her at least one hundred times since they heard she was going that they were proud. And surprised. Raisa never talked about how much she loved math. Her mama hated it while Baba and Pop-Pop revered it. Admitting how she felt out loud would be equivalent to taking sides, and even though she was angry, furious with her mother, she could never choose between her grandparents and Mama. She knew it was strange to hide this, but her family wasn't like other families and now her secret was out. Her grandparents and everyone at school knew the results of the qualifying exams. Raisa hadn't just earned a spot in the competition; she had scored highest in the state. Her grandparents bragged every chance they had because, she figured, in the USSR being a mathematician was one of the highest honors. The profession came with power, private apartments, and even cars. Raisa didn't feel any particular interest or affection for that country, for her family's past, but she did love that if Soviets had any religion at all, it was math. Like Raisa, they seemed to understand that numbers and algorithms were skeletons that held the skin of the universe together. They defined space, orbits, the dimensions of the room, the length of the day, the weight of the marrow bones in Raisa's bowl.

Moscow's bells rang through the radio's speakers, announcing six a.m. Raisa wanted to leave in the next ten minutes. She walked down the hall that skimmed the living and dining rooms, to the bottom of the stairs where the gold carpet was frayed. "Pop-Pop, please hurry," she yelled. If only Raisa hadn't failed her driver's test, she could have driven herself.

"Nine minutes," he called. His voice scraped with age and cigarettes. "We're fine."

"Then do my hair," Baba called.

"I don't need distractions. I need to leave."

"Ten minutes. You have time to do my hair."

"Fine." Maybe it would help. If she didn't do her grandmother's hair, she would pace. She would feel nauseated. Besides, she liked doing Baba's hair. When Raisa moved in she had watched Baba spend hours dyeing, straightening, and twisting it into all sorts of styles, but she had arthritis now and that made it difficult. Raisa had taken over for her when she was twelve. At first her fingers were clumsy, but Baba was patient. She would sit as Raisa tried and tried again. She did Baba's hair slowly because she'd learned it was a way to sit with her grandmother and touch her, to be with her without saying a word. But this morning, she was rushed. "Eight minutes. That's all I have."

She picked up the brush. She divided the hair into sections, worked through knots, and twisted it into a bun. "Such soft hands," Baba said. "Your husband will be lucky." Raisa pinched her, but she laughed, too.

"I'm coming," Pop-Pop called from down the hall. Raisa finished just as her grandfather stepped into the kitchen. He was still wearing his blue pajamas. He had white wisps of hair around his rectangular head and deep lines around his eyes that made him look both older than he was and softer than he wanted to be.

"Why aren't you dressed?" Raisa asked.

"Change of plans. Daniel's driving you out to that fancy school hosting the competition. I have to be at the store today. Inspector's coming for a *surprise* inspection." Pop-Pop paid extra every month for advance warning of these "surprise" visits. Daniel went to school with Raisa and worked at the Market, was hired when he'd arrived from the USSR in 1986.

"Daniel doesn't have a license, either."

"But he did in the Soviet Union. He passed somewhere and that counts." Pop-Pop kissed her. "He's outside. Besides, you don't need an old man. You need energy. He'll stay the whole time, take you home." There was no time left to argue. Raisa started toward the door. "Daniel will take care of you. We're paying him extra," Pop-Pop called after her.

Raisa grabbed her backpack and checked the mirror next to the front door. She never left the house without one last look to make sure her bangs were straight, that they covered the scar she got all those years ago at Wanamaker's. She took a deep breath and ran down the cement walkway they shared with their neighbors. Daniel was at the van's sliding side door rearranging crates. Raisa heaved herself into the passenger seat. She rolled down her window for fresh air, hoped it would keep the smell of meat off her. "Please, go fast," Raisa said in Russian after he climbed in next to her. Russian was the language they spoke with each other outside of school.

"I can't get pulled over," he said.

"I know."

Daniel turned the key. The engine caught. "You never told me you like math."

"It's no big deal," she lied, because she still could not admit to anyone how much it meant to her. There was peace in the way equations came together and had an answer, the way they were predictable and never changing.

He pressed the accelerator, eased them toward the stop sign. "Math is important. You can earn good money. Respect."

"Not in America. No one cares about math here."

"Then why go to this contest?"

"There's a little bit of money in it, and I need it to pay for college." Her voice sounded weak, and even as she said it, she knew he wouldn't believe her. Still, he didn't push and she appreciated that. She hated talking about her real feelings, about how math soothed her and that she was excited to be with other people who might feel the same way. He drove without saying anything else, without the radio, only the sound of the tires rolling on asphalt between them. She knew he liked it that way, quiet, like her. He had fled from the Soviet Union with his mother just after Chernobyl. Pop-Pop saw them moving into the tiny apartment across the street from their store, watched Daniel carry the only suitcase he and his mother had between them. Pop-Pop didn't even wait for them to try the key in the lock before marching over to introduce himself and offering Daniel a job. Baba called the job tzedakah, charity. Pop-Pop called it good business. "That boy and his mother are hungry. That means he'll work hard, and we need that," he said. "Besides, his mother said a friend in the USSR told them to look for us. I never heard of the man, but it doesn't matter. Like I said, that boy will work hard."

Even though Raisa spent more time with Daniel than with anyone else in the world, working every afternoon side by side with him, she didn't know much about him. They passed their time in the back of the Market, in what they called the Chopping Room, where they cut and quartered, flayed and ground all the meat her grandparents sold. He was polite, kind, conscientious, but he never initiated a conversation.

Baba tried to pry, to dig into why he and his mother fled, how they paid for the airplane and found the apartment, found the Adelsons, but Daniel only shrugged and told her to ask his mother. The single fact Raisa knew about him was that he was two years older than he claimed and she wasn't supposed to tell anyone. His mother lied to give him more time in school to learn better English. His hair was dark and his eyes were green. He had been thin when he started and could barely lift a crate of chickens, but Pop-Pop was right. He worked hard and now he could sling cow quarters across his shoulders. Russian weightlifting, her grandparents explained. Baba made a show of pinching his biceps. Women asked him to help carry bags to the car. Girls giggled around him, but he never seemed to like it. If anything, the more attention he got, the more he shrank. Like Raisa, he seemed to want to be left alone.

Daniel eased the van through their maze of a neighborhood, where every house was cut from the same mold. Three stories. Four bedrooms. At Roosevelt Boulevard the street widened and Daniel went faster. Sunday was the busiest day in the Northeast, the day when bakeries, supermarkets, and flea markets made their money. Delivery trucks were already unloading. Blankets and tables were being propped up and weighed down with treasures.

"Don't you need to practice or something?" he asked.

"It's a math competition. I know it or I don't."

"But you seem nervous. You're biting your nails. Do you need to memorize equations?"

"Math isn't about memorizing. It's about knowing, knowing the language." She looked at a billboard advertising a pawnshop. A car sped past. "Teachers shouldn't quiz kids on multiplication tables." Numbers weren't something to regurgitate. They were a way to communicate and describe what was happening in the world around them. "Memorizing defeats the whole purpose."

"How did you learn the language?"

"What?"

"You called math a language. I never heard anyone say something like that. How did you learn it?" Raisa didn't answer because she wasn't sure she wanted Daniel to know something about her that no one else knew, that she taught herself. When she was little, her mother couldn't afford a babysitter and left Raisa at the library all the time. The librarians liked Raisa because she devoured books and didn't cause trouble. They let her wander through every section. One day she found a math book, and while she already knew this was the thing her mother hated, that math represented all the ways her life hadn't turned out well, Raisa couldn't resist looking. She could read in Russian and English, but she didn't understand any of the symbols around the numbers—only she saw there was an elegance to them, and she kept paging through. When her mother came to pick her up, Raisa panicked, slid the book into her bag, and took it home without checking it out. There was a thrill to having and reading something she wasn't supposed to touch. She could remember that even now, the rush she felt that first night she snuck the book from her bag and into her bed. There was another layer of excitement, too. The symbols and diagrams were the most beautiful things she had ever seen, and she knew she had to find a way to understand them. The next time she went to the library, she asked the librarians to help her find easy math books and Raisa started to learn. She didn't dare check any out under her name, couldn't risk her mother knowing. Instead, Raisa snuck them into her bag, returned them later, and if the librarians ever knew, they didn't say a word. By the time Raisa got to high school, she pulled off a perfect score on the hardest exam the advanced placement teacher had. They threw her into community college classes, but she was beyond those, too. She continued raiding the library because it was a habit by then, but also because she liked the rush she felt when she stole the books. Besides, she brought them back.

Raisa didn't *read* books; it was like she absorbed them into her bloodstream. It was the only way she could describe how she understood. Not that she ever explained it to anyone. It was better to be tough than smart in school anyway, and so she kept it all to herself.

"Why didn't the teachers know your talent?" Daniel asked.

"I don't know. I mean, they must have known something, right? I don't take math at school. Besides, aptitude isn't talent. Finding the right answer on a test means I studied. It doesn't mean I'm smart. To be smart you have to have ideas of your own." Raisa wasn't sure she had any.

"Only a smart person would say that. You have ideas. You just don't recognize them yet. That's something my sister would say. She was smart." And then, "Her name was Vera." He looked out the side window. It was the only time he ever looked away from the road.

"I've never heard you talk about her."

"It hurts." He changed the subject. "How much could you win today?"

"A lot. For me." The first-place prize money would cover a good chunk of her first year, and she had to go to college. She had to get a real job that paid real money and wasn't at a butcher shop or a coin-op because she didn't want to be like her parents or grandparents, counting every penny. Even more, she wanted to find people to challenge her, who thought like her. She wanted to find the people who wrote the books she stole.

When they arrived at the suburban school that was hosting the competition, the walls were immaculate and covered with ivy, not graffiti, like her school. Instead of having bars and steel grates, all the windows were clear, unobstructed glass. Daniel cut the engine. "It looks peaceful," he said.

"Your elbow looks close, but you can't bite it." She repeated the old Russian proverb Baba used.

"You'll be okay," Daniel said, smiling. "You don't have to be so nervous. You're good at math. I've known that for a long time. I've seen all those notebooks you write in, all the books you steal from the library."

She slid to the edge of her seat and took a hard look at him, maybe for the first time. Without her realizing it, he had gotten to know her. She hadn't paid him nearly as much attention, and for a split second she wondered if that was a mistake. He had her off balance and this was the one time, more than any other, when she needed to be steady. "Are you spying on me?"

"I just keep my eyes open, that's all," he said, hands up in the air.

She looked away, told herself to push this distraction out of her mind and concentrate on the competition. It was better to change the subject. "I'm the only girl here today."

"Doesn't matter. You'll kill them all. You'll win."

"Maybe." She jumped out of the van and made her way toward the school. Daniel kept up as she hurried.

"Do you mind if I watch?"

"You don't have to. My grandfather will pay you the same either way."

"I just thought…" He put his hands in his pockets. "I have nothing else to do anyway. I'll sit in the back. And I know you like company."

She stumbled on a stick and looked at him again. It was strange that he had watched her so closely, that she'd never realized it, and as much as it unsettled her it made her feel good. She didn't even want to admit that, but the idea that someone other than her grandparents cared was exciting in a way she didn't expect. And it wasn't just someone. It was Daniel. Her face flushed. "Sure. It's fine. I mean, I'm okay alone." She knew she didn't sound convincing.

"Great. I'll watch. I want to."

At the front door, Raisa paused to smooth her hair and bangs, her skirt. Her grandparents taught her to never attract attention outside of Little Russia. Blend in, they said. It was the Soviet in them, and she tried but she could never be as strong as they were. Already her stomach was so tight she worried she might throw up. In her skirt, she would never blend in today. She hated that.

"Do you need some water?" Daniel asked. She shook her head and closed her eyes, thought about the beach. She had lived two blocks from the ocean back when she was with her mother and father in Atlantic City, and the smell of sea water, the sounds of the ocean had always been her escape. She could hide in plain sight on the beach, yell without anyone hearing her over the waves, bury herself in sand. If she concentrated, she could put herself back there in the sand. And when she felt calmer, she went inside. The entryway dazzled with black-and-white floors and an oversized clock. The auditorium was dim and smelled like wood polish. Twenty tables were jammed on the stage. A timer was attached to the wall, set to mark two hours. As the highest scorer, Raisa was seated at the first seat at the first table. She took out the pencils and paper from the envelope they gave her and sat down. Daniel waved from the back, and she closed her eyes, thought about the beach again.

The shells were the most beautiful things in the world. Fibonacci explained the beauty in a way that made sense. She'd learned about him when she was six, pictured a spiral and tried to count the lines in her head.

"Ms. Adelson!" a man said. Raisa opened her eyes with a start. The proctor handed her the test. Behind him, in the front row, a group of three old men, the judges, took their seats. This was the semifinals. The top three scorers would proceed to the finals after a break.

The problems were a series of simple equations that grew into harder proofs. None of it was difficult. As Raisa worked, the world fell away, and when she came to the end, she looked at the clock. She had taken only half an hour to finish. Around her the boys were all still scribbling. Some moved from side to side in their chairs, looking like they were trying to remember something. Others tapped their feet or their pencils. It was clear most were finding the questions hard. Even though Raisa was done, she knew from experience that if she handed her work in so far ahead of others, people would think she had found a way to cheat. Starting with a clean sheet of paper, she did every problem again. She compared her new answers to the originals and found they were all the same, all correct. She turned her answers in to the proctor and made her way outside, walked across the parking lot to the van. She leaned against it, soaked in sweat. Nerves. Why did all those boys think it was so hard? What was she missing?

"Chocolate?" Daniel asked. Raisa flinched. She hadn't heard him coming, hadn't expected he would look for her.

"What the hell? You scared me."

"I only asked if you want a piece." He held out a square and pointed to the front door. "I called out to you back there, but you didn't hear."

"English," Raisa said. "They speak English here."

"Who cares? We speak Russian."

"I care. I like being American and Americans don't speak Russian."

"Fine," he said, but he continued in Russian. "Russian when it's secret. English in the open. Was it hard?"

"I don't know if I did horribly or aced it. I hate that. And I want it, I really want it."

"You want this life?" He gestured to the immaculate school, the polished houses.

"No." She could never feel comfortable in a neighborhood like this, but she did want something bigger than she had, people who understood her and math. She didn't want to worry about paying for college.

"I heard some boys talking trash. They think a girl can't know math. Little shits." He smiled and she laughed. It caught her off guard the way Daniel could make her laugh. He'd never done that.

"You keep surprising me," she said.

All of a sudden, he stopped and pointed to the soccer field behind them. On the edge of the woods, something was glowing. "Do you see that?" Daniel asked. It looked like a distortion, somehow, as if the grass and trees behind it were too bright and stretching. Then there was a gust of wind and static covering a portion of the field. Raisa blinked, and suddenly she felt like she had been punched in the stomach because she remembered seeing something similar before. The stretching and distortions were exactly what Raisa saw on the beach around the old woman, the day her father died and her mother went to prison. She squinted. Now that same old woman was in the middle of the static, in the field. It couldn't be.

"Do you see her?" Raisa asked. Daniel nodded and they started walking toward her, stopping a few feet away, at a distance Raisa thought was likely safe. The woman was holding a comic book, an issue of *Atomic Anna*, just like she had on the beach. Black-and-white static blurred her outlines. Her words were garbled. "I think she's saying my name, that she's been waiting for me for two hours. And something about Chernobyl and needing help," Raisa said. Then she heard something else about waves. Maybe ripples and space-time. Suddenly there was a thud. The static expanded toward them and they both covered their heads and huddled down. They stayed still, pressed together near the ground until the field went still. Raisa looked up and the woman was gone.

"Are you okay?" Daniel asked. He was out of breath like Raisa, pale from shock. He looked behind them to the side. "Where is she?"

"Gone," Raisa said. It had happened exactly the way it did on the beach. "Were her hands burned? Did you see?" Raisa gulped for air. "Last time she wore strange clothes, just like those."

"This happened before?"

"Maybe, I'm not sure." Still breathless, adrenaline making her shake, Raisa ran to the spot where the woman had stood, but there was no trace of her. The field was pristine, untouched. Daniel was next to her, turning around as if he thought she might return, pop up on another part of the field. "She's not coming back," Raisa said. Her knees went weak. Chernobyl. Waves and space-time. That was what she'd heard. She was sure of it. She remembered they'd talked about waves before, too. But on the beach the woman was whole, real. This woman in the field seemed more of a ghost. It felt like her words and the comic book were clues, but Raisa had no idea to what, and all she could focus on was the fact that the last time the old woman came, Mama was arrested. Papa was killed. The stranger had saved Raisa by giving her Baba and Pop-Pop's phone number, but she had been a harbinger, a marker for the worst day of Raisa's life.

"Are you okay?" Daniel asked. "Do you want to sit down?"

"No. No," she said. "I need a pay phone. I have to call my grandparents." She was sure it meant bad things were coming again, that Baba and Pop-Pop had been in an accident.

Raisa ran back to the school with Daniel following on her heels. The phone booth was just off the main hallway. She slid inside, Daniel waiting while she fumbled in her bag for a quarter. If her grandparents were dead, she had no one. She couldn't lose them, not again. The seconds it took for the line to connect felt like an hour. Baba answered. "Did something happen to you? Are you and Pop-Pop hurt?" Raisa said. She didn't recognize her own voice. It was pitched too high and she slipped into Russian.

"Raisele, I'm fine. We're all fine. What happened?" Baba asked.

Raisa leaned back against the glass. Her chest hurt too much for her to say anything else. Baba kept asking Raisa to explain while Raisa slumped and cried. She turned her back to Daniel, to anyone else who might see. "It's nothing," Raisa said. "Just nerves. Please. Be careful." Raisa stood in silence, listening to Baba trying to calm her until the phone beeped to warn they were running out of time. She told Baba she loved her and hung up, stood holding the receiver in its cradle, telling herself again and again that everything was fine. "They're okay," she said as she stepped out. She was sure she looked as rattled as she felt.

"What happened?" Daniel handed her a tissue. It was a little crumpled but clean.

"Nothing." She bent at the waist, put her hands on her knees. It was all going to be fine. That's what mattered. And now she needed to get her head back into the competition, back to math in case she made the finals. "I have...I have to forget about that woman and concentrate on the competition. Win." Daniel's face was red and worried. "Look," she said, "I really appreciate that you're asking, but right now I need to pull myself together, see if I made the finals, and if I did—then I need to win." He nodded and walked her back to the auditorium to wait for the results. She made her way toward the stage, and he returned to his seat in the back. Other contestants made their way back inside in clumps. Raisa never understood how it seemed everyone had friends, people to laugh and joke with; that they found so much to be funny. When she was younger, she never had anything to laugh about, was always worried for her mother. Now she was too concerned about her grandparents to feel so light. She envied those kids, the way they floated through life. She closed her eyes and tried imagining the seashells.

Eventually, the proctor returned to the auditorium and marched onstage. "All of you should be pleased with yourselves and proud," he said. The microphone buzzed. "To make it this far means you are gifted and talented. Keep working hard." No one at Raisa's school ever said anything like that. Tests were returned without a word, a grade slashed on the paper. "We have three finalists. First and most impressively we have Raisa Adelson, the first girl to ever qualify for the final." Raisa cringed and one person clapped. It had to be Daniel. She hunched her shoulders and tried to shrink into herself. The judge read off two more names and Raisa was directed to sit at a table dead center, between the other two finalists. The judge handed them each a manila envelope. "The final problem is advanced," he said. "I thought too difficult, but given the results from the written test, there was no choice. All three of you scored perfectly.

"James Maxwell was a Scottish mathematician best known for his formulation of electromagnetic theory. This veers slightly into physics, but the two disciplines are intertwined. Maxwell's work was groundbreaking. Doubtless the three of you have heard of him." Raisa had not. "For the purposes of this competition, we'll ask you to start with his equations in differential form, for empty space. There are four equations. Your task is to decouple them as a one-dimensional solution and then as a two-dimensional solution. We'll see how far you get."

Raisa tore into the envelope. Electromagnetism. She loved radios and amplifiers. She was hooked on television and transmission, had just cracked cable boxes, and math would take her mind off that old woman. It would soothe her as it always did. The equations were short. Simple. Surprisingly simple. Raisa absorbed them and flowed through their structure to their meaning. No, they weren't simple. They were extraordinary, elegant and complex in a way that wasn't obvious until she understood them. The boy next to her scribbled lines and lines of math, but there was no need. He must not have understood. The expressions were descriptions for understanding the wavelike nature of electromagnetic fields and their symmetry—describing them as two sides to the same coin, as interwoven. The math described the behaviors of electric fields; how electric and magnetic forces can be both positive and negative, can attract or repel. Once she understood this, she could decouple them. It took time because the formulations had to make sense. Raisa didn't notice the timer working its way toward zero. When it buzzed, she didn't stop because she was wrapped in the realization that electromagnetic waves propagate at the speed of light—that light itself is an electromagnetic wave. She knew this. It was basic, modern science. But knowing something as a fact you've been told and then understanding the math that explains it are completely different.

"Ms. Adelson!" the head judge said. He stood over Raisa. "Put that pencil down." He took her paper and carried it offstage to the other judges. The old men huddled. They didn't bother to speak quietly.

"He didn't get past the third line."

"This one's not even close."

"This one, she has it," the head judge said, nodding. "Looks like she was taking it a step further, ran out of time. And she's right."

Raisa won and was crushed with an excitement and pride she'd never experienced. It put her on a high, left her flying on adrenaline that made her feel invincible, and she loved it.

After the contest, Raisa and Daniel walked back out to the spot where they had seen the old woman, only there was nothing there but mud. It had rained and Raisa's shoes squelched in the grass. Daniel spoke in Russian. "Maybe we were seeing things."

"Both of us seeing the same thing? That's impossible," she said.

"Try not to worry."

"You don't get it." She didn't even know where to begin, but she tried. "The woman in this field, she said something about waves, right? And Chernobyl?" Daniel grimaced, nodded. Waves were the central part of the competition, too. Maxwell, his equations and his work were around electromagnetism—electromagnetic waves. There was a connection to that woman, and like the last time she appeared, it had to be signifi-cant. Raisa was sure. She couldn't explain it yet, but she would. "That woman knows things," Raisa said quietly. "I have to figure it out."

"Raisa, I believe you." Daniel nodded toward the van. "But it's getting late. Should we go home?" He unlocked the passenger door and held out a hand to help her step inside. He had never done that before. She took his hand and realized she had never touched him before, either, except for bumping into him at work, and she thought he felt solid, like he wasn't going anywhere. While she knew it was a strange thing to think about someone, about Daniel in particular, somehow it made Raisa feel good. "Raisa?" he said. "Why are you hesitating?"

She reached for the keys. "I'm driving home. You're too slow." They both laughed and he let go, climbed into the passenger seat himself. While Raisa drove she thought more about waves and Maxwell. It couldn't be a coincidence. She ran through her memories of that unspeakable day on the beach, the old woman's bleeding hands, the principal's face at school when he called her into his office and told her Papa was dead, Mama was in jail.

And then there was Chernobyl. It was strange to think of Chernobyl and Maxwell simultaneously. The connection was radiation, but Raisa couldn't see how it all mixed together, why the woman talked about the meltdown. All Raisa could think was she needed more information, that she didn't know enough to understand. A few miles along the expressway, traffic slowed. There was an accident near the ABC station and the van crawled past the lot where five giant satellite dishes gleamed. They had her thinking there was a way to study waves and electromagnetism with dishes like those. She had read about an experiment once in a journal.

"Do you mind if I stop at the library? I mean, before we go to work?" she asked Daniel. She needed books on Maxwell to research the idea forming in her head. "I'll just grab a few things."

"What's so important that you have to do it now?"

"What do you care, anyway? They're paying you by the hour."

There was a pause. "Yeah, sure, that's what I was worried about," he said.

Back in their neighborhood, Raisa turned into the library and pulled up to the curb, then handed Daniel the keys. "Meet me around back." Inside, it didn't take her long to find tomes covering electromagnetism. In a few minutes, she and Daniel were off to the Market. "Don't you want to know why you picked me up in the back?" Raisa asked.

"Probably not," he said. His lips tilted up to a hint of a smile.

"That's good." She felt the same small smile creeping over her face. He pulled the van into the alley behind the Market and parked. It was filled with dumpsters and wooden crates, plastic milk cartons. He pointed to the back wall of the butcher shop. An old mural was still there, the outlines of Atomic Anna and Mighty Minerva faded but clear. They were drawn on either side of the door and the door itself was a gleaming, glowing portal of some sort that they were both headed toward. "Who painted that? I've always wondered. And why do the characters look angry?"

"My mother. A long time ago," Raisa said, and slipped out quickly to cut off more questions.

Her grandfather ran toward them as they came to the door. Raisa heard him yelling to Baba that their granddaughter had won. The trophy was impossible to miss: tall and gaudy and fake gold. Raisa thought it was atrocious, but Pop-Pop loved it. He crushed her in his thick arms against his wide chest and brought her inside. She had been tense, scared since she saw that woman, and with him she could finally relax, lean in. He was safe. Baba was safe.

Pop-Pop knew her so well, he pulled back, looked her in the eye. Under the harsh fluorescents, the strings of broken blood vessels along the tops of his cheeks were brighter. "We're fine," he said. "Baba and I aren't going anywhere for a long, long time." Baba rushed out from behind the cash register, holding a hand towel. She threw it over her shoulder and kissed each of Raisa's cheeks twice.

"So proud," she said, and crushed her with a hug, too. Raisa lingered, slipped her hand into Baba's and leaned on her shoulder.

"She was really impressive," Daniel said. Raisa had almost forgotten he was there. He was so quiet, so gentle.

Baba leaned in and kissed his cheek. "Thank you for taking such good care of her."

"Please, Yulia. We paid him for it," Pop-Pop said.

"I would have taken her anyway," Daniel said. He sounded embarrassed but Raisa couldn't be sure. He was headed back to the Chopping Room.

"You're a good boy," Baba called; then she kissed Raisa again and asked for more details. Raisa told them about the fancy school and the problems being easy. She didn't dare mention the field or the old woman.

Baba put the trophy on her special shelf, next to the old photo she'd taken of her and Raisa the day she came home with them. The photo was taken in front of the van back when it was new. Baba stood with her arm around Raisa and while Raisa wasn't smiling, she remembered feeling flooded with relief that she'd found them and sadness for everything she'd lost, and how much she'd loved the old green sneakers she was wearing.

In the Chopping Room, Daniel told Raisa he would cover for her, that she could read the library books while he worked for both of them. "Really? Are you sure?" she asked.

"I can see it's important. And you had an idea while we were stuck in traffic, right?" he said. She nodded and still, she hesitated. She wasn't comfortable taking Daniel up on his offer. Was this what friends did for each other? She wrapped her apron ties around her waist and knotted them in the back. The cotton was stiff from bleach and smelled like chicken fat, a smell she could never escape unless she soaked her hands in vanilla. She tucked her hair into a plastic net and put on the metal glove that protected her fingers while she carved.

"I'll get to it later," she said to Daniel. Out front, Mrs. Mandel, the woman who ordered capon necks every week for her soup, was at the counter. Her voice was loud because she didn't hear well and so they heard her. "What kind of contest?" she asked.

"More than multiplication," Baba replied, equally loud. They went back and forth while Raisa pulled out a crate of chickens.

Mr. Kestler, the man who ordered two pounds of marrow bones every Sunday, called back through the curtain, "You make us all proud, Raisele."

Daniel slid a side of beef out from the cold room, dragged the carcass on a hook running on rails in the ceiling, and as they started to work, Raisa went back to the idea of waves. They dominated the universe, rode through and around everything that existed. How were they connected to Chernobyl? Daniel worked on the ribs. He was meticulous but fast. "Want to tell me about it, what's bothering you? The old woman?" He placed a slab of bones on the counter and waited for her to answer. Busy now, she found it easier to talk.

"Did you ever feel like you're meant to do something, but you can't figure out what?"

"No. I'm not like you. There's nothing I can do especially well."

"That can't be true."

"I've seen you tinkering, building radios, cable boxes. You work through things. You experiment and it helps. Trying again and again. That's what you need to do now."

She was surprised, again, at how well he knew her. "You pay attention to everything."

"To my friends." He smiled and her cheeks went warm.

"So we're friends?"

He laughed. "Of course. What's the experiment?"

"I do have an idea. Can you drive me to Radio Shack? Or grab the van so I can drive us? You know my grandfather won't give me the keys."

"Tomorrow?"

"No, but soon. Once I figure out what I need." He hesitated and she figured it was because he was supposed to work and money was tight for him and his mother. "I'll pay you."

"I won't take your money." He pulled the carving knife out from between the ribs he was working through. "But I'll drive you if you'll help me with math."

* * *

One week after the competition, Raisa hurried to get dressed for school while thunder clapped and lightning exploded so bright it made her room look like it was under a spotlight. The circuit boards and transistors, capacitors and diodes on her desk, parts for her cable boxes, glittered. "Electromagnetic waves," Raisa said to herself, thinking about Maxwell.

They were everywhere. Light itself was an electromagnetic phenomenon, streams of photons. And those streams were everywhere, in every inch of space: radio waves, X-rays, gamma waves. Raisa already knew how to build radios and cable boxes. From the library books she'd found, she realized she could use those skills and build a radio telescope to study waves coming from planets, stars, comets, and more. That was the idea that came to her on the expressway when she saw those satellite dishes. She could build a radio telescope. It would be small, but that's how all good experiments started. Raisa was going to figure out what that old woman was trying to say.

In the kitchen, Baba and Pop-Pop had herring, yogurt, and orange juice on the table. Baba stood at the counter nodding her head in time with the bells ringing on the radio. She had taped the program from the math competition to the refrigerator. Daniel must have given it to her. Raisa kissed her grandmother. "Can I do your hair now?" Raisa asked, wanting to be close.

"Not today. I'm tired. Eat." Baba pointed to the table. "I'll sit with you."

Raisa nodded and grabbed the orange juice, put it back in the refrigerator. She couldn't stand seeing it on the table. It made her think of Mama. "Stop buying this," she said as she slammed the fridge door. "I've asked so many times."

"I know, but you have to talk about her. Your mama loves you."

"Then why doesn't she write?"

"She sends comic books. That's her way of writing."

"Comic books are for kids," Raisa said.

After she ate, Raisa went for the door, checked her bangs, and made her way toward the bus stop. She found Daniel waiting under the graffiti-riddled plastic shelter. He usually rode the later bus, liked getting to school right when it started, not early like Raisa. Rain balanced on the ends of his brown hair. His jacket and boots were soaked.

"What are you doing here?" she asked.

"I thought I'd come early to talk about this afternoon. Radio Shack, right?" She nodded. The bus pulled up, and they jumped out of the way of the puddle it sliced and then got on, slid their tokens into the machine. They sat in seats across from each other.

"What do you want at Radio Shack? What's your plan?"

"Will you please speak English?"

"We're still in our neighborhood." He pointed through the window to the bagel store.

She continued in Russian because she had learned that week that no matter how good his English sounded, he wasn't comfortable in the language. "I'm going to build a radio telescope," she said. "I need the parts to build it. You were right. I need to experiment, and I figured it out. If I build this, I can study those waves that the old lady talked about. Remember, you heard that word, too. I think it was a reference to electromagnetic waves. Space-time."

He looked surprised, but he didn't laugh like kids at school probably would. "You really think we saw her, then?"

"I'm sure of it."

"And you're convinced it's important, that you really saw her before, too?" She nodded. "Where are you going to put it, the telescope?"

"On our roof."

"You're going to need more help with that, aren't you?"

The bus bucked and Raisa slid forward. "Maybe."

"What'll you tell your grandparents?"

"I'll tell them it has to do with the competition. That'll be enough."

"If I keep helping, you'll keep tutoring, right?"

"We haven't even started. You have no idea if I'm a good teacher."

"I already know you're better than anyone at school."

At Radio Shack the man working, Henry, stared at her like he always did, grinning as if she was the only girl who ever came into the store. She was glad Daniel was there. "What the hell are you up to now?" Henry asked after she handed him her parts list. His voice was too high-pitched for his size. The store was empty and it smelled of old grease, stale takeout. Cardboard displays dominated the floor. Daniel must have sensed Henry made Raisa nervous because he stood closer than usual. "We don't sell satellite dishes," Henry said.

"I've seen your back room. You have piles of them. The kind cable companies use."

"You know it's illegal for anyone to use them but the company."

"Cut the crap," Raisa said. "You steal them and sell them. Every penny is profit. I've seen you do it. And I have enough to pay for one." She surprised herself by being so forthright, but he was gross and he deserved it. Besides, she was using a little of her prize money; she was giving away a piece of her tuition.

He wiped his forehead with the back of his hand, looked at the front door like he was suddenly nervous. "Usually people place orders. They're all spoken for." Daniel stepped closer, not quite a threat but not friendly, either, and Henry took a deep breath. "But I'll sell you one."

He led Raisa and Daniel back to the loading dock. Behind the dumpster, covered in tarps, he had a stack of six satellite dishes that looked brand new. Raisa handed him one hundred dollars and he pointed to the one at the bottom. "All yours," he said. She bent down and picked it up. It wasn't so much heavy as it was awkward. When she stood up, she realized Henry had been watching her bend while Daniel glared at him. "Where's the LNB?" Raisa asked. That was the low-noise block, the nub that sat in the receiver and focused incoming rays.

"Yeah. Almost forgot."

"Bullshit," she said, and Henry laughed. He walked over to another tarp on the other side of the loading dock and dug out the part, along with the signal meter, coaxial cables, and connectors, handed them all to Daniel. "You need a computer to download everything."

She was going to build a basic model to aim the dish and another to receive and capture the signals. They wouldn't look pretty but they would do what she needed, maybe. Daniel must have noticed her hesitate. He stepped in. "How much for the computer?" he asked. "You want more money. That's what this is about, right? You want more money?" His accented English came with an edge that intimidated most Americans, and Raisa was glad for it in that moment. Henry put his hands up.

"Relax, man," Henry said. "What did you bring this guy for? Where you from, anyway?"

"None of your business," Daniel said.

"Fine," Henry said. "I won't charge much."

"You mean it won't cost anything more," Daniel said, walking toward Henry. "This is all profit for you. All stolen goods anyway. She paid you one hundred dollars. That's fair."

Henry stepped back, tripped on a cord connected to a fan. "Sure. Fine. It's all included." He reached under the tarp and pulled out a cardboard box that looked heavy and clunky. Daniel took it. "I'm not including any damn monitors."

"You sure?" Daniel said.

"One fucking monitor." Henry pointed to another tarp. "Make sure no one hears about this. No one."

"Sure, sure," Raisa said. By then they were using a hand truck, had everything piled on, and as they headed for the door, she wasn't sure if she was more excited by what they had just done or scared that Henry would come after Daniel with a bat. Outside, Raisa walked quickly while Daniel took his time. There wasn't a line of worry or fear in his face. "You're different," she said to Daniel after they had it all in the back of the van and she started the engine.

"How am I different?"

"I don't know. You're not scared. And you stood up to that creep. You're not like that at school or work. I mean, it's not like you're scared, more like you're indifferent, but here you were sticking up for us."

"That's because no one is trying to rip you or me off at school. That guy was disgusting."

She laughed, felt herself loosen. "I could have handled it on my own, you know."

"I know, but it's better with me. I mean, better not to be alone."

She looked at him and he didn't look away. He really had confidence in her, that she could handle it even though she wasn't sure she could. "Anyway. Thanks for coming," she said awkwardly.

"No big deal." Daniel smiled and she realized she was having fun, despite Henry's sliminess. She hadn't spent time with anyone but her grandparents in years—and she liked being with Daniel, the way he stuck up for her and made her smile. She turned at the light. "Can we go to the library?" he asked. "We don't have to be at work for another hour and you could start tutoring me."

"Are you sure you don't have something else to do?"

"Something better than passing math?" And then, "Come on. Please?"

She agreed and felt giddy as she parked. Not only did she have the equipment she needed, but she had a friend. She'd never walked inside the library with anyone before, was sure the librarians would notice. And they did; they waved. One raised her eyebrows. Raisa took Daniel to the back stairwell that led up to the private study rooms and found a nook that was open.

"I don't understand the idea of a proof. If an answer is correct, why does it require proof?" Daniel said.

Raisa dug into her bag and pulled out a pencil and a piece of paper. Daniel didn't just need a tutor. He needed a teacher to start at the beginning.

"One person knowing an answer isn't enough," Raisa said. "You need someone else to check your work, confirm the answer. Otherwise, you could be wrong. A proof is something everyone can agree on." She continued, "I like proofs because they show we don't always know the answers. They can fail. Like, Isaac Newton. For hundreds of years everyone took his ideas as gospel. Then Einstein threw it all out the window. Using logic—and proofs—he showed gravity isn't just a force that pulls an apple to the ground."

"I didn't know that."

"That's because people still aren't comfortable with it. And gravity. We don't really understand how it fits in. It's such a weak force, but it's everywhere. Anyway, that's where proofs come in. We can theorize that gravity exists, but math and proofs explain how." Raisa leaned back and organized her thoughts, ran a fingernail over one of the symbols carved into the desk, a stylized *P*, for the Phillies. "Gravity can change time. That's what Einstein discovered." She paused. "Change time. Isn't that incredible?"

"That doesn't make sense."

"It defies logic. In order to understand it, we have to think beyond what we know. We have to step outside of the problem, think from a different angle. He showed that gravity alters how we understand the world. Here on Earth, we think we can mark ten years. But what we mark and experience as ten years, a woman in a black hole might mark and experience as a second, or half a second. See what I mean, it defies logic, but it's right?"

Daniel sat back and pressed his lips together. "That's brilliant, Raisa."

"I didn't make it up. Einstein did."

"Yes. But not everyone can explain it." He pushed the math book between them. "The Pythagorean theorem. Can we start there?"

This was something Daniel should have learned years ago. Where he had looked so confident earlier, in front of Henry, now he looked small, embarrassed.

He held his pencil so tight his fingertips went white. The point hovered over the paper. "You don't know where to start?" she asked.

He shook his head. "English," he said. His voice was so quiet. "I...I know words on the bus, in the halls. I can hang out with kids. But the words teachers use, they don't make sense. Hypotenuse? Every time it comes up, I have to remember. By the time I have its meaning, the teacher is two steps ahead and I lost everything in between."

"It's nothing to be ashamed of."

"But you, you speak perfect English."

"I was born here."

"But you speak Russian like you were born there."

She realized then that though they'd spent so many hours together, she had no idea how much he was struggling, how hard his days must have been, feeling lost in every class.

"We'll go slowly. I know you can do this." He was smart. She had seen him add and multiply easily in the Chopping Room. He filled orders, manipulated fractions without pause, had learned the anatomy of every animal, how to hold the knife, when to force the blade, when to relent. "We'll work in Russian."

MOLLY

Mount Aragats

olly couldn't sleep. She couldn't concentrate or even eat because all she could think about was Raisa. Anna said she had saved her, only Molly couldn't fathom what she had been saved from, how bad her life had been, and Anna wouldn't tell her. She said it wasn't worth introducing memories of something that no longer existed. But that wasn't good enough. Molly needed to make sure Raisa was okay. She'd already made so many mistakes, she had to try to take care of her daughter now.

Molly had seen Anna activate the time machine enough to know how it worked, and she used it while Anna was sleeping. For the first time, instead of watching, she experienced the flash of light and the thud when she pulled the trigger. There was a vibration that shot through her from her toes to her head, then she felt herself stretching, thought she might be pulled apart, but then she saw static, and black and nothing. She opened her eyes after what couldn't have been more than a few seconds and found herself in Mama and Papa's house in Little Russia in 1981. She'd traveled back eleven years to catch Raisa right after Molly had been arrested. Raisa would have only been with her grandparents for a few days and she would have been starting at her new school. Molly wanted to be there when Raisa got home, to kiss her and apologize, only the machine still wasn't precise enough. She'd landed in the old living room just as the clock on the sideboard flipped to ten a.m. Raisa wouldn't be home for another four hours. Molly would miss her.

"Damn it," she said, feeling like a fool. Somehow she had spent her whole life that way, just a little late or a little early, working a little too hard or not quite hard enough. Her hands were slightly burned and they hurt. The newly designed amplifier in the box on her belt was sleek and light, nothing like the old satchel Anna used to carry.

Molly started walking through the living room. The house looked exactly the same as it had the day she left, with the mustard-colored wall-to-wall carpet, the velour couches, and the rosebushes. Memories came for her, had her thinking about the day they moved into the house, going to the flea market to find furniture, bumping into her parents in the cramped kitchen and sneaking cigarettes in the narrow alley behind the building. She thought about all of it in flashes as she made her way through the dining room, thinking about the last Shabbat dinner she'd had with Viktor. He'd never admitted he was drunk that night and it still bothered her that she'd ignored it and even made excuses. She'd still believed him when she should have been smarter about him, about all of her choices. As she walked, she trailed her fingers on the smooth, worn dining room table. Hanging on the wall, above the samovar, was the drawing of the two bears she had made after seeing that woman in Wanamaker's—Anna, she knew now.

"Mollushka!"

Molly let out a yelp. Her mama's voice came from the stairs and scared her. She didn't think anyone was at home, and hearing her mother after all that time made her think, for a moment, that she was a teenager again, like she was getting caught sneaking into the house too late. "Mama?" Molly said quietly. She was sure Mama would be angry about all her mistakes, but in a heartbeat Molly was enclosed in one of her mother's tight, full-body hugs, the kind she had hated as a teenager. It used to feel overwhelming, but now it was what Molly wanted and she fell into it, leaned hard.

"I miss you every single day," Mama said. She angled her head back to get a better look. "You look older." She squinted. "You found Anna. Her machine."

"You know about all of that?"

"Wanamaker's, remember? You must have put it all together by now." And then, "What year did you come from?"

"Nineteen ninety-two."

Mama pulled her even closer. "My god, you're alive. You're out of prison and still alive." She kissed the top of her head, her cheeks, her neck, and even her hands.

"I'm fine. Where's Papa?" Yulia and Lazar were rarely apart.

"I told him I wasn't feeling well so I could make him a surprise. Don't you remember—"

"It's his birthday." Of course. She couldn't believe she hadn't thought about that.

Mama hugged Molly again. "I'm proud of you. So proud. You've been through too much."

Molly couldn't believe what she was hearing. It brought on a wave of relief that her mother wasn't angry, but also regret and her own indignation. "Why weren't you proud of me before?"

"I've always been proud of you. You...you just never heard me say it. I'm sorry I didn't make my voice louder. Being a mother, you never know what's right until it's too late." Mama kissed her again. "What matters is that you're here and you're clean. And I'm proud of you."

"It wasn't easy, it's not easy," Molly admitted. She still thought about alcohol, the drugs every day, every hour, sometimes every minute. When she was angry or bored, tired or cold, she thought about getting high or drunk. It was simpler than being sober. And without a sponsor, she had to go to Anna when she needed to talk about the pull. At first Anna didn't understand, but she'd come around and listened without passing judgment. She even listened to Molly telling her about the times she thought about jumping off the cliffs of Aragats. It would have been easier, she told Anna.

"Easier for who?" Anna shook her head when Molly said that. "Life isn't easy. Stop always talking about easy." Molly had come to think Anna was right in that. Molly was always looking for easy and it didn't exist. She wanted to tell Anna that, only she had changed after that last jump. She was colder, didn't listen in the same way. And her mind was going. She left the stove on, forgot to button her blouse or even to eat sometimes.

"Anna's not well," Molly said. "The time travel, it's killing her, eating her mind. Why don't you look surprised?"

"Because I'm not. I told her years ago time travel was a dangerous idea. She never listened to me. It wasn't the technology that I thought was dangerous. It's the whole idea. I knew, really knew, that one way or another it would take her. Time travel. It's crazy that we're even talking about it, that she did it, built that damn machine." Mama crossed her arms over her chest. Tears were starting in her eyes. "I love her."

"I know." Molly nodded as the memories from her life in that house continued washing over her. "I was a fool to hate my time here," she said to her mother.

"You were a teenager."

Molly took a deep breath and said the words she'd wanted to say for years. "I'm sorry."

Mama looked her in the eye. "Life is about choices, and no matter which ones you make, I love you. Don't ever apologize for going one way or another, just know you can always change. You're living proof of that, aren't you? I've learned from my mistakes, too. Your papa and I, we both did. We should have let you do what made you happy, not what we thought was best." She led Molly to the living room and they sank low into the couches, the cushions giving way.

Tears started running down Molly's cheeks.

Yulia leaned in to wipe them, to hold Molly. "More than anything, we have to keep looking forward, for Raisa."

"But why couldn't we apologize or speak this way before?" Molly said. "And why didn't I realize what I had? You and Papa, you were always there for me. You were always at home or the Market where I could find you, and I never lived a day in this house when I didn't feel safe. I didn't give Raisa any of that."

"You gave her more than you think."

Molly had so much more she wanted to talk about, ask about. She wanted to tell Mama about all the ways Molly wanted to be like her. She wanted to tell her everything she regretted. She also wanted to tell her that she was healing, that she loved and hated Anna and was more grateful than she ever would have anticipated for their time together. Most of all, she wanted to share all the things she wished she could do for Raisa. "I came back for Raisa. I don't want her to be angry, to hate me. I need to talk to her, to tell her everything will be okay. She's such an anxious child. I need her to know she's going to be all right."

"You can't do all of that."

"Because she's at school? I'll go. I'll find her class. I need to see her."

"What would you say? 'I'm here for half an hour and then I'll disappear again for a long, long time'? Think about how it will make her feel, what it would do to her. Do you think she'll understand? Do you think she'll jump into your arms and everything will be okay?"

"Now you're being cruel."

"No. I'm treating you like an adult, like an equal, the way I should have treated you. And I'm keeping her safe. You can't see her and disappear. It will only make things worse."

"Mama, you're wrong."

"You know I'm not. Please, just let me hug you for a little longer." She held on tighter and Molly didn't fight it. She leaned into her mother in silence, thinking about what she'd said. Molly had rushed up to the tower, jumped through time to see Raisa because she told herself it would help her daughter, but now, she realized Mama was right. It would confuse her, likely make her more angry when Molly disappeared again. This whole idea, the jump, was selfish.

"I guess...I came for myself," Molly whispered through her shame. She'd come to assuage her own guilt, to make herself feel better. "I'm still an idiot," she said.

"No." Mama kissed her. "Raisa loves you. She just needs time. And you, you're healing. You need time, too."

"I need her to know I love her, that I think about her every single day."

"Then draw for her, keep drawing for her. She loves your comic books. She won't admit it but I caught her up late last night reading them." Mama smiled and squeezed Molly's hand. "I think if she could wallpaper her room with them, she would."

"Wait," Molly said. She pushed out of the cushions and stood up. "Draw for her. You're right. I should draw for her. Do you still have my old paints in the basement? My supplies?"

Mama said of course and Molly ran down to the basement to collect what she could, then upstairs to her old bedroom, which was now Raisa's. It was different. A small brass bed was along the far wall, tucked under the window. A white desk was next to it, along with matching drawers. Molly checked the stopwatch. One hour and four minutes. That was all she had. "Help me?" Molly said to her mother. She needed to move the desk and drawers away from the wall.

Mama smiled and went to hold one side of the desk. "What's your plan?"

"I'm going to draw for her. A mural like the one I made on the outside wall, in the alley, at the butcher shop." She grabbed a pencil and began to sketch. She planned to paint the Radioactives for Raisa: Atomic Anna, Mighty Minerva, and Rocket Raisa. She worked quickly and Mama stood nearby, watching every pencil mark and brushstroke.

"Three superheroes," Mama said. "It's perfect."

"I thought I'd add you as a fourth."

"No. This is for you, Anna, and Raisa. Not me." Mama smiled. "I want to see the three of you happy that way, together." She lingered there next to Molly, handing her paints and brushes when she needed them. "You have found some kind of peace, finally, and that's all I ever wanted. Just be careful. You think you want answers, but sometimes it's best to leave the past in the past."

"Maybe," Molly said. She had never felt closer to her mother. "I really love you." At that, Mama's smile reached her eyes, her whole body, and Molly felt calmer than she had in years.

RAISA

Philadelphia

'm upstairs," Raisa yelled to Daniel from her room. It was late fall, a month after they had been to Radio Shack together, and he was there to help her install the dish on the roof. It had taken her all that time to build the computer and program she needed to track the data she wanted to collect, and to retrofit the dish to collect it. She didn't think she would be able to receive actual cosmic rays, but any information would help her learn. It was unusually warm and the leaves had turned, so having the window open, wearing short sleeves, felt off. The door was unlocked and she heard Daniel let himself in and take the stairs two at a time. "Raisa? Where are you?"

"Turn left. Second door," she called. He was wearing shorts. He never wore shorts, and she found herself staring at the wisps of black hair on his legs.

"What?" he asked. "Did I wear the wrong clothes?"

"No." She turned her back so he wouldn't see her turn red.

"Sorry I'm late. Nina showed up." Nina was in Daniel's homeroom and she was curved in every way Raisa wanted to be but wasn't. "I had to carry a brisket to her apartment for her."

"Is that all you did for her?" Raisa meant it to sound like a joke, but it came out sounding mean. "I'm sorry," she said.

"Are you jealous? You know, I'm not into her." Raisa only nodded. Nina was one of half a dozen girls from school who had him carrying chickens and anything else from the store home for them. Raisa could never compete; she wasn't nearly as beautiful.

"Of course I'm not jealous."

"Okay. So, all that is going up to the roof?" He pointed to the far corner where she had a pile of wires, cables, and the dish stacked and ready. Then he took a few steps into her room and stopped when he saw the mural. It was partially blocked by a privacy screen with a cheap Japanese print peeling off the front. Raisa had bought the screen at the flea market to hide the painting, but it wasn't perfect and Daniel pulled it away to get a better look. "What is that?"

"Nothing. It doesn't matter." Mama had come, somehow, soon after she was arrested. Baba said the courts gave her twenty-four hours to get her things in order. It was just after Raisa moved in and Mama had painted it without even bothering to see Raisa. It was just like her mother, Raisa thought, to slink away without saying hello or goodbye. If Raisa had been braver, she would have painted over it. "I hate it," Raisa said. "They're my mother's characters. She calls them the Radioactives. They're the women on the back of the store. It's all stupid. Made up. She wrote all of these books and no one ever published them. She used to read them to me every night."

"You used to like them?"

"Yes," she admitted. "They used to make me feel like there was something special about our family, but it was ridiculous." She pointed to the background, to a building and mountains that spanned her wall from the window to the corner. "This is their hideout on top of a mountain. It's supposed to be an old Russian station where Atomic Anna worked on nuclear science. The USSR has a bunch of top-secret weapons sites."

He leaned closer and ran a finger over the youngest character's hair. "She looks like you. What's her name?"

"Rocket Raisa. Anyway, we should get to work."

"The old comic books, do you still have them?"

"Yes." She kept them in her closet in a box she'd decorated just for them. She used to think the box was the most beautiful thing she'd ever made, covered in glitter and gold foil, but now she thought it was as dumb as the comics themselves and she didn't want Daniel to see anything so juvenile. "I haven't looked at them in a while and—" She stopped herself abruptly, because she had never told anyone that much. "I don't like to talk about my mother."

"Where is she?" Daniel asked.

"Prison." It was the first time Raisa said it out loud in years, and while it made her nervous to admit it, Daniel was the one who looked embarrassed. "Did you see the framed bears downstairs? My mother drew them, too. I love those. The bear at war, the bear at peace. They're not her style, not like anything else she made." Raisa looked down, shook her head. "We should get started."

"I didn't mean to push," Daniel said.

"It doesn't matter." It did, but she just wanted to stop talking about her mother. Raisa walked toward the pile of equipment. Daniel followed, pulling out a rope from his bag.

"We can't climb a roof without a rope. It's not safe."

"How do you know about ropes?"

"It's for the army. I want to be in special forces one day. They use ropes, so I learned."

Raisa was surprised. "You want to be in the army. Why? To kill people?"

"It's not that simple," he said as he started packing her wires into his backpack. "Killing is the last thing I want to do, but sometimes you have to scare people to keep them from killing you. You know, counter a threat with a threat. It's what the Soviet Union and America do to one another. By pretending you want to kill, you don't have to do it."

"Mutually assured destruction," Raisa said. She knew that was what it was called but she didn't believe in it. She'd realized that while reading *Atomic Anna*. The characters in the comic books tried to make the same argument, but Anna kept building more and more weapons even after she had more than enough to destroy the world a dozen times over. "If you build a weapon, or join an army, it's because you want to fight. That means you need to be ready to kill someone, or support people who are doing the killing. If not right away, then one day."

"I think you're wrong, but we should keep talking about it." He finished tying a rope around his waist, held up another to tie around hers. She had watched him butcher and slaughter. He was aggressive with the knife, but as he tied the rope around her, there was a new softness to him. His hands were calloused, but they moved gently. His knuckles brushed her stomach. She hoped he didn't see her suck in her breath, or that she started to sweat. He'd never been that close before and she liked it more than she would have anticipated. She took in the smell of his deodorant, what must have been his aftershave, and she thought about those wisps of hair on his legs. "You okay?" he asked.

"Fine," she said, and tried to shake it off. They climbed up into the attic and secured the ropes to the rafters. Raisa took the pack and Daniel carried the dish. They climbed through the window and onto the eaves, made their way to the expanse Raisa calculated had the best exposure. Every few feet Daniel adjusted the ropes. Instead of the temperature cooling off as the sun dipped, it got hotter. Raisa felt the skin on the back of her neck burning when she started drilling holes as leads to bolt down the dish. Across the street there was the thwack of a baseball on a bat, and then a thud as the ball hit something it shouldn't. Whatever it was toppled.

"What the fuck!" yelled Leonid, the father across the street. Raisa knew his boys were about to be smacked, that they would cry. She jumped when she heard it happen. Daniel took over, finished tightening the screws for her.

"In the Soviet Union you live on top of several families at once. You hear things like that enough that you learn to block it out."

"You should never block that out. You don't want to be numb to that, do you?"

"You have to," he said, finishing up.

Raisa started connecting the wires. When she was done, she sat back with Daniel. From this new angle, looking out over the rooftops, she saw that the house was worn, the paint peeling near the roof. She closed her eyes and tilted her head back toward the last remnants of sun. Daniel took his shirt off and she drank him in. His stomach was tight like his arms and there were thin hairs on his chest that matched the ones on his legs.

"What? It's hot," he said. "Tell me why this is so important to you. Not just this project but school, too. Why do you work so hard?"

Before, when her grandparents asked the same question, she'd shrugged. It wasn't just that she wanted good grades, it was that she wanted answers. She didn't know when her mother was coming back, if she was coming back. She didn't know anything about her family's past in the Soviet Union, or even why they left. She knew Mama was adopted, but not why or how. There were so many things she didn't know—at least there were concrete reasons for most phenomena when it came to math and science. And working hard gave her a way to focus and stay calm. "I like explanations," she said.

Raisa had never talked about her childhood before, and she didn't understand why, but sitting there with him, she wanted him to know just a little. "I started grocery shopping for my mother a long time ago. She would forget to buy milk, cereal. Fish sticks. I loved fish sticks. And I was always hungry." Not just for food, for Mama's attention, for company, but she couldn't admit that to Daniel. "When I was little, I had to walk myself to school. Mama and Papa were too high." She took a deep breath and closed her eyes to make it easier. "My kindergarten teacher was the first person to really help me. Somehow my parents got it together to sign me up and take me for my first day. By then I could read a clock and a calendar. Once I knew my way to school, I knew I had to be there every Monday through Friday at eight a.m. I didn't know when we had vacation days, so I showed up every single weekday. I didn't have anything else. My kindergarten teacher recognized how thin I was. She called Mama, asked her to meet at the school, but Mama never came. My teacher told me that if my mother wasn't coming, she would take care of me herself. At first, I thought that meant she wanted to take me to her home and that scared me. I mean, my parents weren't around, but they were my parents." Raisa forced a smile, looked at Daniel and saw he was listening.

She kept going. "My teacher walked me to the church next door. The two ladies who worked in the back office didn't care that I was Jewish. They held out their arms and told me if I came before school, they would give me breakfast every day. After school they would give me a big snack so I wouldn't be hungry in case I didn't get dinner. Bonnie and Vivian. I haven't thought about them in years. They told me I was safer at home and spending time with them than I was in the system, that nosy neighbors and teachers did more harm than good most of the time. So long as I kept coming to them, wasn't home alone all afternoon every day, I wouldn't have to go to a foster home."

"Raisa, I had no idea."

"It's not a big deal." She stopped. "I mean, it was. But those women saved me because they took care of me. Bonnie was from Puerto Rico. She kept her hair back in a handkerchief and wore a jean skirt every day. Vivian wore big, elaborate wigs that never sat straight. They gave me clothes from their donation piles. Mama and Papa never said anything because I don't think they even noticed. Bonnie and Vivian taught me to tie my shoes, brush my teeth and hair. 'Sometimes God gives children parents who watch too closely, and sometimes he gives them parents who don't watch at all,' Bonnie said that first day I met her. There was a tray of muffins behind her and I was hungry. She told me I could eat as many as I wanted. They were blueberry and chocolate. 'The ones who have parents who watch too closely, they'll never learn anything. You think they're lucky. They're not. It's the ones like you, with busy parents, you're the strongest and smartest because you've got to learn to survive on your own. You'll be just fine.' That's what Bonnie said." Raisa dropped her head down to her hands and pictured them, Bonnie and Vivian, could still see them and smell the cream they slathered on their skin. "The morning my father died and my mom went to prison, I was wearing this pair of green sneakers. They were my favorites and Bonnie and Vivian had given them to me. I don't even know why I'm telling you this, about those sneakers, but I can't think about that day without thinking about those shoes. I was so proud of them."

"You were lucky to have Bonnie and Vivian."

"I was." She looked at him. "My grandparents showed me there's more to life than surviving. I don't know much of what they lived through, but enough to know they're qualified to say that." She looked out over the roof, at the smoke coming from the neighbor's grill, and wondered if she had said too much. "Anyway, you know that woman we saw on that soccer field? I saw her before. The day everything fell apart, when my dad died and Mama went to prison. She mentioned Chernobyl then, too, before anyone had ever heard of it."

Daniel sat up and leaned closer. "What are you talking about?"

"When I lived in Atlantic City, that woman. I saw her and she said it then, too. Chernobyl. I forgot about it or pushed it away. A lot happened the day I saw her, but then on the news I saw the meltdown happened and I remembered it. I couldn't believe it. I mean, why was she talking about it before 1986? It's like she was warning me or something, but I didn't tell anyone. I was too scared my grandparents would think I'd gone crazy." She took a deep breath and pointed to the dish. "That's why I'm building this. To learn about it, maybe figure it out, whatever she was saying. The waves and space-time, it all goes together with Chernobyl. Somehow." She looked down at her hands. They were clenched in fists. "Do I sound totally insane?"

Daniel looked her straight in the eye. "No. You sound brilliant. And if you think this is important, then it is. Period. You don't have to be worried about how it sounds." He looked out over the rooftops. "Chernobyl killed my sister, Vera, and my father. It's why we came here, to America."

PART V

Where do you come from?…
Where are you going?…
Before whom will you have to give
an account of reckoning?

—Pirkei Avot

RAISA

March 1988

Four Years Before Molly Dies on Mount Aragats

Philadelphia

Raisa's data collection was marred by fits and stops. Several times she had to climb back up to the roof to adjust the angle or clean the dish. Still, information came. She was able to image the sun during cloudy days and clear days. She picked up satellites in orbit and then set her sights on other objects. Every day, after school and work, she hurried home to check her data. She compared results in warmer temperatures to results taken during snow and rain. She thought she found something she couldn't quite explain, and she needed more data to understand it, but by March, the dish stopped working. She didn't know if it was because the computer she was using wasn't powerful enough, the satellite dish was a piece of crap, or the software she'd programmed wasn't up to the task. Frankly, it didn't matter. What mattered was she was getting nowhere, and she was frustrated. She needed to find a better way to learn and experiment, and she found it by chance one day at work.

Two weeks after disassembling the dish on her grandparents' roof, while Mr. Kestler was ordering marrow bones, she heard him complaining about the old derelict Public Broadcasting Service building he owned just off the edge of Penn's campus. He had been trying to sell or rent it for two years, but had no takers because of the hideous satellite dish on the roof. That comment was enough for Raisa.

"Mr. Kestler?" She stepped out from behind the curtain that separated the Chopping Room from the front of the store. Baba and Mr. Kestler both looked surprised. "Can I talk to you?"

"Anytime," Mr. Kestler said. He came behind the counter and into the back with her. Mr. Kestler was short, thin, and pale, but what he lacked in stature, he made up for with his voice. It was a deep, loud rumble. "What can I do for you?"

Raisa tried to stand tall, knew what she was about to ask would sound ridiculous. High schoolers didn't make these kinds of requests. Still, she couldn't back down. "It's about that building you own, up near Penn. The one you were just complaining about."

"The old PBS station?"

"Yes. You see…" Her nails were digging into her palms. She forced herself to just say it. "I'm studying electromagnetism. Telescopes." She shook her head, knew she had to do a better job explaining, even though she was feeling more and more nervous that she was doing this. "I want to understand electromagnetic waves. To do that, I need a big dish like the one on that old building, and I need space to install smaller dishes near it."

He crossed his arms over his chest. "That old thing hasn't been used in years."

"I can fix it. And I can pay you for it." She still had the money from the math contest. Surely using some would be worth it.

"Pay me?" He waved a hand to dismiss the idea. "I won't take your money. You're Yulia and Lazar's granddaughter. The problem is I don't know if it's safe."

"It is. I know how to make it work."

As she told him why, explained some of the details and her ideas, he slowly came around. "Okay. Meet me there next Sunday morning at nine. Bring Daniel. I don't want you in that neighborhood alone."

One week later, at 8:15 a.m., Raisa stood outside Daniel's apartment, waiting. Daniel had agreed to come, but he was already thirty minutes late. His mother was at work. She cleaned houses downtown and left by seven a.m. every single day. "Daniel!" Raisa called as she banged on the door with her fist. "Daniel." She was about to knock again when he opened the door. He wore checkered pajama pants and no shirt. His hair was loose, not slicked back like usual, and she saw for the first time that he had curls. Not tight corkscrews like her, but waves.

"I'm sorry I overslept," he said. "I was up late training."

"For what?"

"Army. After high school, I'm joining the army, remember?"

She nodded. "But what about college?"

"I'm not college material. You know that. Hold on. I'll get dressed." Raisa waited on the deflated red couch that doubled as Daniel's bed. The apartment was spare, but it felt warm to Raisa, smelled like her grandparents' and was filled with pictures. There was one of Daniel and his mother at a McDonald's, pointing to the sign, more American than America, only neither was smiling. There were pictures of someone who must have been his sister, Vera, and others of his parents at their wedding. They looked like a happy family in the USSR, but in America Daniel's mother was more stooped, like she carried the weight of her dead daughter and husband on her back. In later American photos, Daniel started to grin, but his smile didn't reach his eyes the way it did in the photos from the USSR.

She and Daniel headed to the back alley for the van. When they got there, everything looked normal. The mural was faded, the dumpster was full, and the mice and rats scurried as they approached. Except the passenger door of the van was open. The lock hadn't been working well, but no one ever went back there or would want that old beat-up van. Daniel looked inside.

"Did you leave this here?" he said, pulling out a new issue of *Atomic Anna*, one Raisa had never seen. She took it from him. Atomic Anna and Mighty Minerva were up in their secret lair on the mountain and Atomic Anna was ill. She was lying on a mattress and Mighty Minerva was cradling her head in her lap, helping her drink tea. Atomic Anna's hands were burned, but that wasn't the real problem. *I can't remember*, the speech bubble said above her. Below, the text explained that Atomic Anna had tried to fix her time machine, but she couldn't remember what she had done, what had gone wrong. Something about the machine was killing her mind, slowly destroying her body, and she needed help fixing it. Soon. She and Mighty Minerva were working to stop the Chernobyl meltdown and they were running out of time. December 8, 1992, was their deadline, but the comic book didn't say why, Atomic Anna said only that they had to stop Chernobyl before then. She'd traveled forward in time, witnessed something terrible she needed to prevent on that day. Under the speech bubble, someone had written a message in handwriting Raisa didn't recognize. *Raisa, help me.* Below that was a set of equations.

"Where did this come from?" she asked, her voice pitched high with alarm. The ink was so fresh it looked like it might smear. Only Mama could have made the comic and left it there. That meant she had been in the alley. It was the only rational explanation, but why would she come so early? Why leave a comic book in the van and not even come inside? "Where is she?" Raisa asked, running from one side of the alley to the next, peering down the street.

"No one else is here," Daniel said, sounding concerned. He was right. Raisa didn't see anyone and that made her realize her mother had done it again. Mama left a message without having the guts to even say hello. "My mother made this for me, and left it without seeing me." She held up *Atomic Anna*. "Who else could?"

Daniel gestured around the alley, confused. "If she's locked up, they wouldn't let her out to deliver a comic book. Think, Raisa. It doesn't make sense. She couldn't have dropped it off. Maybe she sent it to your grandparents, and your Pop-Pop left it there? Sometimes he sneaks into the van when he needs a break. You've seen that, right?"

She had. "But this is different. This is meant for me. Look." She pointed to the equations, to Atomic Anna saying she needed Raisa's help. "This is all related to Maxwell, to the work I'm doing now. And it says Atomic Anna worked at Chernobyl, is working now on a mountain-top somewhere to go back in time and stop the meltdown. That she survived. That can't be true. It's crazy." She was speaking quickly. "But it's not in the van by accident. I don't understand. None of it makes sense." She was shaking and he put both of his hands over hers. They were so warm, padded with calluses from work, and they steadied her in a way she didn't expect, made her calm down faster than she would have on her own.

"The simplest answer is almost always right. That's what you tell me," Daniel said. He wasn't laughing at her or making fun the way anyone else would. He believed her, seemed to really want to help. "The simple answer is that your grandfather left it in the van. And your mother, she wants your help. That means she wants you to visit her in prison. That's all. Stopping Chernobyl, what Soviet doesn't dream about that? It's an easy fairy tale. Let's think about it while we drive or we'll be late."

She hesitated, tried to think of an alternate explanation, but nothing came because Daniel was right. A simple answer made sense. Of course *Atomic Anna* didn't have anything to do with the real Chernobyl, and of course Mama was still in prison. She didn't get days off, couldn't deliver a comic book. And Raisa knew the day she was due to get out and it was still months away.

Raisa handed Daniel the keys. She was too upset to drive and she wanted to read the comic. Atomic Anna was tinkering with her time machine. It used nuclear power to access ripples in space-time. The ripples were rolling at a steep angle that burned her hands as she traveled through them, perhaps also were breaking down her core molecular structure. It was Rocket Raisa who had realized that problem by comparing the ripples to waves in the ocean. There was even a frame where a young Rocket Raisa stood next to an old Atomic Anna staring at the ocean. Rocket Raisa pointed to the surf. *The waves are sharp like glass. If you break through, you'd shatter the glass and they'd hurt you. Maybe cut your skin and make you bleed.* Atomic Anna was working to correct the angles. She was certain Rocket Raisa was right, that was why her hands burned, why her brain function was diminishing, but she couldn't figure out why on her own. She needed Rocket Raisa to come back and help her again so they could stop Chernobyl together. Rocket Raisa was the only person she trusted, the only person brilliant enough to figure out how to fix her machine so it stopped harming the people using it. "It says Atomic Anna is dying, that she needs Rocket Raisa's help. That's me. She's asking for my help. Like I'm the character in this comic book. She's even using my idea, something I said a long time ago."

"I told you, you look like the Rocket Raisa in the mural on your wall. It's you. It's your mother asking for you."

"But the stuff in here, a part about waves being like glass, it's something I said to that old woman on the beach. The same old woman we saw in that field. My mother never heard any of it. That's what's so weird. What if it's Anna, Mama's mother, asking for help?"

"I thought Baba Yulia is your mother's mother?"

"It's complicated," Raisa said. She leaned back in the seat and watched the city pass by. Simple answers were almost always correct, she told herself over and over. The van bumped through potholes. She must have told her mother about the conversation somehow. She saw her once after she was arrested and her mother looked dazed, high.

They were in a blank, sterile, white room and Mama didn't say a word. Raisa filled the silence by babbling and she must have talked about that old woman on the beach, the waves. She must have explained that was how she found her grandparents. Yes, that had to be it. Daniel was right, she decided. Mama drew the comic book and sent it home. Pop-Pop likely left the issue in the van, and probably left the door open, too. Without another hypothesis, she accepted it and turned her attention back to Kestler, to the PBS building. She forgot about the date and the equations, even the message.

The old headquarters were wedged into a neighborhood lined with dilapidated row houses. Most were Victorians, marked by picture windows and wooden flourishes that must have been gorgeous in their day but now were stripped down to husks and had become crack dens. Men stood on street corners, dealers or lookouts. When the van pulled up to the building, Mr. Kestler was already waiting. "Damn it," Raisa said. "I hate being late."

"We're early," Daniel said. "It's eight fifty-five."

"On time is late."

The front of Mr. Kestler's building was barred by a fence topped with razor wire and secured with three locks, each on a cord that wouldn't split with regular bolt cutters. "Raisa! Daniel!" Mr. Kestler called. He opened the gate one lock at a time and ushered them inside. "Don't touch anything," he said as they walked through the front door. "We'll go straight up to the roof." The lighting was haphazard. Only one out of every few bulbs worked; most buzzed and blinked. She didn't see rats, but she imagined they scuttled over the linoleum. She didn't even realize she was walking so close to Daniel until she bumped into him at the stairwell.

"It's okay," he whispered. He put an arm on her elbow and she felt herself relax just a touch, didn't even realize she'd been that nervous. They climbed seven stories and onto the roof. Stepping outside, she saw Philadelphia from an angle she had never experienced before. The buildings all around were low enough that Raisa had a panoramic view. Then there was the dish itself. It was bigger than she'd imagined, at least thirty feet in diameter. It was a beauty beaten by time and weather and Raisa couldn't imagine anything more perfect. She stepped closer, her feet crunching on ground asphalt, and ran her hand over the bottom lip. It was hot to the touch and rough, like sandpaper, but to Raisa it gleamed.

"I wanted to strip it and sell the parts, but no one wants them," Mr. Kestler said.

"Is there electricity?" Raisa asked.

"Lenny, he comes to the Market on Fridays. He tapped in, quietly, for you. He owed me a favor." Mr. Kestler pointed to a wire dangling off the end of a pole near the dish. "You can't use much. Little bit and no one will notice."

"It's fantastic," Raisa said. "Just what I need."

They shook and the deal was done.

"That was stupid, Raisa," Daniel said on their way back, inside the van. "Illegal electricity? You can't use it."

"He said no one's looking."

"How would he know? We can't afford to break the law in this country." Daniel was driving again. He slammed the accelerator and they stormed onto Roosevelt Boulevard. "I can't be involved. And you shouldn't do this. When people say things like 'Don't worry, no one will notice,' like Mr. Kestler, you should run. Governments change. Ideas change. They like Jews here now; they won't forever."

"Come on, listen to yourself. You can't really believe that."

"I do." They drove in silence the rest of the way and Raisa sat stewing in her own head, unsure what to say, scared this would be the end of their friendship because she'd never really fought with anyone other than Mama over something so big. The tension was thick, the potholes felt twice as large, and the traffic three times as slow. When he parked, they both sat still. Raisa's chest hurt and she couldn't think of the right thing to say because she didn't want to lose Daniel. At the same time, she didn't want to give up that roof, that dish. "I can't break the law. Not in America," Daniel said, his voice as strained as Raisa felt. "You speak perfect Russian and sometimes I forget you have no idea about what the USSR is really like because you were born here. Raisa, my mother and I, we got out. I have asylum, but nothing is permanent. If I break the law, they will take it away." He spoke faster, took off his seat belt and turned to face her. "You never talk about your mother or how she got here with her parents. I'm sure they're like us, that they can be sent back, too. I'm right. I know I'm right. Have you ever been scared?" Daniel asked. "I mean really scared?"

Terrified, Raisa wanted to say. The day her mother was arrested and her father died. All the times she sat with her mother, thinking Mama had taken too many pills, wasn't going to wake up. In the field during the math competition, when she saw that old woman and thought it meant her grandparents were going to pass away. "You have," Daniel said. "I see it on you. I know you understand fear. That's what I feel when I think about breaking American laws." He took a deep breath. "What makes this worth it?" Raisa hesitated. "Tell me."

"My mother, she was adopted. Yulia and Lazar, Baba and Pop-Pop, snuck out of the USSR with her, brought her to America." Raisa pointed to the comic book. "My grandmother is Atomic Anna, and this work, it's what she did. My mom drew her story in these books. My grandmother believed science was progress—the future. She was a nuclear scientist. She built bombs. I know that for a fact. It's part of why we left. The guilt, knowing what she'd done. I think she didn't want my mother growing up under that, maybe. That day we saw that woman in the field, it meant more than I admitted. There's a connection to my family."

"Chernobyl?" Daniel asked, his voice still taut.

"According to the comic books, Atomic Anna was the lead engineer, in charge of it all. And you remember that day in the field, she said something about it, only her words were garbled. It wasn't clear."

"Your real grandmother was in charge of Chernobyl?" Daniel went pale and sat back, took a series of shallow breaths like he'd been struck.

"It's what the comics say, and I don't think Mama made it all up, but at the same time it's a comic book and I never believed it was real. I didn't...I didn't really put it all together. I guess she was in charge, but that seems crazy, doesn't it?" Raisa felt idiotic for not realizing it all earlier. She'd always kept Anna, Atomic Anna, and her mother in a separate bubble, tried to bury them so they couldn't weigh down her real life, but now she saw that was a mistake. Real or not, Daniel was too close to Chernobyl for her to have kept it from him. "I'm sorry. I just, I never really thought it was real. I didn't think."

"You didn't think? How?" She could feel Daniel getting more upset as the information sank in, and with that she felt even more lost and unsure of what to do. She thought maybe the more she spoke, the better he'd feel, that maybe even he wouldn't run away, because that's how he looked in the moment, like he wanted to get as far away as he could. Only he stayed, and she kept going. "Anna did everything she could to make sure there were safety measures in place, protections to keep the plant from melting down, the comic says. That had to be true. No one would ever build something that powerful without being careful. She believed nuclear power was progress, better than coal or oil. And good science always has a failsafe, mechanisms for protecting from the worst. The beauty of science is that it takes a team to operate and build. She ran millions of tests to make sure it was safe and—"

"Vera," Daniel interrupted, his voice so deep and still it made Raisa freeze. "My sister is proof that it wasn't safe. So is my father."

Raisa tried to pull herself together and finally said, "Anna, the Soviets say she died there, too. She worked for this ideal power source, for the beauty of a better future, and yes, she made mistakes. But what if she was onto something?"

"Wait. She's dead? Or you think the Soviets made a mistake and she's alive on that mountain painted in your room?"

"I'm not sure. It's confusing. My grandparents won't say either way and I don't know what to believe. I looked up the list of the dead once. She was on it, but I know my mother thinks she's alive from the way she draws her. And that woman on the beach, in the field. How could that have been her?" She saw that Daniel was still struggling and so she kept talking. "I'm sorry. I'm so sorry she...killed Vera and your father." Raisa was getting more and more scared that Daniel would never talk to her again. "I'm sorry."

"Shh," he finally said. His eyes still appeared sad, but he was looking at her, with her. "You don't have to apologize. It's not your fault. It's your grandmother's. And I get that she was an idealist. It's very Soviet of her. Communism started from idealism like that. A society of equals. No one going homeless or hungry. It is a utopia that can never exist. Reality never matches the dream," Daniel said. "Of course she didn't build or design Chernobyl to kill people."

"Science is different from politics."

"But look at what happened at Chernobyl, all those people who died. Vera. My father."

Raisa took a deep breath. "You never told me what happened to them."

Daniel bit his lip. "She was a nurse. She was the first to give out iodine tablets. She was at the hospital when the firefighters came in. She was the one who realized their suits and boots were radioactive. She collected them all and carried them to the basement, threw them into a cement stairwell. It killed her. Less than twelve hours later, she saw the burns. That's what her friend wrote in a letter to us. His name was Valery Legasov. He was the one who found us afterward. The radiation ate through her skin." He wiped a tear off his cheek and Raisa wanted to comfort him but wasn't sure how. He kept talking. "She was lucky it was fast. My father didn't understand how something no one could see could kill her. He thought the Soviets were lying. They always lie. He went for her, ducked under all the barriers to get to the hospital. He didn't even know it had already been evacuated. By the time he made it back out, his skin had blistered. He died before we heard he was sick. We came here, to America, because of Valery. I don't know how or why. The man gave us money and your grandparents' address, told us to find them. Then your grandfather showed up at our door and offered me a job, said he didn't even know Legasov. I don't know why my mother trusted that man or how she could leave everything based on that one small moment. Maybe he was with us for ten minutes, then he was gone, back to work, and we were on the run." Daniel took a deep breath. "That man said something else. He said, 'Just because you can do something doesn't mean you should.'" He took Raisa's hand as if he'd held it dozens of times before. He kissed her palm so quickly it was almost as if it didn't happen. But it did.

* * *

After talking about Chernobyl, Raisa felt awkward around Daniel. He must have felt the same, because aside from their tutoring sessions, he stopped talking to her. He jumped to make deliveries, to get out of the Chopping Room. Nina, the beautiful girl from their class, started spending more time in the store and he seemed to want to help her more than necessary. Raisa was jealous and she hated it. She and Daniel had made it through that awkward time in the van and were still friends—just friends—but then she thought about how he came with her to Radio Shack, to the roof, how he touched her hand and elbow, how he kissed her palm. *Friends* don't touch each other that way. But then she told herself she was being ridiculous; there was nothing there.

Two weeks later, Daniel handed her an envelope. She was taking a break, seated in the back of the Chopping Room under the sign for the old fallout shelter in the basement. He pointed to the envelope. "It's an invitation for my bar mitzvah."

"You go to synagogue?" she said, surprised.

"Every Monday and Wednesday morning before school. You're on the bus too early to notice my schedule is different those days."

"Since when?"

"Since we got here. In the Soviet Union no one has bar mitzvahs. Mama wants this to be a big celebration."

"Aren't you too old?"

"You don't have to be thirteen. A guy last week, he was sixty and he had a bar mitzvah. He also grew up in the Soviet Union." He hesitated. "Will you come?"

"I wouldn't miss it."

For his bar mitzvah, Daniel wore a suit he borrowed from Mr. Kestler. It was too small, so the pants didn't hang right. The jacket, shirt, and tie made him look older, more serious than she knew him to be. From the balcony where Raisa sat, the sanctuary looked empty, but when she walked into the celebration and kiddush afterward, she realized the size of the synagogue had dwarfed the crowd. Nearly a hundred people had come. Daniel's mother brought out trays of cakes and cookies. Yulia and Lazar added three briskets. As guests gushed through the door, they deposited fruit and potato kugels. They ate off paper plates, rubbing up against faded pictures of Jerusalem.

"Was I awful?" Daniel asked Raisa when he caught her in line at the buffet table. His hair was pushed back and he had left some of his curls loose. He had a lipstick stain near his mouth.

"You were fantastic." She handed him a napkin, pointed to the lipstick. "You need this."

"Come! Dance!" Baba called from the front of the room. She bumped her way through the crowd and put their plates down, dragged them out to the dance floor. The musicians scrambled to catch up.

Raisa had never seen her grandmother so excited, so filled with energy from a party, and once she started twirling, it was clear she loved it. Mama had told Raisa once that Baba loved to dance and now Raisa believed it. A smile broke over her grandmother's face as big as any smile she could remember. More people joined and Baba made Raisa link hands with Daniel in a smaller circle in the center. Soon his mother joined them; then even Lazar came out on the dance floor. Daniel was ripped away to lock elbows with the rabbi. They lunged down to a squat, then stood back up with a cheer. The vodka flowed as easily as the music and laughter. Raisa had never seen Daniel happier. Nor had she ever seen him watch her so closely. She looked up when she was pouring soda and found his eyes on her from across the room, even while he stood in front of the rabbi. He followed her when she dashed to the kitchen for more vodka for the adults.

"Raisa, where are you going?" he asked.

She reached into the freezer and pulled out a bottle. "For my grandfather."

"Want to share some first? He won't know the difference." Daniel grabbed two glasses from a shelf, not waiting for a reply. "There's a balcony, the fire exit. Here." His sleeve brushed her arm. "Come on," he said.

They sat down on a stone ledge on the landing just outside the door. The sun slanted against their backs. It was cool, and two stories up, she felt like they had privacy. Daniel poured for both of them. "L'chaim," he said.

"L'chaim."

He sipped and pointed down to the street. "Do you like it here in America?"

"I don't know anything different. Do you like it?"

"Most of the time. I still can't read English well. I hate that. It's the alphabet."

"You need to practice. That's all."

Klezmer music leaked from behind the door next to them. Daniel was close. The edge of his pants touched her skirt and she felt self-conscious in her white blouse, the one Baba insisted she wear even though Raisa said it made her look like an old lady. She hated that her hair was pulled into a quick ponytail from when they were dancing, that her mascara had run. She put her glass down and raised her arms to smooth the curls that had come loose, but Daniel stopped her. "You look great."

"You're kidding, right?"

"No." She couldn't remember him ever looking at her before the way he did then. He focused on her lips, not her eyes, and he leaned closer. It had her off balance, thinking about the moment in the van when he kissed the back of her hand. She couldn't understand why he was looking at her that way. All those girls who came to the Market looking for him wore tight pants and short shirts. They had big, full breasts, and Raisa didn't have any of that. She was thin, awkward, and flat. All the curves she wanted in her body were confined to her uncontrollable hair. It was probably better for her to go back inside than embarrass herself. She got up, but before she could take a step toward the door Daniel was up next to her and he didn't hesitate. He leaned down and kissed her. He wrapped an arm around her waist and pulled her close. At first she held her breath, but then she tasted him, the vodka and cookies, and she followed his lead. They fumbled a little. Their teeth clanged, but the kiss grew smoother. She put her hand on his cheek, ran it down his neck. She felt him shiver.

"Raisa?" They jumped apart just as Baba peered around the side of the door. "What are you two...?"

Daniel ran a hand through his hair and looked guilty, Raisa thought. No, embarrassed. "We're just—" he said.

"Drinking?" Baba smiled and pointed at the bottle of vodka on the ledge. "You know she's too young for that." She swayed and Raisa saw she was drunk. "God, I sound American." She laughed. "Come back inside at least." Baba stumbled over the threshold. Daniel caught her, and Raisa watched her grandmother go stiff for a moment. "It was only the light," Baba said. She waved her hands and forced a smile. "For a minute there, Daniel, you reminded me of Yasha."

"Who?" Daniel asked.

"Anna's husband. Not at Chernobyl. They had split by then. Before."

"So it's true, Baba Anna worked at Chernobyl?" Raisa whispered.

Baba laughed again. But it was her forced laugh. "Forget you heard that. This isn't party talk!" She took Raisa's hand, pulled her back inside.

At the edge of the dance floor, Raisa whispered to Daniel, "She never told me any of that. Never admitted Anna worked there or said her husband was named Yasha."

"We still don't know how real any of it is," Daniel said. "But maybe Anna knew Vera." The musicians were still at it, the pace slower. They were drunk like the guests. Daniel and Raisa went to the dance floor, Daniel still holding Raisa's hand. Baba saw it and made a funny exaggerated face to say she approved, and Raisa laughed. "You're giggling," Daniel said. "I never heard you giggle before."

"I was not giggling." And then, "Maybe."

He pulled her close to dance slowly and instead of feeling awkward the way she would have anticipated, she felt relaxed, like they fit. "I'm sorry I've been acting strange since we met with Mr. Kestler. I really want to spend more time with you, to be with you. It just scared me."

"I get it."

"Yeah, but. I'm trying to say I'll help you on that roof, with that dish."

"Daniel, I know you don't want to break the law."

"I'll help. For you. Maybe for Vera and my father, and for Anna, too. If Vera and your grandmother were both there, maybe we're after the same thing."

"What's that?"

"Answers."

ANNA

July 1992
Five Months Before Molly Dies on Mount Aragats

Mount Aragats

Y ou're going too fast for me," Anna said to Molly. They were outside at the lake that bordered the station. It was summer. Warm. They had stripped down to their underwear to swim. Molly was slender and strong, her body lean, but her skin was marred from all the needles and infections from using while in prison. It hurt Anna to see that, knowing she had sent her daughter to America, to the drugs. Ever since coming back from her jump to the prison, Anna had tried to be softer, kinder, the way Molly said she had been in Molly's timeline. At first, she had felt awkward about it, but the more she pushed herself the more she realized the warmth Molly had described came more easily than Anna thought. It made her realize that for decades she had been holding back, pulling away in order to protect herself, but with Molly she didn't want distance. She wanted to get to know her, to apologize, only she wasn't sure how to start their conversations. "You can't come back from a jump and be Betty Crocker or a good mother," Molly would say.

"Who is Betty Crocker? Did you tell me?"

"Yes, a dozen times. It's getting worse, your short-term memory." She was right, but Anna still hadn't figured out what part of her machine was killing her brain cells. Whenever she wasn't working on it, she focused on Molly, made herself available so that when her daughter came to her and said she was fighting a craving, the darkness, Anna could drop everything and listen. That's what Molly needed, someone to sit and be there with her as she worked through it. Sometimes Molly would talk about a memory she had with Viktor or guilt she felt for leaving Raisa. Other times they just sat in silence in the big chairs in front of the picture window, watching the mountains.

"Did we talk a lot before I jumped to save Raisa?" Anna had asked once during a silent moment as they sat at the window.

"Yes. It was hard at first."

"Why?"

"I felt like you were judging me. But I told you that, and you worked so hard to change. You would bite your lip to keep from scowling or stare at that old picture in your pocket, the one of Mama, Papa, Raisa, and I in front of the Market. That photo was like magic. You looked at it and somehow you started listening without judging, and that was when I even started to like you," she said, the hint of a grin lifting the edge of her lips. "That's all I want. I want you to listen. And make me tuna fish sandwiches because I love tuna."

One week later, Anna had put out a can of tuna for Molly along with two slices of bread. She had no idea how to serve it or how Americans ate it. When Molly saw it, she had scooped it out onto her plate, added olive oil. "Thank you."

"Will you tell me about that American now? The Bonnie Cracker?"

Molly had laughed hard and sat at the table with Anna, started eating next to her. Today, for the first time, she had invited Anna to come out to the lake and swim. The water was melted snow and so cold it hurt Anna to put her toes in, but Molly ran right in and dove under, swam to the middle. "Just go for it," she yelled. "Whenever you hold back it hurts more." The water was clear and when it was still, Anna could glimpse the bottom, the sharp stones below.

"I've seen you sketching your experiments," Molly called.

"It's how I know what to build," Anna said. "I've always sketched them."

"You know what's funny?" Molly was treading water, her head bobbing. "My whole life I felt like a failure because all I wanted to do was draw and I thought my parents were telling me not to. Only up here, I realized they never told me anything like that. They told me not to rely on art for my future. I was the one who thought I was a failure. It was me all along, not them. I never even really put myself out there. I mean, I sent off a few panels to this magazine called *EVO*, but no one gets their break like that. If I wanted it, I should have moved to New York. Really moved. Or showed up at their office. That's what you did, right? You kept showing up to Laboratory Number Two in Moscow, to get to Igor Kurchatov?" Anna couldn't remember telling her about that, but it was how she had found Igor and Yasha. Molly went underwater, bobbed back up. "I was scared. I'm still scared. And I regret it, blaming my parents for all those things I did wrong. But it was easier that way. Do you know what I'm talking about?"

"I think I do," Anna said.

"When I draw, I'm lost to the world. In a good way. Everything else seems easier to deal with. I get it from you. Mama must have known how much you draw. You told me once Yasha helped you with your work because he saw things from a different angle." He did, but Anna didn't remember talking about that with Molly, either. "Why won't you tell me more about him?"

"The past hurts," Anna said, because it was the truth. Yasha, in particular, was a deep memory that could still cut her now with the same sharp edge it had all those years ago. But she'd thought about him a lot since living on that mountain, and how she felt about him, about

them together, had shifted. "I don't talk about him because I feel guilty.
I took you away from him. I had my reasons. What I thought were good
reasons at the time. He was spying on me, reporting on me, it was all
atrocious. But I took you away. I became judge and jury."

"I don't understand," Molly said. Of course she couldn't. She hadn't
lived it. Anna started to swim toward Molly. The cold wrapped over
her chest, made it hard to breathe. It didn't help that her pulse was
racing. She was sharing the past, unsure of where that would leave her
or Molly. She forced herself to keep talking. "You're my daughter. I
won't push you away again. I know that now. Back then I was such a
mess. When I sent you to America, I told myself I was doing the right
thing. But I was hiding or running and I needed help. I was in such
a deep fog after you were born. I was miserable and feeling guilty for
that. The cycle was devastating and embarrassing and no one seemed
to understand, least of all Yasha. It took years for it to lift, for me to
think clearly again." Anna waited for Molly to reply, but instead Molly
went underwater and stayed there for what felt like too long. Anna
wasn't sure if she'd said too much or not enough. When Molly came
up, finally, Anna said, "I didn't mean to hurt you or your father."

"You hated him."

"In some ways. But I also loved him very much." She kept going
even though she was getting tired from treading water, too old to be
out so long in that cold, but she didn't want to lose this moment
with Molly.

"What did you love about Yasha?"

"He helped me simplify my designs, like my work on the gun
assembly for the bomb. He looked over my sketches and streamlined
them. The problems that were obvious to him were invisible to me.
You did the same for the amplifier, simplified it for me."

"I asked what you loved, not how he helped."

Circles rippled out in the water from Anna's fingertips and broke over
Molly. Anna thought about how Yasha had acted when they walked in

on Lazar and Yulia that first time, when Anna's heart broke because she realized Yulia was no longer just hers. His instinct was to protect her then and every day after that. "He did what he could to help me feel better, what he thought was right."

"He sounds kind."

"He was, but there were other sides to him, too. It's why Yulia and Lazar probably never told you about him. You were his project. He thought you were the future, that you would lead the Soviets to greatness. Yulia never wanted that for you. She wanted you to be happy, and Lazar wanted you to be American, to be free from the suffering we all experienced."

"They never thought I was smart enough." Molly winced as she said it.

"No. No, no, no." She jerked up higher in the water. "That's not right. They thought they were keeping you safe. It's what I thought, too. Mollushka, we had a different life before you came along, before you went to America. Yulia, Lazar, and I, we grew up never sure if we might have food one day to the next. In our childhoods, it was never a question of *if* our parents would die, but *when*. I can't remember a day when I wasn't terrified before I met your mother. Living like that, well, no one should have to live that way, and so your parents did everything they could to make sure you had a better life. They pushed you away from art because they were scared you couldn't earn a living from it. They didn't want you to know hunger. Do you know how hungry your mama was as a child?" Molly looked stricken, and whispered back that she had no idea. "Hunger can distort the way you see the world. Pain can, too. Yulia and Lazar may have made bad choices for you. I know I did, but they came from love. You have to know that."

Molly floated on her back for a long time as the sun reflected off the water, bounced along the surface. Anna could sense her thinking, considering, the weight of what she'd just been told sinking in. "I'm glad you shared that with me," she said. "I guess I did the same for Raisa. In a different way. I gave her all the freedom I wanted, but maybe it was too much."

Anna took a deep breath. "Raisa," she said. She was running out of time, needed Raisa's help, desperately. "Why won't you let me ask Raisa for assistance?"

"We've been through this." Molly swam closer, looked Anna in the eye. "She can't be involved. Ever. She's happy. She has everything you said you want her to have, security and food, family and a future. Bringing her here, it could take it all away. What if the Soviets find us, arrest us? Or she freezes hiking up here? Who knows what could go wrong, maybe she's irradiated in one of your experiments. No, I'd never risk bringing her here."

"By keeping her away, you're repeating my mistakes. What if she wants to come?"

Molly waved her arm at the station behind them, at Anna. "She deserves better than anything here. Swear you won't go near her," Molly said. "Swear it."

The two of them treaded water, facing each other as if in a standoff. Anna broke away and turned to swim back to the shore. She didn't want to face Molly when she lied to her. "I swear," she said, but it was too late. She had already set her plan in motion, delivered the latest two copies of *Atomic Anna*.

RAISA

Philadelphia

The summer after Daniel's bar mitzvah, Raisa and Daniel were rising seniors and expected to work forty hours a week at the Market, chopping and cleaning, butchering and selling up front. At night, Raisa planned to study for the SATs and sort the data coming through the dish in west Philly. The strange anomalies she had found on her grandparents' roof were there again in the data here, but she couldn't explain it, not yet. It could have just been a blip and so she focused on collecting and analyzing. She even added four more satellite dishes because she learned that an array was what made radio telescopes more powerful. All the while, the comic book they'd found in the van the day they went to meet Mr. Kestler was in the back of Raisa's mind, something she thought about every day. When she looked at it more closely, tried to parse through the equations, she realized they were incorrect but she wasn't exactly sure how to fix them. It seemed a variable was missing, but she couldn't isolate it or identify it. The woman on the soccer field had said something about waves, ripples, and space-time. Raisa researched, found papers on the theory behind ripples in space-time, but they were only theories. No one had been able to prove or detect the ripples. And Raisa couldn't help but think the problem with all the theories was that none melded electromagnetism with gravity. Some tried, but not even Einstein could fit them together, and even though she had an idea where to start, it required equipment far beyond anything she had. So instead, she focused on her small, growing experiment.

"The big satellite dish is loose, wobbling in the wind," Raisa said to Daniel one night in July. They were on the roof of Kestler's old building. Below someone was blaring Run-DMC. They had been up on that roof almost every night that week. The sky was clear and a soaking rain that afternoon had erased the smog. She had to climb underneath the dish to tighten the bolts. As she slid in under the base, her shirt caught and rode up, exposed her stomach. She felt him put his hand on her bare skin. He kissed her belly button.

"Let me help," he said. He rolled under with her, so they lay side by side on their backs, their hips touching. She moved one of her legs over so it was between Daniel's as he took the wrench. "That's how you like to work?" he asked with a grin. "By distracting me?"

"Yes," she said, giggling. They shimmied out from under the dish and she pulled him to her. They had learned enough about each other that there was no hesitating anymore. She bit his lower lip because it drove him crazy. He licked her neck down to her collar bone. They had been inexperienced at the bar mitzvah, but as Daniel said, they had Soviet blood and Soviets weren't prudes, and they certainly weren't virgins now. They had explored every inch of each other since that first kiss, and she couldn't get enough of him.

"Hold on," Daniel said. The music from below was louder. He went to his backpack and retrieved a blanket, spread it out for them. She wanted to make a joke because he wasn't that guy who pushed. He was patient and slow with her. If anything, she was the one who wanted more. She should have been the one bringing the blanket, and when she opened her mouth to say it, he kissed her and she pulled him down and straddled him.

Up on the roof like that, Raisa felt like they had the city to themselves. It was the only place Daniel stopped pressing his curls flat, where he seemed to feel most comfortable in his own skin. He took off his shirt. She did the same. Then came their shorts. In the locker room at school she was self-conscious, but never with Daniel. He told her she was the most beautiful woman he could ever imagine, and the way he looked at her, she believed him. He made his way down her body, kissing her everywhere: her shoulders, her arms, her breasts. He kissed her over the cotton of her bra and panties and the effect was an electric shock. "Keep going," she said.

"Where?" he asked. "Where should I kiss you?"

She loved the feel of his nakedness against hers, loved the sound of his breathing so close. "Here." She pointed between her legs and he didn't hesitate.

Later, they slid back under the dish and Raisa returned to work, tightening the bolts. While she downloaded new data, he did push-ups and sit-ups. He was a citizen now. His papers had come through early in June and he was more determined than ever to join the army. She had pushed him toward ROTC and he was finally thinking about college. "My mother used to exercise like that," Raisa said. "She loved Jack LaLanne, the old guy with the funny track suits. I used to watch him with her, sometimes. She said doing all those exercises made her feel better."

"You haven't mentioned her in a while."

"You know I don't like to talk about her." Raisa went back to her telescope.

"Do you want me to go with you to visit her sometime?"

"No." She took a deep breath. "I don't even know what I'd say if I saw her."

"You'd figure it out."

"She's being released soon."

"Why didn't you mention it? Why do you still keep things from me?" His voice was gentle, concerned.

"I can't talk about it yet."

He kissed her lightly and held her. Later, while she was packing up, they kissed again. Before they got into the van, they kissed. At the door, they kissed good night. Raisa loved kissing him and he seemed to feel the same. They were always trying to find places where they could sneak time alone, in private. She pulled him into the office at the back of the Chopping Room while her grandparents weren't looking. She dragged him downstairs to the fallout shelter. He pulled her up on the desk in the private room at the library where they were supposed to be studying.

"You're more like your mother than you know," Baba said when Raisa got home after fixing the satellite dish. Her lips were swollen. Her back was scratched. "She used to creep inside after her dates with your father, too." She paused and looked like she wanted to smile but was holding it back.

"I wasn't creeping. You knew where I was."

"You're right." Baba let her smile come and spread across her face. "Of course I know what you two are up to. You have the same look on your face that she had when she came home after being with Viktor. But Daniel, he's a nice boy. It's different."

"Why didn't you like Papa?" Raisa leaned on the door. The lock clicked into place.

"He was a drug dealer. What mother wants her daughter with someone like that?" Baba's smile disappeared and she came closer, ran a hand over Raisa's cheek. "You're being careful, right? You can't have a baby."

"Baba! Please. I'm not an idiot. I won't get pregnant."

"Anyone in love is an idiot." The smile returned to Baba's face and made her look younger, happier for a second. "Maybe it's the best part of life."

Summer spun through July and had Raisa dizzy by August. She hadn't studied enough, hadn't collected enough data, and hadn't had enough of Daniel. And while she felt off-kilter, she reveled in it. She loved all the new sensations, the way he made her feel, the way her body responded to him. But there was another, bigger reason for feeling off balance: Mama was going to be released soon. Raisa knew because she had intercepted a letter in early 1983, opened it before her grandparents. It was the last letter Mama sent from prison, and in it she wrote that she was being released on October 7, 1988. Raisa had run upstairs holding the letter. She expected Baba to be excited with her, but instead Baba took the letter and told Raisa to forget what she had read. Many things had to happen before the date was final, before Mama walked out without handcuffs. "This could all change," she said. "And when she comes out, she's going to rehab. Don't set your heart on any date."

"It won't change. I know it won't," Raisa said. She stomped back to her room. Mama wouldn't write with a date unless she was sure, and while Raisa still didn't want to visit her in jail, she did want to be there when she was released. Raisa had been counting down ever since. She wanted to make sure she was there to meet her mother, but over the years, every time she had tried to talk to her grandparents about it, they had told her the date hadn't been confirmed, that she shouldn't get her hopes up. She knew they were only trying to protect her, and so she had stopped talking about it.

On October 7, 1988, Raisa woke up excited and scared because she planned on being there when Mama was released—with or without Baba and Pop-Pop. "Why are you so nervous?" Pop-Pop asked when he saw her in the kitchen getting ready for breakfast.

"Don't you know what today is?" Raisa asked.

"Friday. Shabbat tonight. Now tell me, why the nerves?"

She went to the refrigerator and pulled out milk, unsure whether her grandparents were being coy or had really forgotten.

"Your shirt is on backwards," Baba said, walking in. "When you're nervous you do funny things like that."

"Baba, you tell me. What's today?"

"Friday. Your grandfather already told you. Come." She handed Raisa the comb.

"I have a test," Raisa said. "I don't have time to do your hair."

"Maybe that's it," Pop-Pop said. "You're nervous for the test. You shouldn't be. You always overstudy." He pulled a piece of toast from the toaster and put it on Raisa's plate.

"Don't you have anything to do today?" Raisa asked. "Any-thing...*special*?"

Pop-Pop paused. "What are you getting at?"

"It's Daniel," Baba said suddenly, like she'd just understood. "You had a fight."

"It's not Daniel." Could they really have forgotten?

"Then why is he here?" Raisa looked over her shoulder at the front door. Through the glass window at the top, she saw his slicked-back curls. "The only reason a boy shows up at this hour is because he needs to apologize."

"You're wrong," Raisa said. "I thought maybe—"

Baba interrupted. "Go see Daniel. It's fine."

Raisa kissed her and turned to go. She checked her bangs before she grabbed her bag.

"Hey," Daniel said before she even finished opening the door. He leaned over to kiss her and she turned so he caught her cheek.

"What are you doing here?" She hiked up her backpack.

"I saw your planner." She closed the door behind her and made her way down the cracked cement path, stopped on the sidewalk. "You're going to New Jersey to meet her, aren't you?"

"You shouldn't snoop."

"I wasn't snooping. It was just open, and I saw it."

She kicked a chunk of broken walkway. "I didn't ask you to come."

"But you know I wouldn't let you go alone."

She took a deep breath. "My grandparents don't even remember today's the day."

"Maybe they're as nervous as you, just better at hiding it. Or maybe the date was never really final, maybe it changed." She walked faster and he kept pace. "Please, let me come. I can wait in the parking lot. I want to be there for you just in case."

"In case what? She doesn't recognize me?"

"You might not recognize her."

Raisa felt her cheeks flushing, anger rising. "She's my mother. I'll know her." There were so many things she wanted to say to her mother, to ask her about, like the mural and the last issue of *Atomic Anna*, the drugs and protests, why she had thought it was okay to leave Raisa alone at night. "You don't get it," she said. "It's just—just—" There were too many emotions getting in the way, keeping her from thinking straight. "Fine," she grunted her frustration.

"She doesn't know I'm coming," Raisa said as they rode the bus to Atlantic City. They passed strip malls and diners, gas stations and farm stands. For years Raisa had thought about going to see her mother, but she was furious that Mama had put drugs before her, that she'd kept Baba and Pop-Pop away. She didn't ever want to imagine what would have happened to her if that old woman hadn't come to the beach and given her their phone number and address. "I think I hate her," Raisa whispered. "And love her." Daniel wrapped his arm around her.

"I used to feel that way about Vera. She could have gotten out. That's what the man said who came to the funeral and gave us money. He said she chose to go into the hospital and help. She died for no reason and took our father with her."

"You really didn't know the man who sent you here? He just came out of the blue?"

"Maybe I was too devastated to ask the right questions. All I remember is he looked very sick, and he spent the entire time smoking. Vera was appointed as a personal nurse for an old woman who worked at Chernobyl. Legasov said he was close to that old woman...I never knew what she did, why she needed a personal nurse. I can't remember her name..." He closed his eyes and squinted. "Ugh, I used to know it so well." He sat up. "Anna Berkova. That was her name."

"Anna Berkova?" Raisa sat up and felt her entire body prickle, the hairs on the back of her neck rise. "Your sister was Anna Berkova's nurse?" Daniel nodded. "Daniel! Anna Berkova is Atomic Anna. My grandmother."

"I've never heard you use the name Berkova," Daniel said. "You always just said Anna!"

Raisa continued. As she spoke, her pulse was rising into overdrive. "It can't be a coincidence. Your sister worked for my grandmother. It's why that man directed you to us."

He shook his head and looked pale, ran his fingers through his hair. "Anna's such a common name. And...after all this time, I never put it together." His voice was too loud. Other passengers were looking. Raisa edged down in the seat. "How could we be so stupid?"

"It wasn't stupid."

"Of course it was. God, I'm blind. Of course we're connected." Daniel was getting louder. She begged him to keep his voice down. "That man, Valery, he said Anna died. What happened?"

"I have no idea," Raisa said. "Remember, I told you everything I know is from those comic books. And I told you, my mother must think Anna is still alive, living in a secret hideout on a mountain, and my grandparents won't talk about her. I can't use a comic book as my only source."

"If Anna's alive, and Vera was her nurse, maybe Vera's alive, too?"

Raisa looked through the window, at the sand swirling on the edge of the expressway. She could feel it scratching at her, like she was about to figure something out, only it was just beyond her reach. "I—I don't have any idea what my mother knows and doesn't. What's real and what's just artwork." She looked at him. "They're probably both dead, Anna and Vera."

"You're right." Daniel kissed the top of her head and looked into the distance.

The bus pushed southeast and the smell of salt water seeped in through the crumbling rubber seams on the windows. The closer they got, the more Raisa's hands turned to sweaty lumps and the less sure she was that she was making the right choice, going without her grandparents, going at all.

The doors leading into the prison were heavy and thick. The guard sitting at his desk had bulletproof glass between him and Raisa. There were three televisions behind him. One played a baseball game. The other two showed views of closed doors and empty doorways. "Can I help you?" His voice came through holes in the divider. He was so round it looked like the buttons on his uniform might fly off.

Raisa told him she was there for her mother. He picked up a thick binder and flipped through page after page, looking for her. Raisa was up on her tiptoes, watching. Every time he ticked past another page she flinched. "She shouldn't be hard to find. Today's the day she's getting out."

"Relax," the guard said. He got to the end of the binder and started at the front again.

"What is it?" Raisa asked. She moved closer, her forehead pressed against the glass. She could smell the guard's gum through the holes between them.

"Just give me a minute, kid." He stood. He hiked his pants up several inches, then walked out through the door behind him. It shut with a bang.

"Something's wrong," Raisa said. Daniel squeezed her hand.

Raisa's first thought was that her mother was dead, but she didn't want to say that out loud. She had read there were lots of drugs in prison, and Raisa could picture Mama in a cell getting high, overdosing. But they would have called.

"Hey, kid," the guard said as he swung back through the door. "She's gone. She was released in eighty-six. Good behavior." He shook his head. "I'm sorry. Guess she didn't go home. We see that sometimes." He leaned against the glass, flattened his palm near the holes, the pudge between his knuckles making his fingers look too small for his hand. That was the detail Raisa focused on because it was better than thinking, really thinking about what he was saying, that her mother had been out all this time and hadn't come for her. Thinking about that would break her.

"Listen, don't look for her. That's one thing I've learned. When she's ready, she'll come home." He paused and gave her a sympathetic smile. "I can see you're one of those kids who's going to run after her. Don't do it. She's not in a safe place. I can guarantee you that. The good news is she's not back in the system." Raisa knew she should turn and leave, but she couldn't. Leaving would mean it was true, that Mama had abandoned her all over again. The guard shook his head. "I'm real sorry."

ANNA

July 1992

Five Months Before Molly Dies on Mount Aragats

Mount Aragats

Tell me more about Yasha," Molly said. She and Anna were out of the lake, had showered and were sitting in front of the picture window in the main compound, drinking hot tea. A fire blazed in the stove, overheating the room. "I saw that picture of you and him at a lake."

"Baikal." Anna smiled and imagined it, the hammock on the front porch. "He was as lost as I was," she said, and her whole body went tense as she filled with regret. A tear rolled down her cheek. "We should have fought for each other."

"Tell me," Molly said.

△ △ △

"My name is Yasha Berlitsky," the man from Laboratory No. 2 said as he stood in their doorway. Anna stared at him. Yulia was next to her,

Lazar and Malka behind her. Anna had asked for this but still she felt herself start to panic, thought about the men who came for Mama, how they dragged her down the stairs. She'd always known they would come for her, too, but somehow, with Yulia she had pushed past the constant fear, even buried it. Only now it came roaring back. If she went, would she ever see her new family again? She cleared her throat, forced herself to sound as nonchalant as she could. "No theater, then?" She forced a smile. "We're leaving now?"

He nodded. "I had hoped to go, too. But new orders came in. For you."

Yulia grabbed Anna's arm. They all knew she had to go with him and Yulia was trembling, holding tight. Malka tried to hand Anna her coat, but Anna dropped it. It fell on her boots, the boots she never took off. Yulia finally let go, helped Anna put her arms into the sleeves, and then she kissed her cheek. "I love you," she said. She pulled Anna so close her lips were next to her ear. "America." It was enough. Anna understood. If Yulia thought they were in danger, they would run to America.

"Can't we go to the play first?" Malka asked Yasha. She was sobbing, had seen more than enough to understand what was happening.

"I wish we could. I thought we could," Yasha said. "But I have new orders."

Anna kissed Malka and Lazar, held them tight, thought about how much her life had changed since she met Yulia. Before, Anna was alone, but now, look at how much she had. They were a family and she didn't want this to be goodbye. "I love you," she said to all of them.

Yasha reached for Anna's arm and held on firmly but didn't pull. She stepped into the stairwell with him and it wasn't until the door closed behind her that she lost control. All those times she told herself Mama was missing, not dead, came flooding back. She started shaking so hard, Yasha had to help her down the stairs. "They killed her. That day they killed her, didn't they? She never made it to a gulag." Anna was babbling from fear.

"Who?" Yasha asked. "Who are you talking about?"

"She never had a chance."

On the landing between the first and second floors he pressed her against the wall. "Breathe, Comrade. Relax," he said. "Tell the truth and you will be fine."

"Truth?" Anna shook her head. If they had already decided she was guilty, sentenced her to death, there was no difference between the truth and a lie. "You carry a gun. Why?" It was possible he'd been sent to kill her.

"Shh," the man said. "You must be strong. I will be there with you." He pointed to the gun. "It's nothing. You asked me for this. Remember that." He was right, but she realized now it had been a mistake.

At the curb, she couldn't get into the car. Two other men who were there to help Yasha had to lift her into the back seat. "I asked for this," she reminded herself, not meaning to say it out loud, barely believing she had pushed so hard. They drove to a brick building. Yasha led her through dark, damp halls so poorly heated she slid on ice. "Please, make it fast," she said. "Kill me quickly."

His hand was at her elbow and it was warm. He leaned close and whispered, "No one wants to kill you. Be honest and you will be fine." He sat her down at a table in the basement. There was no fresh air, only the smell of cigarettes and sweat. A rat scurried past, slipped into a hole. Yasha left and a different man in a uniform she didn't recognize came into the room. He shackled her hands to the table. Her heart was beating so fast she felt it jumping in her chest. He unbuttoned his cuffs and rolled his shirtsleeves up high. Anna was cold but covered in sweat. Her clothing was plastered to her skin. She thought about Yulia, Malka, and Lazar, the rosebushes. She had said *I love you* when she'd left, to leave a meaningful last memory, and she realized she really did love them. And she wanted to live for them, to be with them.

She tried to focus on the man in the unfamiliar uniform, to answer everything directly, honestly. After all, she had nothing to hide. He posed the same questions again and again, wanted to know how she got back to the USSR, why she left Berlin, if she had any help. Anna couldn't remember how many times she answered, what details she shared, or when she started talking about Yulia, but at some point, she was aware that she was both imagining her first night out with Yulia and describing it at the same time. By then she was delirious and felt like she was really dancing, could even hear the music and smell the sweat and tobacco. The man questioning her was angry, his voice was rough, and he tried to pull her back, to keep her in the basement, but she resisted and her mind drifted to Berlin.

The first man was replaced by another who didn't react when she went back and forth between her life in Germany and in the USSR, her personal life and her lab. He had dull eyes and hair that needed to be washed. He drank glass after glass of water but didn't offer Anna any. "Can I have some?" she begged. She couldn't remember a time in her life when she'd felt so parched, so helpless. He didn't give her a sip. Occasionally he came so close she could see the hairs in his nose. She didn't understand how she was still sweating, how she had any more liquid in her. They wouldn't even let her up to go to the bathroom. Instead, they started dousing her with ice-cold water. Finally, they left her alone, shivering, and she was even more certain she was going to die.

Hours passed. Maybe days. She had no sense of time and tried to survive by thinking about Malka helping her make dinner, Lazar and Yulia hunched over an English book as she taught him the language. And then a man came into the room with a cattle prod. Anna let out a yelp. "No. No," she begged. "Please. No." He put it on the table between them and sat down.

He spoke. "Dual surface electrodes produce a high-voltage, low-current electric arc between them. It causes pain, like a gun, only with electricity rather than bullets." She was sweating again, had peed right there on the seat. Her clothes reeked of urine. "Why Berlin?" the man asked. "Why Otto Hahn?" Again he went through the same questions she had already answered. Anna was so tired she couldn't even reason her way through an argument. She just answered and eventually even Yulia fell away. The man didn't use the cattle prod. It sat there between them and that was as terrifying as anything Anna had experienced in her life. She was left waiting, imagining. The man across from her stood up with the cattle prod in his hand and circled her. He came up behind her and leaned down to whisper in her ear. "Why Berlin?" That was when Anna heard the electricity, felt the current close to her cheek, and she screamed. It never even touched her, but she broke. She looked up at the stained, yellowed ceiling and screamed and screamed. She didn't remember passing out, but she must have because someone put a hand on her shoulder and she woke up with a start. At first, she thought she was a child again back in Petrograd, that the door to their flat had just closed.

"Mama!" she yelled. She felt herself in that old flat, running through the rooms, past the newspapers to the balcony doors. "Mama!" Anna needed to catch her, only then someone slapped her face bringing her back to the basement, and she tried to pull her hands up to protect herself but the handcuffs bit into her skin. The man who had slapped her was still standing over her holding the cattle prod. She tried to kick but her legs were shackled, too. She couldn't remember when that happened.

"Enough," another man said. He sat across from her at the table. He wasn't wearing a uniform and he was rounder than the others. His hair was black and swept back from his forehead. He had a mustache and a long beard that reached his collar. His eyes were dark and while he had no wrinkles, he had circles so deep they looked carved into his skin. "I am Igor Vasilyevich Kurchatov," he said. "After all this, please, call me Igor." He said more as he took a key from his pocket and unlocked the shackles at her ankles and wrists, but Anna couldn't hear it over her own crying. The welts under the metal restraints were bloody and bruised. He gave her a glass of water, but she was still sobbing and shaking. "Please, Comrade," Igor said in a loud, clear voice. "Tell me how you discovered uranium cleaved in two."

For a long time she had tried to get to this man, to find a way to work with him, and as she sat there finally staring at him she had to ask herself if the price she paid for this meeting was worth it. She used to think no price would be too high, that she was willing to sacrifice herself, everything she had, but going through the questioning made her realize she had more than she knew, a whole family, and that was too high a price. "Please, let me go," she whimpered. She should have run. Mama should have run. Anna had spent her whole life angry that her mother went with the soldiers, and now Anna had done the same thing. "I'm a fool," she said.

"No. You're brilliant," Igor said. "I'm sorry you had to go through this, but everyone does. I must trust my inner circle."

"By torturing me?"

"They didn't touch you, did they?"

"They didn't have to." She fell into a long silence. "Maybe it would have been better if they did. Just got it over with."

"Yes." He nodded. "The mind creates as much pain and fear as the senses."

"I don't want this anymore," she said. "I want to go home."

"You'll sleep. You'll eat. You'll feel better. You didn't lie about anything and that was all I needed." He pointed to the glass of water in front of her. "Drink. Then tell me how you discovered uranium cleaved in two." She obeyed like an automaton, even though she didn't want to. That was what the Soviets did, she realized; they coerced control. Igor could ask her to do anything at all and she would. She hated her country in that moment and she wanted to spite Igor, refuse the water, but she needed it so badly and above all she still wanted to live, to get back to her family. She moved her arms to reach for the glass, but they were so sore from being in restraints that they shook and she had to hold the glass with both hands. Slowly, she raised it and it spilled everywhere. "Uranium," Igor said without moving closer or offering to help.

"Uranium isn't right. Not for a bomb. We need plutonium."

"Tell me." Someone in the corner of the room, someone she hadn't noticed, coughed. It was Yasha. He looked concerned and upset. He held a tray with food and more water. Igor nodded and Yasha brought it to the table, quickly.

"Can I help?" Yasha asked. Anna couldn't answer with words. She only looked at him and he held up the water and eased it to her lips. "Slowly," Yasha said, but after only three sips she starting retching, couldn't hold it down. She wanted to cry but didn't have any tears left.

Eventually, Yasha took her upstairs, far from the basement. He led her into a white tiled room with a bare ceiling. New clothes and shoes, even a new coat, all her size, were there for her. She washed and changed, was given more food and water. Surely this meant she was going to live, and she relaxed enough to eat on her own and sleep. Later, Igor and Yasha came back and Igor asked her to talk more about her discovery of fission. "All my observations proved it," she said. She told him about the tram accident, about the blood rippling and how she realized that when the atom cleaved in two it interacted with ripples in space-time, opened access that wasn't usually there. They discussed fission and its potential as a weapon. Igor asked, "Dr. Anna Berkova, could you live with yourself if you built an atomic bomb? If your invention murdered millions of people, could you live with yourself?"

"Murder? I wouldn't use that word."

"What word would you use? If you make a bomb, it won't just target bad Germans. It will kill anyone near them. Even if you could justify killing Hitler, what about his cook? Or the children in the nursery next door?" Igor took a long pull on a cigarette. The tobacco singed. "No weapon can be so accurate as to spare innocents. How do you feel about that?"

"I don't know." That was the truth. She had thought about it countless times. It was an obvious dilemma and there were days when she could accept the guilt, convince herself it was for a greater good. But there were other times when she couldn't. Times when she imagined Yulia or someone like Yulia next to Hitler, translating a message for him when the bomb fell.

"Think hard, Comrade," Igor continued. "Make no mistake. Whoever has it first will use it. Death will come quickly for some and agonizingly slowly for others. The radiation will disfigure anyone it reaches, maiming and killing. You will have to decide if you can live with that before you come to work with me."

"How can anyone know if they could live with that guilt?" Anna rubbed her wrists, the torn red skin where she'd been cuffed. And then she shared what was in her gut. "I've seen what Hitler's men are doing. Women and children disemboweled, shot in front of ditches, infants murdered. When I was hiding in the woods, I witnessed too much. I want him dead."

"Fair enough. Now ask yourself, how will you feel if *you* build the worst weapon ever unleashed on humanity? Yes, we may beat Hitler, but then who do we face? Tyrants, evil like him is far more common than you might want to admit."

Anna closed her eyes, thought about the look on Yulia's face when they saw Nazis beating Jews in the streets in Germany, Lazar and Malka shaking after their parents were killed, and she realized, she would fight. If Hitler took the Soviet Union, Yulia, Lazar, Malka, and Anna would be murdered in the blink of an eye for their Jewish blood. "I'll do it," she said. "I might hate it, but I'd hate it more if I didn't."

Igor's laboratory gleamed. The walls and floor were covered in pale tiles. Tables on the perimeter were polished. Computers that looked like large closets had blinking bulbs. They hissed and emanated so much heat the room felt like summer in winter. Anna was the only woman who ever set foot inside those four walls, and none of the men let her forget it. She was second in command, behind Igor, but the pressure and condescension were relentless. "Do you need to rest?" the men asked her often. "My ovaries are fine," she shot back. "Do you need me to help lift that part?" they would ask. "I can lift it with my pinkie finger," she replied, even when she couldn't. When Yasha was around, no one dared treat her that way. Already he was feared. But he couldn't be by her side every minute of every day.

The guards were even worse. She had to pass through security to get into the building. The men went through with a cursory glance and occasional pat-down. Anna was often pulled aside, off into the main office where they ran their hands over her body. The only time they let her pass unhindered was when she was with Yasha, and so she walked with him more and more often. Igor objected on her behalf, but security was managed by the military and the scientist had no say. "I'm sorry," he said. "It shouldn't be this way." Anna cried in the bathroom often, kept telling herself all of these small inconveniences were worth it because she was going to defeat Hitler and her position secured larger rations. She was now feeding Yulia, Lazar, and Malka, plus the family in the flat next to theirs, every night.

Igor and Anna led a team of ten. Yasha, it turned out, was a chemist with the strict assignment of watching Anna and the lab. That was why he carried the gun, was trained to use it. He was the last line of defense inside those four walls, in case security was breached. At first, she worried he would crowd her, but he gave her all the room she needed. When she required a notebook or anything else, he was quick to get it for her. He was the only one who complimented her work or sat near her during lunch. Not once did he seem to object to his assignment. If anything, he made it clear he adored working with Anna.

"Over here," Igor said as he blasted through the door and into the lab one day, six months into Anna's tenure. The room was steaming with heat from all the computers running at once, and dust distorted straight lines. No one and no room in Moscow could escape all the dirt and rubble, the coughing and burning eyes that came with the war. Igor had news from their American spy working on the Manhattan Project. "Our source says the Americans are working through the problem of separating U-235 from U-238," Igor announced. He spread the notes across the table and Anna stood over them, front and center.

"This is brilliant," she said when she got to the schematics, designs for a gun assembly to start the chain reaction in uranium. "But we need more. They're incomplete."

"Then you must figure it out," Igor said.

Anna worked tirelessly, experimenting with the information from America and with her own twists and changes. Yulia was worried about her, nagged her to sleep. "You work more than you did in Berlin," she said. Anna insisted there was no choice.

"How many Jews has Hitler killed?" she asked.

"You're not fighting him alone," Yulia said.

"No, but my bomb can make all the difference."

"You want to destroy him for the Jews or for the Soviets?"

"For both," Anna said. "Aren't we both?"

"There's an old philosophical argument you should know," Yulia said one cold night as she climbed into bed wearing every sweater she owned. "Can there be good without evil?"

"What does that have to do with my work?"

"You think you're doing good because you work in the face of Hitler. That's how you judge what you do. But what if you're looking at the wrong mirror? I'm asking you to think about how you'll feel after he is defeated."

"Igor asked me something similar. My work goes beyond Hitler. I know that, but it doesn't mean I can stop. Getting through this war will be a luxury."

"Lazar agrees with you. I'm not sure I do," Yulia said.

"Lazar? You speak to him about things like this? He's a child."

"Child? He's twenty-six. A man. And he's smart. You're so busy at work. We talk about a lot of things." She turned on her side. "Tell me, how's Yasha?"

Within the next year, Anna and Igor understood better how to control a nuclear reaction and it was time to bring it to life, to build the first Soviet nuclear reactor. They put it on display for an elite group of generals, and afterward Igor turned to her. "We walk a very thin line," he said. "With this success, we weaponize the technology. With failure, well, they'll probably kill us. Either way, with this experiment, we are unleashing a new evil today." Anna couldn't help but think about her conversation with Yulia, the idea that once she let others see this science she would lose control of it. She'd have no say over how or when it was used, who would be playing God. She wondered if it was already too late to stop it.

"Not evil," Yasha said. He was by her side, always. "It is Soviet destiny."

Anna, Igor, and Yasha were the only people still working at Laboratory No. 2 on the night of May 9, 1945, pushing furiously to finish their prototype of a bomb. The war was ending; that was clear. And while Hitler was on the edge of defeat, the Americans were on the edge of producing the bomb first. Anna couldn't let that happen. They were allies, but she didn't trust them. She'd read the Soviet papers, knew Americans were beholden to money above all. Dollars were a source of corruption only made deeper by their culture of films, jazz, and pulp magazines. These poisons distracted their attention from the real struggle of the lower classes who needed food and education. She couldn't let that nonsense spread to the USSR.

She bent over a sketch she'd made of an improved gun assembly, one Yasha helped her simplify. Igor sat across from her. His eyes were closed, deep in thought. Yasha dozed at his desk in the corner. After almost two years, he was still tasked with trailing Anna, and like everyone, he was showing signs of wear from the war. His features had always been bunched too close, but they seemed even closer now, his forehead higher.

"The radio! The radio!" the night guard yelled suddenly in the hallway. Igor startled awake and hurried to the tuner sitting on a table in the corner. Yasha jumped to his feet, hand on his gun. A moment later, there was an explosion. The lights flickered. The tables shook and Anna slid under her desk, put her arms over her head.

"An invasion," she yelled. A searchlight scraped through the window, ran across the top half of the lab. Were Yulia, Lazar, and Malka safe? Then came another explosion and this time she recognized the sound. It was a cannon. The floor shook.

"The war's over!" the guard yelled. Igor turned the radio volume up as high as it would go. "Zhukov has accepted the surrender. It is over. Over." Anna sat still, though she knew she should jump and celebrate. She thought about how she and Yulia had barely made it to the USSR from Germany, how they'd spent months huddled in the woods, running to avoid dogs and searchlights and farmers who could have reported them or killed them. She still didn't even know how they had been so lucky. Now it was all over. She curled into a ball, hugged her knees to her chest. "Over! It's over!" the guard kept yelling.

"Anna." Yasha slid down to the floor next to her. "Anna, it's okay," he said. "The cannons are a celebration. That's all." He took her hand and helped her up and over to the window so they could see the excitement outside. But a thick fog hung over the city so she couldn't see much. Her heart was racing; her hands were sweating.

She spotted a group of people walking down the middle of the street, singing. Cheers rose behind them. "How can they celebrate?" she asked. "So many, too many, died to get here."

Yasha held her hand as he walked her home, kept them together. They dodged rowdy soldiers and women flirting, everyone drinking and celebrating the end of the war. She showed him into an alley, a shortcut to her building. It was quieter and private. Tucked in between cement and bricks, he wrapped an arm around her waist and pulled her close. "You're beautiful," he said.

She slipped away but he caught her hand and held her in place. She felt a flash of panic. Even though she held a higher rank, it meant nothing. He was bigger and stronger, a man tasked with overseeing her. He had power over her and she was a fool for leading him into that alley. No matter how high she rose or how hard she worked, she could never escape being a woman to her colleagues, even to the kindest of men like Yasha. "Please, let go," she said, hoping she sounded forceful.

"I'm sorry," he said, quickly realizing, pulling back. "I scared you. I didn't mean to." She hurried out of the alley, into the wider street. A man and a woman walking arm-in-arm passed them, laughing. Someone was playing the accordion. "I'd never hurt you. Never," Yasha said, running to catch up. "I know you're underappreciated in that lab." They dodged a swarm of people dancing. "They should all look up to you. Realize what you've done for our country. We need comrades like you to lead us forward. The USSR is so new and there isn't a man anywhere who's better than you." This was the praise she had dreamed about for years, but coming so close to what happened in the alley, she couldn't take it in. She looked to the side nervously. He kept talking. "The Soviet Union, we are destined for greatness. My parents were starving peasants. They left their land, made a life for their family working in factories, and look what they got in return. My sister and I, we're educated. Look at my job. What else could anyone want? The Czar was a curse." He stopped and she knew he was waiting for her to say something, anything. "I'm sorry," he said again. "I really didn't mean to scare you."

"I know." She believed him. "That doesn't mean you didn't."

"I meant what I said. That I think you're beautiful. The most beautiful and smartest woman I've ever met." He cleared his throat. They were at the entrance to her building. The wind swept through the half structure across the street with a sound like whimpering. "You don't have to say anything now. Maybe. I mean, I hope one day you will. Can I walk you inside?" She hesitated. "Just to make sure you're safe?" She didn't want him to come with her, but the night was chaotic, out of control with too many people drinking too much vodka, and so she nodded. He was safer than what she might find inside. They made their way up one flight and another. She thought about the last time he was on those stairs, the night he came for her. He must have been thinking the same. "We've still never been to the theater together," he said. "I hated taking you in. The way you shook and babbled in this stairwell."

She stopped to ask him a question that had been bothering her ever since. "The play. It was illegal, an underground performance. Why would you take me there? Was it a test?"

"No." He shook his head and dropped his voice to a whisper. "I can't tell them everything. And I'd read your work, notes in your file from Berlin. There was a line about time travel. I wasn't sure if you thought you could actually research it, but I guessed, maybe you were interested. That you'd like a play like *Ivan Vasilievich*."

She took a closer look at him then, at the way he faced her, what he had said to her. The only other person who had ever thought so much about her and what she might like was Yulia. "Thank you," she said. It wasn't enough or even the right thing to say but it was all she could manage.

When they reached her door, she took out her key. Already she could smell Malka's roses. She wanted him to leave then, needed space and time to think about everything that had happened. "Everyone's asleep inside. Good night."

"Trust me," Yasha said, "no one is sleeping tonight. We're all celebrating!"

"Annushka?" Yulia called from inside. Her voice sounded different, deeper, like the voice she used when she spoke to men in the cafés in

Berlin, and Anna felt a flash of panic. Was there someone else inside with her? Where were Lazar and Malka? She opened the door quickly. There was the click of a lighter, then a flame as Yulia lit a candle. Wax was cheaper than electricity. That was when Anna saw Lazar in Yulia's bed, under the blanket with her. Malka was sound asleep in the other room, snoring. Yulia and Lazar should have been embarrassed but neither of them tried to hide anything.

"You're...together?"

"Maybe give them a minute," Yasha said. Anna had forgotten he was there.

"How long?" Anna demanded, sounding angry, feeling hurt.

"A few months," Yulia said.

"I love her," Lazar said, and Anna's knees must have buckled because she felt Yasha holding her tight, felt the gun at his belt press into her hip.

"Who's that?" Lazar asked, pointing to Yasha. "The man who came for you, right?"

"Yasha," Yulia said. Anna wanted to disappear, to run back downstairs, out to the street, but she couldn't move. Yulia. Her Yulia in bed with Lazar. She had always known that Yulia had never really been hers, at least not in that way. And now that she found them together, she realized she had noticed how Lazar looked at Yulia. It was something she'd cast aside as innocent infatuation, but if she was being honest, hadn't Yulia been talking about Lazar more, wanting to be with him more? "Hello, Yasha," Yulia said, filling in the silence.

"Hello," Yasha said. He gave a small bow. "It is my privilege to work with Anna. I requested the post specifically to meet her."

"To be with her?" Yulia asked.

"Of course," he said. Anna still couldn't manage a word, but Yasha seemed unfazed. He took up the conversation exactly where she could not, and she was grateful. "We'll leave you two for a little longer," Yasha said, taking her hand.

Anna wanted to close the door, to run and scream and cry all at once. The family they had built, the security Anna finally knew felt like it was crumbling, leaving her on the outside, exposed. Yasha somehow must have understood because he helped her down the stairs and onto a bench in the park across the street. There he wrapped her in his arms while she cried, let go of tears she didn't even know she still had. They were from heartbreak and betrayal, from surprise, perhaps tears she had held on to waiting for the war to end, too. And Yasha, the man she'd hated for keeping her from Igor, for watching over her every move, who was only a part of her work life, was the one who held her close. "It's better this way," Yasha said. "He was too young for you. Obviously not smart enough for you." Anna didn't dare correct him.

"It hurts," she said, and he only held her tighter.

"We can work through this together. We can work through anything together."

* * *

The next day, Yasha was waiting for Anna at the park bench when she left for work. He held her hand as they walked to the lab. "You'll be stronger because of this," he said. That day she and Igor activated their first actual reactor—not a prototype. It worked, and where Igor jumped with joy, Anna pushed herself to smile, terrified by what they'd built, by how quickly she was losing control of everything she had constructed. Yasha walked her home again that afternoon. "Time will help you heal," he said.

Soon they were eating lunch together every day. Then he invited her to dinner. When Anna came home after that meal, she found Yulia and Lazar curled together again. This time they didn't wake up, and after that, they spent every night in that small bed. A month later, Yasha kissed Anna for the first time. It was in the park, what she had taken to calling their park. It wasn't rushed and drunken like the kisses in the cafés of Berlin, or the sloppy kisses when she was a student at the university. It was slow and quiet. The air was crisp, just warm. Anna leaned in because he tasted sweet and he was so tender, and she was surprised that she wanted it. She wanted him to kiss her, to hold her. Later, before he walked her to her door, she said, "I won't be your mistress. I don't just want an affair."

"I don't want that, either." He laughed. "So, you want to get married?"

"No. I just meant I don't want to be a woman you sleep with here and there and then move on. I need more than that."

He kissed her again. "I would never, could never think of you that way. We are a team. I can support your brilliance. I can get whatever you need to run your laboratory. I have the eyes and ears of powerful men and I want to use that for you, for us."

She liked that he thought of her, of them, that way—as a team. Though she didn't like the idea of him writing reports, asking for permission on her behalf. She wanted to do it on her own, be beholden to no one. But she understood the world didn't work that way. She was only a woman. "When you write your reports about me, do you tell them everything?"

"Obviously not *everything*."

It wasn't obvious to Anna what that meant. "Explain. You mean like the tickets you bought for the play?"

"Yes." He grinned. "And I've never told them I'm in love with you." She hadn't expected that. She stepped back and put her hand on her head. He *loved* her. It was a word she only ever used to talk about Yulia and Mama. Before Papa had become a drunk, she'd loved him, too. But all of them had broken her heart. "Why is it so hard to believe?" He smiled. "Actually, that's part of what I love so much about you. You doubt yourself. You never believe you're as great as you are. If you were a man, you would brag. You would lord it over everyone." He paused. "You would expect love. And if you were like other women, you would wear more makeup, spend time flirting with the men in our lab instead of working side by side with them as strict colleagues."

"I didn't think—"

"You don't have to say anything. When you're ready, you can respond." He leaned over and touched his lips to hers. "Don't worry, I won't report this," he said with a smile. He deepened the kiss and she let herself fall into it.

Another month passed with them spending time together and Yulia invited Yasha for dinner. He and Lazar joked with each other while they ate cabbage soup flavored with marrow bones Yasha had somehow delivered that morning as a surprise. He had such an easy way about him that made people comfortable. It was why he was a perfect spy, he confided once. He was funny, too. He did impressions of Igor and of what he thought Americans were like. They all laughed easily, but when Yasha started to talk about his love for Stalin, everyone around the table went quiet. "He came from humble beginnings and rose up to greatness," Yasha said. "He robbed banks, the rich, was exiled over and over, but he always escaped. The will to return, to fight for his people is the most admirable of all."

"He murdered millions," Lazar said.

"It was a sacrifice for the greater good. Not murder," Yasha said.

Lazar leaned back and put his napkin on the table, looking Yasha in the eye. "I want to go to America one day," he said.

"That is a dangerous thing to say," Yasha replied.

"But they have it all. You can start with nothing and work to become a very rich man. No one asks for your papers. No one cares. And they don't have to sacrifice millions of their people, endure Siberia, to do it."

"What you describe doesn't actually exist. It's what they want you to believe. You're giving in to their propaganda."

"Are you giving in to ours?" Lazar stood up and walked to the window. Anna looked at Yulia nervously.

"Maybe we should start the dishes," Anna said. She fumbled with the bowls.

Yasha held her hand, stopped her and continued as if reciting a speech, but with so much conviction his eyes were rimmed with tears. "I will pretend I didn't hear that," he said. "That instead you said you agree and embrace our new five-year plan. We will rehabilitate the devastated regions of our country, restore industry and agriculture to the prewar level, and then exceed it. The rationing system will be abolished. We'll pay special attention to science, of course to science." He looked at Anna. "I have no doubt that our scientists will, in the very near future, not only overtake but even outstrip the achievements of science beyond the borders of our country." He stopped. "Our future is better than any of the American trash they try to peddle as success."

△ △ △

"So, Yasha was a kind man," Molly said. The fire had burned down by then, their tea gone cold. "I don't understand why you grew to hate him."

"I don't hate him. He made choices I wouldn't, put country over family."

"But you're putting science over family."

"What do you mean? I used science to save Raisa, to bring you here."

"Those are excuses. If family was more important, you'd be in America with Mama and Papa. You would have found a way to work there. You're hiding here."

Anna shook her head. "There's so much you don't know." Molly begged her to keep talking, to tell her everything, but Anna couldn't. She needed a break. "Later," she said. "I'll tell you more later."

PART VI

Do not be moved to anger easily.

—Pirkei Avot

RAISA

Philadelphia

A re you sure Baba Anna never said anything about a nurse?" Raisa said to Baba and Pop-Pop at breakfast the day after she got back from the prison. She never told them she went because she knew how upset they'd be to hear Mama had left again without telling any of them. Better to just leave everything as it was, she figured. Only first she needed answers about Anna and Vera.

"No. She didn't have a nurse when we left, and we haven't heard from her since."

"It can't be a coincidence that Vera's job was to watch over my grandmother. That Daniel and his mother came here."

"No, it's not," Baba agreed. "Anna did things for people she loved. She likely made arrangements because she knew they would be safe here, we would help. That man who came to Daniel, he must have been a dear friend of Anna's."

"Everyone lands in America near someone they know," Pop-Pop said.

"That means she really designed and built Chernobyl. It's all real?"

"Probably," Baba said without looking her in the eye. She and Pop-Pop both went back to work, to their day, like it wasn't a big deal, refusing to say any more. But Raisa couldn't just drop it. She didn't understand how they could take this information in stride. She wanted to know why Anna loved Vera so much that she took care of her, what they did together, and more, much more about her role at Chernobyl. For Daniel, she wanted to know what happened in the end, and she wanted to know if maybe, just maybe, Vera escaped with Anna, if they were both alive. Any hope was worth holding on to for Daniel and his mother. She didn't understand why her grandparents couldn't see that, didn't want to know more.

"It's infuriating," she said to Daniel while they were working in the Chopping Room later. He handed her the bleach to wash down the counter. "Why won't they talk about it?"

"What's there to say? They worked together; she sent us here. I guess that's all there is."

"But where were they when Reactor Number Four melted? Maybe they both survived."

"Maybe your grandparents are right, best to let it go." He put down the knife he was holding and walked over to Raisa, took her hand. "I've thought a lot about it since we figured out their connection and I know, knew, Vera. She would never disappear like that. She's dead and I don't think your grandparents are hiding anything. I was holding on to hope as a kind of dream but it's not real. I have to accept that she's gone and Anna did this one incredible thing for our family. She sent us here to Philadelphia, to your grandparents, and we found each other. We need to be grateful for that."

The next week, Mr. Kestler came to the Market to see her. It was a Thursday and he never came on Thursday. Her first thought was that something must have happened. She and Daniel both put down the crates of chickens they were carrying to the cooler. The smell of fat was heavy in the room. She braced herself for him to tell her he'd sold the building, remembering he had been trying for years. And she was hit with regret that she hadn't done more with what she had. She still needed time on that roof to add more satellite dishes, to increase the power of the telescope. While most of what she found was expected and fascinating, there was a small anomaly she couldn't explain. She'd researched it and discovered a few astrophysicists had found the same, suggested it was echoes or the reflection of light from novas or super-novas, but she was sure they were wrong. The anomalies Raisa found were too bright to be explained away so easily, and she had to keep studying them, to figure out what she'd found, because she couldn't help but think they were the ripples in space-time described in *Atomic Anna*, only she wasn't sure yet.

"What's going on, Mr. Kestler?" Raisa asked. Her voice sounded high-pitched and as nervous as she felt. Before she'd finished the question, another man stepped through the plastic flaps behind him. That man was tall, with brown skin and hair cut so close his scalp broke through. What struck Raisa was his perfect posture, his creased pants, and the fact that he was Black; Black people rarely came to Little Russia.

"I was up on my roof this morning," Mr. Kestler said. "All those wires you've hooked up, and screens. Computers. I found them under your tarps. There's enough equipment up there to wire a city." He shook his head, but he was grinning, showing he was impressed. He was also waiting, it seemed, for Raisa to say something. It occurred to her it was possible she was being busted, was in trouble for using too much electricity, but he kept talking. "You're panicking. Don't. You're not in trouble." Mr. Kestler laughed. His mustache went askew at a hard angle. "You see, the University of Pennsylvania is expanding. They've bought up most of the block, including my building. They'll be tearing it down. The electric company is coming soon to disconnect all the lines, so I went up to see what you have been doing before they did. It's astonishing. Which is why I brought my friend with me to see it, then here. This is Philip Stocken. He's a professor at Penn. Physics. I took him up there to see what you'd been working on because I couldn't explain it, but I knew it was brilliant."

"Astrophysics," Stocken said. He walked toward Raisa and held out his hand to shake hers. "Kestler and I go back a long way. Who helped you with your work?"

"No one."

"Incredible," he said, shaking his head.

"I've always loved radios and I'm learning about electromagnetism," she said. Daniel was next to her. He crossed his arms over his chest and she knew he was scared, too. This was what he'd warned her about, getting caught. "You're sure we're not in trouble?"

"Positive," Kestler said, and Daniel's shoulders inched down but only slightly.

"You've been discovered. I see you. You can't hide anymore—and you shouldn't," Stocken said, cutting in. "Here's how I see it. On the roof of a run-down old building, a seventeen-year-old kid built a radio telescope in the city of Philadelphia as powerful as anything we have on campus. To top it off, that kid built her own parts and programmed computers she juiced to parse whatever data she collected, to control the thing." He paused to make sure Raisa was following. "What the hell was she doing up there? I asked myself." Raisa opened her mouth to launch a defense, but he held up a hand and stopped her. "You didn't have passwords on those machines. I'm assuming it's because you didn't expect anyone up on that roof. Am I right?"

She shrugged, still not sure if she could trust him.

"What are you searching for up there?"

"I was learning, that's all. I wasn't sure what I'd find. That telescope gives me the pieces, creates images I can't see."

"Any amateur or hack could say that," Stocken said. "No one would spend all that time and effort up there just to learn without a goal. What are you after?"

She bit her bottom lip and considered how much she should share. Talking about ripples in space-time would sound strange, off-the-wall. And there was no way she was ready to share her larger theory, that she thought what she was seeing had to do with gravity, when no one, not even Einstein, could figure out how gravity fit into electromagnetic theory. "I've been looking at anomalies, at light echoes in particular," she said quietly. It was a partial answer. "Our understanding of what they show or how they manifest themselves in the universe is inaccurate."

"Okay. All right," he said. He put his finger up to his lips and seemed to be thinking. The quiet in the room was punctuated by the ding of the cash register. Mr. Kestler stood there grinning.

"I told you, she's smarter than both of us combined," Mr. Kestler finally said.

"Have you thought about college?" Stocken asked. Of course she had. She'd thought about the bills, about leaving her grandparents, about what would happen to Daniel. The money from the contest wouldn't go nearly as far as she had planned, and while she knew she would work as hard as it took to send herself, she was still worried it wouldn't be enough.

"Can you help her with a scholarship?" Daniel asked, knowing she stayed up at night running through budgets and scenarios to pay for everything.

"Daniel," Raisa said, trying to pull him back.

He faced her and spoke in Russian. "Raisa, he could help. Mr. Kestler wouldn't bring him here unless that was the case." He turned back to Stocken, to English. "Well, a scholarship?"

Stocken stared at Raisa for a long time. Finally, he said, "Those anomalies might be because you don't understand. Or maybe you're confusing concepts. We can look into all of that." He took a step closer. "If you ask big questions, you might get big answers and those aren't always easy. I have a math problem for you. I'll leave it here." He made a show of taking a folded piece of paper from his pocket and placing it on the counter. "Work through it, then come and see me. Because yes, I think I can help."

* * *

Raisa stood on the threshold of Professor Philip Stocken's office. She hesitated before she knocked. She had the answer to the problem he'd given her in her bag. She could still turn around, go back to the Chopping Room and forget all of this. A part of her wanted that, because she knew her solution was correct, and she knew bringing it to Stocken, stepping into his office, was going to point her in a new direction, a direction Daniel, Baba, and Pop-Pop couldn't follow—that she would face it alone. She leaned against the doorpost, saw that Stocken's window looked out on a brick courtyard framed by old trees. The hum of lawnmowers snuck through the glass. The top of his shiny scalp poked out from behind a five-screen computer array that curled over in two levels. She could still turn around and forget all about this, go back to the life she loved with her grandparents and Daniel, keep running through budgets to make college happen. Or she could step forward into a life where she would finally be challenged by the people who wrote all those books she stole. Stepping forward felt like stepping away, and she didn't want to leave what she had. *You want this*, she reminded herself. Daniel, Baba, and Pop-Pop were only a few miles away if she needed them. She cleared her throat, spoke up. "Professor?"

Stocken leaned to the side so he could see her. His glasses were halfway down his nose. "Raisa. Already? It's only been four days."

She pulled out the piece of paper with her solution. "You asked for tree structures, so I drew them. The answer is there are ten homomorphically irreducible trees with n=10. They're here."

"Did anyone help you?"

"Who would help me?"

He laughed and pushed his chair back and stood up. "Take me through it."

Raisa hesitated. She wasn't used to explaining her work. Her teachers had only ever wanted to know the answers; so long as she was right, that was all they cared about.

"Nothing fancy, just show me your steps. Show me your logic."

She didn't use logic. She felt her way to the answer. She visualized the solution. Once she could see the tree structures, she manipulated them. She jotted down notes, but none of that was a cohesive line-by-line proof. She realized how ridiculous that was now. And she thought about that first day she sat at the library with Daniel and explained to him how important proofs were. Yet here she was, staring down a huge opportunity, and she hadn't even worked through the proofs that of course he'd want to see. "I didn't think you'd care how I got to the answer," she said, cringing.

He chuckled. "No one asks you, do they?" He shook his head and she knew he saw how nervous she was. He continued, "Okay. Show me what you've got." He walked over to her, ushered her inside and took the paper, used his finger to trace line after line of her work. She held her breath, wasn't sure if she was supposed to say anything. "Yes," he said. "Yes. You saw that. And that." In the hall, a pair of students walked by. The lawnmowers went silent. "How do you know Cayley's work?"

"Found it in a textbook." She looked down at the linoleum.

"You're self-taught." It wasn't a question, more of a realization. "It's why you don't use conventional notations. That makes sense." He pointed to one of the lines where he had stalled. "I wouldn't express the equation this way, but you're not wrong. It's just not conventional."

"I'm right, though," she said. "Maybe my notes aren't normal, but my answer is right. There are ten and this is what they look like." She knew it because the numbers flowed. She hadn't forced any of it.

"Absolutely correct. Please, take a seat." She didn't sit. Instead she watched him carefully as he walked back toward his computer screens. He didn't sit either. He walked to the window and looked out at those old trees. "I have another student who's also in high school. A senior like you. He was one of the finalists at that math competition you won. Anyway, I volunteer at a youth center. That's where I met him. I invited him to start coming here twice a week to work with me. He's extraordinary. Is there any chance you would be interested in joining us? His name is Vito. He speaks Russian. He learned because he plays chess." Stocken smiled. "He told me good chess players know Russian."

"I have to work at my grandparents' store," Raisa said, thinking she might regret what she'd done, that she would miss Daniel and her grandparents if she came every week because already her decision was taking her farther away from them.

"I'll pay you for your time. I have a grant to cover you, bus fare." Raisa still hesitated. "I bet you've never had a math teacher who challenged you, did you? You have no idea what it will be like to sit in a room where you don't know the answer. Are you scared?"

"No," she lied. "I'm in."

* * *

Raisa returned one week later. She arrived an hour early and was shocked to find the other student already there. He was small with short dark hair and round wire-frame glasses. He fidgeted with the strap on his backpack and smiled when he saw her. "Welcome. I am Vito Sicarelli," he said in Russian with a thick American accent. She already knew he wasn't used to speaking the language, that he had practiced his introduction. They shook hands. His palms were soft; he had no calluses like Daniel's.

"English is fine," Raisa said.

"I don't mind Russian." But his words came slowly and she could see he struggled.

"You know I was born in America, right?"

He looked to the side, started playing with the strap on his bag again. "I'm sorry. At the math competition, I heard you speaking to that guy in Russian. Anyway. Great. English. To be honest, I'm relieved. I hear you live in the Northeast. I've been to the flea market there. All that junk." He laughed. "My parents don't like to go but I do. The things you can find."

"Treasures," Raisa said. She had neighbors who sold anything they could in order to make rent. "It's not junk in those flea markets."

His neck flushed and he looked down. "I live in Roxborough. Do you know it? It's not that far." Already she could tell Vito had the American habit of talking to fill silence. But Roxborough she knew. The local paper there had published Mama's comics. He continued, "Stocken, he's been tutoring me for a while. I have to take three buses to get here, but it's worth it. My father says opportunities like this are how you get ahead. Edison, Ford, and Morgan. He says they weren't first, they just pushed the hardest. History remembers those who push and—"

"You have a lot to say."

"Sorry, I'm nervous. Stocken, he's a big deal. Bringing you in, it's a big deal, too."

"What does that mean?"

"He could get us in, here, to Penn."

"I couldn't afford to go here."

"They have financial aid."

"Ah, you're both early," Stocken interrupted. He stepped into the hall and pointed to a door farther down marked MAUI. They followed him inside. The space was square and as large as a classroom. There were three overstuffed black chairs in the middle of the room. The walls were blackboards from floor to ceiling except for three windows. Two posters were taped to the blackboards; one featured an enormous wave and the other a beach scene framed by palm trees. Stocken settled in, crossing his legs. Raisa was struck by the way he moved. He was fluid and at ease the way she wanted to be. "Relax," he said with a smile. "There are no more tests."

"Yeah, but you're Professor Stocken. And—" Vito started, but Stocken cut him off.

"Next time, you'll leave your backpacks outside the door. In this room, we don't bring in any baggage or books or even notes. We generate ideas and put them up on these walls. Please, take a seat."

Vito went first, hurrying to follow orders. Raisa was slower, easing into a chair. "Is that sand on the floor?" she asked.

"Yes." Stocken laughed. "You saw the name of this room, right? Maui is my favorite place on earth. When I go there, I let my mind run free. And the waves, they're terrifying. I don't surf, never want to because I have too much respect for the ocean." He gestured to the walls around them. "In here, the only thing I do is think." It struck her as a waste of space. And she felt like a child at the grown-ups' table, having sunk so deep into the black leather chair. She was relieved to see Vito looked as uncomfortable as she was. "Science at its highest levels isn't about math," Stocken continued. "It's about ideas and observations. We must understand the world around us first. We use math to describe it, to show what we can already see. We won't use textbooks or calculators or computers together. We're here to think. It will be months before I see any numbers enter this room."

"But I'm here for math," Vito interrupted.

"This is math. That's what I'm telling you. If you want to memorize equations or times tables, please. There's the door." He paused. "Tell me, either of you, what do you know about Einstein? Not his crazy hair. Not his famous formulas. How did he work?" Raisa had no idea. She assumed he sat at a desk and read a lot of books, went to lectures. Stocken continued, "Ideas. That's how he worked. Ideas first. Math later. That's what we'll do here. Ideas. Then math. Both of you have already proven you're exceptional, that you can follow and re-create what's already been done, but what about pushing those boundaries? Einstein, he was a revolutionary because he dared to daydream. That's what I want the two of you to do. Daydream. We'll begin with the idea of simultaneity. Einstein didn't start by working through equations. He couldn't. He had to know the problem before he could translate it into math.

"Imagine two women arrive at a train station together. They are friends. One is bidding the other farewell. Perhaps one sheds a tear because she knows it will be a long time before they see each other again. Or maybe their goodbyes are hurried because they are late. The train is already on the platform. Is it a cold fall day? A hot summer afternoon? Tell me about it."

"Why?" Raisa asked. "I don't understand what this has to do with math."

"I'm teaching you to think. To understand a problem, you need to see it. Every detail is a part of what you must solve." Stocken stood up. "Close your eyes." He pressed a button on the wall and shades came down over the windows. He turned out the lights. "Two women are at the train station. Make it an afternoon in August. What are they wearing, Vito?"

"T-shirts and shorts."

"They're young?"

"Yes."

"It's hot. Very hot. And the air is thick. It feels like rain. What does that smell like?"

"Sewage," Raisa said. "And asphalt."

"Okay, Philadelphia hot." Stocken laughed.

They went through this process for nearly an hour. Stocken had them imagine every detail from the laces on the women's shoes to the gum stuck on the cement platform. At first Raisa thought it was pointless, stupid, but the longer he persisted, the more she fell into his experiment. She felt like one of those women on the platform. She got onto the train that left the station while her mother, not a friend, stayed behind. Mama didn't wave, didn't kiss her goodbye. She just turned around and left as Raisa pulled away.

"There's a storm coming," Stocken said. "Raisa, did you hear me?" Raisa shook her head. "Two strikes of lightning break across the sky. Is the sky dark now? Or light?"

"It's light, gray. There are lots of clouds," Vito said.

"Good. Good. Both women see the lightning, but how? What's different for the woman in the train that's speeding out of the station?"

"Nothing," Vito said. "Lightning is lightning. It strikes. Nothing's different."

"No. Feel the wind, the rain. Look at the lightning from both perspectives," Stocken said. Raisa squeezed her eyelids together. What did he want her to see? What did Einstein see? She felt the rain, the wind, even the vibration of the train under her. Pigeons cooed, perched on rafters. What did each of the women see? "I'm going to leave you with this problem. I'm not going to tell you the answer. I know you can go to the library and look it up as soon as you leave this room, but I'm going to trust that you won't. I want you to figure it out on your own because this is where real math starts."

It took Raisa a full month to find a solution that was elegant, not forced, to see it: While the woman on the platform witnessed the two lightning strikes as simultaneous events, the woman sitting in the train saw one strike a moment before the other. The two women perceived the event differently. Who was right? That was the point. Neither of them. There was no correct time—only relative time, which meant the present, past, and future were blurred. It was such a wild idea that it scared Raisa. It approached some of what she'd found in the latest copy of *Atomic Anna*, where Anna said the same. There is no difference between past, present, and future. That was what enabled her machine, why she was able to bend time.

* * *

A week before their high school graduation, Daniel called Raisa and said he wouldn't be coming to school or to work that day. "I love you," he said before he hung up. He had said it before, but it sounded different that morning. She heard it in the lilt in his voice, in the way he hesitated. Later, after the store was closed, he came into the Chopping Room while she was washing down the counters. Pop-Pop was up front closing out the cash register, waiting to take her home. She still never liked to be alone.

"Raisa, I'll leave you two," Pop-Pop called.

Daniel wore an army uniform, camouflage pants with a matching jacket and black boots. He smelled like shoe polish and his hair was cropped so short she couldn't see any hint of the waves that used to be there. All of it caught her off guard and she dropped the five-gallon bucket of water she was holding. The dirty gray liquid soaked Raisa's sneakers and lapped up the side of Daniel's boots, but she didn't move. Seeing him there, in that uniform, made her picture him being shot, bleeding. She could imagine him trying to do something heroic, jumping up to pull a man to safety or trying to provide cover for a soldier caught where they shouldn't be—and Daniel would die. She was sure he was going to die and she couldn't move. She couldn't lose him, too. He was the one who grabbed a mop and pushed the spilled water toward the drain in the middle of the floor. "I signed up for ROTC," he said. She knew he was waiting for her to say something, to move, but she couldn't. Yes, they had talked about it. They had gone back and forth. Raisa was going to Penn in the fall. Stocken had helped her apply and secure full funding. Daniel was just off the waitlist at Temple and had a scholarship. It covered tuition but not room and board, so he would live at home and work twenty hours a week. It would be hard. Money would be tight, but he could do it and Raisa would see him Friday through Monday. She'd helped him work through the numbers, the accounting. He didn't need the extra money ROTC would provide. He didn't need to be a soldier. But now he was.

"It's better this way," he said. "You know I want this."

"They're going to make you practice killing people. Can you live with that?" she asked.

"Learning to shoot isn't practice to kill. I'm not going to kill anyone."

"The purpose of an army is to fight and kill. If you're a part of it, you're killing whether you're pulling a trigger or stuck in a laundry room. It's all the same purpose."

"It's not that simple. An army is a deterrent, too. We've been through this. And not everyone uses a gun or shoots missiles. They need my language skills, more soldiers who speak Russian. I'll be translating."

"Then they'll send you abroad," she warned. "You'll translate documents they need to plan how and where to kill people." She tried to slow down but she couldn't, couldn't stop herself from imagining him bleeding in the snow, dying. "You'll be overseas."

He put the mop down and reached for her hand. "You know I've wanted to do this for a long time. Plus, my mom and I, we need the extra money." Raisa's heart was beating so fast it hurt and her hands were shaking. "I won't die."

"You will. And they're going to send you off somewhere. You're going to leave."

"I'll see you as much as I can. We'll make a schedule."

"I can't lose you. I can't." She knew he meant what he said, that he believed he'd see her often, but she also knew that wasn't true. He'd be busy. The army, his superiors, would realize how smart he was and give him more to do. She could already feel him slipping away, the world changing under her. It was bad enough that she was going to Penn, that they wouldn't be together every day.

"You won't lose me," Daniel said. He reached for her and hugged her so tight his ribs pressed against her. It didn't feel close enough. "Raisele, I'll be fine."

"It's not worth it."

"Raisa, you're not being fair. You have your own work, your own future. You have something you love, and that you're good at—your math. I don't. This is the first time I might find it. I could find my place, really do something that matters." He sounded so passionate and convinced. She'd never heard him so sure of himself.

"You're smart. You can use your brain. You don't need to fight."

"I am using my brain the best way I can. I'll be translating."

She pulled away and reached for the mop because there was nothing else to say. He had already made his decision, cut his hair, signed his name. Daniel stopped her, put his hand over hers, moved the mop to the side. He wound his fingers through hers the way he had more times than she could count, and then, without warning, he reached into his pocket and pulled out a gold chain with two pendants, two golden bears. "My mother, she gave me some old gold jewelry. I had it melted down and made into this, for you." He held it up. "It looks just like the bears in your grandparents' house. You've told me you love all they symbolize and it's everything I can give. We can fight together, we can be at peace and love together. It's my promise to you that I'll never leave you. That nothing will ever pull us apart," Daniel said. He took a deep breath and Raisa kept staring at the necklace. It was the last thing in the world she expected from him, and her mind was spinning. The bears sparkled under the light and she remembered something. He kept talking. "I just want you to know that we can make promises to each other for later." She closed her eyes, and she wasn't standing in the Chopping Room anymore. She was back on the beach with the old woman with the bloody hands. Was it her grandmother, Anna? She also wore two bear pendants—the same pendants. Raisa had never put that together before, that the bears in the dining room matched that woman's pendants.

"Raisele," Daniel said. "What's wrong? You're shaking."

"The bears," she said.

He dropped his head. His chin fell to his chest. "If you don't like them, you don't have to keep them. I mean, I just wanted you to know how much I love you. That I can't see my future, my life, without you."

She didn't want to explain, not then. She could see how terrified Daniel was, that he needed her to wear that necklace. She had always thought she needed him more, but maybe she had that wrong. They needed each other. She asked him to help her put the necklace on her and then, after he did, he kissed the back of her neck.

ANNA

Mount Aragats

Anna and Molly were sitting by the picture windows in the main compound, watching the mountains topped in ice. "Do you remember telling me about Yasha last month?" Molly said. "You told me about how you started dating, but you never said why you married or when. Why you pushed me away."

Anna smiled, relieved to go into the memories she could still retrieve easily. Instead of healing, her mind was only getting slower, and now larger lesions were also opening on her skin. They hurt, wouldn't heal like her hands did after a jump. "Are you sure you want the answers?" Molly nodded and Anna started, "You weren't something I ever thought I'd have. Especially not in the way it happened." She kept her eyes on the mountains, away from her daughter's gaze. It sounded unnatural to admit she was a woman who didn't want a child. It made her feel shame. But she had seen women who were poor and begging on the streets with toddlers pulling their skirts and babies wailing in their arms. Surely those women never wanted children like that, did they? It was easier to live on your own, to worry about yourself. That way you couldn't lose anyone, either. "Even if I kept you, I would have lost you. The Soviets looked at family as unimportant. The collective was what mattered most. I couldn't live with myself if I let them take you. Worse, it was what Yasha wanted. He wanted you to go to them." She blinked. "You resemble him, you know, the way you open yourself to the world, open your heart. You even bite your lip in the same way. But you fight like my mother." Anna looked at Molly. "Did you always want a child? Did you imagine having Raisa before you found out you were expecting?"

"I wanted her." It wasn't a complete lie. Out of fear, her reflex had been to ask for an abortion. But it wasn't what she truly desired. "Almost immediately, I wanted her."

"I envy that confidence. Never believed I could make a good life for a child. I have lived terrified of the Czar, the Nazis, and the Soviets. No government can be good in this world. They don't want to govern, they want to control."

"Where is he now, my birth father?"

"Moscow." Anna paused and Molly stood, went to the steaming samovar and made them tea. Anna turned and perched on the back of the couch to face her. "It's taken me a long, long time to really understand what happened between us, Yasha and I, but I think, maybe, over the years, we destroyed each other." She leaned back. "The truth is we pushed each other away. I never let him in, but there was such an imbalance. He had power over me because he reported everything I did to the KGB. With one missive he could have me thrown in prison. Last I saw him was at a restaurant in Moscow. He never stopped missing you, thinking about you."

"Why?"

"Why what?"

"Why did you push him away? Why didn't you run with me? Why did you send me, Yulia, and Lazar so far away?"

Anna tried to keep herself steady. "I always thought my own mother had all the answers, too. Now I wonder if she had any at all. I'll tell you the rest."

△ △ △

Yasha and Anna married the same day as Lazar and Yulia, in August 1945. They went together to the office where marriage certificates were issued. The clerk behind the desk looked bored. Malka threw flowers and cried for all of them. Afterward, Lazar wanted them to go for lunch to celebrate, but Yasha thought that was a waste. "Splurging is a capitalist vice," he said, and Anna agreed. Better to go back to work, so she and Yasha went to the laboratory.

"Lazar's an idiot," Yasha whispered as they walked away. "Look at the size of his feet. Anyone would know he was a fool with feet like that." His silly comment, the hint of jealousy, made Anna laugh. That was what she needed to break from Yulia, the laughter. He made her smile more and more often, whereas she had so rarely smiled since leaving Berlin. That day he kissed her, in front of security, in front of everyone. It wasn't hesitant or soft but full of passion. Anna had come to enjoy his kisses, crave them even. She liked feeling him, his skin next to hers, filling the spaces in her heart she used to hold for Yulia. After that kiss, security never once pulled her aside again, even when Yasha wasn't around, and the comments in the lab stopped, too. She and he sat close at work, their chairs touching, their thighs often pressed together.

Anna worked tirelessly on her amplifier during those early years. She was terrified of the power a nuclear bomb would release, or an accident at a nuclear power plant. Surely there was a way to make as much energy with less risk. One day, Yasha came running home from a meeting. He had requested more funding for her amplifier project, for the cosmic ray station. The wind that night cut through the cement of their building and whistled around corners. "I'm sorry," he said, out

313

of breath, his trench coat still on. He looked sad and beaten down, not angry the way she wanted him to be, like he'd come at them with everything he had. "I tried for more money, for space. They said the project is a pie-in-the-sky dream."

"You fought hard?" Anna asked. She was at the kitchen table, which doubled as their desk. Papers were strewn across the top. Burned toast sat on a cracked plate.

"Yes, but you know I can't push too hard."

"You can," she said. "You need to push harder. I know I'm right. This amplifier, it will make nuclear power safer. As it is, I think nuclear weapons are a mistake."

"How else would we keep the Americans back?"

"Weapons aren't the answer, Yasha," she said. "I used to think they were, but I've moved on. I thought you did, too. After what we've lived through."

"Living like we have has made me realize we need weapons more than ever. We have to be ready to fight, to defend ourselves. Anna, how can you be so naive?"

"How can you call me that?" Her voice rose. "After all the work I've done, we've done. How do you still not understand that this bomb makes us as bad as Hitler?"

"Never say that. Nothing is as bad as that man."

"I've come to realize I was wrong, that's what I am doing. Admitting my mistake."

Their voices rose and they went back and forth with increasing passion, rising anger. The more Anna pulled away from weaponizing her work, the more he dug in. Around and around they went that night and then night after night until they were exhausted. And then, spent, Yasha would reach for her, touch her waist. "I love you," he would say. She'd try to push him away but he'd hold on tighter.

"We have to build our station on Aragats," she'd say.

"I'll keep trying," he'd say, and kiss her deeply. Anna loved it when they went from cold to hot like that. It made her head spin, her heart dance. She would pull at his clothing, his pants, and he would hike her dress up, help her onto the table, where they would make love. It was hard and fast and everything that made her feel strong, everything she wanted if she couldn't have Yulia.

For five years, Anna kept herself from getting pregnant. She didn't want a child, and besides, she was already in her late thirties when they married. Her method was simple oral contraceptives. Not the Soviet kind, which were infamously ineffective. The Hungarian kind. Igor's wife, an unexpected ally, helped her source them. And while Anna did everything she could to keep herself from building a family, Yulia's dreams grew. At first Yulia wanted a daughter to name Ruth and a boy to name after Lazar's father. Later she wanted four children, then five, but year after year she failed to get pregnant. Anna helped her see a line of doctors. She even traveled with Yulia and Lazar to East Germany to visit the world's foremost fertility expert. He told them children were not in their future, and while Anna felt sadness for their pain, in the most selfish part of her, she was relieved. If Yulia had children, she would have even less room for Anna. As it was, Anna barely saw her, only for weekend meals.

At work, Yasha and Anna became a renowned duo, the envy of Soviet scientists. Anna planned and sketched experiments while Yasha wrote them up as proposals and helped her secure and prepare equipment. They woke early and stayed at the lab late. The biggest surprise to Anna was their sex life, how she grew to love touching him, being with him. It wasn't what she imagined she might have with Yulia, but it was its own kind of love and Anna was happy until she missed her period one month and then the next. She told herself it was likely cancer. A pregnancy was impossible. She was in her forties and didn't want it, only nature doesn't care what you want and her whole life she had defied the odds.

Anna went to the hospital for a diagnosis. She was told to take off her clothing and wait on a stretcher in a dull yellow room. The sink in the corner leaked. The ceiling was stained. She was cold, but they wouldn't give her anything to cover herself. "The doctor will be in soon," the nurse said. When he finally came, he didn't make eye contact. He told her to lie back and spread her legs. "Lower. Move lower," he said. He poked and prodded while she shivered. "Stay still." When he removed his hands from her body, he didn't help her up. "It's not cancer. It's a geriatric pregnancy. You'll have to be careful. No work. Bed rest." He left without another word, and when the nurse came in, she thought Anna was crying tears of joy.

At home, she locked herself in the bathroom. Yasha pleaded with her to tell him what was wrong. "Are you dying?" he asked. Anna leaned against the wall and cried more. She stopped only when she had to vomit. A baby. She had no idea how to tell Yulia. "Please, tell me," Yasha begged. She could hear him leaning against the door, terrified and wanting to be close.

"I'm pregnant," she said. Then she opened the door, and he came in to hold her. "I can't do this." She sobbed and leaned into him, and he wrapped himself around her. He was the only person who let her break down, who never shied away when he saw her cracks, and she loved him more for it, held on as tight as she could. Even with Yulia she always had to be strong, but not with Yasha. He always understood some portion of Anna's pain.

"I already love this child as much as I love you," Yasha said. "We will make it work."

The day she told Igor, they were sitting in his office, crowded with piles of papers and a desk too large for the space. The Soviet flag hung on the wall behind him, along with a portrait of Stalin and one of Gorbachev. Anna's legs hurt. Veins bulged around her ankles and felt like snakes cutting off her circulation. Igor told her she could come back to his lab as soon as she was ready, but she looked at Stalin glaring down at her and wasn't sure she believed him.

She never mentioned that the doctor had recommended bed rest. Instead, she went in to work every day, and while Anna's dread grew, Yasha's excitement ballooned. He skipped around their flat, made every meal, wouldn't let her lift a finger. At night he read to her stomach. He started with Marx and Lenin, moved on to speeches by Stalin. "We are going to have a comrade to make us all proud," he said. "She'll have your brains and my cunning." Yasha's joy never grew into her own. Anna was terrified she couldn't protect a child. Becoming a mother would likely lower her status at work; she would have less power, less potential, less independence. Her own mother had failed, so how could Anna do any better?

Keeping the news from Yulia hung over Anna like a black cloud. By twenty weeks, Anna still hadn't told her. Finally, one bright night in spring, she forced herself to go to Yulia's. "I haven't seen you in months. You're luminous," Yulia said as she dragged Anna inside. She was a translator now for the KGB, tasked with turning stolen intelligence into Russian. Lazar was out, working at a butcher shop, the tank factory long since closed. Malka was living in a dorm, attending the university. Anna couldn't remember the last time she and Yulia were alone. When Anna took off her coat and revealed her belly, Yulia dropped into silence and minutes gaped between them. Every second felt sharp like a knife.

"You're pregnant," Yulia said finally. Her face was still, her whole body unmoving.

Anna opened her arms and tried to take a step toward her, but Yulia held up a hand.

"I never wanted it," Anna said. She felt growing guilt splitting them apart and she couldn't lose Yulia, not ever. "I'm sorry. I'm so sorry."

"Funny how you don't see that's what makes it hurt so much more." Yulia turned to face the window. Outside, men were laying the foundation for a new building. The cranes inching into place made the glass vibrate.

"I didn't ask for this." Anna's mind raced as she searched for something, anything to say to make Yulia feel better. Already she felt herself crumbling while Yulia turned harder, crueler. Jealousy, she realized, is as powerful as fear.

"Please. Go," Yulia said. Anna hesitated. She reached for Yulia, touched her arm, but Yulia jumped back. She had never recoiled from Anna before, and Anna couldn't bear it.

Sixteen weeks later, Anna tripped and fell when she felt the first real birth pains. Yasha rushed her to the hospital while she screamed. She was certain she wouldn't survive. "She's tearing me apart," Anna cried. A doctor, an older man, came and went. Yasha kissed her and the world around her melted into a blur. Eventually came the worst pain of all, so intense Anna didn't know anything else. It took over her body, her mind, and she was sure this was her end. She went in and out of consciousness. There were forceps, stitches. And then it was over. Anna didn't feel any elation or relief. She had no rush of happiness like she'd heard some women describe. For her there was only a fear of death and then nothing. She couldn't remember the afterbirth or even hearing her daughter cry. She didn't feel the overwhelming sense of relief or love, either. What she did feel, when the baby was in her arms, was protective. The child was hers, and this small, helpless creature needed her. "Take care of her," she said over and over to Yasha before she fell back into the blackness.

"Annushka. Annushka? Please, come back to me," Yasha said some time later. He was kneeling next to the bed. Anna was in a clean smock, lying on crisp sheets. She heard a baby whimpering. "You need to feed her." Their daughter was pink and wrinkled like an old woman. Her fingers were long, her cheeks were round, and she looked perfect. Anna turned away, toward a woman in the next cot, so close to hers that she could see the sweat on her upper lip.

"What's her name?" Yulia asked. Anna startled, looked up.

"You're here?"

"Of course," she said. She took Anna's hand and kissed it. "Her name?"

"Manya. Call her Manya," Anna said. It was her grandmother's name.

"A perfect name," Yasha said.

When Anna and Manya left the hospital, Yasha took control and Anna found herself happy to relinquish it. She let him feed them, bathe them. Anna couldn't get out of bed anyway. She was bleeding too much and walking made it worse. She stayed under the sheets and watched the world through the window, regarded Yasha and Manya as if they were characters on a screen. Yasha kissed her, urged her to hold Manya, to feed her, but Anna couldn't bring herself to do any of it. Manya was safe and so Anna slept. Yasha sat next to her for most of the day, every day, holding Manya and reading Marx and Trotsky the way other parents read fairy tales.

Yulia and Lazar came and tried to coax Anna out of the bedroom again and again, but she didn't move. Instead she cried into her pillow, especially after they told her they'd lost their jobs because they were refuseniks now. They'd applied for permission to emigrate to Israel and were denied—which meant they wanted to leave her. Now, trapped in the USSR, they were miserable, both applying for menial jobs so as to avoid being charged with social parasitism. While they searched for work, they took Manya for walks and Yasha stayed with Anna, climbed into bed next to her and held her, told her jokes and stories, tried to make her smile. He assured her they were doing their duty, that their baby was the Soviet future, but none of it helped. Anna didn't feel like she had any future at all. Everything had changed. She had no control over her body. Her mind was too tired to work, and even though Yasha took care of Manya, the baby was always there. Anna had no quiet. No peace.

Four months after giving birth, Anna went into her lab. It looked different, older, like it had withered without her. "Anna, you should be home with the baby," Igor said.

"Yasha is with her."

"Your family needs you."

"I don't want it." The lab went silent. Anna felt the other scientists stare, stop their work, and her own heart stuttered. "Not every woman is a natural mother," she whispered so quietly no one else heard. If only all these people in her life could understand that. And as she stood there, the center of attention, in that space that used to glitter for her, she tried as hard as she could to control herself, but tears ripped down her cheeks and made it all worse. All she felt and saw was fog. For decades she had held herself together, made sure she was always composed in front of her male colleagues. It was how she attained her place, proved she was worthy, and now she was shattering, throwing away all of that effort. Igor tried to hand her a handkerchief and put an arm around her, but she pushed him away. "I don't need anyone to take care of me. I can do this by myself." He tried to tell her she needed to calm down, but she shook him off. "I want my old life back. I want it all to go back to the way it was."

"The beauty of life is that it pushes forward," Igor said. "You can't fight it."

Only Anna had been fighting, and she wasn't winning. Could he see that? She walked home in a fit of rage at herself for breaking down in the lab, for getting pregnant in the first place. She elbowed strangers, crossed at red lights. She had put herself in this position, but Igor, Yasha, and Yulia were all treating her like she had delivered Manya and handed over her brain at the same time, as if she couldn't make decisions for herself. She knew better than anyone what she needed, what she wanted. At their flat, she burst through the door.

"Annushka," Yasha said. He was holding Manya. While he put her down in the crib, Anna stormed to the window, feeling like she couldn't breathe. She flung it open, leaned out, and gulped air.

"I'm suffocating," she said. Yasha had his hand on her back. "You...you think you know better than me. You all do. I just want to go back to where I was, to what we had. I don't want all of this. All of you looking over my shoulder, checking in on me. Hovering." The words came so quickly she wasn't used to it, but it felt good to have them tumble out and she didn't slow down. "I need space. I need you to leave me alone. And more than anything, I need to go back to work. I—I..." She took a deep breath. "I need my brain to work again." She slumped against the side of the window frame because that was really it, what she needed. She hadn't admitted it before. "I can't think clearly. Can't see in a straight line. That's never happened to me before." She felt useless, far from the person she knew she was. Before Manya, she could always map one point to another, define it with an equation that described the trajectory, the slope, every characteristic, but now she was lost and felt like she was drowning.

Yasha helped her away from the window, back to a chair. "You need to give yourself time," he said. "Your belly is still swollen. The doctors said recovery would be prolonged." She opened her mouth to interrupt, to tell him that was exactly what she didn't want to hear, what she was trying to fight against, but he held up a hand. "Please, trust me. You need time. You can't see clearly, and I know you're terrified. You must trust me."

"This is my body. I decide when I'm ready to return."

"You share your life with me and Manya. It's not just you anymore."

"But I want it to be just me," she said, and she saw the way her words cut him, left him reeling like a wounded animal. Manya started wailing, her cry quickly crescendoing into a high-pitched scream that made Anna's ears ring.

"Help her," he said, pointing to the crib.

"No," Anna said.

"You're pushing me too far." For the first time since he'd been with her in that basement after her questioning, his voice was cold, devoid of any warmth or sweetness.

Anna knew she would regret what she wanted to say next. But he wasn't really listening. No one was listening and she couldn't help herself. "I don't want this. I don't want any of it."

"If you leave us, I won't let you back into our home." He paused and took a deep breath. "I won't let you back into the lab, either." Anna felt the warning like a bullet in her gut and she stumbled back. He had used the one weapon he had in their relationship, the power he held over her but had never wielded. She had felt it that night in the alley, the night the war ended, but then he had let her go. Now she knew he wasn't going to let her slip past, and she felt a turn in her feelings, a tear between them. The anger and frustration she had felt standing in front of Igor, walking home, boiled up into a rage that left her shaking and her mind a flash of white fury like she had never known.

"You put it in one of your reports, didn't you? You told them I need more time."

At first he puffed out his chest, looked like he was going to defend himself, but then he let all the air go and rolled his shoulders forward. His face fell. He looked down and she knew he regretted what he'd just said. He walked to her with his arms out to hold her, to apologize, but she stepped back. He must have felt that tear opening between them, and she knew he didn't want it because he kept coming like he wanted to sew them back together. "I love you." And "I'm sorry. I'm so, so sorry. I thought you needed more time. You're so sad, every day."

Anna started toward the bedroom. "Yulia wanted a baby, not me," she said as she slammed the door behind her and locked it.

"It's always back to Yulia," Yasha said through the plywood. "Sometimes there isn't room for us. Only for her and Lazar. No matter what I do. I can never be enough to fill that void."

"You did. For a long time, you did," she said, but maybe her voice was too soft. Maybe he didn't hear. She cleared her throat.

Not long after, Yulia and Lazar came to the flat. They whispered with Yasha. She overheard bits and pieces from the bedroom, didn't dare come out to face them because she was embarrassed and ashamed. They talked about medicine, therapies. Then Yasha said, "We'll find someone to watch the baby."

"Time helps everything," Lazar said eventually.

Somehow, that night, it was decided that Yulia would watch over Manya, that next to Yulia, Anna might heal. Yasha wrote letters and he was senior enough by then that it was agreed: Even as refuseniks, Yulia would be permitted to become Manya's caregiver while Lazar worked in maintenance. After all, Anna was the Soviets' foremost expert on nuclear power. She was their way forward with atomic energy and weapons, and above all else Stalin wanted her back.

On her first day as Manya's caregiver, Yulia came to their flat with a smile so wide Anna didn't think she had ever seen her happier. Yulia was thrilled to spend her days with the baby, and Anna was even more excited to try to return to what she had lost. Even so, her life continued in a blur of fatigue and fights. Yasha never gave up trying to push Anna to care for Manya, and Anna never gave up rallying against it. Manya's second year of life was even worse because at Yasha's request, Anna was assigned a new security detail. Anna had two men following her everywhere. "To make sure you're safe," he said, but she knew they were spies, tasked with reporting her every move back to him. They checked her notes, her bag, and escorted her to the bathroom. Any freedom she had was gone. When she fought against them, Yasha countered by saying she didn't even know she needed the help, that she still wasn't herself. Only every time he said that, she felt like she was getting less oxygen. She didn't need to be watched or told what to do; she needed freedom. The constant surveillance and all the reports he wrote about her were squeezing the life out of her. Ideas she had for her amplifier, for advanced forms of power, had started fading. When she confronted Yasha, he told her he wasn't taking anything away. He was giving her the chance to work again—safely. "Maybe we can even get back to our dream, to Aragats," he said, but she didn't believe him. She yelled and cried more, told him he was making their lives unbearable.

One morning, instead of going to her lab, she walked Yulia and Manya to the park. They left Anna's guards at the gate after Anna pleaded for space. They agreed only if she promised to stay where they could see her. Anna leaned into Yulia as soon as they were far enough away that she thought no one could hear. She took a deep breath, knowing that what she was about to ask was enormous, that it risked all their lives. She knew it might even sound insane, but in that moment, she was sure her life couldn't get any worse.

"You know I'm not happy," she whispered to Yulia.

"Give it time," Yulia said. "You're getting better."

"Everyone keeps saying that. Please stop telling me to give it time. That's not what I need. What I need is quiet. What I need is time to work, space." She looked back at the gates, made sure the guards were keeping their distance. "I need my life back."

"Anna, you have a new life now. A better life with Manya. She's incredible."

Anna didn't understand how Yulia was missing the point. Yulia, the one person who used to know her better than anyone, who always understood. "Why can't you hear me? I don't care."

"Don't say that. You'll regret it. I know you."

Anna's whole body trembled. "I know what I'm about to say is going to shock you, but please, listen. I wouldn't say it if I wasn't desperate. Yasha and I, we're terrible parents. We'll never give Manya what she needs. I'll resent her because she's keeping me from the life I want and had. And Yasha, he'll push her to be the super Soviet. He'll teach her to despise me, to think of me as a cruel villain, probably even lean on her so hard she'll hate our country and him, too."

"You both love her too much for any of that."

"You're wrong. Listen to me, I used to see the world in details, every piece fitting together with an explanation. Now my brain is stuck in a slog of gray. It moves too slowly, never gives me answers I need. I used to know exactly where to go, what to do, and now I'm lost. I can't live this way." She stopped herself and shook her head. "We'll ruin her if we keep her here. I want—I *need* you to take Manushka and Lazar and run."

"Annechka, listen to what you're saying." Yulia's face went pale, her eyes wide with shock. Anna threaded her arm through Yulia's, pushed her to keep walking.

"Yasha watches my every move." She nodded back toward the guards. "He has power over me, always has. And he's using it. My world is getting smaller, closing in. I swear I think he suspects me of spying, but he won't admit it. He keeps telling me what I need to do for Manya, for our family. What about what he needs to do?"

"He loves Manushka. And you. He wants your old life back, just like you."

"I think we're past that." She looked back at the guards one more time. "And he can't see past that to give her what she needs—a better mother. I don't want her growing up like this, being watched, with a mother who resents her. Or even with a father who only sees her as a Soviet tool for the future. With parents who grow to hate each other." Yulia started to object, but Anna kept going. "I've given it two years. I don't have any more time to give. Take my money and go."

"But, Anna. You wouldn't see Manya ever again. Even if we made it out, we'd never come back."

"I know. It hurts, but you have to run. Think about what she will see or become if she stays. Lazar, he's always wanted to go to America. Your English is already perfect." Anna closed her eyes, could barely believe she was suggesting they flee to the one country she hated. But the fact that she detested it meant it was the one place Yasha would never look. "You see what I've become. I hate it. You hate it, too. I see it in your eyes. In your face when you look at me." She pulled Yulia even closer. "You know what they did to my mother. To your family. If I go on like this, I will disappear, too."

"Shh, you're upset. This will pass."

"It won't."

"He loves you and his daughter more than anything."

"That's the problem. He wants us to be his perfect family, not the one we are," Anna said. "You must take Manya and go."

"I can't imagine my life without you." Yulia's voice was trembling, on the verge of tears. Anna hadn't expected that. A part of her thought Yulia would jump at the chance to have her own child. The fact that she didn't made Anna feel a wave of sadness, of regret for pushing Yulia to take Manya to America. She hugged Yulia tight.

"I love you. I love you more than you can imagine. Please do this for me. For Manya."

"I can't."

Anna refused to accept that as an answer. She began walking with Yulia every day, pleading with her to run to America. To wear her down, she described in detail the ways in which her life was crumbling around her. "I have to lay out every step of every experiment," Anna said, accusing Yasha of treating her like a child in her own laboratory. When Yulia asked why, Anna admitted she had been sloppy. There was a fire, but everyone makes mistakes. "He lords over me. Every half hour I have to tell him what I'm doing."

"But at home, what is it like?" Yulia wanted to know.

"He's choosing my clothing. He said I was wearing summer dresses in winter, but the lab is so hot. I can't stand the wool. Surely he must understand."

"Does he let you hold Manya?" Yulia pushed.

"Only when he's there. He never leaves us alone. I would never hurt her. You know that. Please, take her and run to America. To Lazar's cousin."

Making everything worse was that as Anna saw herself falling apart, Yasha rose higher than ever. He wasn't only reporting on Anna anymore, but becoming an important party member himself. "Look," Anna said during one of their walks. "You see?" She held up a stolen page from one of his reports. She pointed to the lines where he detailed her breakfast. "That's not even the worst." She read the contents: "'Considering her mental condition, it might soon be time to place Anna in a mental institution for recovery.' He wants to send me away. There's even a line in here saying I might be a spy, but they have no proof."

"He wouldn't."

"He will. Please, I'm begging. Take Manushka. Run. She deserves a better life. She deserves you."

Eventually, three months after Manya turned two, Yulia agreed. The morning she was set to leave started like any other. Yasha and Anna kissed Manya when Yulia came to their flat. Lazar was there, too, but he often came to drop Yulia off. Both of them looked relaxed. They wore thick coats and regular clothing. They couldn't bring any bags, photographs, or mementos, anything that, if they were captured, might hint they were fleeing. Anna knew they had sewn the little jewelry Yulia had into the lining of her skirt. Yulia's face was calm. Lazar's too. How far he had grown from the young man they found destroyed and sobbing, holding his sister the day they were orphaned.

Anna had organized their escape for them, and her plans were meticulous. Every minute of their time from Moscow to America was mapped out. They were going to cross the border into Finland on a wagon, take a boat to Sweden and then a plane to Philadelphia, where Andrey, Lazar's cousin, had landed. Anna lingered at the door, wanting to tell Yulia that they had been through worse, that given they had endured and survived through so much already, landing in America would be easy. But Anna's mouth was dry. She told Yasha to go ahead, she would be down soon, and he nodded. When he was out of sight, Anna's tears started in a steady stream. Her tongue was thick and she didn't know what to say. She kissed Yulia on the forehead. "I love you," she said, realizing her plans were no longer theoretical; they were actually happening, coming to life. Anna held her breath. She bent down and kissed Manya, put her palm on her chest. It had always amazed Anna how her entire hand covered so much of the baby's body, how someone so small had managed to take up all the space she had in her life. "I'm sorry," she whispered, and where she expected it to be easy, a relief to say goodbye, she felt herself second-guessing the decision. The doubt was like a needle under her skin, something she wasn't used to that made her squirm. She resisted the urge to scoop her daughter up, thinking perhaps if she held her she would change her mind. And she could. She could still stop all of this, but she knew she would regret that, too. She kissed Manya again. "I know this is the right thing to do."

"Are you sure?" Lazar asked.

"Yes." Still, she wanted to linger, to stretch the goodbye longer, but it was safer to let them go. Yulia's handbag was on the table by the door. Anna poked inside and took her gold lipstick case, the one she'd had in Germany. Then she took the extra blanket from Manya's pram, the one they kept just in case it got cold. She smelled them both, kissed them both, and was about to give them back, but instead held on to them. They were tokens she couldn't keep for long, but a few more hours was more than nothing.

"Annushka," Yasha called.

"Coming," she said. She tried to push her lips into blowing another kiss but couldn't. She was losing control, couldn't let that happen. She made a fist around the blanket and lipstick for strength. Lazar turned away. He was crying, too, and it surprised her, made her hesitate once more.

"Find us," Yulia said, and then Anna left. The latch clicked quietly. It should have slammed and rattled the walls. Anna wanted to fill the silence that followed with her screams. But she didn't. She walked to work hoping she looked like nothing had changed at all.

That night, Anna saw rage and hatred in Yasha that shook every dish in their cabinets. He tore through Manya's room and threw her clothing on the floor, ripped her diapers and dumped her toy box as if he might find her in some overlooked nook. Then he shredded their plans for Aragats and walked out.

△ △ △

Molly leaned into the couch by the window as she absorbed the story. Her face was calm but Anna knew her well enough to know that inside she was rumbling like a storm, trying to figure out if she was angry or sad. Anna gave her time to wrestle with it, to decide. When Molly finally turned to face her, Anna was surprised to see pity. It was in the way her eyebrows arched, her body leaned toward Anna's, reached to touch her hand as if to reassure. "Anna, don't you see? All this time you've been asking me what I want to fix. But maybe it's you who needs to change the past."

"You mean your past?" Anna asked.

"No. Yours."

RAISA

October 1989
Three Years Before Molly Dies on Mount Aragats

Philadelphia

After graduation, time seemed to speed up. Raisa moved into a dorm. Daniel stayed with his mother and Raisa saw him on weekends. She knew that compared to other students in her dorm who were in committed relationships with people living across the country, that was a lot. But for Raisa, only three days a week with Daniel was a shock. She was used to having him beside her at work, at school, on the bus, on the roof—everywhere. Without him, without her grandparents, she was alone. It reminded her of nights she spent in the apartment in Atlantic City when her parents thought she was asleep and they went out. Nights when the apartment was dark. Now at Penn, she heard the wind slam into the bricks and rustle the ivy, just as back then the wind had rattled their storm windows and sand pelted the glass in wisps that sounded like finger taps. The insomnia came back along with the fear. She worked until she fell asleep on top of her books. She had a single, didn't have a roommate to distract her, and Kestler's building had been demolished, so she didn't even have her experiments. She felt empty, spent all her time in her room, at class, or with Vito and Stocken in Maui. Other students introduced themselves and she tried to imagine how it would be to share dinners in the cafeteria with them, to trade stories about their parents and prom, laugh about drunken nights out or whisper about first dates and losing their virginity, and realized she couldn't. She was sure they all had shiny pasts, as clean and expensive as the school she had visited for that math competition. They would never understand that she started in Atlantic City, that her parents were addicts and were no longer there. That her family fled the Soviet Union. What if people called her a Commie? What could she possibly share with these people; how could they understand her? Being a wallflower, not being noticed was easier. She had done it all her life. She didn't take classmates up on their invitations to join them for a party or even for a study group.

It was during her first month at school that Raisa received a new issue of *Atomic Anna*. She had just come out of the shower, her shampoo and conditioner in a plastic caddy in her hand as she walked down the hall in her towel. Her door was locked. Most of the people on her hall left their doors wide open at all hours, but Raisa had grown up where it was dangerous to leave a door open and so she always locked hers. When she went into her room, there it was, sitting on her pillow. Raisa was sure she smelled Baba's roses, but any hint dissipated as she stood there staring at the comic book. Her mother had come to her room, Raisa thought. She came and left without saying hello, without even laying eyes on her daughter. But the door was locked and the comic book was on her bed, not shoved under the door. How was that possible? Raisa didn't know, decided she didn't care. She grabbed it and flung it into the closet. "How could she?" Raisa said. Getting dressed, she punched her arms into a sweater and kicked her feet into jeans. She wanted to believe her mother wouldn't leave without seeing her, but she had. Her mother was a coward.

Raisa was due at Stocken's office in fifteen minutes. She pulled on her shoes, made sure her bangs covered her forehead. She applied lipstick and eyeliner, a little mascara. Baba had taught her how, and every time Raisa blotted her lips, she thought about Baba's makeup table with a sadness she preferred to bury. Raisa was about to walk out, but she stopped. The comic book was bent, the cover ripped, half in and half out of the closet. She grabbed it and flipped through, angry at herself for looking, even angrier at her mother. The issue was focused on an amplifier for the time machine. It was the core of the technology, the piece that required nuclear power. The amplifier controlled gamma waves and used them to step through time. Anna's work wasn't going as well as she expected because of the amplifier. Somehow it was malfunctioning, she thought, because time travel was killing her from the inside out. Lesions had spread over her body and her mind was eroding to the point where she couldn't remember what she'd done to try to fix it, had to keep copious notes that she reviewed again and again. In a speech bubble, Anna called for Raisa's help. Scrawled on the top of the page in big black letters was a date: December 8, 1992. The same date that was in the issue she had found in the van that day with Daniel. There was no explanation or drawing to explain why the date mattered. "This is stupid," Raisa said. She wanted to throw the comic book out, but she couldn't bring herself to do it. Instead, she jammed it into the back of her closet and tried to walk away, only there was something to the idea of using an amplifier. She'd seen it in other issues of *Atomic Anna*, and it was something she'd thought a lot about. In fact, she'd already had an experiment in mind, a way to use one.

Raisa found Stocken in Maui sitting in one of the deep chairs. The lights were off, his legs were crossed, and his fingers were steepled. He was still, thinking. Her first impression of Stocken had been that he was perfect. Perfectly dressed, perfectly coiffed, and perfectly spoken. Even his handwriting was perfect. He told Raisa once it was because he never wanted to give anyone a reason to stare or scrutinize him.

He was a Black man in a white world, he already stuck out enough, and in the smallest of ways, she understood what he meant by that. She was white, but she had Soviet blood, came from a Soviet family and a Soviet neighborhood. Even more, her parents were drug addicts, felons. She felt like she stood out, that she wasn't like any of the students here. But unlike Stocken, even when she felt like an outsider, she had the luxury of receding into the crowd, finding a way to be invisible.

She cleared her throat and he looked up. "Professor, I want to talk to you about my research." She closed the door and sat in the chair across from him. Einstein's field equations for relativity were on the board behind him. "I want to get back to radio telescopes."

"I'm not surprised." He smiled. "Tell me why. Back to the anomalies you found?"

She held up her hand so it was in a stream of sunlight cutting through the windows. She angled it one way and another. "Yes. Exactly. Light waves, sound waves, all these make it possible to see my hand and for us to talk about it, and yet we know so little about them. Except they're filled with energy, and sometimes they're distorted. Gravitational waves, they affect results; at least some people think they might. I can't stop thinking about that, about the waves that make our universe and how we drill and frack trying to produce energy when it's already all around us. We're wasting time, killing the earth for nothing. What if we can use waves as power and—" She took a breath, told herself to keep going. The comics weren't real, but good ideas could be inspired by anything. "What if we could build an amplifier and use gravity and electromagnetism together?" She knew it was a radical, fringe idea, that a unified field theory was something most said was impossible. It was crazy to think her small rooftop experiments might have taken her in that direction, but she also thought she was onto something. "This is Maui. I can say anything, right?" Stocken nodded. His eyes were wide and he made no effort to stop her. Nor was he laughing. She kept talking, explaining because she didn't know what else to do and Stocken was still completely silent, not even moving to start taking notes. "I think there's an important clue in a nuclear blast. A way to bring them together. And I know that sounds crazy, but we're missing something in all our papers and studies. I saw it in my data. It's too much. Is that what you're thinking? I'm pushing too far ahead?"

"No," he answered quickly. "If anything, I'm in shock because I missed it. That I didn't know that's what you were working toward." He leaned his head back. "There's an old Soviet theory. I read it a long time ago. It had to do with waves and amplifiers, bringing gravity around to fit, but the theory didn't go anywhere."

"A Soviet theory?" She sat up and her voice went loud. "Who was working on it? Do you remember? Where?"

"I don't remember." He shook his head. "I can look into it. Tell me more about the anomalies you saw in your data. Why weren't they echoes of light, reflections?"

"What I saw, it just didn't fit with the explanation of light reflections. Einstein, he fought against Newton for tiny, minute corrections. That's what I found. Tiny, minute differences. But I think they're massive in what they mean." She paused because what she was about to say was big, bigger than anything she'd ever admitted. "Gravity. I think if I account for gravity the results are precise. There is no margin of error. What I'm saying is..." Her heart was racing. She was sweating. Others had worked on this problem for years, decades, and here she was, a college freshman, proposing her own solution. "The *graviton*. I think I'm witnessing the graviton and I know how it affects, interacts with electromagnetic waves. I can harness it with an amplifier."

Stocken didn't blink. He didn't move. She waited on the edge of her seat for some kind of reaction, for him to say something, anything. Finally he spoke, quietly. "The graviton. It's only a theory."

"Until it's not," she said. "Obviously I wouldn't tell anyone else yet. But this is Maui. And I think I can prove it. I need more data. More time."

"You realize how radical this is, what you're saying?"

She took him through the data, what she'd found. It took hours and he sat there listening, watching as she drew it on the blackboards all around the room. She wound her way through sketches and equations, demonstrations. "You see how it doesn't fit. How it's not quite right. And not quite right isn't enough. There has to be a better explanation. Only, I don't have a final answer. That's the problem," she said. By then the sky had gone dark. The rest of the building was quiet, the courtyard below, too. "I need more data."

Stocken rolled his hands around one another and started pacing the room. He looked as if he was running through her equations again in his head and the more he paced, the more energized he became. "You need to come to me with ideas like these sooner. That's why we're here. We have to break down the old and find the new." He smiled and Raisa felt a wave of relief that she hadn't expected. She had wound herself up so tight, was so scared he would reject her, that his smile radiated deep inside her and for the first time in hours she felt her chest loosen, a shot of adrenaline taking hold.

"I know it's not finished. I have a long way to go. It's a hunch. A good hunch."

He paced to the window and looked out, but it was so dark the glass showed only his reflection. "I have a friend working at Arecibo, in Puerto Rico. You know it?" Of course she did. It was the largest radio telescope in the world. "I can ask him to share his data."

"Thank you. Oh my god, thank you," she said.

They reviewed the information she'd need and talked through a research plan. Just before she was about to leave, he said, "This is all exciting, but your English professor contacted me after she read your first essay. She and I are friends, she knows you're working with me, and she reached out as a favor. If you keep handing papers in like that one, you won't graduate. And if you flunk out, you won't have access to anything. You won't have the future, or answers, you want. Ask Vito for help. I'll get the data, you work on your grades."

The next morning she approached Vito. They hadn't spent time together outside of Maui. She'd been a recluse and he'd been busy pledging a fraternity, going to parties, and playing Frisbee, but he agreed and spent hours explaining something he called the "Five-Paragraph Formula." He edited every one of her papers. In return, she helped him with math. What came easily to Raisa in their advanced classes, he often needed to review two or three times before he understood.

"Can I take you to lunch tomorrow?" he asked one day in Russian. It was nearly midnight. They were at the library, huddled in a corner of the reading room. The lights were dim, and the librarians had started turning off the desk lamps one at a time, getting ready to close.

"Can you drop the Russian? I don't like everyone knowing I'm different. They'll look at me funny, think I'm a Communist."

"All these people around us"—he gestured to the other students still at the library—"they all wish they spoke a second language half as well as you. I bet at least one of them is taking some kind of intensive Russian so they can read Dostoevsky in the original, or some Ivy League crap like that. You should be proud."

"Come on. They hate Communists."

"Americans romanticize the Czar. The beautiful buildings, the balls, those stupid jeweled eggs. I'm telling you, the language makes you interesting. People here like it."

"Is that what you're doing?" Raisa laughed. "Attracting the ladies with your language skills? Seducing them with Russian?"

"Ha! Well, I wouldn't complain if that happened," he said. "So, lunch?"

"Maybe next week."

A week later, he asked again. "Lunch? Or dinner?" He was standing at the door to her room, had caught her in her room, huddled over a tray from the dining hall. In the corner was a stack of trays, plates, and glasses, all neatly arranged. She only took them back to the dining hall when Daniel was coming. "You have to get out of this cubbyhole," Vito said. "And not just for classes or the library." He pointed to the corner where she kept her packed single suitcase. The lid was open, clothes folded and ordered inside, but she couldn't bring herself to put them in the dresser. "Move in already. Have fun. If you don't want to go to the dining hall, I'll take you out. My father's business is good. He gives me an allowance and I'm not embarrassed to take it. Come on, let me show you what it's like." She refused. He stepped closer to her desk. "What are you working on?" Her notebook was open to a design she had for an amplifier based on images in *Atomic Anna*. She felt strange about using a comic book for a guide, but the sketches her mother drew were detailed and Raisa was convinced she needed to build an amplifier to enhance gravitational waves, to find the graviton. "I like that you sketch your experiments. You're pretty good."

"You're surprised that I have a good idea?"

"No." He jabbed her shoulder gently. "Surprised you draw so well. What is it?"

"Equipment. For my research."

"Tell me about it over lunch or dinner. Whatever you choose." Vito smiled. He shifted his weight from one foot to the other. "Fine. No food. How about hockey? Russians play hockey. I play hockey."

Raisa was stunned by the suggestion and laughed. The sound was quiet at first, but it felt so good that she let it escape, a laugh that made her shake. "I don't know anything about hockey." But she hadn't laughed in so long that she relented. The next day he took her to enjoy her first cheesesteak from a food truck on the corner of Chestnut Street. Drowned in fake orange sauce and fried onions, it was delicious. They sat perched on a bench facing a check-cashing convenience store, and Raisa realized Vito was the only person who made her feel comfortable at Penn. She never worried about what she wore or said around him, or if her notes were laid out strangely. He was gentle in correcting her and only did it because he knew she didn't want to stand out.

"How about another food truck?" she asked him a week later.

"Perfect."

There were lines of food trucks covering blocks of campus, and together they started sampling one and then another. They compared cheesesteaks and strombolis, soft pretzels and water ice. In November, the dorm and classrooms baked with heaters that clanged and hissed. Raisa tried to open her window, but it was sealed shut, making her feel suffocated. Vito showed her how to cut through the paint so she could get fresh air. He had her join his study group and she found herself having fun, laughing. She even chipped in to buy pizza one night so she could help a group of students through a problem set.

Raisa enjoyed her time with Vito and the study group, and when she tried to explain it to Daniel on weekends, he didn't understand. "Vito's an idiot American who's had everything handed to him on a silver platter," Daniel said. "He's not worth your time."

"You're not giving him enough credit," Raisa said. "His family is Italian and they're not rich. He's had to work his whole life, like us."

"I know what he wants. It isn't math."

"He's my only friend at school."

"I don't want you to be lonely. Have you tried meeting other people? Because trust me, he doesn't want to be just a friend."

"I kind of like it when you're jealous." She smiled and kissed him. It was a side of Daniel she had never seen, and it made her feel more desirable, more wanted, than she ever had. As it was, she was back at the Market with him every Friday afternoon, Saturday, and Sunday. While her classmates were drinking and then recovering from hangovers, she was at home and at the butcher shop, chopping and slicing, helping her grandparents. At night she and Daniel went back to her dorm room. She helped him with math and science, tried to offer advice about his English class. His language had come far, but it still wasn't automatic or easy for him. By Monday, she was back to Penn. She spent her afternoons, outside of class, poring over the data from Arecibo and designing her amplifier. While Raisa worked, Vito spent his free time with his new fraternity brothers. He had let his hair grow long and messy and started wearing a baseball cap to hold it back. "You're a shaggy American," Raisa teased him when they ran into each other on Locust Walk one day.

"Only on the outside," he said. There was a lot Raisa envied about him, about the way he fit in, about the way he got along with other students and had so many friends. And she was grateful for how he kept trying to include her. She continued joining the study groups, accepting invitations to go out.

By January, Vito and Raisa were laboratory partners. One night, they were in the library. It was Vito's turn to write up their notes. While he worked, Raisa flipped through a bound index of the library's collection of scientific papers. She focused on papers written on amplifiers designed for radio telescopes. She had already found a dozen designs in various back issues of science journals, but nothing that looked promising until she uncovered a recently declassified report out of the Soviet Union. Raisa opened the summary and gasped loudly. "What?" Vito asked.

The few people still in the library looked up. "Nothing," she whispered. She didn't want to explain. She wanted to get to the report as quickly as she could. There was a chance, a slim chance, that Anna had written it. Raisa had already found enough to know large chunks of the comic books were based in reality. She wrote down the information she needed to retrieve the paper and took off to locate it. The library was closing in twenty minutes. She expected to find it on microfiche, but the library had a copy of the actual report. Raisa riffled through the file drawers looking for it, grabbed the one she wanted, and pulled it out. She wasn't supposed to take it outside of that room, but she was running out of time before the library closed and couldn't wait to read it. She snuck it out with her and hurried back to the reading room, sat down and started paging through. It was in Russian, which slowed down her reading.

The librarians flicked the lights to signal they were closing just as Raisa read the author's name: Anna Berkova. She froze, hadn't noticed it in the index. The hair on the back of her neck stood up. She went cold. This amplifier was like the one in *Atomic Anna*. Raisa was touching something her grandmother wrote, and not only did it discuss the amplifier, it showed the schematics, described the actual theory and science behind it. It meant all the science in those old comic books wasn't just based in reality but was probably real—how?

"Raisa, we have to go," Vito said. He was standing in front of her. She blinked, felt her pulse climbing, the itch of adrenaline flowing in her veins. Anna Berkova. The amplifier. The comic books. It was all—*real?*

Vito looked at the paper in her hand. "Isn't that like the design you've been working on?"

"It's similar, better," she whispered. The overhead lights were going out, and Raisa did something she hadn't dared to do on campus. She slipped the report into her bag and walked out. There was no magnetic tracker or sticker on it to catch her, and it was just as easy as it had always been.

"I saw that," Vito said once they were outside. He was jogging to keep up with her. "You just stole that report. It wasn't even supposed to be out of the back room, was it?"

"You didn't see anything," she said.

"Wait up! I'm not going to bust you." She was walking as fast as she could along the red-brick path that wound through campus, past the blue emergency phone stations. She didn't slow down. The report in her bag felt heavy and hot.

"I just need to read more tonight. I'll bring it back."

"What's going on? You're running and speaking so quickly. What the hell did you find?"

"It's nothing."

They passed a fraternity blaring music. Red plastic cups littered the lawn. "Can you slow down, please?"

"I can't." She needed to read the report, think about what she'd found, what it meant. At the very least, it showed that Mama really had been in touch with Anna, that she wasn't directing Raisa to amplifiers by accident. She hurried into her dorm. Vito followed.

"I can help you think this through, whatever it is," Vito offered. They were on Raisa's floor by then. As Raisa took her key from her pocket, Daniel opened her door and stepped out into the hall. She wasn't expecting him. She could tell he had been in her room for a while because he was shirtless and in socks, wearing his jeans with the hole at the knee. His hair was a mess of curls, the way she loved it, not the way he ever wore it in public. Raisa was in a T-shirt the football team had handed out during the first week of school when they were trying to get kids to come to their games. It hit just above the waist and his hand went straight for the slip of skin that was exposed, sliding along her stomach. "Hey," she said.

"Hey." He kissed her deeply, in a way he never did in public. She pulled back, embarrassed.

"Hey, man," Vito said. He was obviously uncomfortable, looking off to the side. "It's been a while."

"Yeah, I've been busy," Daniel said in Russian.

"Yeah, well. Anyway, we were at the library. I just wanted to make sure Raisa made it home okay." Vito hiked his backpack up higher. "I'm exhausted. I'm gonna head out."

"I'll see you tomorrow," Raisa said. Daniel was already pulling her inside. As soon as the door closed, Daniel was on her. He pushed her against the wall and kissed her. He ran his hands up her back, along her sides, like he couldn't touch enough of her. She loved feeling him that excited and she kissed him hard, leaned back so he could lick her neck. But then she stopped him. "You can't do that," she said. "Treat Vito that way." He pulled her to the bed and fell back so she landed on top of him.

"Treat him what way?" he asked as he kissed her neck.

"He's my only friend. You can't scare him."

"He doesn't want to be your friend."

"Stop saying that." She pushed him to the side but understood there was some truth to what he said. Even though Vito knew she was with Daniel, he still kept asking her to lunch and dinner. She picked up her backpack and pulled out the report from the library.

"You're stealing again?" he asked.

"Why don't you think I borrowed it?"

"'Cause I know you. And it's covered with a million canceled confidential stickers."

She smiled, loved that he knew her so well. "I'll return it. The library was closing. But look!" She pointed to the author line, her finger shaking. "Anna Berkova. This paper is about an amplifier, one she wanted to use with the nuclear reactor. The idea was to expand and also contain gamma rays, to use them as a power source." She could see Daniel squinting, trying to follow what she was saying.

"You're losing me," Daniel said.

"In *Atomic Anna*, my mother's comic book, my mother drew an amplifier that looks just like the one in these specs, in this report. She drew my grandmother's amplifier." She pointed to the paper. "It's like nothing I've ever seen. How did my mother know?" She took a deep breath, put the papers down. "My mother has seen Anna—seen this amplifier, taken the time to replicate it exactly. We keep finding more and more evidence that what she draws exists. That means some parts of those comics are real. It means *Atomic Anna* isn't just a hobby or something my mother drew or draws for fun. The pages are filled with formulas. None of this is a coincidence." She took a deep breath. "In the last issue Anna said she needed my help. She needs me. Daniel, I have to find them."

PART VII

*Do not judge your fellow man until you have
been in his position.*

—Pirkei Avot

RAISA

Philadelphia

Raisa was outside her dorm, on the lawn, one day during the summer after her freshman year. The grass was thick and so clean it looked like the gardeners washed it every morning. That was what money did, Raisa had learned. Spread out on a blanket with her notebook on her chest, she was going over notes from her last section meeting, working as a teaching assistant for Stocken's summer course. It was the first June, July, and August she could remember that she didn't spend fifty hours a week at the Market, but Stocken paid her double what she would earn working at the Market and so she couldn't refuse. Nor could her grandparents. But she missed them, called home every day. It was also her first time away from Daniel. ROTC had shipped him off to the south, extended his basic cadet training, and she had spent most of her summer without seeing him, speaking on the phone only every Sunday and only for ten minutes. Without Daniel, and in her new role as a TA, she had started spending more time with

Vito and making other friends of her own. Three girls had even invited her to move off campus and share an apartment with them in the fall. A year earlier she would have thought she had nothing in common with them, but now she saw that everyone had messier lives than she anticipated. No one was as perfect as they seemed.

Raisa had fallen asleep on the lawn, and she felt someone block the sun, their shadow spreading over her. She opened her eyes and saw Daniel. She gave a yelp and jumped at him as he leaned down to kiss her, wrapped her arms around his neck as tight as she could and inhaled him. Taking in his smell of sweat and aftershave that she adored made him feel even closer. She kissed him the way other kids at school kissed each other in public, a way she had never dared. The two months they had been apart felt like three years. She ran her hands up over the back of his neck, felt his curls were still all cut away. When she came up for air, she leaned back enough to see he wore a green army jacket, pants, and boots. He buried his face in her neck. "God, I missed you," he said. She was wearing a bikini top and he ran a finger over her stomach. "I never thought you'd wear a bikini outside on a lawn like this." He smiled. "I love it."

"I do, too," she said, knowing she had changed. "I don't have anything to hide, do I?" Her smile grew. It was Andrea, one of the girls who'd invited her to join the apartment, who pushed her to wear the top outside to tan. She'd felt shy at first, but now she'd been wearing it for a month and it made her feel more powerful than when she hid in a big T-shirt, because people were looking and seeing her. Even if they were noticing her body, she wasn't invisible, and that was a strength she'd come to understand. It reminded her of Stocken coming to the Chopping Room, telling her he saw her. She couldn't hide anymore. She shouldn't hide anymore. "What's with the jacket in this heat?"

"I was hoping you'd like it," he said sheepishly. "I missed you so much." As he said it, she realized she'd missed him even more than she'd let herself admit. He had sent letters, one every day, but they were short and barely said anything, didn't hint at how he'd changed, too. Already she could feel he was physically stronger and that, like her, he wasn't hiding, either, wasn't trying to blend in, or he wouldn't have worn that uniform. Instead, he was standing tall and taking his space. There they were, two full-blown Americans in the middle of campus where the whole world could take them in and neither of them were looking over their shoulder or trying to slink away to privacy. He leaned down and kissed the bear pendants at her neck. She hadn't taken them off once.

Someone across the lawn whistled. It was Andrea, waving. She was with another friend, Michelle. "You know them?" Daniel asked.

"My new friends." Raisa smiled. "Can you believe it? We even go to parties together."

"Raisa Adelson. I like this new you."

Raisa held up her arm to invite her friends over, to introduce them to Daniel, but before they came, he scooped her up and whispered that he wanted to take her back to her room, have her to himself. She giggled, waved at her friends and was happy to realize there was still no one she wanted more than Daniel. It wasn't until after she had stripped him down and made love to him that they started talking. Naked, in bed, they wove their legs and arms together and began to work through all they had missed. "Raisele," he said. His eyes were so dark, even in the sun-soaked room. She ran a finger along the soft skin under his eyelashes. "You're not scared the way you used to be."

She smiled. "I know." She took a deep breath and held him tighter, exhaled. "I don't know why but I feel free in a way I never have. I've opened up, found friends who respect me for my work, for being good at math, instead of teasing me."

"Here it's better to be smart than tough?"

"Something like that." Her smile grew. "For the first time, people talk to me like they want to know as much as I do. Can you believe that?"

He pushed a strand of hair back from her cheek. "Of course I believe that."

"You're stronger," she said. "Bigger." She ran a hand over his chest.

"It was all of the push-ups and sit-ups." He hesitated, went still.

"What?"

"I need to tell you something. I could go to jail for saying it."

"Then don't tell me. I mean it. Don't tell me."

He leaned closer so their noses touched and he spoke in a voice so soft, if she moved she couldn't hear. "I can't keep anything from you. You know that. I...I studied Chernobyl this summer. It's why I stayed longer than the other cadets. They used my Russian. They never let someone like me access documents like those, but they were desperate for translators. They were looking for information on the cleanup, on the lunar modules used on the rooftop, thought it could help with our weapons research." He bit his bottom lip. "I found something. You would have put it in your bag and walked out with it, but I couldn't."

Raisa nodded, couldn't help herself even though she knew he shouldn't be saying any of this, that it could get them both into trouble.

"Valery Legasov, the man who came to Vera and Papa's funeral, who sent Mama and me here. He worked with Anna in one of the Soviet black sites. They had dozens around the country, cells where scientists worked secretly on weapons." Daniel took a deep breath. "Legasov was also the one placed in charge of the cleanup after Chernobyl. He ordered a full recounting from anyone who had been at Chernobyl that night, wanted to know what they saw, felt, heard, even what they ate. Every tiny detail." Daniel closed his eyes and rolled over on his back. He threaded his fingers through Raisa's. "None of it could be fact-checked or proven. All those testimonies came from dying patients using their last breaths to describe the explosion, their terror."

"What did you find?"

"Raisele, you're not going to believe this. I barely could. Dozens of people reported the same experience. They felt a shudder. They heard something loud, a bang, and then...most saw a flash of light. Get this:

They said it looked like a wave ran through the room they were in. Not a wave with water, a wave where everything around them stretched and crested. Their descriptions were identical. Independently, they all used the word *wave*."

"Spaghettified?" Raisa said. Daniel nodded. "The static? Did they talk about the static?"

Daniel held her tighter. "Yes, exactly. They described what we saw in that field, what happened when that old woman appeared, disappeared. It was as if they had all been there with us, seen the same thing." Raisa leaned her head down and burrowed against his chest. It was as terrifying as it was exciting because it meant whatever happened around that old woman wasn't an anomaly—it was real. And there were implications for *Atomic Anna*. Were there more parts in the comic books that were real, too? She got up and pulled out the issue she had stashed in the back of her closet.

"There's a connection," she said. "That's what you're thinking, isn't it? Whatever my mom is up to with Anna. It's connected. I mean, that old lady, Anna, Atomic Anna, they're all the same person. She gave me an issue of *Atomic Anna* back on the beach all those years ago. And when she was in that field the day of the competition, she had a copy then, too."

Daniel ran his hand over his shaved head. "Are you saying you think the time machine might be real?"

"I don't know. It sounds crazy, right? But so much of the comics is real and if this is, then my grandmother, Anna, is working with my mom on a time machine. How else would my mom know what to draw?" She started speaking faster, her mind whirling through possibilities. "And if the time machine is real, then it's killing Anna. And they really are asking me to help. But all of that is just...just wild. I mean, really? Am I really even talking about this?" Raisa came back to bed and flipped through the pages, showed him the equations in the new issue. "You know I have this theory I've been working on. From the data I found in my telescope. I told you there were things I couldn't explain. They could have been static, light echoes—but I've gotten tons of new data from Arecibo and seen the same disturbances there. I have a hypothesis."

"The graviton?"

She smiled because he remembered, because she loved how closely he listened to her and never dismissed a single idea. She kept going. "Yes, the graviton. No one thinks it's real. All these respected scientists say it's farfetched. But here's the thing. The unexplained phenomenon in all the data coming from Puerto Rico, it's exactly the same as what I collected on Kestler's roof. Tons of experts have made excuses for it, but their explanations don't make sense. It seems like everyone is too scared or confused or I don't know what to look at what's really there. Gravity. The problem is it's such a weak force. And gravitational waves are so enormous, they're nearly impossible to detect, but they're out there and I think those waves, and the graviton, are what I've found."

"What does this have to do with Anna and the time machine?"

"If her time machine is real, and that's a big *if*"—Raisa smiled—"then her equations aren't accounting for the graviton, for gravity. The waves are clashing and breaking down her cellular structure. That's why she's dying. Okay. I'm just going to say it." She felt nervous knowing that once she said what she was thinking next, she could never take it back. "Let's assume this is all real and I have identified the graviton. Then, I think I can fix the time machine."

"If you did, you could stop Chernobyl. Isn't that Anna's goal?"

"Yes. I'd do it by figuring out the equations to account for gravity. I can't be sure. I've been working on it. Haven't told anyone, but—"

"But, Raisele, you're a genius. I'm sure you can do it."

"But should I? Even my mother asked that in one of the issues. I mean, should a time machine exist? What if I fix it and then I can't even save Vera or stop Chernobyl because my mom and grandmother have other plans? Or someone else takes it and uses it for something else? Just because you can doesn't mean you should."

"But what if none of that happens and you use it to save my sister and all those other people? It's worth trying, isn't it? You'd be saving thousands of people, all those animals, and the forest itself." Daniel's voice was rising as he got more and more excited.

"I guess; I mean, I can't even tell Stocken this is what I'm thinking. He'd tell me I'm nuts adding a time machine into the mix." She put the comic book down and faced Daniel. "I want to save people, I really do. But I have older issues of *Atomic Anna* where Mighty Minerva and Atomic Anna are out for revenge. They said it was all for good, to make people pay, but it got ugly. They did bad things. What if I do the same? I could see using a time machine as a tool for revenge."

"You wouldn't."

"Others might." She leaned back and closed her eyes, thought about the older issues, all the destruction Mighty Minerva and Atomic Anna caused, even sometimes hurting innocent people as they destroyed the evil headquarters or crashed the plane carrying the villain. "There's still a lot to process and figure out. I have to keep working through the data. I need to read through all the old research, see if I can find more of Anna's papers. The equations would be for the amplifier, so I'd need to understand her designs better."

"Her old papers, they're all in Russian. I can read quickly, help you sort through to pinpoint what matters. You can understand the science," Daniel said. "We can work on this together." Raisa ran a finger along the soft edge of his cheek. He must have shaved for her, but the stubble was already poking through. It broke her heart to see how badly he wanted this to work, how he wanted to save Vera.

"I can't promise anything. I might not even figure out the equations."

"Trying is more than enough for me. Trying, together. I can cross-register here, at Penn. I'll make it an independent study. Maybe Stocken can sign off on it and I can get credit."

Raisa brought his fingertips to her lips and kissed them. "Okay," she said. "It's worth a shot. But not yet. I'm hungry and I want to show you something."

"Since when do you shy away from work?" He laughed.

"Since I haven't seen you in so long. Also, I changed, remember? I'm doing more than work all the time. I want to show you what I found."

They went outside to one of the food trucks. She held his hand and he kissed her knuckles and her shoulder while they waited in line. She leaned close so there was no space between. She ordered cheesesteaks first, water ice later. "Tell me about your summer," she said, sitting in his lap. She'd never sat that way in public before and he seemed to love it, held her tight as they claimed each other. "I want to know where you slept, what you ate, who you talked to. I even want to know where you went for vodka," she said.

He started telling her about training, about the sun. "It was hotter in Virginia than anywhere I've ever lived." He told her about the eggs every morning, that he couldn't imagine how they scrambled and cooked so many every single day and how they always tasted like nothing. He told her about the afternoons spent in an office reading through Soviet documents, early mornings filled with running, the endless push-ups and sit-ups, the drills and obstacle courses. "It was fun," he said. "Part of it, until they taught us to shoot. Aim to kill, they said." He paused, probably because he felt her go tense. She hated thinking about him with a gun. "Remember you asked me if I could kill anyone?" She nodded. "I don't think I can."

She slipped off his lap so she could look him in the eye. "What if someone was coming to kill you, or me? Would you shoot then?"

"Of course I would."

"But if you didn't know how to shoot, you probably wouldn't."

"How can I say?" And then, "What is it, what's worrying you?"

"There is something," she admitted. "Going through all the data from Arecibo, thinking about the universe, being away from my grandparents...I used to think I could control things, but now I know I can't really predict anything outside of the Market. There's no Mrs. Mandel ordering capon necks or Mr. Kestler coming for his marrow bones. I used to love that order, that I knew what would happen and when." She paused. "Now I think I love knowing the universe doesn't stick to any kind of schedule like that. And I can't believe I'm about to admit this, but it's exciting. I realized, I want to break out of our Soviet neighborhood. I want to even get out of Philadelphia. With you." She took his hand. "Come on, I still have something I want to show you." He laughed, was still drinking the melted juice from his water ice. She took him across campus and toward a seedier side of West Philly where none of the rich kids dared set foot, to a club named Shay's.

"Been wondering where you were," the bouncer said to Raisa.

"Right here," she said, smiling. "This is my Daniel."

"No Vito? Or the girls?"

"No, just us," Raisa said. She felt Daniel tense at Vito's name and she leaned over and kissed him. "He's just a friend," she whispered to Daniel, and then took him inside. It was early, but there were no windows and so the place was dark. The bar was half-full. She felt Daniel hesitate. "We're not here to drink," she said. She pulled him down a narrow hall.

"Room two," the bartender called. Raisa pulled Daniel in with her. There was a beat-up couch and a sticky table. She reached for the control board. It was set up at the back of the room and a curtain peeled aside at the front, revealing a screen. She pressed play and the music started. "Karaoke," she explained, laughing. "Come on." She put on a song by the Beatles, "Let It Be," because she knew Daniel had heard it before. The words danced on the screen.

"What are we doing?"

"We're singing. Read the words and sing. It's how you can learn to be American, how you can practice English," she said. She started singing and Daniel joined her, quietly at first, then louder, laughing. They'd had fun together before, but never like this, never being goofy and carefree, enjoying youth and silliness like she'd always seen her peers revel in, and Raisa loved this new side to both of them, that they were growing together.

*　*　*

That fall, Daniel got special permission from Temple to cross-register for an individual study with Stocken. He and Raisa dug into everything they could find on the accident at Chernobyl, convinced it might help Raisa understand the graviton and work on her equations for the amplifier. The university's access to old Soviet documents was limited, but Stocken had contacts around the world and he was able to get colleagues to send reams of information. Scientists everywhere had tracked the fallout, the cloud and ash, and dissected every detail the USSR released. Raisa and Daniel found that hundreds of people reported seeing static and waves. Most labs tracking the event called the waves pressure waves, but that didn't describe everything Raisa found. And the more she read, the more convinced she was that she had found the graviton, was on the verge of describing it through math, because every single anomaly could be accounted for by incorporating gravity.

"Look, look, look," Raisa squealed one day while she and Daniel were in the library. She had just uncovered a long, thin tube from a box a colleague of Stocken's had sent from Sweden. It was a map of Pripyat and Chernobyl. She rolled it out on the floor, anchored it down with books on each corner. They had read countless descriptions of the closed city, and seen dozens of photos after the disaster, but this was the first time they were looking at a pristine schematic.

"A pool and a school," Raisa said. Somehow, she had never thought of that side of Chernobyl, that there were families and lives outside of the plant.

"Vera loved to swim."

She pointed to a playground. "We never even talked about all the children who died."

"Or the farmers." Daniel pointed to the plots designated as farms outside the town. "Some of them were probably there for generations." They leaned over that map for a long time, taking in all those details of the dead. Each new piece of information made Raisa quieter, sadder.

"You remember I can't promise to save Vera, to stop Chernobyl?" she asked gently.

"I know."

In early spring, Raisa was working in the server room on the machine Stocken had given her permission to use for her research. Daniel was there reading through Soviet papers for their work together while she reconnected some wires that had come loose. The room was cold and sterile, lined with row after row of stacked towers humming and blinking. She leaned over Daniel's shoulder, pointed to the paper he was holding. "What is it?"

"A paper reviewing Anna's amplifier. This model looks different from others."

"It is," Raisa said. "Looks like a newer schematic." She read quickly and stopped dead when she saw the authors listed at the end. "Daniel," she said in a whisper, her chest tight. "Yasha Berlitsky. My grandfather. They worked together? Baba and Pop-Pop never told me that."

Daniel flipped to the notes at the end of the paper. There were references to several papers they published together, experiments they ran together. "They were a powerhouse," Daniel said. "Wait." He read the next part very slowly. "There's an addendum from the editor. He wrote he's disappointed they didn't push the project further, especially their work on cosmic rays. Wait, listen. He says they lost a child, that she was kidnapped, and then their work stopped. All the questions posed in their research together went unanswered."

"Kidnapped? That doesn't make sense," Raisa said. Mama had talked about being pushed away, how her birth mother never wanted her. Did Baba and Pop-Pop kidnap her? The servers around her suddenly seemed louder, the room smaller, and Raisa's head started to spin. She couldn't bear to think of her grandparents as criminals. "I need to talk to my grandparents."

YASHA

November 1992

One Month Before Molly Dies on Mount Aragats

Moscow

Yasha sat in his office on the top floor of the Kurchatov Institute and stared out the window, down at the Moscow streets. The Soviet Union was gone. Russia had risen in her ashes, but for Yasha there was no difference. The same men were at the top, science was still the heart of the country, and his work allowed him to keep all he had. Cold seeped through the bricks around him. He wore an extra sweater these days. He never used to need it, but now his arthritis had become painful. He felt old looking down at a city that hadn't even existed when he was a child. What hadn't been destroyed during the war had been bulldozed to widen the boulevards, stop anyone from demonstrating. If he closed his eyes he could still imagine the destruction and carnage of the war, what it felt like walking Anna home. Anna. Even after all these years, he missed her more than he thought possible. What a mess they had made together. Age had turned his anger more toward regret than fury. Without much to do, he spent hours running through *what ifs*.

What if he had let her return to work when she said she was ready? What if he hadn't insisted he knew what she needed? What if he hadn't agreed to let Yulia watch their Manya? What if he had told her more often how much he loved her, that he needed her?

"Professor," his secretary interrupted. Irina was young, without a husband or a wrinkle. Her job was to tend to all the old men on the floor, the retired scientists who had nothing left to contribute but knew too many secrets to be allowed to fade into the sunset. "A package for you."

"A package?" Yasha sat up. He held out his hand to signal her to bring it to him. He reached for the letter opener and saw the censors had already opened and resealed the envelope, probably at least twice. He expected a few sheets of redacted papers, but instead, a hand-drawn comic book spilled onto his desk. *Atomic Anna.* The cover featured three women wearing capes. The silhouette of Chernobyl's power plant was in the background. The facility was still sparkling and new. He shook the comic book, expecting a note to fall out, but nothing came. He leaned back. The office was so small the top of his chair rammed the wall behind him. Plaster spilled as it did every time. He turned to the first page and found a date scrawled across the panels in thick black marker. December 8, 1992. Underneath was a message: *Be here by then.*

That was only a month away. He started reading. The superheroes had a secret lair, a cosmic ray tower built on the top of a mountain. There were a series of towers surrounding a main compound, a small lake, and majestic views. There was no denying he knew exactly what he was looking at. His hands started to shake. His whole body trembled. "Irina," Yasha called. "Irina!" he yelled. Then, even louder, "Irina, I need to leave!"

He kissed the comic book. "I'm coming, my love."

RAISA

Philadelphia

Raisa and Daniel sat at the table in Baba and Pop-Pop's kitchen. Their knees were crammed together and Raisa was flush against her grandmother, pressed into her soft side. Steaming borscht sat in bowls in front of them. Pop-Pop's hands were stained purple from peeling the beets. "You're pregnant?" Baba asked. "Is that why you both have serious faces?"

"What? No." Raisa shook her head. "Why are you always worried about that?"

"Because you have a big life in front of you."

"Would you please just hear us out," Raisa said, feeling annoyed by the comment, nervous about what she had to say. The window was open. Someone had hung a basketball net in the alley and kids below were playing. Daniel squeezed her hand to push her to start, but Raisa's stomach hurt. Her head, too. She'd never doubted her grandparents' love, not even for an instant, for her or for Mama, or even for Anna.

That was what made this so hard. "This is really difficult. Daniel and I, we found something." She shook her head, hated that she was stalling. "Anna and Yasha stopped working together after their only child, a daughter, was kidnapped." She stopped to let the words sink in, watched her grandparents go pale and look at each other. She waited for them to reply, hoped they'd tell her she was wrong—or say anything, but the room was silent save for the ball dribbling outside. Raisa couldn't remember the last time she felt this anxious, couldn't understand why even Baba kept her mouth closed. Baba always had a fast reply, and seeing her so still, looking petrified, rattled Raisa. "You...you said you adopted Mama," she said slowly. "You know what I'm asking, right? Did you do it? Did you kidnap my mother?" They still didn't say anything. Raisa wanted to beg them to answer, but she willed herself to stay put, to let them take the time they needed to explain because she wanted them to give her an explanation. She wanted to believe this was all a mistake. Pop-Pop reached into his pocket for cigarettes, flicked his lighter. Baba never let him smoke at the table, but she didn't say anything.

"Sounds...sounds like a good game outside," Baba said in a hoarse whisper.

"You did it?" Raisa asked, her own voice shaking now. It was the only reason Baba wouldn't answer, didn't rise up to contradict her, tell her this was a terrible insult. "Say something, please. What happened?"

"Give them a minute," Daniel said.

"They've had years," Raisa said, and it started to sink in for her, too. Her grandparents had a whole side to them she had never imagined. They'd done it. They'd kidnapped Mama, torn her away from her birth parents. And where she'd always been so scared of losing them, too scared to ever really even be angry at them, now she let anger come. It washed over her in thick swells that rattled her chest, had adrenaline coursing, making her feel like she was out of control. Pop-Pop's cigarette singed; his cheeks went concave. Baba was still staring at the window.

"Tell me," Raisa said, her voice sharper than it had ever been with them, her anger rising even more.

"The answer isn't easy," Baba said, and she looked down at her untouched borscht.

"We imagined we were protecting you and your mother," Pop-Pop said. "Anna gave your mother to us. We would never steal a child. There was no kidnapping. The Soviets called it that to protect their reputation. The story also kept Anna out of prison because giving her daughter away like that, it was illegal."

"Anna and Yasha, they were in a bad place, using everything they had against one another," Baba said. "Anna wasn't well. Yasha wasn't helping. There was nothing we could do to reunite them. Once it was done, it was done."

"So, you just took her?" Raisa said; the edge in her voice was sharp.

"I told you, we didn't take her," Pop-Pop said. "Nothing about it was simple. It was a complicated disaster. When Anna asked us—and I'm being clear, she asked. When she asked, we knew she was out of options. We said no again and again, but she wouldn't accept that as an answer."

"You have to believe we had no choice," Baba said. "Anna was like my sister. Family. And we truly thought we were saving your mother, that she was safer away from her parents."

"Is that what you tell yourself?" Raisa said, letting her voice sound bitter. "She's a drug addict. She couldn't even drag herself over here to see me, not even once. That's better than the USSR?"

"Raisele," Daniel said.

"What? I should be polite after all these years of lies?"

"Just hear them out."

Raisa paced to the refrigerator, then back to the table. She hadn't realized she had so much bottled up inside, but now she was letting it come out and she couldn't stop, even though she knew so much of her rage was actually for her mother. But hadn't her grandparents' lies made Molly into the woman and mother she was? Raisa's voice went even louder. "There is nothing good about her life now, is there? You remember she came to this house, back when she was arrested, she painted that damn mural and didn't even wait for me to come home from school. I bet she ran out to get high instead. And she still does that. Drops into my life and leaves comic books without seeing me. Did you know that? She puts them in my room, even left one in the van once. She delivers them and won't even face me. She's a coward."

"You have no idea what her life was like, *is* like," Pop-Pop said.

"Then tell me. Tell me how this is better than what she had with Anna and Yasha." She saw her grandparents shrinking, cringing, and still she couldn't stop. "You made her into what she is."

"I'm sorry," Baba said. She reached for Raisa's hand, but Raisa pulled away.

"Why are you saying sorry?" Raisa asked. "What is it that I should forgive you for? Because as I see it, there's a long string of lies and bad decisions, years of you not telling me what was really happening. Yes, you gave me a home and took care of me, but at what price? Why? Why all the secrets and lies?" She looked at Pop-Pop and Baba while they looked at each other. There was an entire conversation taking place between them, in silence. She had seen it so many times before and she had no idea what they were saying. And she needed them to tell her, to treat her like an adult. "What else are you holding back?"

"Your grandmother, Anna, is a great woman," Pop-Pop started.

"She's alive?" Daniel interrupted.

"We think so," Baba said. "She is brilliant and troubled. She has seen too much. And your mother, we held on too tight, made so many mistakes. That's true. That's what I'm sorry for. But I'm not apologizing for keeping it from you, Raisele. Children don't get to know everything. You can't. And you shouldn't. We want to give you the future, not trap you in a past we ran from." Baba's words hit like weights that sent Raisa reeling back into her seat because even through all her anger she could see that her grandmother was right. Her mother lived in darkness and Raisa didn't want to know the details. She never had, only wanted to know Mama was coming home, was going to wake up.

"We thought math was a future for her. She was so good at numbers when she was little. I hated to admit she didn't like them even if she had talent. And we never told your mother not to pursue her art," Pop-Pop said. "Not in the way you think. She made her own choices."

"Did she?" Baba asked. She dropped her head into her hands and Raisa saw pain in her grandmother that she hadn't seen before. It made her feel ashamed for pressing so hard, for unleashing so much anger. Still, she was torn between wanting her grandparents to feel better and wanting answers. She had to keep pushing.

"I don't know," Pop-Pop said. "That's what I've learned through everything. I just don't know." He went quiet. And then, "Maybe we made many wrong decisions, but at the time we thought they were right. We thought we were giving her what she needed. And I think that was what mattered. We couldn't have done better."

Raisa sat, not knowing what to do or say, her head spinning through too many ideas, her heart reeling with emotions she couldn't handle, and above it all the looming realization that all of this was more complicated than she had imagined. She hadn't been prepared for that complexity, the mess. Unlike life, science and math had easy answers. She had been looking for a simple answer to wrap her head around when they started this conversation. She should have known there was none.

Quiet expanded and filled the room. Daniel squeezed her hand and broke the silence, finally. "Tell us about Yasha. He didn't want to give Molly away?"

"No. But he was cruel back then; they were both spinning out of control," Baba said. "We couldn't leave Molly with him."

"We really did our best," Pop-Pop said, and Raisa realized all her fury was slowly being replaced by sadness. Pop-Pop meant what he said. They both did. And now her grandparents, whom she'd always looked to as rocks, who always had all the answers, were broken into more pieces than she had ever realized. They had done everything they could to put themselves together, to be whole for her. She had never appreciated that before.

"Did you know Mama got out of prison early?" Raisa said. "I went to meet her. Remember, she sent that letter saying she was getting out. The day I went, you thought I was nervous about a test, that Daniel and I had a fight."

Baba leaned back, sucked in air. "I didn't put it together." That was when Baba started to cry, long sobs heaving from her chest. "We wanted to tell you. We really did, but we weren't sure we could explain it. And we didn't want you to know where she was going. Following her would be too dangerous."

"Where did she go? Are the comic books real?" The questions poured out of Raisa. "Did Mama go after Anna, look for her and Yasha? Is she back in the Soviet Union? Aragats, the station, it exists? The time machine, too. It's real, isn't it?" Her grandparents had another long, silent conversation between them and Raisa couldn't stand the quiet. She kept pushing. "They're trying to stop Chernobyl, change the past? Tell me. Just tell me."

"Perhaps; I can't be sure." Baba sniffled. "Anna's past was so painful for her. Her mother was taken during the revolution. Then she lost her father. He was a drunk for years before he slipped off a bridge. The ice was thin. He fell through. All of that grief, everything we saw during the war, none of it left her. She never let it go. Pop-Pop and I, we buried our dead, but not everyone can. I can't explain it. I can't tell you why some people recover and some don't. To meet her, you wouldn't even know it. On the outside she is strong and brilliant, the best scientist the world has ever seen, greater than Einstein and Newton, all those men that came before her." Baba smiled. "She looked up to Marie Curie, thought Yasha was her Pierre. It was Pierre, you know, who helped

Marie rise. She was brilliant, the brains in the marriage, but she was a woman. The world wouldn't let her be anyone without Pierre. They worked as a team."

"Anna and Yasha, they were in love," Pop-Pop said. "It was a strange love. I'm not sure everyone saw it, but we did. She was devoted to him and he was always holding her. She never showed her vulnerabilities with anyone else."

"Not even really with me," Baba said, and the more they explained, the more they said, the calmer Raisa felt, the more the adrenaline faded. It left quickly, she thought, because she didn't want to be angry. She was more frustrated with her mother. But perhaps, above all else, anger scared her; it always had. Baba continued, "Anna fought that love at first, but he was a constant, always at her side. He took her for who she was. Among scientists it was known, well known, that they were passionate. They worked next to each other in their lab, their chairs touching." Baba pointed to Daniel's and Raisa's chairs. "Like you two, only that passion was killing them. It was like the air around them was charged. They kissed as much as they fought. They clawed at each other, tore each other to bits, but then they found their way back. Always, a fight followed by love. Anna had so much bottled-up pain from her childhood and she unleashed all those feelings onto Yasha—the good and the bad. He must have had the same inside him. I can't say. He was very private."

"Anna was forty-three years old when she got pregnant," Pop-Pop said. "I don't think she had ever thought about children, about being a mother. Maybe because hers had destroyed her. Anna was convinced that her mother chose to leave her, not that she was taken and executed. I don't know why. All I know is that after your mother was born, Anna and Yasha's life together turned toxic in a way I had never seen."

Raisa pressed, "You never told me any of this. Why? Why hold it all in?"

Baba reached for Pop-Pop's hand. "You have to understand. We lost everything. We all saved each other, but somehow Anna and Yasha forgot that. After your mother came, they fought over everything. We heard them tear into one another, but nothing cut deeper than your mother. Each had their own plans for her future. There was only bitterness and hate in that house. We didn't kidnap your mother. Anna gave her to us and we didn't know how to explain."

"And Yasha?" Daniel asked.

"He never would have let her go." Pop-Pop leaned forward. "That was part of the problem. He wasn't letting Anna go, either. She started to slip away and he held on tighter, tried to control her every move. It was horrible watching him hold on so tight, knowing Molly was stuck between them."

"We should have told you sooner," Baba said. "You're going to look for them, aren't you? I can already see it in you. Your mother has the same look when she's determined."

"Chernobyl," Daniel said. "Raisa thinks she can help Anna stop it from happening."

"You want to save Vera." Baba reached for Daniel's hand and covered it with both of hers. "I don't know anything about Vera, but I do know the past is best left in the past. No matter how much it hurts."

"But I can fix Anna's equations, her time machine," Raisa said. "And Anna, she's dying. I can save her, too. Save Vera and all those other people who died in the meltdown. Where are they? Tell us."

Baba dropped her chin to her chest and took a deep breath. "I can't be sure. If your mother has been leaving you comic books and clues, follow them. You need more than coordinates or an address. Think of it as a journey. Find her through *Atomic Anna*. But be careful. Just because you can doesn't mean you should. I know I can't stop you, but I can warn you. You might be able to change the past, but does that fix it? What will you lose?"

YASHA

Mount Aragats

asha stood at the base of Mount Aragats and looked up at the wind-ing, narrow path. It was early morning. He wore his military uniform, hoping it might impress Anna or at least keep locals from bothering him. It was black, with snow gear that matched. He was more nervous than he'd anticipated. He had read that comic book, the *Atomic Anna* that arrived at his office, hundreds of times. It was tucked inside his jacket, in the pocket at his breast.

"I'm coming," he said to the wind, and he started up the path. His driver had taken him as far as he could. The snow and ice would make the rest of his trek on foot dangerous, but it was worth it. He knew Anna must have sent the comic book, that it was her way of apologizing. Aragats was their design. It was their station, the one she conceived, and they'd dreamed of building it together more than forty years earlier. He could remember them talking about it in the hammock next to Baikal like it was yesterday, how soft her skin was, how delicious she tasted.

He'd built this station for her, always knowing they were meant to come back together here. It was fate, he told himself, something he'd never believed in before but now knew without a doubt was real. Anna was bringing him here to reunite, to rekindle and rebuild their love.

He had already mourned her, thought she died at Chernobyl along with everyone else. The loss almost took him, too. He had spent months locked in his flat, in the dark, refusing to work. He had pulled out of it by convincing himself that Anna would have wanted him to carry on. He still thought about her every day, sometimes every hour. And then that comic book arrived and had allowed him hope. She had to be alive. Who else could have sent it? She must have been in hiding all this time and now she was opening herself to him. He would forgive her. He already had, years ago. The anger wasn't worth it; it had taken away too much of his life already. In hindsight he would have been better off forgiving her from the start, trying to understand what she was going through and keeping them together. After all, he wasn't the only one suffering. Losing Manya was the worst thing that had ever happened to both of them. Now, whatever time they had left, he imagined it would be best spent researching and exploring together. Side by side as they once were. He wasn't naive. He knew it would be hard. They wouldn't just fall into each other's arms, but this was a start. They didn't have to die alone. And he was prepared for her to be different. Surely the radiation at Chernobyl would have affected her appearance or made her ill. He would take care of her. They would take care of each other.

The snow was light now. The wind traced gentle arcs with it, leaving curved patterns on the surface. They were predicting a blizzard to start that night. "Sir," the driver called after Yasha when he was a few steps up the path. "Sir?"

Yasha turned. "Yes?"

"Radio. Use your radio. Check in once a day."

"I told you that won't be necessary. I'll be safe."

"Still, I'll be at the inn here if you need me." Yasha was a state treasure, too valuable to slip away. He was guarded all the time the way Anna used to be. He'd now come to understand how wrong he'd been to hover over her the way he did.

"She's waiting for me," Yasha said to himself, and smiled. He kept walking toward Anna.

ANNA

October 1992
Two Months Before Molly Dies on Mount Aragats

Mount Aragats

Wake up," a woman said to Anna. She was shaking her. The sun was high and it was cold. Anna was huddled under a heap of blankets, had been deep in a dream she didn't want to leave. It put her in the Moscow flat with Yulia, Malka, and Lazar. The dream was so real she could smell the rosebushes on the floor and the cabbage cooking on the stove, see Yulia's dress hanging on the back of the door. She felt happy and calm, and it had been a long time since she'd felt that way. But the woman trying to wake her up wouldn't relent.

"Leave me alone," Anna said.

"You need to get to work," the woman said, and Anna realized it was Molly. She was on Aragats. "You need to keep working to stop Chernobyl from melting down. Remember?"

Anna opened her eyes and pulled herself out of the dream, back to the mountain, back to her daughter. Yes, she remembered. "AZ-5," she said. Fixing the failsafe was the key to saving all those people. Only she couldn't remember what she'd worked on the day before. The memory loss was a side effect of all her time jumps. Her time machine was broken. AZ-5 was broken. She stood up slowly and rubbed her temples.

"Don't worry," Molly said. "You keep careful notes, recorded everything you did yesterday so you can read it, and remember, then start where you left off. That's what you do in the mornings, review and push ahead." She handed Anna a notebook. Anna reached for it and saw her exposed arms, how bad the lesions had become. Most were bandaged but the edges had expanded, leaked through. Somehow she hadn't felt any pain from them before, but seeing them made them start to ache. "What's the date?"

"October eighth. You have two months until your deadline. December eighth. Are you going to admit why that date is so important?"

"I can't." Her feet felt unsteady in her boots. She leaned on the dresser. At least the memory of what was going to happen in December was deep and old; it came easily. "We should leave this mountain, go somewhere safe. We can't be here on December eighth."

"I'm not leaving. I told you that." Molly went still and Anna tried to remember what Molly had said. She could see in the way Molly's shoulders were back, her jaw set, that something important was keeping Molly there.

"What is it?" Anna asked.

"For starters, I sent Yasha a copy of *Atomic Anna*. He's coming. Yasha is coming here." The three words, *Yasha is coming*, had weight well beyond their size. Anna sank back toward the bed and sat on the mattress, felt her lungs closing. It had been decades since she'd seen him, and while she'd imagined their reunion hundreds of times, she'd never thought it would actually come. She used to think she'd yell and scream, tear his eyes out, but now she was tired and not even sure she had the energy to still be angry. And if he was on his way, what did he expect to find? Would he try to drag their daughter back with him to Moscow, arrest Anna?

"When?" Anna asked. It was all she could manage.

"I told him to be here by December eighth. Your made-up deadline." Molly's voice got louder as the truth spilled into the room and she told Anna how she'd tracked him down, drawn the comic book just for him, and sent it to his office in Moscow. And as she spoke, Anna felt herself splitting into two. On one side she was relieved to see her daughter taking action. But at the same time, she had to get Molly out of there. December eighth wasn't a made-up deadline; it was the day Molly was going to die. "Anna, listen to me," Molly said, bringing Anna back. "When I started going to meetings, when I was sobering up, my sponsors told me I needed to face what scared me most. That was the only way I'd beat the drugs, the urge to drink. I did it. I even came here, but you. You haven't done that. In all of this." She motioned to the room around them, to the towers through the window. "In all of this tremendous work, you've taken yourself out of the equation. I know, you've admitted it was a mistake to push me, Mama, and Papa away, but that was easy. You haven't done the hard work, dug deeper. You're still looking outside of yourself for answers, but the answers you need are inside. They're buried. You need to look at the mistakes you made before us. That's why I'm bringing him here. You need to face what scares you most, starting with Yasha. Tell me. Why are you scared of your own past?"

Anna pulled a sweater tight around her, not because she was cold but because she heard Molly loud and clear. "Yasha," she said. Molly was right. She was scared to see him, to face the pain and anguish he might bring with him. She didn't have much time left and what she had, she wanted to spend on her work, on her daughter.

"How did he make you happy?" Molly pushed. Anna had admitted she and Yasha destroyed each other, but Molly was right. There was a time when he made Anna happy. Only it was so long ago. "Tell me about being happy," Molly said.

Anna closed her eyes and went back to memories with Yulia in

Berlin. "In Germany, I was gloriously happy with Yulia. It sounds terrible to say that. Now we know Hitler was killing and maiming, but we were ignoring all the signs. Living there, I never wanted it to end."

"Now tell me when you were happy with Yasha."

Anna opened her eyes. "Everything ends. My time with your mother ended, and my time with Yasha is over, too. Besides, it doesn't help to think about time as swaths. Single moments are what matter, what we're going to change with the time machine. A split second can shape a life. Or take a life." She was thinking of the moment she met Yulia, the moment the trolley car crashed, even the moment she sent Molly away. "It's why we need to leave, whether Yasha is here or not. We can't be here on the eighth."

"Come on, Anna. You keep talking around the date but won't tell me why. And you're still avoiding what's important. A single moment can make a difference, but real mistakes span years, not the two hours we have to jump and fix them. To really change anything we can only look forward, apologize, and move on, not go back."

"What if you're wrong?" Anna asked.

"I'm not. I've never been more sure of anything in my life. Being sober has taught me no one mistake is ever the problem. The real problem is not looking at the arc of bad decisions. I've spent my life as a pawn, haven't I? I've been caught between you and my parents." She shook her head. "I deserve my own life, to make my own decisions. All this time we've spent together, I've been waiting for you to let your guard down, to admit you were happy to have me here. I thought the more you saw me, the more you would realize the mistakes you had made. But I made the same mistake again and again up here. I thought I might change you, or help you see the light, or something like that. But it'll never happen. Yasha is coming because I want to meet my birth father and have him in my future. You see, I have the power to change things for tomorrow, for Raisa and for me. Yasha and I can help you with the time machine and Chernobyl and then I'm going back to

Philadelphia. To my family." Molly gestured around the room. "This is where your life took you. You're up here alone, living in memories of the past. I don't want this for me."

Molly's words held Anna with a strength she never thought her daughter possessed. While she wanted to say a dozen different things in response, the one that rose above all came quickly. "I'm proud of you," she said. "I'm so proud of you."

"That's it? That's all you have?" Molly said, and to Anna's surprise, her face fell. "Don't you want to tell me anything about Raisa?"

"No," Anna said, feeling guilty that she was letting Molly down again, but what else could she give her? She raced to think of more, to figure out what Molly wanted, wished her mind would work faster the way it used to. "You're right. I always hide behind my work, always have. It's easier, you know. But single moments do matter. Like this conversation."

"This conversation was years in the works."

"But it's happening now over the span of minutes. What I say next matters more than you're admitting."

"You're making excuses." Molly stood and started walking toward the door.

"We don't always get a second chance, even with a time machine. A heart can already be too broken to mend," Anna said. Her own heart pounding in her chest, working so hard the wounds on her skin felt like they were also beating. "I do have something else to tell you." Molly stopped with one foot over the threshold. The faster the better, Anna told herself. "Raisa is coming. I gave her your comic books, added my own notes. I need her help to fix my time machine, to stop Chernobyl."

Molly turned around and faced Anna. Her jaw was still set, her shoulders squared, but where Anna expected surprise all she saw in Molly was relief. "It's about time you admitted it. Mama told me. I got a letter from her last week. She said you wouldn't warn me, that you'd continue making the same mistakes again and again, thinking you could control everything. And Mama wanted me to know so I could prepare to take care of Raisa, get her home safe. Yasha and Raisa are coming. And I know why you're scared of December eighth. Mama told me about that, too. That you think that's the day I die. Can't you see that'll never happen? If you'd just told me from the beginning, we could have made a plan together, figured it out together. But now I've prepared on my own. I always thought I needed you, but I don't. I realize that now."

RAISA

March 1991

One Year Before Molly Dies on Mount Aragats

Philadelphia

After talking to her grandparents, Raisa was more convinced than ever that she needed to find her mother and Anna and help them. Daniel agreed, and since Baba told them to look at the clues Mama had left, Raisa went back to the only primary source she had: her collection of *Atomic Annas*. She and Daniel lugged Raisa's glittery box filled with the comic books to her dorm room and read them one by one, starting at the beginning. The comics were crude at first. The colors weren't consistent, the lines weren't straight, and the characters varied from panel to panel. Raisa had never noticed that before. Still, the story was clear. It began with the Russian Revolution in 1917. Mama drew the mobs, the crush of people flooding the streets, demanding bread. They didn't want their precious Czar dead, Mama wrote; they wanted him to change. Xenia, Baba Anna's mother, was a leader. She was arrested, taken by soldiers, and thrown into a deep, dark pit of a prison.

Raisa and Daniel read sitting on her floor, their backs against the bed. "The first time I read this," Raisa said, "I didn't know Xenia was my great-grandmother. I thought it was all an elaborate story." She ran a finger over the figure of Xenia being dragged away. "Now I know it's my family history."

Daniel kissed her cheek and pulled out the next issue. There was no question Mama, Molly, was Mighty Minerva. She had the same body, the same straight jaw and blond hair. Mighty Minerva grew as an artist, her abilities increasing with each issue as she learned to conjure more elaborate designs on the page and then lift them off of the paper and into real life. Rocket Raisa's power was speed, and as each issue progressed she flew and ran faster and faster, accelerating beyond anything or anyone on earth. Dozens of issues detailed Atomic Anna, Mighty Minerva, and Rocket Raisa saving the world together, fighting off evil bad guys. Eventually, Rocket Raisa's origin story changed and she became Mighty Minerva's daughter. After giving birth, Mighty Minerva's appearance changed and softened. Her angles turned to curves.

"The day you were born, her life changed," Daniel said. "That's what she's telling you."

Raisa quickly flipped the pages depicting her mother in labor. "She's trying to paint over the past, make it seem better than it was," she said.

They kept reading and Raisa realized she'd never consumed the comics that way before. In the past she read single, isolated issues, but now seeing them as a whole body of work was overwhelming. She alternated between pride and anger, sadness and confusion. Mama had always left her on edge, never knowing what to expect, and here she was doing it again with these comic books.

Raisa reached for the issue her mother had left in the van, the one she'd found on their way to Kestler's roof. This one was different from the others because a dozen of the text bubbles were covered in

Wite-Out and new dialogue was written in a different handwriting. The letters looked old-fashioned and practiced, not smooth like Mama's. Even more, it was the first issue set on top of a mountain with six watchtowers.

"This one has bothered me for years," she said, opening to the page with the speech bubble that had caught her attention the very first time she read it: *Raisa, help me.* Below it were the equations. "Help with what? Why? I never understood why she didn't spell it all out. It's like a cipher that I'm supposed to decode."

"Maybe it's like your grandmother said, they want to take you on a kind of journey. Like you need to know something before you get there. Look, there's a lake in the summer," Daniel said, pointing to a frame near the equations. He sat up straighter. "There are seasons in this one. None of the other comic books have seasons. There's even a sign that says Anna Maksimovna Berkova and Yasha Ivanovich Berlitsky Cosmic Ray Station. Raisele, the name is horrible and exactly how Soviets name places. There must be an acronym for it." He shook his head. "The point is, I think this is a drawing of a real place. She's trying to tell you where she is—giving you equations and a location."

"Then where are the coordinates?" Raisa took the comic book and held it closer, as if that would help, opened it to the page with the date. "Look. December 8, 1992. If you think she's trying to tell me something, then that date is important for some reason. I'd put it out of my mind because it never made sense, but now, looking at it, I think something's going to happen on December 8, 1992. The thing is, I have no idea what it means or what it'll be." She groaned. "She's only giving me half of what I need, tidbits to string me along."

"Maybe it's because she doesn't want you to come until you've worked through the equations. You're still trying to understand the graviton."

"True." Raisa's heart was beating hard. Thinking about it made her anxious, made her want to work faster. "I guess December 8, 1992, is my deadline."

"In the meantime, how do we find this place?" Daniel pointed to the watchtowers.

"Maybe Stocken can help," Raisa said. "He has contacts. He might be able to locate an old cosmic ray station."

ANNA

December 1992
One Week Before Molly Dies on Mount Aragats

Mount Aragats

nna was sitting in the kitchen, alone. Scared. It was early evening, close to dinnertime, and she'd spent the whole day working on a fix for the time machine, had spent the last few weeks barely sleeping, waiting for Yasha and Raisa on edge, dreading the moment they arrived and whatever would happen after that. Now she was exhausted. Molly was already asleep in the bunk room. She had written out a calendar and nailed it to the wall, counting off the days to December 8. Seven days to go and Anna wanted more than anything to get off that mountain, but she wouldn't leave without Molly, and Molly wouldn't leave until Yasha and Raisa came. What would Anna even say when they arrived? She had no idea what they'd talk about, wished they could skip over the dramatic reunion and get straight to work. Only she also wanted to hold Raisa, talk things through with Yasha, and so she'd grown more and more anxious. Making things even worse, there was a blizzard in the forecast, with days of snow and ice predicted. And since they were going to be stuck on Aragats, to defend them, Anna had assembled an array of alarms. She was in the middle of making herself a snack when one of the alerts started blaring, lights flashing. Someone was there. Anna jumped and grabbed her coat, but her hands weren't steady and she dropped it, tried again. Her boots were already on, always on. While she zipped up, Molly came to the coat rack.

"It could be Raisa or Yasha," Molly said. She still sounded half-asleep but was moving quickly. She ran out the door first and Anna followed as best she could, nervous and wary. They were so close to the eighth.

The lesions on her skin made it painful to move quickly. The air was dark and bitter. Cold sliced her cheeks along with the snow that had already started. She made her way past the six watchtowers, saw Molly disappear over the crest of the hill. "Mollushka," Anna yelled, "slow down." Anna pushed through a snow drift, ignoring the growing pain from her wounds. She narrowed her gaze as if that would help her navigate better through all that snow, but it didn't. She didn't see the man until she was standing right in front of him. He wore all black so he blended into the night sky. Still, she knew him instantly. Yasha. Molly stood behind him, strong and tall, unharmed. She must have missed him in the dark. Anna didn't move, didn't breathe. Fear overtook her, along with relief that he was finally here, that the moment had come. She raised her arms out of habit, because she always used to open herself to him, and as she did she realized she wanted to reach out and touch him, to feel him. He looked like he might cry.

And as he stepped toward her, he said, "I love you." The words were a force she hadn't expected. So was his voice. She hadn't heard it in decades, but it pulled her back to the first time she saw him, to the time she stood with him in front of the clerk and signed their marriage certificate. She looked closer at his face, at the shadows and features she knew so well. And she took in the way he looked at her, a way no one else ever did because he was the only one who saw all of her, who let her be strong and fall apart at the same time. "I never stopped loving you," he said. Anna's heart hammered in her chest. She had spent so many years hating this man, despising him, and now that he was here, she was melting back to the way she felt before the hate, back to the softness and love. How did all that anger leave her so quickly? It didn't make sense, and yet she didn't want to fight it. "I thought I would have more to say. I planned a speech," Yasha continued. He didn't look down. "Now I don't have any words."

"Papa," Molly said. She stepped forward and he looked at her and gasped. He held out a hand and reached for her arm, touched her gently.

"Manya. You brought her home," he said to Anna.

"No," Molly said. "I brought you here. I sent the comic book." Yasha leaned toward her, looking like he wanted to say a thousand things at the same time. Anna knew the look because she felt it, too, only all the things she had to say were caught and clogged with emotion or fear, that intangible flood that kept her still and quiet. "I came to help. And I'm Molly," she said. "I'm not Manya anymore. I'm an American."

He started to cry, thick tears that raced over his cheeks and spilled onto the snow. "You made it. They made it," he said, and his posture broke; his chest was racked with sobs. "I couldn't check on you, couldn't take any chances that might lead them to you. I never knew if you made it to America. If you, Yulia, and Lazar were alive."

"You knew?" Anna gasped.

"Of course I knew they had her. I put it together that same day because they were gone, too. It couldn't have been a coincidence. And I didn't say anything because I knew they'd arrest you, blame you." He held out a hand to take hers. "I'm not angry, not anymore. We don't have time for that, do we? But the three of us, we can be a family again. Now."

Anna was crying, overtaken by a flood of relief and the realization that she'd been lost. Maybe he felt it, too. She saw him shaking as he reached out and pulled Molly to him.

Anna wasn't sure how long they stayed there like that, together. It was Molly who said it was cold, that they needed to keep moving. The three of them marched over the ice in silence, sliding and slipping under the weight of all that hovered between them in that dark field. Once inside, they took off their coats.

"The blizzard will lock us in here for at least a week," Yasha said. Anna opened her mouth to explain that the snow couldn't keep them there, they needed to be off that mountain by the eighth, but then she saw his black military uniform. She put it together with the black parka and she remembered her first jump to the station, the same uniform and parka soaked with blood.

"It's all coming true," she said.

"You mean the snowstorm they predicted?" Yasha asked. "Yes, they say it's bad."

"No. You don't understand yet. I have to explain."

"Let's get warm first," Molly said, already walking down the hall, toward the kitchen. Anna followed with Yasha at her side. He was as solid next to her as he'd been the night she'd found Yulia and Lazar together.

"I made this all for you," he whispered.

"I know," she said, and a memory of their first kiss in the park touched her from the past.

"When I got that comic book, I thought you were inviting me back into your life."

"I wish I had," Anna said, realizing it was true. "Raisa's coming."

"Who?" Yasha asked.

"Your granddaughter."

Yasha looked hopeful, excited even. He sat down in one of the chairs near the picture window, and where he had been calm outside in the snow, now he appeared as overwhelmed as Anna felt, like he was full of things to say but didn't know where to start.

"Maybe none of us have been fair to each other," Molly said.

"If anything, we're the ones who weren't fair to you," Yasha replied. "It took me a long time to realize that, but it's true. And now I know I'm old enough to leave the past behind, start again. That's all I want." He looked at Anna and his eyes were as dark as ever. New wrinkles she hadn't seen before made them look even closer together than they were when they were young. He gestured to Molly. "You're Mighty Minerva. You drew the comic book, didn't you?" Molly nodded. "I love it. I love you." And then, "Molly, really?" He couldn't hide his expression of dislike, said the name like it was a dirty word. "What was wrong with Manya?"

"Too Soviet," Molly said, and they all laughed. For a split second, Anna saw through the old man in front of her to the younger man who used to press his thigh against hers in the lab.

Yasha continued, "I've imagined you millions of times and never did I think you would look so much like Anna. Not in your coloring or your hair, but in your presence. You're determined like her. Stubborn like her. I see that already." Anna smiled at that, and relaxed, waited for Yasha to keep talking because she knew he would. It was what he had always been good at, filling the space, making everyone around him feel comfortable.

He spoke late into the night, until the three of them almost fell asleep in their chairs. Then Anna told him about their deadline. "We only have until December eighth," she said. "That's the day Molly dies, here on Aragats. I saw her bleeding to death on my very first jump. I have to fix my machine, stop Chernobyl before then—to save her."

He reached for Anna's hand and kissed it. "We're a team. We've always been a team. Show me what we need to do."

RAISA

November 1992

One Month Before Molly Dies on Mount Aragats

Philadelphia

Raisa was tucked into her office, a cubbyhole Stocken had given her at the end of his hall, working on equations to define the graviton. Papers and books were stacked on the floor. Her desk was overflowing with notes. She was frustrated. She couldn't find an answer and she needed one to fix and improve Anna's time machine. She was close, examining the power of gamma waves resulting from nuclear explosions, and just on the edge of figuring out how gravity interacted with those waves, but she still wasn't there, couldn't quite meld it into the amplifier. Even the smallest margin of error could be what was killing Anna.

"Raisa," Stocken called in an excited voice. He walked out of his office, made his way down the hall. "I have something for you." He grinned and held out a cardboard tube covered in Soviet stamps. "You're going to love this. I had to pull strings, trade some favors, but I got it." His smile grew as she took the tube. "You know, I doubted you.

I didn't think this old place existed, but you sounded so convinced. You were so sure the Soviets built that cosmic ray station that I had to look. And goddammit, you were right. It's the exact one you asked about, the one with the long name I can't pronounce. Here, the plans, the details. I got them for you."

Raisa's hands started trembling before she had the tube open. Even as she believed Anna was alive, that the math and work portrayed in the comic books were real, there had always been a part of her that doubted, that wondered if this was all too farfetched. But now, as she held that tube, the uncertainty was blown away. Before, she had let herself believe parts were real, but now she saw it was all real and it was terrifying and exhilarating all at once. When she pulled out the plans, the first thing she noticed was how thin the paper was, that it was old, and she forced herself to slow down. This was an important moment. It was about Anna and her mother, her family's past and future. And Daniel. He was wrapped up in the middle of it all, too, maybe even the most important part. When Raisa saw Cyrillic, she started thinking about her mother and Anna together, safe and alive on the mountain.

The plans were from 1950, labeled ANNA MAKSIMOVNA BERKOVA AND YASHA IVANOVICH BERLITSKY COSMIC RAY STATION. Just as she'd seen in the comic books, there were six watchtowers on the edge of a lake, a main compound, and even a path leading out of the woods. All of it was arranged exactly as Mama had drawn, on a mountain called Aragats in what was now the Republic of Armenia. "They really built it," she whispered. Her heart was beating so fast and her hands were shaking so hard that she had to put the plans down, anchor them with books. She kept studying them. At the bottom was a stamp that said CANCELED. A handwritten note reported that construction was halted, but there were coordinates and Raisa knew it had never been canceled.

She called to tell Daniel, huddled in the corner of her workstation with the phone cord wrapped around her fist so tight it cut off her circulation. She was so excited she was speaking in a loud voice and the sound bounced off the blackboards. Daniel didn't need to see the plans to be convinced, to start talking about plane tickets. "I knew it," he said. "When do we leave?"

"You don't want to talk about going, what it means?"

"No. Of course we're going. You know that. We'll make it there by December eighth."

"I'm still not sure I have the equations figured out, if I know how to account for the graviton. I need to keep working."

"Then work while we travel."

"What if we get there and I haven't solved it?"

"Then you'll work with your grandmother and solve it."

The next day they boarded a plane. The flight was long, and Raisa had never felt so excited and terrified at the same time. She knew it would sound crazy to anyone else that they were going to Armenia, to a mountaintop, chasing down a narrative pulled out of a comic book, but it was the most important thing she had ever done. Before leaving, Raisa had gone to the library, planning to scoop up every travel guide she could find on Turkey and Armenia, the countries they would pass through, only she couldn't bring herself to take more than a map. She wasn't going to explore, she was going to work, with a mission, and it was dangerous. Not only were they unsure about what they'd discover or if they'd even find Mama and Anna, they also had to be wary of the Russians. Daniel was convinced the Armenians would turn him in, that even though the country was no longer Soviet, the same people were at the top, and they still wanted him and his mother to pay for their escape. That was why Raisa and Daniel planned to fly to Turkey where they'd be safe, and cross into Armenia at a remote, unguarded border near Aragats.

On the plane, whenever she needed a break from math, she studied that map, thought about their route because it was easier to plan each step from Ankara to the mountain than face the decisions she'd have to make once they got there. The closer she came to Anna and her mother, the farther she would be from Daniel. If she made the time machine work, then she would stop Chernobyl from melting down, and if all the *ifs* fell into place, she and Daniel would come out on the other side living different lives. It was possible he would never come to America, that she'd never even know she'd lost him.

When they got off the plane, she felt heavy with fatigue and worry. She wanted quiet, time to think about the choices that might be coming, time to spend with just Daniel, but instead she was bombarded by an overload of new experiences. Voices all around chattered in Turkish and Arabic, perhaps Persian, mixed between occasional English and Russian. At home her fair skin helped her blend into most crowds, but in Turkey it made her stand out and put her on edge. People stared. And as she and Daniel went through passport control, the smell of fake floral deodorant and stale beer she had grown accustomed to in her dorm was replaced by sweat and a mixture of spices she couldn't recognize. Standing there feeling like such a foreigner also made her realize she had spent her entire life between Pennsylvania and New Jersey, had never been so close to the place where her parents and grandparents were born. It made her remember how much they hated that land, how much they had given up to escape it, and that made her even more anxious and self-conscious in the crowd. She knew Daniel felt the same because he held her hand tighter than usual as they pushed forward, and like her he mostly kept his head down. Raisa didn't make eye contact with anyone.

After their passports were stamped, they gathered their luggage and went out to the curb, where they were surrounded by men on small scooters and motorcycles, old buses and taxis belching black soot, and open trucks covered in dust. Men selling foods Raisa had never seen or tasted came toward them. One sold a pastry he called börek, layers of dough and cheese folded together. Another had simit, a bagel-like pastry crusted in sesame seeds and something sweet. Raisa and Daniel were hungry and ate before stepping onto their first bus. They took seats in the back, huddled close. Raisa was keenly aware that they were the only Americans, the only ones who didn't speak Turkish—and likely the only Jews. Her grandparents always said they weren't safe if they couldn't disappear in a crowd, and it was all she could think about in the back of that bus.

"We'll be fine," Daniel said, but he didn't sound confident. Like her, he knew that either their Soviet or their Jewish blood could get them killed in this country if it came up at the wrong time with the wrong person. A man who carried a pitcher of water and a bowl helped every passenger wash their hands as the bus bucked forward through traffic. They rode in silence. Raisa bent over her notebook and kept at her equations, trying to untangle the graviton.

One bus led to another and Raisa continued working. They spent days lumbering through narrow passes and potholed dirt roads. As they traveled, they tried to look and act like everyone around them. Daniel started to grow a beard. Raisa wore long tunics and covered her hair and people stopped paying attention to them. Slowly, Daniel began smiling at her again, and she was able to put the danger out of her mind for small stretches, even look up from her notebooks. She let herself be swept away by the new rhythm of the Turkish language, by the intensity of what she learned were cumin and mint, sumac and cinnamon lingering in the air, flavoring the food. At night, often the buses drove without headlights, without music. More than once Raisa was convinced the driver would fall asleep or careen off the road, but the closest they came to danger was a tribe of goats that blocked their way. Once they left the larger cities and bus depots, the map Raisa had was useless.

The more time they spent on buses, the more Raisa became accustomed to locals sitting across from them with makeshift cages that held chickens, or goats that boarded the bus and stood in the aisle on leashes like dogs. She and Daniel told everyone they were husband and wife, and when the buses finally stopped, when they had to transfer, they took breaks and rented a room above a café or a space in a barn where they tried to get some rest. In public, they were reserved, careful not to attract attention, but once they were behind a closed door, they tore at each other. They couldn't get their clothing off fast enough, couldn't get close enough.

"I know you're scared, that losing your parents, living in Atlantic City was hard," Daniel said one morning as they lay in a bed in the back of a café that doubled as the bus stop. They were near the Armenian border. The building was made of mud bricks. The bed was a wooden platform covered with pillows and blankets and Raisa lay on top of him with her arms crossed on his chest. They had been on the road for ten days. Coming from outside she heard the sounds of animals. He ran a finger over the edge of her shoulder and continued, "I know it was terrible and you've always had to keep it bottled up inside. In America, you hold it in and walk tall, but you've always held on to that fear. And I see it growing in you now. Maybe because I'm scared, too. So I'm just going to say it. Whatever happens on that mountain, we're going to be okay."

She put her head on his chest, listened to his heart. It was strong and steady and everything she loved about him. "We never talked about what happens when we find Anna, when I fix the time machine." She paused. "God, it sounds so crazy to say that out loud."

"You figured it out, then?" he said, and she heard his heart beat faster, felt his abdomen flex as he raised his head to look at her. "You know how to account for gravity?"

"I think I do. Yes." She let herself smile, just for a moment, recognizing the enormity of it. But then she was struck by the potential tragedy. It was why she hadn't told him earlier. Fixing the time machine would break them and she didn't want to face that yet. "Daniel. Say I can make the time machine safe and we go back to stop Chernobyl. If we do that, everything will change."

"I know." His voice was quiet, but she could feel he was excited, that perhaps he'd been waiting for this conversation, too.

Raisa started speaking quickly, letting everything she'd been holding in come out. "Vera will survive. The entire world will be different. What we know will be erased. You and I, we won't be here, we'll have never had this moment, this trip." Her voice went quiet. "We might never meet." He wrapped his arms around her tighter. "I don't know if I can live with that."

"Would you rather let all those people die?" he asked.

"How can I choose?"

"Maybe we can have both."

"To have everything? It doesn't work that way."

"Are you telling me you want to stop, that you want to turn around and go home? Raisele, I've thought about this a million times. We could save so many people."

"You thought about it, but didn't tell me," she said, because it was the first time she realized he'd held something back from her and it stung even though she'd done the same. He kissed her, his lips lingering on hers.

"Of course. I know you did, too. That's my point. I know you, and you, you know me better than anyone. I believe in us. It's why I gave you the necklace. I believe we will find each other. We just need a plan to make sure our lives cross in an altered future. We can do that. We can do this. We have to do this."

"You're not understanding. If we can really go back in time, really change things, then we erase us. We'll never even know we're missing. This. Between us. We'll never know it existed. That's the most terrifying part. We won't know what we've lost. I'll never know about this room, this trip, our time on Kestler's roof, your bar mitzvah, or even that time in the van after the math competition when you kissed my hand."

"God, I was mortified that I did that." He smiled and she felt him lean back, relax just a touch. "I was so scared it would send you running out of that van, but you stayed. Then the way you looked at me when I took my shirt off on the roof of your grandparents' house, I knew." His smile grew. "I miss being on both of those roofs with you, those nights we had that summer. But I know what we're doing is the right thing. We won't regret this. We'll find each other. When you fix your grandmother's machine and go back to Chernobyl, you'll meet Vera. You'll convince her to come to America. You'll tell her to find your grandparents. That I need to work for them." And then he asked, "What will you say to your mother when we see her?"

"I don't know."

"Do you want to talk about it?"

"No." She didn't want to think about it yet, had been avoiding it for the entire trip. She preferred to hold on tight to Daniel, only she could tell he was still holding something back because his jaw was still tight. "What is it? What else?"

"See, you know me," Daniel said. He eased out of bed, walked to his bag. She saw the glint of the metal before she made out the whole form of a gun. "I bought this at our last stop, at the souk. I thought we might need it." She gasped and he held a finger to his lips. "I don't want to use it, but things are different here. We're not in America, and on that mountaintop, we're not really sure what we'll find."

After that morning, Raisa and Daniel were closer in a way that Raisa felt as deeply as any ache she had ever known. She hated comparing this new feeling to pain, but every step closer to Aragats was potentially a step away from Daniel and so that's what it was, pain.

At the border, there were no buses going the way they wanted to go, and they had to hire a guide. He drove them through Armenia in his private car and didn't slow down except to refuel and sleep. His only request was that they wear stolen, black military uniforms. No one would dare ask questions if they believed they were soldiers.

At the end of their first day on the road with their guide, the snow started. The wind and intensity picked up and their pace dragged. What were supposed to be flurries morphed into a blizzard, and when they reached the bottom of Mount Aragats on December 3, the guide told them he couldn't drive farther. The snow was too thick. There was an inn nearby. For a hefty price, he left them there with snow gear for their hike the rest of the way up once the storm cleared.

The inn was small and had a café. Raisa and Daniel changed into their regular clothes and ordered stew and vodka, taking a table next to a raging fire. The flames danced off the brick walls. Candles sat on every table. Warm and nervous, Raisa couldn't eat much. Daniel finished their bowls for both of them. Raisa held her notebook in her lap, bending the corner back and forth as she went through her equations again.

The innkeeper told them it would likely be a few more days before the snow stopped. "A few more days," she echoed. Her words were a whisper because she still didn't know how she'd decide, how she'd choose between Anna's time machine and Daniel, and it terrified her because it was up to her. From the comics it was clear Anna was too ill to do it and her mother would never be able to handle it. Raisa was the one with the equations. She was the one who had to travel back to Chernobyl to stop it.

"We'll find a way back to each other," Daniel said over and over, and she wished she had his confidence.

Another guest came into the restaurant about an hour after them. He wore the same black uniform their guide had given them and so Raisa thought he was likely military. Raisa and Daniel both sat up straighter. More than anyone they wanted to avoid soldiers, anyone who might bring Daniel back to Russia, and so they watched closely. Raisa was shocked when he spoke because his accent marked him as Russian, and she realized she'd assumed the uniform was Armenian, and had been wrong. She regretted that now, that she and Daniel had never asked for details, demanded to know where the uniforms came from and who wore them. If only she knew more about the other guest, if he even really was a soldier. Scared, her throat went tight. She squeezed Daniel's thigh under the table, and she saw he was rigid with the same fear. There was no reason for a Russian soldier to be at Aragats. It couldn't be a coincidence that he'd come, but at the same time she tried to convince herself he might be no more of a soldier than she was. Besides, no one else knew about the station. The chances he was there for Anna, Mama, or them were minuscule. She guessed Daniel was also thinking about that, weighing the possibilities, imagining being caught and dragged back to Russia, because his jaw and shoulders were growing more tense by the minute. "Let's go to our room," she suggested.

They stood up just as the waiter came in with a bowl of stew and set it down for the man in the uniform. Raisa couldn't help but overhear their conversation. "Your dinner, soldier," the waiter said in Russian, and Raisa slowed her pace to eavesdrop. "He's still up there on top of the mountain, the old general you dropped off?"

"Yes. The old fool," the solider replied, smiling. "He thinks he's up on that mountain with his old lady, that he's making some kind of grand gesture. But here's the thing: His wife died in eighty-six. At Chernobyl." The soldier laughed. "I'm just his driver and I'm guessing he went up there to die like an old dog. He's not a general. He's a scientist. Was important back in the day. Now he's a dinosaur."

The waiter chuckled. "Love and grief make us all blind. Did you say he's after his wife?"

"Yeah, but she's not there. I'm sure of it."

"I thought there is an old woman living up there, with a younger one."

"Can't be," the soldier said. "Maybe just hikers."

"Maybe," the waiter agreed.

Raisa and Daniel were just outside the door by then. The last thing they heard was the soldier saying, "I'll go up there and check on him when the snow stops. Bring me more vodka."

And then they hurried to their room.

"You heard that, right?" Raisa said as soon as their door closed. She was shaking. Daniel was, too. "His wife died in eighty-six at Chernobyl. An old scientist. They must be talking about Yasha and Anna. My grandfather came. He's there, too. And that waiter, he's seen Anna and Mama."

"From the way he was talking, they're alone up there." Daniel paced across the room and back. "It sounded like no one else is up there. I mean no other soldiers. Yasha came with his driver. No one else. That's good."

"It is. But if that soldier does go up, if he finds Anna and Mama, they could both be in trouble. He'll bring them back to Russia. Maybe that's why December eighth is so important. Anna saw them being captured that day. We have to warn them, get to them first."

"When the storm breaks, it'll be a race," Daniel said. "We'll have to go up before the soldier, try to bring them back down before he gets to them."

Raisa didn't sleep that night, and barely slept the nights after that while they waited for the storm to blow over. When it finally did, it was December 8, 1992—and they hurried to leave. At least the soldier wasn't in a hurry, Raisa told herself. He thought Yasha was out of his mind or had gone up Aragats to die. That meant he wouldn't rush and so she was sure they had a chance to make it up there before him.

Raisa and Daniel layered on their black snow pants, parkas, mittens, and snowshoes and hiked as quickly as they could. "This is the right thing to do," Raisa said, even though she wasn't sure she actually felt that way. They stumbled and made slow progress, had a hard time picking out the path, were grateful for the infrequent painted marks on trees directing them. Only she was still torn, scared that every step she took to save her mother and grandparents was taking her away from Daniel.

"I'm still not sure I can do this," she said as they took a break, huddled under a rock that jutted out over the path.

"We won't lose each other," Daniel said, kept saying.

They pushed forward. The wind blew hard. Snow scratched at the small bits of their exposed skin. Their boots sank deep. Daniel stayed close. Ice had formed on the edge of his beard. "We have to keep moving," he said. "Raisele, how could we live with ourselves if we knew we could stop Chernobyl and we didn't?"

"But what if my math doesn't work and that soldier catches us all?"

"He won't."

"How are you so sure?"

"I'm not, but in my training I learned to accept the mission, to push ahead even if I have doubts, so that's what I'm doing. I'm telling myself this will work out because I know it's the right thing to do."

Every step was exhausting and they stopped to rest again and again, going slower as they rose higher.

"You think that soldier is awake, hiking up the mountain yet?" Raisa asked.

"Maybe," Daniel said.

He turned to continue, but in a flash, she caught his arm, pulled him back. Just over the ridge in front of them she knew they'd break through the trees and reach the top. They were so close she thought she could even smell smoke that must have been coming from the station. "I changed my mind." Her voice was hard; she spoke quickly. "I don't want to choose Chernobyl over you. I know that makes me selfish, maybe even an immoral person, but all those people who died—I don't know them, but I know you. I love you. I want to choose you."

"Raisele, you don't really mean what you say. I know you don't. Believe in us."

"If this all works, there is no us. Can't you see that?" She motioned to the space between them. "If I go back and change things, then what we have, had, it never even existed. And I don't want to live without this. Without us."

A tear slid down from the corner of his eye, tangled into his beard.

"We can't afford to think this way. We have to keep our eye on the greater good, on saving all those people because that's the right thing to do. That's what matters."

"You sound like a Communist putting the collective first."

"No. I sound like I'm choosing morality. And I know you couldn't live with yourself if you turned around here. Maybe tomorrow or next week you would feel fine with it, but next month, next year, you'd hate yourself for making the wrong decision. Please, keep going. I trust Vera. If we ask Vera to go to America, to take me to America, she will. She'll take me to you."

The wind picked up and Raisa didn't want to continue. She was sure that if she did she would lose him forever, but she also saw that he'd resent her if she turned around, and then she'd lose him, too. Besides, he was right, saving all those people is what they *should* do. "We'll find each other," she said over and over and put one foot in front of the other. They trudged ahead. Soon the trees thinned. The birds fled, and eventually Raisa and Daniel made it past the tree line. Over one more crest and the top of the mountain rolled out to a breathtaking view. They were surrounded on all sides by mountains that loomed with jagged cliffs and iced peaks. The trees themselves were topped with pillows of snow. Raisa should have been in awe but all she could think about was changing the past, losing Daniel.

She pointed ahead, out of breath, and said, "The watchtowers." Daniel came up next to her. They were there, just as Mama had drawn them, all six. So were the main compound and the vast flat expanse that had to be the lake. She wanted to admire it all, but she was too worried, too sad to even take in the importance of what they were facing, what was unfolding. Even more, she was terrified of everything that could go wrong or right.

"The soldier could be behind us," Daniel said, urging them forward. He was correct but still Raisa hesitated. She reached for his hand and held him close.

"Another minute," she said, and she kissed him. It wasn't a long embrace, but they both lingered before they continued. They passed the first tower, the second, and Daniel stopped. He didn't say a word. He just pointed. Fifty feet in front of them, a man in a black army uniform like the one Raisa and Daniel were both wearing was headed straight for them. Raisa's first thought was that they'd been wrong all along. They hadn't beaten the soldier to the top. They had trailed him the whole way. The man was saying something, but she couldn't hear, not through all the wind, not while so much ice and snow still separated them. He kept trying, had his hands around his mouth like he was calling to them. Raisa wanted to move closer, but Daniel held her back, made them stand their ground. The distance between them was narrowing. Forty feet, thirty. It was impossible to see him clearly, to make out anything but his uniform.

"That can't be Yasha, right?" Daniel asked. "He's not a soldier."

"That's right," Raisa said. Her voice shook.

"But that looks like an old man."

"Yasha wouldn't be wearing a uniform like that. It has to be the soldier from the inn. Which means he already has my mother and grandmother."

"Then where's your grandfather? Why isn't he with the soldier?" In the blink of an eye, her whole body went cold and numb as she was seized with the realization of just how much danger they were in. This man approaching them was a real soldier with real power. He had already captured her family and now he was about to take Raisa and Daniel, too. They still had time to run, but she couldn't move, couldn't even think clearly enough to find a way around him because she kept coming back to the idea that he already had her mother and grandmother, probably Yasha, too. And while Raisa shut down, Daniel kicked into high gear.

"Get down!" he yelled. The soldier was only ten feet away and his face was covered. "Down!" Daniel repeated. She'd never heard his voice go as cold as it did in that moment. Nor had she ever seen him act so quickly. At the same time, the soldier and Daniel both reached into their jackets. Raisa knew what was happening, but her body and mouth couldn't catch up fast enough. "Gun!" Daniel yelled before she could. Daniel and the soldier were both aiming at each other, only Daniel was ready a split second before the soldier. He had the first shot, but he hesitated. The time came and he didn't take it. She dove for Daniel, tipped them both backward into the snow and heard the shot as they fell.

"Daniel!" Raisa screamed. "Daniel!"

ANNA

December 8, 1992

The Day Molly Dies on Mount Aragats

Mount Aragats

Anna stood in the kitchen facing Yasha and Molly on the morning of December 8, 1992. A blizzard had raged for days, keeping them in the compound, and Anna had stayed calm by telling herself they were safe because no one could brave that storm and get to them, kill Molly. She had spent the time working; listening to Yasha and Molly talk about their lives, their regrets and loves; avoiding their questions about hers. And now the storm had cleared. The morning and the mountain were quiet, and the sun was glorious, streaking through the giant window. Anna's arms and legs were bandaged and the lesions hurt, were getting worse. "We need to leave right away," she said to Molly and Yasha.

"Nothing is going to happen," Molly said. "Whatever you saw on that first jump, you've changed enough of the past that we're not headed in that direction; it won't happen again. We have plenty of time to stop Chernobyl and I am not going to die today." She looked at Yasha. "I know it because Yasha is here now and he wasn't on your first jump. Now we're a strong team. Together. And we're safe. Let's concentrate on Chernobyl."

"Maybe," Anna said, taking in Molly's words. She had a point, but still Anna couldn't relax, couldn't shake the feeling that she was missing something.

"Anna, to stop Chernobyl you don't have to be the one to jump," Yasha said, bringing her thoughts back to the room, to the present. "I'll do it. I will jump for you." His voice was deep and had the serious timbre Anna loved. It took her back to a time in the lab when they built an early reactor. Someone had to pull the graphite rods out from the pile and it was Anna's job, but Yasha had volunteered using that same voice. "I will go back to Chernobyl."

"No." She couldn't let him do that. With the machine still not working properly, it would kill him. Plus, the Anna living in 1986 wouldn't trust Yasha. "It's not that simple," Anna said. "If you find me in 1986, I wouldn't listen to a word you said. You know that." She turned to face her daughter. "You think everything has changed, that we're safe, but I can't shake this feeling that I'm missing something. We should leave, err on the side of caution. We can come back in a few days." She looked Yasha in the eye. "The storm cleared. We have to leave. Now. For Molly."

"I'm not leaving until Raisa gets here," Molly said.

That was when the alarm started to blare. Lights flashed. Someone had breached the perimeter. "My driver?" Yasha said. "I was supposed to check in once a day. With the storm, I couldn't get through. It must be him."

"Not necessarily. It could be Raisa," Molly said quickly, sounding nervous.

"Whoever it is is going to shoot Molly," Anna said, feeling the claws of fear start in her gut. "This is what I warned you about."

"No," Yasha said. His tone was calm but Anna knew him well

enough to hear it was a forced calm. "It's nothing. We shouldn't panic until there's a reason. The simple answer is it has to be my driver. I'll deal with him. Stay here." He hurried for his coat and boots, spoke louder like he was scared. "If he sees you, Anna, he'll take you back with him. There are still people who want you to pay for the meltdown. You're supposed to be dead. If he brought you back, it would be a coup for him, a major notch in his belt. I can't let him near you or Molly. Do you understand? You need to wait here."

Anna understood. She knew they were after her as soon as she realized what had happened at Chernobyl. It was why she ran. She knew that if they found her, she would be blamed, tortured, and sentenced without being able to say a single word in her own defense. She was the one who had spent days in that basement being questioned according to Soviet protocols, chained to the chair, and she couldn't do it again. The USSR had been dissolved on paper, but Yeltsin was a Communist born and bred in the party. He wouldn't show mercy.

"Let's see who it is before we panic," Molly said, hurrying out the door. Anna hadn't even seen her putting her boots on, grabbing her coat, and before Anna could object, Molly was gone, calling over her shoulder that it could be Raisa. "You can't be sure it's your driver."

"No!" Anna yelled after her. The claws in her gut were digging deeper and she knew something bad was about to happen, felt the same loss of control she had experienced the day the soldiers came for Mama and the day Yasha first came to her flat. Anna's lesions were bad, the pain intense, but she pushed through it to follow. "I'm not staying behind," she said to Yasha. He understood there was nothing he could say or do to stop her and so he offered his arm and together they trudged through the deep, thick snow. The wind was loud. Anna was holding on to Yasha so tight her hands hurt. "You weren't in the compound, Yasha. The first time I jumped. But maybe you were still there. I somehow missed you."

"You still think our daughter's about to die?"

She did. Everything else matched. The walls with the murals were the same, the wires were all tucked in and the construction finished. There were even plates out on the counter, the same plates she had seen smashed when she jumped for the first time. "I *know* it. Someone is about to shoot her."

"Then we need to go faster," Yasha said. She tried but couldn't. The pain was too intense. She fell and screamed. Yasha scrambled to help her up but he was old and slow, too.

"Anna, are you okay?" Molly said, running back. She was out of breath, flushed when she reached them.

"Why did you come back?" Anna said, wincing in pain. "You believe me now, that you're in danger?"

"Maybe. I also heard you scream." She took a deep breath. "I saw. I saw two soldiers coming. Up ahead. They just broke through the trees. Maybe you were right, Anna. Maybe not enough has changed. Soldiers are here. Of course they have guns. We should hide before they shoot."

"Yes. Yes, of course," Anna said. Her whole body was shaking. Molly was alive, there was still time, she tried telling herself. "We can hide."

"Where?" Yasha said. "In the snow? In the woods? We'd freeze or fall from a cliff. We can't hide. And they don't know you're here. They haven't seen you. I'll stop them," Yasha said. He kissed Anna's cheek, stood up, and passed Anna's hand to Molly, pushed forward. "I have a gun," he said. "It's always been my job to protect Anna, to protect both of you." Anna blinked and saw a flash of a memory from her first jump, the blood in the snow, the blood on the floor in the main compound.

"Yasha, no," she said, but he didn't stop. He moved faster and Anna turned to Molly. "We need to run. Now." Anna could see Molly wasn't sure what to do, but she still helped Anna back to her feet. They both stood and watched Yasha. The big black parka he wore made him look younger than he was. Anna tried to pull Molly toward the trees, to take cover, but her daughter wouldn't budge. In the distance, she saw the two soldiers in black emerging over the horizon. "Listen to me. You're going to die," Anna said. Her voice was pitched high and panicked. She stared straight into Molly's eyes, pulled her as close as she could so their noses were touching, as if that would make her listen. "Those soldiers are going to shoot you. And then I'm going to try to save you. I'm going to drag you back to the compound, to the kitchen. That's where I saw you on my first jump. You were slumped over in the kitchen, shot in the gut. There was blood everywhere. You were dying. I saw it and still didn't prevent it. It's about to happen. I can feel it. Run. Please. Run."

"Yasha is here this time. He'll stop them. He has a gun," Molly said, but she didn't sound convinced.

"Those soldiers also have guns. Something is going to go wrong. I know it be—" Anna stopped mid-word because it hit her. Everything else was exactly as it had been. Now there were even guns. Someone would shoot Molly and she'd make her way back to the compound but Anna and Yasha wouldn't be there. No one would until Anna from 1986 jumped. What Anna had witnessed was inevitable, time turning back on itself. It was the ouroboros Molly had mentioned before. Her daughter had been right. In another, parallel timeline, Anna was asleep in her bed in Pripyat. Reactor No. 4 was about to melt down and she would rip forward in time, to Aragats. She would wake up in the snow and make her way to the main compound. Her head would be pounding with pain because the Anna from 1986 would be too close to the Anna of 1992. It was all happening again and again. "It's a loop," she said, and she went still. Her voice fell. "It's the guns, mentioning the guns. That made me realize it's already too late. All the pieces are in place. We can't stop them. Even though we know it's coming, we can't stop them."

"We know better than most that you can always restart your life," Molly said. A small smile cracked across her face. "It's something Papa said once, that I've always held on to."

In the distance, one of the soldiers yelled. It was a female voice and Molly jerked forward when she heard it and ran like a starting gun had been fired. At the same time Yasha, who was standing close to the soldiers, was reaching into his parka for his gun. Anna knew he was going to shoot and she couldn't stop him. It crushed her and she sank to her knees, felt like she couldn't get enough air, that she was suffocating. The rest unfolded as if in slow motion. The metal body of one of the soldier's guns struck sunlight first. The glare made it look like it ignited. Then came Yasha's gun, a beat later. The soldier aimed and had a kill shot before Yasha, only he didn't take it. He hesitated, and when he did, the other soldier jumped in front of him to protect him and Yasha fired. The sound was like a scream. It sent birds scattering and echoed off the walls of the mountains around them. The second soldier, the one who'd jumped in front, fell into the snow, a limp heap. Anna felt like Yasha's shot had ripped through her own body because she knew something terrible had happened, that somehow this was all part of the loop. She knew it even though Molly was alive and running toward the soldiers. And now she realized the blood she had seen in the snow was the blood Yasha just spilled, not Molly's. More than one person was going to die. The soldier who had been first to draw his gun dropped to the snow and leaned over the other. His wails of pain were so intense they shook Anna and a switch flipped, throwing her from slow motion to high speed.

Anna followed Molly and ran for the two soldiers and Yasha as fast as she could, stumbling, bumbling. As she got closer she heard one soldier wailing, "Raisa, Raisa," and Anna's blood went cold. She collapsed and couldn't stand, couldn't move. She shook so hard her teeth chattered. Save Raisa, Molly had told her when Anna found her dying in the kitchen. This was what Molly meant. Anna was gripped with horror, realizing she had been wrong this whole time. Saving Raisa wasn't about keeping her out of foster care, helping her find Yulia and Lazar. Molly's warning had been about this moment. And she'd failed, failed miserably. After a lifetime of striving to be right, of chiding others for sloppy work, she had made the biggest mistake of all.

"Raisa!" Molly yelled as she ran. Anna pushed up to her feet, continued forward. She couldn't catch her breath, didn't see anything around her, only Raisa as a black heap bleeding in the snow.

"No. No," Anna said over and over again. Shame mixed with horror when she finally stood over her granddaughter. She searched her face, tried to see the child she had met on the beach. She looked for the round cheeks and wide eyes, but all of that was gone. Raisa had grown into a woman. In her mind Anna was cursing herself, trying to figure out how she could still make this right. The young man holding Raisa, crying and hysterical, the other soldier, had to be Daniel. She recognized him from the photos Yulia had sent. In the last picture he and Raisa were on their way to their senior prom, smiling. She wore hot pink sequins, he wore a tuxedo, and both were beaming with happiness. Now Daniel was broken, shattered, Raisa's face was pale and blank, and Anna felt the same.

"I'm so sorry," Anna said over and over. No one looked at her or listened. She felt as though she'd pulled the trigger herself, her whole body still shaking hard. Not once had it occurred to her that *Save Raisa* meant saving her from something happening that day.

"Raisele," Daniel said. "Come back. Come back." Yasha was starting to pull himself together by then, reaching for the radio in his pocket. Molly was bent over Raisa's head, her tears falling on Raisa's cheeks.

"I need to get her help," Daniel said. His voice sounded numb, and like Yasha he looked like he was trying to recover, to think. "I need to stop the bleeding. Stabilize her. I have to save her." Daniel was breathless, his words staccatos. "It should have been me," he said. He looked to the side and must have realized Anna was next to him because he locked his gaze on her. "You can fix this," he said. "You can change it all." He reached for Raisa's bag, fumbled with the clip. He pulled out a notebook and shoved it toward Anna. A streak of blood smeared the front. "She did your work. Fix this!" He stood and picked Raisa up in his arms. Blood dripped, left more red blotches in the pristine snow, and she realized what Daniel was telling her. Raisa had worked on the equations to fix the time machine. She'd come up with something.

"The snowmobile," Molly said. "We can take her down the mountain quickly and get her help."

"I'll radio for an ambulance to meet us," Yasha said.

The rest happened in a blur while Anna stared at the notebook. Molly and Yasha rushed Raisa and Daniel onto the snowmobile, sent them back down the mountain. Raisa had a pulse, but the bullet had hit her chest and she wasn't conscious. How could she possibly make it? Anna went back inside the main compound, telling herself she could still save Raisa, end this loop. She clutched the notebook to her chest so tight she felt it bend. And she steeled herself not to think or feel, told herself she needed to push all emotion away and concentrate on logic. Reason was what would get her through, what would save Raisa. In a daze she pulled herself out of her coat, made her way to the chairs at the picture window where she planned to read Raisa's notebook, only her mind was as broken as her heart because this time she couldn't push emotion away. She had known for years that today would be a catastrophe and yet she hadn't been able to stop it. The warning was wasted. She was a waste. She looked down at her hands. They were covered in her granddaughter's blood and she knew no amount of washing could ever clean it away.

When Molly and Yasha came in, Molly collapsed on the bench. Yasha was soaked and it took a moment for Anna to realize it was all blood. He left his stained parka hanging near the door, his drenched black uniform on the floor, and put on a robe, put his gun on the counter, and came to sit next to Anna while Molly remained motionless. Yasha's face was pale and stricken. "It's my fault. All of this is my fault," he said again and again. He looked down at the bloody notebook in Anna's hand. "Annushka, you can change this. You have a time machine," he said. "I can help you go back and change all of this. Raisa brought what you need, didn't she?" His face was red with tears and cold, and those eyes that Anna had always thought were too close together looked softer than she remembered, sadder than she could have imagined.

"I don't know which of you is worse than the other," Molly said in an eerily quiet voice. Under it Anna heard anger, fear, and doubt. She'd heard something like it before, on nights when Molly came to Anna and said she needed someone to listen, to keep her from jumping off the cliff or drinking. Only on those nights, Anna heard Molly trying to restrain herself, and as she sat on the bench staring at the blood on the floor, it sounded like something had snapped. Molly wasn't trying to control anything, was instead letting it all come out. Anna sat on the edge of her chair, waiting, trying to think of something she could do or say. She wasn't used to dealing with so many emotions, had spent her life running from anything overwhelming, and as they sat there in silence she hated herself for it, cursed herself as a coward. She was supposed to be the parent, the one to help, and she didn't have a single idea, was paralyzed.

It was Molly who moved first, who let out a primal scream. In one violent motion she jumped up from the bench and stormed past the murals, toward the kitchen. She swiped everything off the table and counters with a violence Anna had never seen before. Bowls and plates smashed to bits. After it had all shattered, she turned over the table and the chairs, all the while screaming. "I'm done. My own daughter is dying because of me and my stupid ideas. I'm done. Do you hear me?" She was speaking quickly, in English, and it was hard for Anna to keep up. "I didn't learn anything from my own past. I ruined it. Ruined it all, have always ruined everything. If she's not going to live, then I can't, either." Molly's eyes were wild. She even threw one of the empty lead-lined fuel pellet boxes into the corner, was lucky it didn't crack or open. Molly was out of breath, out of control by then. She picked something up from the counter, the only thing she hadn't touched. It took Anna another beat to realize it was Yasha's gun.

"Don't!" Anna yelled, but it was too late.

Molly held the gun up and turned it on herself. "Anger," she said, her lips twisting into a strange smile. "I shouldn't have wasted my time on anger. Nor on regret. Maybe I shouldn't have even bothered getting sober. I mean, what was the point?" She let out a cruel, dark-sounding cackle and used the gun to motion around her, around the room. Anna looked at Yasha for a split second. He was up on his feet, poised to move toward Molly. "Don't even try coming closer," Molly said to him. "You can't stop me now. No one ever could. Isn't that the point, Anna? Isn't that your brilliant, incredible discovery? You've spent years up here working. Working. Working. Always working. For what? You couldn't save Raisa. You said you did. Remember that? You told me you saved Raisa, now we would stop Chernobyl. But you didn't save her. And you haven't stopped Chernobyl, either." Molly turned the gun on Anna. "You said you saved her but you killed her. It's your fault. All your fault." Molly stepped back, seemed to lose her balance for a moment. Yasha took advantage of the stumble and started toward her, but she held up the gun and fired into the ceiling. It stopped Yasha and sent him and Anna down. They cringed. The sound left Anna's ears ringing. When she looked up, Molly was steady again, still pointing the gun at Anna. "There was no escaping this, was there?"

"Mollushka, you just told me we know better than most that you can always restart your life. We have the time machine. We can change this."

"How? It's killing you." She motioned around the room with the gun again and then pointed it at her own chest. "It's killed all of us, hasn't it? I—I always knew I'd end my own life one way or the other. I can't fix anything. I can't even fix myself."

Anna took a step toward Molly, and Molly pulled the trigger. Anna and Yasha dove to get to her as Molly staggered from the sink, to the exact spot where Anna had found her on her first jump. "No. No!" Anna said. "No!" She must have been screaming because her throat hurt, her mouth was wide. "No! No!" Anna panicked, had no idea what to do, while Yasha started moving. He gathered towels, used them to apply pressure.

"We can save her," he said. "I know we can save her."

Anna still didn't move. There was already too much blood and he hadn't seen what she'd seen. He didn't know, or really understand, what was happening. Anna did. She stepped back. "Not like this," she said, her voice quiet. "I won't let you die like this again."

"I'm sorry," Molly whispered. "Please, tell Raisa I'm sorry. Save her. Promise. Go back and save her."

Anna kneeled next to her daughter and pushed Molly's hair back, off of her face. She ran a finger down the soft skin of her cheek and kissed her, told herself to remember every inch of Molly's skin, how soft it was, how strong Molly had become. The room, the blood. Everything was now exactly as it had been when Anna jumped from 1986. "The loop is starting again," she said. The sequence of events, their lives were coming back to the beginning. Molly had been right when she told Anna her problem was she hadn't stared down her own fears, hadn't dug deep enough and tried to change her own self. Anna had refused to hold herself responsible for any of the dozens of things she had done wrong—and letting today happen was her biggest mistake of all. She could have stopped it, not with a time machine but by working to restore her own life, by confronting what really scared her, all her mistakes with Molly, Yulia, Lazar, and even Yasha. She could have looked in the mirror and changed herself, built a life that didn't put her anywhere near Chernobyl or this mountain, if only she'd faced the things she'd done wrong.

But why had she been too terrified to look fear in the face? What had stopped her? She remembered something else Molly had said. She'd already apologized for her more recent mistakes, faced the fact that she'd been wrong to send her daughter away, cut everyone out of her life after that. But she'd never faced her earlier fears, what really scared her most. "I think I know what to do," she said to Yasha. Molly's eyes were closed and Anna felt a strange calm take over, a quiet she hadn't felt since celebrating her tenth birthday with her mother. She reached up to her neck and took off the bear pendants her mother had given her, put them around Molly's neck. She leaned close. "When you see me, remember I'm coming from Chernobyl. It's my first jump. Tell me we failed again. That the bears mean I can trust you. Mention my birthday cake. You remember that story?" Molly nodded. Anna remembered the photograph, the one Molly had given her on her first jump. It was still tacked to the wall in the kitchen. Anna grabbed it and put it in Molly's hand. "Give me this and tell the younger Anna that an older Anna is really fixing things this time. You won't have to die again. I'm going to change things by fixing myself."

Molly's hands went to the bears. She smiled.

"I love you. I always have," Anna said. "Never doubt that." She was surprised that she really meant it, truly felt it in a way she never had. She stood and turned to Yasha. "Will you help?" He nodded and they walked, together, toward her time machine, slipping into the tunnels and up the ladder into the watchtower.

"What do I need to do?" Yasha asked once Anna was ready to jump.

"Don't let anyone move this machine," she said. "I need two hours."

"You're sure this is what you need to do? It could kill you."

"I have one more jump in me," she said. She had never been more sure of anything in her life, knew that the one thing she had avoided, that her biggest fear and biggest regret, was the doubt she felt around her own mother. She was going to confront Xenia. Through the window, in the distance she made out static at the edge of the forest. She took a step closer, watched the trees stretch and snap back, and then she saw her younger self lying in the snow and felt an unbearable pain in her head. It knocked her down even as she realized what was happening. She had just witnessed her first jump from 1986, the moment she was torn from Chernobyl. And she was experiencing one of the law of twos—was too close to the Anna from 1986. Yasha helped her back up.

"I love you," he said.

"I love you," Anna said. Through the window she saw her younger self stumbling into the door of the main compound. Anna pulled the trigger and jumped.

PART VIII

Who is wise?
Those who learn from all people…
Who is strong?
Those who control their passions…
Who is rich?
Those who rejoice in what they have…
Who is honored?
Those who honor others.

—Pirkei Avot

ANNA

February 1917

Seventy-Five Years Before Molly Dies on Mount Aragats

Petrograd

nna jumped to 1917, to the day before her mother was taken. She must have been far enough away from her childhood self because her head didn't hurt, and she was thinking more clearly than she had in a year. Her plan was to find Mama before she went home, and so older Anna tucked herself into an alley next to the Dubinskys' house, where Mama would get hurt, and hid, waited for Xenia to come. The city was loud with protestors, rioters, and screams. Anna tried to control her nerves and fear of all that could go wrong or right, told herself to be patient, that she was doing this for Raisa, for Molly. She was going to confront Mama and ask her why she pushed Anna away and put the revolution before their family, why she sacrificed herself for a cause that would never even recognize her, would leave her out of every historical account. Even more, she would tell Mama that it was Anna's younger self that needed to hear her answers. She would tell her mother to say it all to the ten-year-old Anna waiting for her to come home—so that ten-year-old would grow up to be the kind of woman she needed to be, not the woman Anna was.

While Anna waited for Xenia to come, she closed her eyes and remembered where her younger self would have been, what she was experiencing.

△ △ △

Younger Anna woke up that morning to the sound of the front door banging shut. The bang, like a gavel, made it final—her mother was gone. "Mama!" She hurried out of bed and ran to try to say goodbye. It was too dark to see where she was going, but the apartment was laid out like a train, one room followed by another, and she knew the obstacles: the overfilled bookcase, the table littered with dirty dishes and the half-eaten birthday cake from the night before. In the sitting room, she hit a pile of newspapers that had been moved while she slept, and they toppled. She ran over them and made her way to the balcony doors, concentrated on prying them open. The frame was encased in ice and while the handles moved, the doors were stuck.

"Please, Annushka," her papa said, pulling her back. From the way Maksim's voice shook, she knew he was crying, had been crying; that even as Xenia had laced her winter boots and piled on sweaters and coats, he had begged her to change her mind and Xenia had ignored him. Anna used the weight of her young body to pull harder on the doors. They opened with a crack as loud as a gunshot. Wind whipped her face and churned loose papers on her mother's desk.

"Be careful, Mama!" young Anna yelled. It was too dark to see the sidewalk below. The street, normally loud with the commotion of workers and crooning drunks, was still. The only sound was Xenia marching, the insistent pound of leather against stone and ice. She didn't pause or slow down at the sound of Anna's voice, and Anna couldn't be sure she heard. Then it came to Anna. "Arise, arise, working people!" Anna sang as loud as she could. It was the "Worker's Marseillaise," the revolution's anthem that Xenia sang when she tucked Anna into bed.

At that, Xenia's footsteps halted. It was too dark for Anna to see her mother, but she imagined that she smiled, and young Anna heard her reply, "Forward, forward!" Mama must have held her fist high over her head, as she did every time she said those words. Anna wanted her mother to linger, to say something else, but instead Mama must have turned away, her bootsteps receding, fading. All that was left was the moan of ice on the Neva, ice that creaked at a pitch so low most people never heard it.

Papa put his arm over his daughter's shoulders. "No one can stop her, not when her mind is set." He sounded resigned through the tears.

Pangs of fear clawed at Anna's stomach. To look away was to give up, to say Mama wasn't coming home. She hung on to the frigid balcony and squinted, leaned as far forward as she dared, hoping Mama might change her mind, but all Anna saw was black. "She might be okay," Anna said.

"She's marching for your future. We should be proud," Papa said, and he held Anna so close, his hip bone jutted against her shoulder.

"I'm not proud. I only want Mama to come home."

"This is bigger than her, than us. You'll understand one day."

"I won't. She forgot we're Jews. We can't do anything important." Anna's words were the ones her parents hated most, the prejudice that kept them down, and she used them now as weapons to make Papa angry, only he didn't let them touch him. He stood unfazed. How could he be so calm? How could he let her go?

Anna finally stepped back into the apartment. Papa latched the doors and went through the motions of starting a fire, his shoulders slouched and heavy. There was the crumple of newspaper, the thud of a log against the irons. It hissed before it sputtered and caught. In the new, thin light Anna saw a fresh crack in the glass on the balcony doors from when she had pried them open. She also realized a plate had crashed to the floor. She had bumped the table when she tripped on the newspapers. She hadn't realized it fell. Her birthday cake lay between shards. Papa had saved flour and sugar for months to make it, and still had to supplement with potatoes. They had stayed up late eating and singing. Young Anna didn't take her eyes off her mother the entire night. Xenia wasn't a beautiful woman, but she was striking. Her skin was pale and smooth like enamel. Her hair was her triumph. It was the color of wheat and it helped her pass for Russian. Her eyes were green and piercing. She had flaws and scars, but no one noticed because when she spoke, she was electric. No one could resist Mama, and Anna understood why. When her mother focused on her, it made Anna feel like she was the most brilliant and important person in the world. Xenia made others feel the same way, and crowds flocked to her speeches in factory basements, in the backs of cafés, and even in their flat every Tuesday night. They came to hear Mama lecturing on Marx, speaking out against the Czar and religion. "Fight," she told the crowds. "We must fight." Anna couldn't remember a day in her life when she didn't want to be like her mother. Nor could she think of a time when she wasn't competing for her attention, and she'd had it entirely while they ate her birthday cake, sang, and talked. Their conversation, of course, was about politics. "We have the power to build our tomorrow," Mama said. Her skin glowed.

"You'll make it extraordinary, Mama."

"No. You will. I'll lay a foundation and you will build on it and make something better."

Anna had wanted the night to stretch forever, but she fell asleep at the table and woke up in her bed when the front door slammed shut and she knew right away Papa had lost the argument. Why couldn't he have done better?

"Annushka?" Maksim said. His hand was on her forehead, checking her temperature. He was a doctor, always worried she'd catch a cold or break a bone. "Annushka?" he said again. His voice dragged Anna away from the memory of her party, back to the present moment where they were both next to the cracked glass doors. "You need to put your coat on. You're shivering." He was leaning down so they were eye to eye. She stared at his freckles, the ones they shared, along with a slight stoop. Where Mama was light, Papa was dark. He was also bone thin with a graying beard that made him look older than he was. He didn't mind people underestimating him, he told Anna. It made it easier. Easier to do what, he didn't say.

He helped her layer on another sweater and coat, all the clothing they had left. One hour ticked past and then another. There was a stillness in the apartment and on the street that made Anna think everyone in Russia was holding their breath. The sun slid up and over the crooked rooftops and finally a man crept along the sidewalk. Every few steps he looked over his shoulder as if he were being followed, but there was no one near him. As it got brighter, it got colder. When the temperature was at its nadir, the noise started. Chanting, then yelling. There was no doubt the crowd had swelled to thousands just as Xenia expected. "Forward! Forward!" the crowds yelled. Mama had done it. All those meetings, all the organizing. It had worked. Anna cheered and pumped her hand over her head in a fist, like her mother. "Forward!" Anna said. "We shouldn't have worried. Right? Right, Papa?"

"The day isn't over."

At some point, she heard a slash of screams. Papa leaned against the glass doors to get a better look at what was happening. "Crowds panic. I told her that," he said. His voice wasn't angry but resigned, sad. They watched a man run past their building.

Then came a gunshot, and all of the calm Anna had felt exploded.

"Something's wrong," she said. Then louder, "Something's wrong."

"Mama will be fine," Papa said, but he wrapped Anna in his arms so tight it was hard to breathe. A clump of boys sprinted past, then more.

Fires started and soon it seemed all of Petrograd was burning.

"Mama!" Anna cried. It was the only word that spilled between Anna and Maksim as dark took hold. Near midnight, Anna spotted Mama's shadow on the street below. At first, she thought there were two shadows, that Mama wasn't alone, but then she came into focus. It was just her, bent over. Maksim ran for her. His footsteps thundered down the stairs. He leaped across the courtyard, bundled Mama into his arms, and ran toward their building.

"Draw the curtains. Light a candle," Papa said as he burst inside. Mama's leg was bleeding. She should have been crying, but instead she was stoic and silent.

"She's going to die, isn't she?"

"Please, Annushka, get a candle."

Anna ran to the hutch while Papa put Mama on the divan. Blood soaked her stockings and spilled down her boots. Too much blood. Papa was pleading with her to speak, to tell him what happened. "A house collapsed," Xenia said. Her voice was quiet. It was never quiet. "I was nearby. Something stabbed me."

"I must sew it up, hold back the infection," he said. He put pillows behind her to prop her up and walked to the corner of the room where he kept his doctor's bag.

"Which house?" Papa asked. "Was anyone else hurt?"

"The Dubinskys' house." Anna knew it well. Her friend Bina lived there.

"Annushka," Xenia said. She motioned for Anna to come close. "The world is shifting. You. You are the key." Anna snuggled against her mother. "Take these. Take care of them for me." Mama put her bear pendants around Anna's neck and kissed her. "I know you'll watch them for me."

△ △ △

Anna had worn the bear pendants every day since. And now, standing next to the Dubinskys' house as an old woman, she imagined how they felt when she ran her fingertips over them, thought about how she'd left them with Molly. Anna's arms, hands, and torso ached from the lesions and she told herself this was her last jump, that she was going to finish what she should have finished years ago. By then, flames had started to devour Bina's house and Anna heard Xenia yelling. "Bina, come down now! You don't have long." Anna hobbled out of the alley and saw Mama standing in the doorway, at the edge of yellow and orange flames. She was leaning forward. "Bina! Now! Run to me!" Mama yelled, and Anna felt like her heart stopped. She'd imagined her mother countless times and now there she was, and not only was she flesh and blood but she was trying to help Bina, not navigate the revolution like Anna remembered. Mama was also shorter than Anna recalled, and she looked ragged and dirt-smeared, not regal the way she was in Anna's mind. But her voice was compelling and Anna had to resist the urge to run to her, knew it would only scare her. Why hadn't Mama told her she'd attempted to save Bina? Anna tried to think of a way to help, but then came a crack so loud it sounded like Petrograd was splitting in two—but it was only the roof imploding. Anna covered her head and cowered down into a ball to protect herself. When she looked up again, Mama was flat on the ground. A giant wooden shard had impaled Mama's calf. That was how she'd been injured, Anna realized. She'd never known. The flames were enormous by then, the heat debilitating. Mama pulled the shard out of her leg and Anna helped her to her feet, dragged her away. It was hard because of Anna's wounds and Mama being dazed. People all around were screaming and pushing, running. Anna had to jostle their way forward, to the alley. Mama leaned against an old barrel, wouldn't let go of Anna.

"You're here," Mama said. She stroked Anna's cheek, running a finger over her wrinkles, and Anna thought the touch was magical. She remembered that Mama used to stroke her cheek that way every night. She leaned into it and despite all her pain, she smiled. "Annushka," Mama said.

"You recognize me?" Anna was breathless, caught off guard. All these years she'd been angry at her mother for putting the revolution before her, but standing there, injured and bleeding, Mama knew her, and it touched Anna in a way she didn't expect. There were more screams from the street. A band of men on horses trampled past. "I'm even older now than you are. How do you know me?"

"I'd know you anywhere, my heart." Mama kissed her cheeks. "I love you with everything I have. I always will. You're here to tell me my time has come. That I'm dying?"

"Almost," Anna said.

"You're a ghost then. A marvelous one I can touch and kiss." Mama folded her into her arms and Anna felt the warmth of her mother's skin, a connection she hadn't remembered. It was so intense, so filled with the emotions she'd hidden away for decades, that without her mother to hold her up, she would have fallen. Anna recalled the nights her mother cuddled with her while they read, while Mama told stories about revolutions past and to come. Those stories made Anna excited for the future, inspired her to be brave as a child, to always fight, and now she felt all of that again as if she were a ten-year-old, not the old, sick woman she was. And quickly, those feelings fell from excitement to regret. "I spent my whole life angry with you," Anna said. "But that never made sense, did it? I was never angry with you when we were together, only when they took you. And they took you. You didn't choose to go."

"It's easier to hold on to anger. I don't know why, but it doesn't hurt as much."

"You're about to leave me and Papa. It kills us both in different ways."

"You're here to warn me so I can change something?" Mama asked.

"Why aren't you surprised or in shock that I'm here?"

"Ghosts surround me all the time, ghosts like you," Mama said. She leaned back harder on the barrel and winced. Blood poured from her calf. "I see my own parents. My sisters and brothers, other people from our village. All those poor souls who perished in the pogrom, I see them all the time. Whether my eyes are closed or open."

"I never knew."

"I'm sure I would have told you if we had more time together."

Anna nodded. "They'll take you. Soldiers. Soon. Not tonight, tomorrow night." Her words came in broken pieces. "When you see me, as a child, I need you to tell me to focus on my daughter, my family. That we should all run together when it's time. Tell me not to be angry."

"I have a granddaughter." Mama smiled. "That means you survive."

"Yes, but I'm not happy. I haven't been for a long, long time. I've held on to so much. You have to go home and tell me you're proud of me, that you're not pushing me away. That I will do great things and when I do, I need to keep my daughter close. Never leave her. Ever. Tell me not to be afraid to face my fears, that avoiding them causes more harm."

"Of course you wouldn't leave your own daughter. I raised you better."

"I need you to go home and tell me. Please. Above all, tell me not to build any weapons, not to think they would be used as anything but instruments to kill. Tell me I'll never be able to control them and I will hate myself for what I create," Anna pleaded. Her mother nodded, and she pulled Mama's arm across her shoulders and walked her out of the alley, back toward their flat. Every step felt like ten with the weight of her mother on her stooped back, pressing against the lesions on her skin. "Mama, stay awake," Anna said.

"I am so, so proud of you," Mama mumbled.

"You never said that you were proud of me before. Not even once."

"You just never heard," Mama said. "You were always busy, wanting to be better, the best. I've always believed in you, in the power you have." One block dragged past and then another. She could see their building. Papa was going to run outside any minute and carry Mama upstairs. Mama took a deep breath. Her eyes weren't focusing. "I'm sorry I'm leaving you this soon," she said, kissing Anna. "I don't want to. I want to live, to see you grow and fall in love. I want to meet your child, my future. That's why I'm fighting. For your future." And then, "I love you more than anything. More than this revolution, more than my work."

"Xenushka!" Papa bellowed from across the courtyard. Anna heard his footsteps, his heavy breathing as he ran, but then she felt the tug of gravity and she knew her time was up, only she didn't see static this time. Instead it was a dark, black wave that swallowed her.

Anna had changed her path.

PART IX

If I am not for myself, who is for me?
But if I am only for myself, what am I?

—Pirkei Avot

RAISA

Philadelphia

My papa dragged my mama inside after the march. She was dazed and only half-conscious. She had a terrible wound on her calf. Papa said she had been impaled by a shard from my friend Bina's house. The roof imploded." Baba Anna stopped. "Bina died that night." And then, "My mother told me a ghost saved her, pulled her from the rubble and walked her home. Before the soldiers took her, she gave me these bears." She held up the golden pendants. "A bear at peace and a bear at war."

"That's impossible," Raisa said. She was sixteen years old and living in a slice of Northeast Philly they called Little Russia. The streets were lined with narrow row homes separated by walls so thin there was no privacy and invisible borders so thick she didn't need to use a word of English until she stepped into a classroom at school. Mama lived in the basement, which doubled as her studio. Baba Yulia and Pop-Pop were on the third floor while Raisa and Baba Anna shared the second, as they had ever since Baba Anna landed on their doorstep in 1975. She had defected, come bearing Soviet secrets and spent her first year being questioned. She never told her family by whom or where, only that the Americans knew how to treat scientists much better than the Soviets. They didn't take her to a basement and they let her use the bathroom. Those were the only details she shared. After the Americans believed her, and released her, she unpacked her suitcase and started tutoring Raisa while looking for a job. They used the dining room table, covered it with their experiments. Together they built radios and amplifiers, cable boxes and even radio telescopes with old satellite dishes.

Raisa loved listening to the story of her great-grandmother's bravery, about how she led the march in 1917 that brought down the Czar. "Keep talking," Raisa said.

"After my papa brought her home and bandaged her up, before the soldiers came and took her away, she told me she had a vision of me in the future." Baba Anna smiled. "She said I would have a beautiful family. That I needed to use my brain for work, but also for love." Baba Anna stopped—she always stopped here because it was the point where she started to cry the most. "Your Baba Xenia said she didn't want me to make the same mistake as her. That when the time came, I shouldn't leave my family behind. 'Don't follow me,' she said. And she told me she was proud of me, that she believed in me, in the power I had. She said she'd meant to put me first, but the accident, the wound, turned it all upside down."

"You still sent us away," Baba Yulia said. She liked to remind Baba Anna that she had made a bad decision, that they should have all left together. Baba Yulia tried to spoon more herring onto Raisa's plate, but Raisa pushed it away.

"Please, no more. I need to leave," Raisa said. She was due at a math competition in one hour and if she didn't go soon, she would be late. They were seated in the kitchen at their Formica table, so close together their knees knocked. The whole space was cramped like that. The refrigerator was flush with the stove, which nestled against a counter that in turn spilled into a sink only one plate wide. Baba Anna never complained about the kitchen because she didn't cook. She spent her time at her lab with her collaborator, Philip Stocken. They ran the Physics and Astrophysics Departments at Penn. He had been the first to hire her, to take a chance on a *Commie defector*, as she was labeled back then, and they spent a great deal of time researching, working on her ideas for an amplifier. That was as much as she would say about that work.

In the Soviet Union, before she ran, she was a famous scientist. She and Raisa's grandfather, Yasha, had worked together. They had sent Mama to America with Baba Yulia and Pop-Pop and planned to follow them in a year, only it took longer before they could try to leave. In 1974 they ran for the border. Papa Yasha was shot in a field defending Baba Anna while she ran with her nurse, Vera, and Vera's family. He sacrificed himself for them, Baba Anna would say with tears and regret when she told the story. She missed him every day.

"Never build a weapon and think you can control it," Baba Anna said wistfully. "All weapons are meant to kill and destroy. Don't forget it. 'If you build a weapon, you will hate yourself for it,' Mama said, almost like she could look into the future. Still, she was right and—"

"Okay, okay," Raisa said. She'd heard that a million times. "I don't want to be late. Pop-Pop, can we go?"

Mama walked into the kitchen and yawned. Her hair was pulled back into a loose ponytail and her mascara was smudged. Most nights she worked late, inking comics for the next issue of *Solar Sokolova*. Sokolova was Soviet, similar to characters in Mama's original series, *Atomic Anna*, but like the rest of the family she had sworn off nuclear power. In its place, she built power plants fueled by solar technology and got all of her own powers from the sun. Mama kissed Raisa's cheek. "I told you that you're going to win this math competition," Mama said. She looked at Raisa. "I'm so proud of you. And I know you'll win. I'm sorry your dad couldn't be here. Maybe soon." He was back in rehab, hadn't managed to kick the drugs and alcohol like Mama. She told Raisa it was never easy, that she still thought about taking a drink or getting high, but she fought it every day.

"Raisele will win the contest," Baba Anna said. "Stocken is rooting for you, too. He has a new student for you to meet. A Vito or something. Whoever he is, he won't be able to keep up with you."

"Enough," Raisa groaned. "I need to leave."

"All right," Pop-Pop said. He stepped into the kitchen wearing his blue pajamas. He had white wisps of hair around his rectangular head and deep lines around his eyes that made him look both older than he was and softer than he wanted to be.

"Why aren't you dressed?" Raisa asked.

Pop-Pop smiled. "Change of plans. Daniel's driving."

"Daniel?" He lived across the street from them, had come to America with his family and Baba Anna. Vera, his older sister, had been Anna's nurse in the USSR and Anna had told Raisa she couldn't bear to leave Vera behind. She'd paid to help her whole family escape. Now Daniel worked in the Chopping Room with Raisa, but they never spoke much. He was shy and quiet. "He doesn't have a license." Nor did Raisa. She'd flunked the test twice already.

"True." Pop-Pop smiled. "But he's a good driver. You don't need an old man. You need energy." There was no time left to argue. Raisa started toward the door. "We're paying him extra for this," Pop-Pop called after her.

Raisa grabbed her backpack and, in another heartbeat, ran down the cement walkway and toward the van. Daniel already had the door open, waiting for her. She grabbed the keys from him. "I'm driving. Let's go," she said. He grinned and climbed into the passenger side.

"Okay," he said. "Let's see what happens."

ACKNOWLEDGMENTS

It took a team of superheroes to pull *Atomic Anna* together, and I can't thank them enough for hanging in draft after draft after draft. Finishing this book was a labor of love.

Eve Attermann is my Wonder Woman. She fell for this book when it was just a glimmer and has cheered ever since. She is my dream agent. The Mighty Millicent Bennett scooped this book up as a rough draft. The Spectacular Seema Mahanian swooped in and picked up the reins. Editing is Seema's superpower and I am beyond lucky that the universe put us together. The Courageous Carmel Shaka pulled apart every line. The Amazing Andy Dodds is a miracle worker and the best publicist a writer could ever ask for. A million thank-yous to all of you.

At WME I am grateful to: Haley Heidemann, Sam Birmingham, and Sian-Ashleigh Edwards. Nicole Weinroth and Elizabeth Wachtel, whose enthusiasm is infectious. Matilda Forbes Watson, Caitlin Mahony, Oma Naraine, and Suzannah Ball.

At Grand Central I am grateful to the incredible Anjuli Johnson and Laura Cherkas. Any mistakes that remain are my own. Thank you to the rest of the outstanding team: Ben Sevier, Karen Kosztolnyik, Kristen Lemire, Matthew Ballast, Beth deGuzman, Brian McLendon, Jeff Stiefel, Alana Spendley, Ivy Cheng, Chris Murphy, Alison Lazarus, Ali Cutrone, Martha Bucci, and Rachel Hairston. Thank you also to

ACKNOWLEDGMENTS

Karen Torres and all of the sales reps at Hachette for being super champions.

Thank you to the Jewish Book Council and CANVAS, a project of Jewish Funders Network, for the emergency relief funds awarded to artists/creatives impacted financially by the COVID-19 crisis. Thanks to the Brookline Public Library, which provided me with hundreds of books while working on this one. Thank you to Lisa Fishbayn Joffe and the Hadassah-Brandeis Institute for offering a community to lean into during COVID.

My unending gratitude goes out to GrubStreet. Without Michelle Hoover and her Novel Incubator, this book would never have seen the light of day. Thank you to Christopher Castellani, Eve Bridburg, and Kitty Pechet for making dreams possible.

Thank you to early readers: Louise Berliner, Susan Bernhard, Janet Rich Edwards, Michele Ferrari, Robert Fernandes, Desmond Hall, Jennifer Johnson, Andrea Meyer, Tracey Palmer, Julia Rold, Rebecca Givens Rolland, Elizabeth Chiles Shelburne, Leslie Teel, and Bonnie Waltch. Some of these brave souls read several drafts, and I couldn't be more grateful. Other Grubbies who have carried me through include: E. B. Bartels, Helen Bronk, Julie Carrick Dalton, Kelly Ford, Kasey LeBlanc, John McClure, Alison Murphy, Patricia Park, Emily Ross, Katrin Schuman, and Sara Shukla.

Thank you also to: Marjorie Gellhorn Sa'adah, who always makes me a better writer. Jenna Blum and Caroline Leavitt, who cheered me through countless edits and the blurb slog. Laura Rossi for getting the word out. Anna Costa for talking through addiction and being honest about the pain. Felixa Eskey for answering questions about Russian and the USSR. Miriam Udel for helping with a touch of Hebrew.

The Hirsch family inspired me as I wrote the first draft. The Rosen family did the same, Deb Rappaport in particular. Tally Zingher and Chavi Eve Karkowsky kept me sane most Fridays. Tally was even there, along with Josh Kaufman, the night this book sold. Thank you.

432

ACKNOWLEDGMENTS

Thank you: Melika Fitzhugh, who gave me the gift of music after listening to my character hang-ups. Jared Lucas Nathanson for launching me into women in comics. Marc Foster for talking Maxwell, and Ed and Nancy Roberts for providing the perfect retreat. Dan Burns for your YouTube video demonstrations and help with electromagnetism.

Linda Kleinbaum, Steve Anderson, and Karun and Judah Grossman are my rocks. I can't thank them enough for slogging through even the worst early drafts. Thank you: Joanna Josephson for having the courage to read everything. Leone Levi D'Ancona for loving books. Beverly Horowitz for pushing me to be a better, deeper writer who understands her characters. Melissa Román Burch and Erin Friedland for cheering every step on every path I've taken.

An article by Dennis Overbye and photographs by Yulia Grigoryants appeared in the *New York Times* in 2020 in which they profiled the real-life cosmic ray research station on Mount Aragats, and I am forever grateful for that inspiration. I used it as a starting point, and what lies in these pages is my imagination gone wild. Steve Sheinkin's book *Bomb* inspired many of my science scenes, and Adam Higginbotham's *Midnight in Chernobyl* informed my writing on the catastrophe. Samson Raphael Hirsch's translation of *Chapters of the Fathers* helped me translate, as did Arthur David's translation of Maimonides's *The Commentary to Mishnah Aboth*.

Thank you to all five of my parents, my amazing siblings, nieces, nephews, aunts, and uncles for the unending support.

Thank you to all of you, my incredible readers.

The biggest thank-you of all goes to Adam, Ezra, Lily, and Jonah. They believe no matter what and cheer even when I cry. You have no idea how much I love you.

ABOUT THE AUTHOR

Rachel Barenbaum's debut novel, *A Bend in the Stars*, was a *Boston Globe* bestseller, a *New York Times* Summer Reading selection, and a Barnes & Noble Discover Great New Writers selection. Rachel is a prolific writer and reviewer whose work has appeared in the *Los Angeles Review of Books*, the *Tel Aviv Review of Books*, *Literary Hub*, and *Dead Darlings*. She is an honorary research associate at the Hadassah-Brandeis Institute at Brandeis University and is a graduate of GrubStreet's Novel Incubator. She founded and runs the podcast *Debut Spotlight*. In a former life she was a hedge fund manager and a spin instructor. She has degrees from Harvard in Business, and Literature and Philosophy. She lives in Brookline, Massachusetts.